Tish was in total darkness. She could still hear the diesel noises, the earth coming down, but these began to grow fainter. She told herself she should scream, but no scream came. She should at least cry, she thought, but no tears came either.

Finally she felt her way through the dark trailer until she found the bed. She lay down on it.

I'm going to sleep, she thought. I'm going to die in my sleep.

Then the scream came. And so did the tears.

Also by B.W. Battin
Published by Fawcett Gold Medal Books:

ANGEL OF THE NIGHT

THE BOOGEYMAN

PROGRAMMED FOR TERROR

THE ATTRACTION

THE CREEP

SMITHEREENS

DEMENTED

B.W. Battin

FAWCETT GOLD MEDAL • NEW YORK

A Fawcett Gold Medal Book
Published by Ballantine Books
Copyright © 1988 by B.W. Battin

Library of Congress Catalog Card Number: 88-91169

ISBN 0-449-13438-5

Printed in Canada

First Edition: November 1988

*To Clarence and Lucille Sherman,
Two of the Nicest People in Minnesota*

PROLOGUE

"I hear you're looking for that cocksucker Gilbert Martinez," the male voice on the phone had said. He had given an address in East Harlem. Then he'd hung up. That's why Detectives Kate Hastings and Tom Napier were northbound on the FDR Drive.

Tom was driving. Glancing at Kate, he said, "Just like the old days. We're looking for a guy whose name I can pronounce who killed a guy whose name I can pronounce."

"What's the matter?" Kate asked. "Can't you say Niem Van Vu or Huyen Troung or Tsang Tran?"

"First time I ever heard Vietnamese spoken with a Texas accent."

They were part of a special juvenile gang detail, and they were running into more and more Asian youths. Not all of the Oriental immigrants fit the stereotype of the ambitious, motivated people who studied, worked hard, became successes in their adopted land. Some formed gangs, robbed, and extorted money from the ones who did fit the stereotype.

The kid they were seeking was one of the lieutenants of a large gang that operated in the Puerto Rican neighborhood known as El Barrio. He was wanted for killing a kid named

Lopez. It was a dispute over turf, who controlled which streets in an area that was claimed by two gangs.

"I don't have a Texas accent," Kate said. "Not after living ten years in New York."

"Maybe not to the casual observer," Tom replied. "But to a native New Yorker you sound suspiciously like hog jowls and turnip greens."

"Hog jowls and turnip greens? Are you sure you're not confusing Texas with Harlem?"

"That's not what you eat in Texas?"

"Tom, I think you need to travel more, broaden your experience a little. There's all kinds of things out there beyond the Hudson River."

"You mean it's not all a barren wasteland?"

Growing up on a farm in West Texas, she had thought it *was* a barren wasteland, which was why she had come to New York. But then, she wasn't going to tell Tom that.

Tom Napier had been her partner for two years now. Tall and broad-shouldered with thick dark hair and a boyish face, he was a hunk. He was also a married hunk who didn't fool around. Not that Kate would have allowed herself to become romantically involved with him. You and your partner were too dependent on each other for that. Romance was an unnecessary complication. It could cloud your judgment, take the edge off your instincts.

Looking across the East River at Queens, Kate wondered how Tom had beaten the odds and remained happily married so long. Being a cop put you in the high-risk category when it came to divorce—not to mention alcoholism, suicide, burnout, and all the other names that were given to what happened when you couldn't cope anymore.

Kate had never been married. She'd come close a time or two, but something had always gone wrong.

Two days ago, she had broken up with a man named Donald. Or more precisely, he had broken up with her, abruptly ending their year-long relationship. They'd been lovers, both physically and emotionally. Although a date had never been set, they'd been drifting inexorably toward marriage. Or so Kate had thought.

And then, the day before yesterday, just like in some damn soap opera, Donald had informed her that he'd found some-one else, someone who worked for the same company. They were both accountants. Maybe they'd sit around in the eve-nings and recite the multiplication tables, Kate thought bit-terly.

But she shouldn't be bitter. Relationships ended. It hap-pened. She was a cop; she was supposed to be tough. But she hadn't felt very tough. She'd felt unloved, unwanted, rejected.

A little bit of it was fear, she supposed. Fear that at thirty-two she had delayed marriage so long that it would soon be beyond reach. Fear that all she would ever have was her job and the lonely apartment that offered only a TV set for com-panionship.

But then maybe she was better off this way. Tish, her twin sister, had stayed in Texas, married a man who turned mean, beat her up so badly that she had to be hospitalized. Finally he did the only kind thing he'd ever done for Tish. He ran off and left her.

"You figure it was someone from the other gang tipped us where to find Martinez?" Tom asked.

Kate considered that. "Seems to me they usually settle their own grievances," she said. "The only thing they hate worse than a rival gang is cops."

"Somebody out there doesn't like Martinez."

Kate said, "Somebody from the neighborhood maybe. Some shop owner who got tired of being ripped off. Or some kid who got beaten up by the gang."

"Most of these people trust cops just slightly more than the kids in the gangs do."

"Could be a phony," Kate suggested. "You know, have a little fun making the cops run around in circles."

"You mean you didn't come in today just hoping for a fun trip to East Harlem, a chance to see the sights?"

"To tell you the truth, Tom, I was hoping to get on the Gray Line tour of the Lower East Side. You know, the one where they point out the homes of all the famous muggers."

3

Tom laughed. "This job's making you too damn cynical, you know that?"

They fell silent, and Kate found herself recalling what had happened two days ago. Donald had sat beside her on the couch in her apartment, looking uncomfortable.

"I don't exactly know how to say this," he said.

Uncertain what was going on, Kate said, "There's nothing you can't tell me; you know that."

He squirmed a moment, then said, "I'm breaking off our relationship."

She stared at him, dumbstruck.

"I've . . . well, I've found somebody else."

"I see," she finally managed to say.

And then the whole story poured out. How he'd been seeing both her and the other woman. How he'd loved them both. How he'd finally decided that the other woman was better suited to be his lifelong partner, making it sound as if he'd worked it out mathematically or something like that.

Kate saw an image of Donald the accountant, pages of figures in front of him, assigning two points to her hair, three to her breasts, God knew how many for her performance in bed. She wondered how badly the other woman had beat her. By two points? A hundred?

Who needs a guy like that? she wondered. But then it wasn't losing Donald that hurt. It was being rejected. It was all the self-doubt.

These things were still on her mind as Tom pulled to a stop in front of a four-story brick tenement. A brown-skinned boy of about five with black curly hair watched them as they got out of the car, staring at them with large dark eyes that were more like an old man's eyes than a child's, eyes that had already seen too much of what life had to offer. FUCK THE WORLD someone had written on the building's wall in yellow spray paint.

As the detectives entered the building, Kate smelled onions and garlic, the scent seeming permanent somehow, as if it had seeped deeply into the walls and floors and ceilings. And below that odor was another, less clearly defined one: the smell of derelicts who had vomited and urinated and maybe even died in the vestibule, the aroma of an old building going to ruin. It was, Kate supposed, the stench of human misery.

They headed up the stairs. Gilbert Martinez was supposed to be hiding out in 2-D. The cracked, yellowing walls were covered with graffiti, much of it in Spanish. LOS BANDITOS was written in bright red felt-tip marker at the first landing. The Banditos were a street gang.

They knocked on the door of 2-D. Kate had unzipped her purse. Her fingers rested lightly on the butt of her service revolver. There was only silence from within the apartment. Tom knocked again, louder.

"Quién es?" a boy's voice said through the door.

"I'm from the welfare office," Kate said.

"What-choo want?"

"I gotta make sure the landlord's doing his job, fixing the stuff that needs fixing, getting rid of the cockroaches."

"I don't want no trouble. It's okay in here."

"You gotta open up. It's the law."

For a few moments there was only silence on the other side of the door, and then it swung open, revealing a skinny boy of about ten or eleven. Dressed in a dirty T-shirt and torn jeans, he eyed them fearfully. His straight black hair was thick and shiny. Kate and Tom displayed their badges.

"You said you were from the welfare."

"We look out for everybody's welfare," Tom said. "We're looking for Gilbert Martinez."

The boy shook his head.

"You know him?" Kate asked.

Again the boy shook his head.

"Whose apartment is this?" she asked. "Who lives here?"

"Me and my mother."

"What's your name?"

"Rudy Ramirez."

"How do we know Gilbert's not inside hiding?" Tom asked.

The boy just stared at him, a strange mixture of emotions

5

playing in his eyes. Kate saw fear and something else, something she was unable to identify.

"Let us take a look around," Kate said. "If Gilbert's not here, there's no problem. We'll go away and leave you alone."

The boy stepped aside, and the detectives cautiously moved into the apartment. If Martinez was here, he could be armed, and the seventeen-year-old had already demonstrated his willingness to kill. To Kate, who didn't smoke, the place smelled of cigarettes. The living-room furniture consisted of a couch, a chair, a portable TV, and a coffee table with two glass ashtrays, both full of cigarette butts. The furniture was old, Salvation Army quality. Blankets and a pillow were piled on one end of the couch, indicating that it doubled as a bed.

Kate could see the kitchen through an open doorway. To its left was a tiny hall leading to the bathroom. To its right was a closed door that presumably led to a bedroom. Tom nodded to her, then moved toward the kitchen while Kate headed for the bedroom. Stepping through the doorway, she found an unmade bed and more shabby furniture. She checked under the bed, discovered no one hiding there. Nor was anyone in the small, musty-smelling closet, although she did find men's as well as women's clothing. The boy had lied about living with just his mother.

Kate considered that, deciding that the boy either didn't want to admit his mother was living with a man or he didn't want the welfare people to find out. Sometimes women would claim the husband was gone when he really wasn't, to keep the welfare checks coming.

Kate returned to the living room as Tom emerged from the kitchen. He gave a quick shake of his head, and so did she; neither of them had found anything significant. The boy was sitting on the couch now, beside the pillow and blankets.

"You were right," Kate said, looking at the boy. "Martinez isn't here."

"Like I tole you," he said.

"Why do you think someone would tell us he's here?"

The kid shrugged.

"He a friend of yours?"

6

"I don't know him."

"Who else lives here besides you and your mother?"

The kid mumbled something.

"What?"

"Nobody. Just us."

"Then how come there's men's clothes in the closet?"

"And a guy's razor and stuff like that in the bathroom," Tom said.

"Carlos," the boy said almost inaudibly.

"Who's Carlos?" Kate asked.

"He stays here sometimes."

"What's his last name?"

"Trujillo."

"You sure it's not Martinez?"

"Trujillo," the boy said again. "You come back later, you can meet him."

Kate sighed. She was just about convinced that the tip on Martinez had been a phony. The clothes in the closet had been the sort of things a man in his thirties or forties might wear, not a seventeen-year-old. She took one last shot at it.

"We could tell the welfare about Trujillo, you know."

The boy stared glumly at his shoes, said nothing.

"But we wouldn't do that," Tom said, "not as long as you were straight with us."

"I tole you the truth," the boy said. "I don' know the guy you're looking for."

Kate's eyes met Tom's, the two detectives silently communicating that they were both ready to go. As they moved toward the door, Kate turned, intending to tell the boy something, and in the next instant she forgot what she was going to say, because the kid's hand was emerging from under the blankets, raising an automatic.

"Look out!" she cried, trying to push Tom out of the kid's line of fire. The gun went off.

Kate heard Tom gasp as he spun around, dropping, and she knew he'd been hit. A part of her wanted to go immediately to her fallen partner, see how he was, but she had to ignore that part of herself, for the kid—the crazy, goddamned kid—was swinging his gun toward her. Instinctively Kate had reached into her purse. Now, as she threw herself to the floor, her hand found the butt of her service revolver. She flung the purse off the gun as the boy fired again, the bullet missing. The boy was standing now, holding the automatic with both hands, the way you were taught at the police academy, and before he could shoot again Kate fired her own weapon. The boy flew backward, as if he'd been hit by a truck.

For several seconds, Kate lay on the floor, trembling, her brain unable to cope with what had just happened. Finally the realization settled over her that she was a police officer, that she still had responsibilities, that both her partner and the boy needed medical help. Getting slowly to her feet, she moved to the fallen boy, kicked the automatic out of his reach. He lay on his back, arms and legs spread, as if he were about to make an angel in the snow. Blood ran from the hole in his neck. Suddenly Kate was confused again, uncertain what to do. A voice somewhere inside her head said, *You can't put a tourniquet on a neck wound; you'll strangle the person you're trying to help.*

Suddenly Kate turned away from the boy, hurried over to where Tom was lying. He was on his side, his back against the door. Blood had seeped through the front of his shirt. And then Kate noticed his eyes, the way they stared at the ceiling, dully, lifelessly.

Kate could feel a strange lethargy settling over her, as if sitting down and closing her eyes would make everything all right, as if it were just a bad dream, a weird horror concocted by her subconscious. She shook her head. She had to take action. She had to get help.

Her eyes darted around the room, but she saw no telephone. Dashing into the kitchen, she saw two wires hanging out of a hole in the wall, where a phone had been once. Nor was there a phone in the bedroom. As she passed the boy, she noticed that the blood had stopped pouring from the hole in his neck. He'll be all right, she thought. The blood's stopped.

And then Kate realized how ridiculous that notion was. The blood had stopped because his heart had stopped. She rushed to the door, which wouldn't open because Tom was lying against it. She realized then that she still had her gun in her hand. Picking up her purse, she slipped the weapon inside, then grabbed Tom's arm and pulled him away from the door.

She banged on the door of 2-C, getting no response. Moving to 2-B, she tried again, and this time the door was opened by a chubby young woman with a bad case of zits.

"You got a phone?" she asked.

The woman eyed her warily, started to close the door.

"I'm a police officer. This is an emergency."

Inside the apartment the phone rang. Kate put her foot in the door to keep it from closing. The woman just stared at her, apparently uncertain what to do. In the apartment the phone was still ringing. Kate hit the door with the weight of her body, flinging it open. Rushing into the apartment, she spotted the phone sitting on the wide arm of the couch. She snatched the receiver.

"Hello," a man said. "Manuelita?"

"This is a police emergency. Get off the line."

"Who you kidding? Manuelita? Where's Manuelita?"

"You've got a wrong number, okay? Hang up." Kate broke the connection, got a dial tone. After explaining where she was and what had happened, she replaced the receiver and sank slowly to the floor. She was shaking all over. The chubby woman stared at her, looking confused. Kate began to cry, and after a while she heard a woman's screams, but distantly, as if they were coming through the walls from another apartment. Then she realized that the screams were hers.

Later—she was uncertain how much later—a uniformed officer came into the apartment, asked if she was Detective Kathleen Hastings. Kate simply stared at him. She was in a nice little corner somewhere deep within herself, a place that was safe, a place where titles such as detective were meaningless, where bad things never happened.

"Are you all right?" the patrolman asked.

Kate smiled at him and said nothing.

ONE

Kate spotted Tish in the crowd of people waiting for arriving passengers at Austin's Robert Mueller Municipal Airport. Then Tish saw her, and the sisters rushed toward each other, embracing, holding each other tightly, finally stepping back to look at each other. For a long moment, neither sister spoke. Tish's eyes were moist, and Kate knew hers were, too.

"Oh, no," Tish said finally. "We're wearing almost exactly the same dress."

Unlike some identical twins, they had always avoided dressing alike. To them it seemed cutesy, an unnecessary calling of attention to themselves. And it seemed to imply somehow that neither of them was a whole individual, but merely one half of a pair, nothing without the other.

Kate said, "Mine came from Bloomingdale's. Where'd you get yours?"

"Sears. Forty-seven-fifty."

"Oh, God."

"What'd you pay?"

"A hundred and fifty."

"You'd better stock up on clothes while you're here."

Kate laughed and realized it was the first time she had done so in a month, the first time since her partner and an eleven-year-old boy had died in an East Harlem tenement. She was on extended medical leave from the NYPD, not permitted to return to duty until the department psychiatrist said she was well enough.

As they headed for the baggage pickup area, Tish said, "How are you doing?"

"Pretty well," Kate replied. "Very well compared with two weeks ago." She let it go at that. There'd be plenty of time to talk later.

Glancing over at her twin—especially with Tish in a similar blue dress—made it seem as though the passageway were lined with mirrors, as though Kate were looking at a reflection of herself. As did Kate, Tish wore her curly dark hair short. She was tall and trim, with breasts that were prominent but still firm. Her face had a scattering of light freckles that were concentrated around her small nose, which had just the hint of a rise at its tip.

Looking at your twin gave you the chance to do something most people couldn't. You could see yourself as others saw you. And Kate saw that Tish was extremely attractive. If there was a continuum, with *beautiful* at one end and *cute* at the other, Tish was somewhere in the middle, maybe a little closer to the cute side. Which meant Kate was, too. And she wondered why they'd both managed to have such crummy relationships with men. But then the trouble wasn't attracting them; it was what happened afterward.

As they passed another gate, a pretty young woman wearing cowboy boots, jeans, and a western shirt let out a scream of delight as she hurled herself into the arms of a man who'd just gotten off a Southwest Airlines flight. Apparently Texas hadn't changed.

Kate hadn't been back to the state in years, not even to see Tish. Though lured by the glamour and sophistication of the city, she'd also gone to New York to get away from the brash cowboyness of Texas, along with the narrow-mindedness of some of its attitudes. She'd worked hard to rid herself of her Texas accent, which always made her feel as though she carried a neon sign that flashed: *hick . . . hick . . . hick.*

She recalled Tom's accusing her of pronouncing Vietnamese names with a Texas accent, and she pushed the painful memory away.

When they were in Tish's car, heading out of Austin on Interstate 35, Kate said, "The boy was eleven years old."

"You told me that," Tish said gently.

"Did I tell you why he did it?"

"No."

"He was trying to get into a street gang. He was trying to prove himself, show he had what it takes. His mother told us."

"You mean she knew ahead of time what he was going to do?"

"No, she'd have tried to stop him if she'd known. But she knew what he wanted, how his mind worked. And that's the whole gang psychology. The older kids, the ones who are already in the gangs, make the younger ones do stuff to prove themselves."

"What an awful place that must be," Tish said.

"There's good people and bad people everywhere, Tish. New York's no different than anyplace else."

Tish eyed her skeptically.

"Really," Kate said. "There was a war between two motorcycle gangs here in Texas a few years back, and the losers were decapitated. Their heads were put on the tops of poles. Their sex organs were cut off and put into their mouths."

"Yuck," Tish said, grimacing.

"I've known a lot of good people in New York. One was my partner, Tom Napier."

"I still think I'm a lot safer here," Tish said. "At least I feel safer, and I guess that's what counts."

When Austin was behind them, Tish left the freeway, headed into the part of Texas known as the Hill Country, one of the prettiest parts of the state. Tish was the librarian in a town called Leap. She'd moved there a couple of years ago with her husband, before he'd run off and Tish had divorced him *in absentia*. This would be the first time Kate had been to Leap.

It was late in the day. Before long they'd be driving into the setting sun. Kate adjusted the vent on the dashboard, directing the flow of air conditioning up at her face. It was summer, which in Texas was synonymous with hot and muggy.

"I never thought it would happen to me," Kate said. "You hear about people freaking out, breaking down, whatever you want to call it. But I guess it doesn't seem real, like maybe it's just a rumor, something that was made up. But it really did happen. I lost it. I just withdrew. I was in there with myself. The rest of the world didn't exist."

She paused to try to collect her thoughts, figure out how to say it. "It's a hard thing to describe. A part of you knows you're not acting right, but you keep right on doing it. You just can't stop. The psychiatrist says it was my mind's way of trying to cope with what had happened. It was so horrible that my mind just sort of tried to hide, stick its head in the sand like an ostrich. That's not the way the psychiatrist put it, but it kind of describes what he said."

"I'm glad you're here," Tish said. "When we get to Leap, I want you to relax, watch TV, do some sunbathing, maybe eat a few bowls of Texas chili—if living in New York hasn't ruined your taste for good food."

Kate laughed. "I'm glad I came. When you need to heal, you go home to your family. And with Mom and Dad gone, you're the only family I've got."

"How long has it been since we saw each other, three years?"

"About that."

"Let's not go that long again," Tish said. "Now that we don't have to."

By that she meant now that Boyd, her former husband, was no longer there. Boyd hadn't liked Kate, and he'd discouraged her from visiting. And he'd refused to even consider taking Tish to New York.

As they drove, the scenery became prettier. The part of Texas in which they'd grown up was farmland, flat as a tabletop, but here there were rolling hills, and the countryside was covered with scrub oak, mesquite, and cactus.

Suddenly Kate felt a tear trickle down her cheek, then another. She wasn't sure why she was crying. Maybe she was just relieved to be here with her twin sister, away from New York and the NYPD and all the reminders of what had happened. Kate pretended to look out the side window, so Tish couldn't see her tears.

It was nearly dark when they arrived in Leap. They crested a hill, started down the other side, and there it was, a community big enough to have traffic lights and maybe a small shopping mall. Kate caught a whiff of something strong and unpleasant while they were still on the outskirts of town.

"Ugh," she said.

"That's the livestock auction," Tish said. "Don't worry, most of Leap doesn't smell like that. Do you see that house?"

Kate said she did. It was on the same side of the road as the livestock auction, an ordinary-looking frame home with a scraggly lawn and a gravel drive. It stood by itself, about a thousand feet from a small subdivision.

"That's the county battered women's shelter," Tish said. "I had to go there a few times."

"Tish, I'm so glad he's gone, out of your life."

"The last time I thought he was going to kill me."

"Tish, I—"

"I'm afraid I don't have anything in the house that can be put together quickly," Tish said, cutting her off. "But I know where there's a pretty good steak house."

"Sounds good to me."

"You want to go home and clean up, or are you ready to eat?"

"I'm ready to eat."

As happened sometimes after the first night in a strange bed, Kate awoke uncertain where she was. Bright sunlight was coming in through a crack between the curtains. Outside, birds were chirping. Her eyes took in the white walls, the pattern of small flowers on the curtains. The window air conditioner blew cold air at her.

Kate's sleep-fogged brain cleared a little bit, and she remembered that she was in Texas, at her sister's house. She was here because she'd had a breakdown after seeing her partner killed, after blowing away an eleven-year-old kid.

She'd had nightmares about it at first. She'd seen Tom Napier falling, the boy turning the gun on her, the blood coming from the wound on the kid's neck. Last night she'd slept well, without bad dreams.

Getting up, she went to the window and looked out at the bright morning. She'd forgotten how intense the Southwestern sunlight was. By comparison the sunshine in New York seemed weak, as if it had never been turned up all the way. Small houses—two- and three-bedroom models—lined the street. Some had clapboard siding; some had a brick or stone veneer. Their lawns were well kept, the houses themselves neat and cheerful. Compared to the streets in New York, this one seemed as squeaky clean as Grandma's dinner plates.

Her things were still in the three suitcases she'd brought. Putting her clothes away would give her something to do today while Tish was at work. Kate located the small case containing her comb and toothbrush and other toilet articles and headed for the bathroom. She met Tish in the hallway.

"What are you doing up?" Tish asked. She was wearing a pink robe. Her hair was tangled, her eyes still dulled with sleep.

"I thought that's what people did after sleeping all night. They got up."

"Guests who have had a rough time are supposed to sleep in."

"I'm not a guest. I'm your sister. Siblings can never be guests."

Tish shrugged. "What would you like for breakfast?"

"What's that?"

"The first meal of the day."

"Oh. I call that lunch."

Tish shook her head. "I'm going to have to reeducate you while you're here. Will you at least have some coffee with me?"

"Coffee I'll take."

Later, after they'd both showered and prepared to face the day, Kate sat at the old-fashioned country table in the small kitchen, watching Tish consume scrambled eggs, ham, hash browns, and toast.

"How can you eat like that and not gain weight?" Kate asked. She took a sip of coffee.

"I can't face the day on an empty stomach," Tish replied. "I tried eating cereal, because it's faster, but the stuff is as satisfying as a bowl full of insulation."

"I've always been amazed that anyone could face food this early in the day. Are you sure you're my twin and not just somebody who happens to look like me?"

"I grew up on a farm near Lubbock, daughter of Todd and Eunice Hastings."

"We must be twins," Kate said.

Both women were silent for a few moments; then Tish said, "Do you want to talk about it, or would you rather just not think about it for a while?"

"I don't mind talking about it. There's a lot to be talked about—by both of us. I guess I sort of figured that some heavy conversations would be on the agenda."

Tish ate a piece of ham; then her eyes found Kate's. "Has there been any trouble in the community or anything like that . . . you know, because a kid was killed?"

"There are always a few cop haters who'll have something to say, but there wasn't too much reaction. The evidence was pretty clear. The kid had killed my partner and would have killed me too if I hadn't shot him. Even the boy's mother took it fatalistically. She was pretty upset, but she'd known all along that the kid was heading for trouble, and that there was nothing she could do to stop it. The kid's father had run off; she had to work. She couldn't influence the boy as much as the neighborhood did. That's what she was the most bitter about, the neighborhood."

"Was there an investigation by the department?"

"Always is when a cop shoots someone. I was cleared. IAD ruled it a completely justifiable shoot. The problem was all inside myself. I couldn't cope with what had happened."

"And now?"

"I'm trying to cope, learning to cope. In two weeks I'll go back to New York, and the psychiatrist will tell me if I'm ready to go back to work. To tell you the truth, I don't know if I'll be ready or not. I can sit here like this and talk to you

16

about it, but that's not the same as being back on the job. There'll be a lot of reminders there. And even if I hold up okay for the run-of-the-mill police work, the big question is what will happen if another tight situation comes along, if I have to draw my weapon. Will I freak out, freeze, what? Instead of seeing some punk with a Saturday-night special who just held up a liquor store, will I see a little kid? Will I stand there while he blows me away, while he takes out my partner or some innocent people?''

Kate took a sip of her coffee. It was cold. Her hand was shaking. She told Tish about Donald, how he'd abruptly broken off their relationship, and how that had primed her for the breakdown that followed the events at the tenement in East Harlem.

"It took two weeks before I started coming out of myself," Kate said. "The psychiatrist told me that some people stay freaked out for months, so I guess I was lucky in that respect. As breakdowns go, mine wasn't a bad one. The shrink didn't use that term, by the way. He called it a short-term mental illness. Apparently breakdown's a layman's term."

Reaching across the table, Tish took her hand, squeezed it. Kate could feel the bond between them, the intense closeness. It had always been like this between them, and Kate had often wondered whether it was an empathy unique to twins.

"You've had some rough times lately yourself," Kate said.

"But you're not going to hear my tale of woe until this evening. I've got to get to work." She carried her dishes to the sink.

"Leave those," Kate said. "I'll wash them."

"You got a deal. You want to drive me to work so you'll have a car?"

"No need. I don't have anywhere I want to go."

"I should be back around six-thirty or so."

"I'll have supper ready. I'm a whiz with TV dinners."

"I don't have any TV dinners."

"I'll come up with something."

* * *

Kate spent the day relaxing. She unpacked her suitcases, took a nap, explored the house. It had two bedrooms, a single bath, light blue carpeting throughout. The furniture was country, but without the clutter that sometimes meant. Everything was spotless. Kate noticed that there wasn't a single trace of Tish's ex-husband. No overlooked bottle of Boyd's after-shave, no golf clubs or fishing poles or pipe cleaners. Although Kate didn't violate the privacy of her sister's bedroom, she'd have been willing to bet there was nothing of Boyd's there, either. Apparently Tish had systematically removed every last reminder. She'd even gotten rid of his name, again becoming Patricia Hastings.

Good riddance, Kate thought. She hoped neither she nor Tish ever encountered Boyd Steuben again.

Kate had only met him a couple times. He was a tall, wiry man, a hard drinker who'd be talking in a gentle drawl one minute and be furious the next, ready to break things—or people. He was your basic Texas good ole boy. Liked drinking beer with his buddies, thought women should be good in bed, respectful, subservient, and have lots of babies. Although Kate wasn't sure how her sister fared in all these categories, she did know that Tish wasn't real good at subservience and that she wasn't able to have any children.

They hadn't liked each other, Kate and Boyd, even before she knew that he was beating up Tish. He'd been uncomfortable with the idea of a woman cop; he kept trying to put her in her place. He wasn't rude exactly. He just sort of tried to make a point of dominating her. And Kate tried equally hard to make sure he didn't succeed.

It was midafternoon before Kate started looking for something to make for dinner. Almost everything Tish had was frozen, so she used the microwave to unthaw some hamburger, then put together a meatloaf, which she served with mashed potatoes and peas. Tish said it was a pretty good effort for someone who'd spent the last ten years in a place where they didn't even know how to fry okra.

"The last time it happened," Tish said, "he cracked some of my ribs." They were sitting on the living-room couch now. They'd watched TV for a while, and then they'd started talking again. It was Tish's turn.

"He'd just lost another job a few days before, and he'd been feeling mean since then. He'd been out drinking with his friends. He's one of those guys that drinks to forget his troubles, but drinking just makes him angrier. I pretended to be asleep when he came in, just hoping he'd leave me alone. He grabbed me, turned me over, said he wanted to do it and that I'd better damn well show him a good time. I should have just done what he wanted, but I didn't. I told him I didn't want to. I told him to leave me alone.

" 'You denying your husband?' he asked. And then he jumped on me and said he'd force me. He was too big to fight against. I just wasn't strong enough. But he couldn't get it up for some reason. That made him furious. And it took him only a minute to figure out that it must be my fault. Actually I think he felt humiliated because he couldn't get an erection. Men are weird about things like that. And he took it out on me.

"He pulled me off the bed and began punching me. When I fell to the floor, he began kicking me. That's how he cracked my ribs. After that, it's all a blur, but I remember him forcing my arm behind my back. I remember I screamed and screamed, begged him to stop. Somehow I got out of the house. I think he must have gone to the bathroom or something like that, giving me a chance to get out. Anyway, I made it to the battered women's shelter, and they took me to the hospital.

"My arm was just hanging there, limp. I thought it was broken, but they X-rayed it and found that it wasn't. The real damage was to my ribs. I was in the hospital for a few days. Boyd came to the hospital to see me, said he was sorry, that he didn't mean it. He always said he was sorry."

As a police officer, Kate had seen her share of battered women. They stayed with the men who abused them out of fear, fear that they'd be unable to make it on their own, fear that their husbands would find them, hurt them even worse, maybe even kill them. To Kate, it made escaping a brutal husband seem akin to informing on the Mafia. In either case, the threat seemed to hang there: *Betray me, and there's no-where you can hide.* She wondered whether that's how it had been for Tish.

These thoughts made Kate think that maybe it was just as well that Donald had broken off their relationship, that maybe staying single wasn't so bad. She put her hand on Tish's, and again she felt that special something that linked her to this person whose genes were identical to hers.

"Why'd you marry him?" Kate asked.

Tish shrugged. "Because he was there. Because that's what girls are supposed to do, get married."

"But not to—"

"You don't always know, Kate. Or maybe you're just too young and inexperienced to figure things out. Or maybe you only see what you want to see. Boyd was real popular. Everybody liked him. He probably could have married half a dozen girls. I was floating along on pure euphoria when he asked me to marry him."

"How do you feel about him now?" Kate asked. She'd seen some battered women who would take the son of a bitch back, again and again, always forgiving him, and she hoped Tish wasn't one of them.

"I don't want to think about him. He's no longer part of my life."

"You'd never take him back?"

"Never."

They sat there for a while, each absorbed in her own thoughts, and then their eyes met. It seemed like one of those moments when you should burst into tears, have a good cry, get rid of all the pent-up emotions. But no tears came. After they'd been looking at each other a moment, Tish giggled. Kate chuckled, and then they were both laughing, just looking at each other and having one of those you-don't-know-how-it-started-and-you-don't-know-how-to-quit laughs.

The time for crying was behind them, Kate realized. Now was the time for healing.

TWO

Standing in the kitchen, Kate studied the cans of soup in Tish's cabinet, desperately hoping to find some cream of mushroom. She sighed. Tomato, chicken noodle, vegetable, and many of the other common varieties, but no cream of mushroom.

Kate had taken over the cooking duties. It only seemed fair since she was here all day with nothing to do while Tish was at the library, earning a living. Today Kate had kept Tish's car so she could buy groceries. And she'd forgotten to pick up cream of mushroom soup, the principal ingredient in the gravy for the meal she was preparing.

Kate considered omitting the gravy, then concluded that the dish simply would not be the same. The chicken breasts sat on the counter, pounded flat, rolled around the ham, held together with toothpicks. She scooped them up, put them on a plate, and put the plate into the refrigerator. She had to go back to the grocery store and get the cream of mushroom soup; that was all there was to it.

It was nearly six. Tish would be coming home soon. The number of the library was written on a pad that hung from a hook on the wall beside the phone. Kate dialed the number.

"Tish, it's me. I've got to run back to the grocery for something. Want me to pick you up?"

"Don't bother. It's no problem for me to ride home with Pam. It's only about half a block out of her way, so it's no big deal. What are you making?"

"Something Mom used to make, if I've remembered the recipe correctly. It'll be a surprise. I just hope it's not so much of a surprise that you don't recognize it."

"Okay. I'll be leaving in a few minutes."

As she hung up, Kate considered the irony of her mother, who was born on a farm and married a farmer, cooking things made with soup that came from a factory in Chicago or some place like that. The image of life on the farm was one of self-reliance. Growing your own vegetables, raising your own meat, canning in Mason jars. But then that was a city person's notion of life on the farm. Kate's dad had been too busy growing sorghum to worry about vegetables or livestock. Her mom had bought the groceries at Safeway.

Stepping through the door that connected the kitchen with the single-car garage, Kate realized how much she missed her mom and dad, even now, more than a decade since she'd lost them. They'd both died while she and Tish were in college. Her father was killed when his tractor overturned, crushing him beneath it. Her mother died a few months later—of grief more than anything else. Picturing her mom's vacant stare, the utter loneliness and misery in her eyes, caused Kate's vision to cloud with tears.

Kate carefully raised the garage door, which had a tendency to stick because the spring on one side was worn out. She backed Tish's white Toyota out of the garage, closed the door, and headed for the supermarket.

Tish had given her the grand tour of Leap. The whole community was as clean and well maintained as the street on which Tish lived. Apparently the town was holding its own despite the hard times being suffered by those parts of the state whose economies were dependent on the oil business. Tish, sounding like a member of the chamber of commerce, said people came here simply because it was such a nice place to live.

Kate paused at a stop sign, then turned right onto a through street. She was in a block along which nearly everyone seemed to be watering the front lawn. Rainbows shimmered in the mist above the sprinklers. A pot of gold in every house, Kate thought, and then laughed quietly to herself. A pot of gold indeed.

The houses in this part of town were mainly brick homes, three and four bedrooms, the sorts of places where assistant managers and schoolteachers and owners of successful small businesses lived. Kate tried to recall whether she'd seen any eyesores in Leap. She had. There were a few shabby buildings, but the real blemish on the place was the foul-smelling collection of corrals surrounding the rusty metal building that made up the Leap Livestock Auction.

Kate drove for another few minutes, and then she realized that the houses didn't look familiar anymore. Should she have turned back at the last stop sign? Or could that be the street she was looking for at the next intersection? She had found the grocery store earlier, when Tish's directions were fresh in her mind, but now she was in a neighborhood she was sure she had never seen before.

Oh, damn, she thought. I can find my way around New York City like a native, and I get lost in Leap, Texas.

Tish waved as Pam's small red car pulled away from the curb. Pam was a high school girl who helped out at the library part-time. She and another part-time worker, a woman in her late seventies, were the extent of Tish's staff. Leap was a small community. It had a small library.

Digging her keys out of her purse, Tish walked toward her front door, noting that the weeping willow tree in the front yard was looking a little bedraggled in the summer heat. She hoped it wasn't diseased, like all the elm trees.

"Kate," she called as she stepped into the house.

Getting no response, she checked the kitchen, which was empty. Opening the door to the garage, Tish saw that the car was gone. Kate was still out getting whatever it was she needed at the grocery store. Tish closed the door. In the few seconds it had been open, stale, sticky heat had washed over

23

her, making her feel exhausted. She wondered how the car survived without melting.

Tish headed for her bedroom, unbuttoning her blouse as she went. The next order of business had to be a shower. She undressed quickly, and a moment later she was closing the frosted-glass sliding door of the tub enclosure and adjusting the water temperature.

"Ahhhhh." She sighed.

Tish's system in the shower was to start at the top and work to the bottom, so she squeezed a handful of shampoo out of its plastic bottle and began washing her hair. She was glad Kate was here. She'd been going through life like an automaton since divorcing Boyd. With him she'd lived in fear; without him her life had seemed aimless. She'd go to work, come home, watch TV, read a little, go to bed. Every day the same: empty, purposeless.

But it wasn't Boyd's absence that made her life that way. Not hardly. It was just the rut, the feeling that she'd made mostly the wrong decisions in her life and that in doing so she had passed up chances that would never be offered again. But then it could be worse, she supposed. Being in a rut beat the hell out of living in terror, as she'd done with Boyd.

And since Kate had arrived, everything seemed brighter. They had needed each other apparently, needed the support, the strength they could get nowhere else. They'd laughed, relaxed, started the process of mending. As she rinsed the shampoo from her hair, Tish decided that if her life was nothing but a dull routine, then she had no one to blame but herself. After Kate went back to New York, she was going to get out, meet people, play cards, go bowling, sing in the church choir, whatever. She was going to put Boyd and the ugliness he represented behind her forever.

Somewhere in the recesses of her consciousness something warned her that Boyd could still come back, but she didn't want to think about that. He'd been gone for over a year when she'd divorced him. The house and everything else they'd owned was legally hers. He had no rights. She could have him arrested if he bothered her. Again, something tried

24

to warn her. *He's violent and vengeful,* it said. *He could hurt you.* She shut the voice out.

And then she thought she heard a thump come from somewhere in the house. The image of Boyd using his key to get into the house popped into her head, and she forced it away. She'd had the locks changed. If anyone was here, it had to be her sister.

"Kate," she called. When there was no response, she yelled, "I'm in the shower, Kate. I'll be out in a minute."

Again there was no answer, and Tish decided that she'd probably imagined the sound. It was impossible to hear anything over the noise of the water spraying from the showerhead, splashing over her body, running down the drain. A number of times she'd thought she'd heard the phone ringing, then turned off the shower only to find the house completely quiet.

"Oh, damn," she said, squeezing her eyes tightly shut.

Instead of rinsing the soap off her face, she'd washed most of it into her eyes. She turned her face into the spray of water, trying to get her eyes to stop burning.

Suddenly the tub enclosure's frosted-glass door was slid back, startling her. But then she recalled how she and Kate used to play tricks on each other as kids. One was to get a glass of ice water, sneak up on your showering twin sister, and toss the freezing liquid onto her, listening to her scream as you ran away, giggling.

"Dammit, Kate, don't you dare," she said, keeping her face aimed into the spray of water.

She braced herself for the freezing liquid, but nothing happened. And then the realization settled over her that Kate and she weren't little girls anymore, that Kate was extremely unlikely to throw cold water on anyone, that adults didn't do things like that. An icy feeling that had nothing to do with a child's prank crawled down her spine.

Abruptly she turned to face the open door of the tub enclosure, trying to blink her eyes into focus. She saw a blurry shape standing there, a shape that was too large to be Kate. A scream started at the base of her throat, but before it could come out, a hand was clamped over her mouth, and she was dragged wet and naked out of the tub.

Kate twisted the handle on the metal garage door, then hefted the door upward and watched it rise crookedly on its tracks. It needed a new spring badly. Kate drove the car into the garage, then closed the door. It was then that it occurred to her that she hadn't needed the key to get into the garage, which meant she hadn't locked the door when she left. Oh, well, she hadn't been gone that long. It was unlikely that she'd find the TV set and all the furniture gone.

"I'm back," Kate called as she stepped into the kitchen, closing the door on the unbearable heat in the garage. There was no reply. Apparently Tish wasn't here yet. Kate glanced into the living room. The TV set and furniture were still here.

Putting the bag containing the cream of mushroom soup on the counter, Kate dropped her purse on the table, then got the chicken breasts from the refrigerator. A few minutes later they'd been sautéed and were simmering in creamy mushroom gravy—just like Mom used to make. She set the table, put on rice to cook, and got some frozen peas from the refrigerator. Dinner was just about ready. All she needed was Tish.

Half an hour later there was still no sign of Tish. Kate called the library, getting no answer, which meant that Tish was probably on her way. Another half hour passed, during which Kate added water to the creamy gravy twice to keep it from getting too thick. She was getting worried. If Tish knew she was going to be tied up, she would have phoned.

But then maybe she had phoned while Kate was out getting lost, trying to find the grocery store so she could buy some cream of mushroom soup. There's no reason to panic, Kate told herself. Then she nervously filled a glass with water. When she started to drink it, she realized how full her bladder was and headed for the bathroom. It wasn't until she relieved herself that she sensed the lingering dampness, as if someone had recently taken a bath or a shower in the room.

Puzzled, Kate looked at the mirror, which showed no trace of steam. But there were a few drops of water on the bottom of the tub, and more water in the tracks along which the glass shower door moved. Had Tish come home, showered, then left? Kate hurried into her sister's bedroom. At first, there were no apparent indications that Tish had returned since leaving this morning. Then Kate lifted the lid of the big white wicker laundry hamper. The yellow dress Tish had worn this morning was on top, along with some undergarments.

Tish had come home, changed clothes, and left, without leaving a note. Which wasn't like Tish at all.

Sitting down on the bed, Kate tried to think things through. It was just unlikely as hell that Tish would run out without leaving a note for her. So if that wasn't the explanation, what was? Perhaps Tish had left a note, but Kate had simply over-looked it. Maybe it had been blown off the kitchen table when she opened the door.

Hurrying into the kitchen, Kate turned off the heat under the chicken breasts, then carefully explored the room, look-ing under the table, behind the refrigerator, on the seats of the chairs. There was no message. Moving on to the living room, she looked under the cushions on the furniture, behind the couch, behind the console TV set.

She checked the two bedrooms, the bathroom, the garage. Finally there was nowhere left to check. Kate returned to the kitchen, sat down at the table. Tish had not left a note. Why would she do something so uncharacteristic? And where had she gone? Another hour passed. Twilight gave way to night.

Very worried now, Kate decided it was time to start calling people who might know where Tish could be. The cover of the small Leap phone book was pristine, without a number written on it anywhere. Nor had Tish written down any names or numbers in the space the phone company provided on the inside of the back cover. Kate began searching for an address book. She found it in the magazine rack that stood at one end of the couch.

Sitting down at the kitchen table, Kate flipped through the book, finding her own name and those of some of the neigh-bors back in the county where she and Tish had grown up. There were about a dozen local phone numbers. Kate called them all. No one had seen Tish. No one had any idea where she might be.

At nine o'clock, just for something to do, she warmed up some of the stuffed chicken breasts and ate. Too worried to be hungry, she picked at the meal. She didn't notice whether it tasted like the dish her mother used to make. At 9:45 she called Leap's only hospital, which had admitted no one named Patricia Hastings. Nor had it admitted any Jane Does that evening.

At ten o'clock Kate watched the news on an Austin TV station. There were no reports of accidents or shootings or stabbings or anything else like that involving a woman who fit Tish's description. She waited until 11:15 before she called the police.

The officer who showed up was a young guy with short blond hair. He was about six feet tall, and stood just inside the doorway, holding a clipboard, his hat tucked under his arm. He looked like a military cadet.

"How long has your sister been missing?" he asked. The name tag on his khaki uniform read "Schultz."

"Since about six-thirty or so. She said she was getting a ride home with a girl named Pam. I don't know her last name." She paused, giving the policeman the chance to fill in Pam's surname if he knew it, but he just nodded. Kate told him about finding Tish's clothes, but no note.

"She came home and went out again," the cop said.

"That's what it looks like."

"No signs of a struggle or anything like that."

"No."

"How old's your sister?"

"Thirty-two."

"Thirty-two-year-old woman comes home and changes clothes and goes out again without telling her sister. No reason to suspect foul play. Ma'am, I gotta tell you that there's nothing here that concerns the police. She's probably out with some fella, having herself a good time."

"Then why didn't she say she was going out when I talked to her on the phone?"

"Maybe she forgot to mention it. Maybe she didn't think it was any of your business."

"You don't know her. She wouldn't do anything like that." As Kate spoke those words, she realized how pointless they were. She was a cop. She'd heard people say similar things, and she always had to say what this officer was saying: that there was simply nothing here for the police to act on.

"Look," Kate said, "I understand where you're coming from. I'm a cop too. So, as a professional courtesy, would you just trust me? I swear to you that my sister would never simply disappear like this unless something's wrong."

He eyed her curiously now. "What department are you with?"

"NYPD. I'm a detective."

"That right?" He studied her with an expression Kate was unable to interpret.

"Can you do anything for me, as a professional courtesy?"

"I don't know what the rules of professional courtesy are, but I can put out a locate if that will do any good."

"It's a start."

"It's all I can do for the moment. If she still hasn't turned up by morning, you can come down to the station, maybe talk to the chief."

That certainly pointed out the differences between the situation here and what she was used to. In New York a person with a complaint like hers would be lucky to get past the precinct sergeant. Here you got to see the chief.

"Give me everything you've got on your sister," the patrolman said. "I need to know what she looks like, social security, date of birth, whatever you can give me."

Kate was vaguely surprised that in a small town like this he didn't know what Tish looked like. But then maybe Schultz wasn't the type to go to the library much. "She looks like me," Kate said. "We're identical twins."

He kept glancing up at her as he wrote things on his clipboard. Kate told him her birthdate, which was the same as Tish's, said she didn't know her sister's social security number, but she could look through Tish's papers, see whether she could find it. The cop said not to bother.

"She have a car?" he asked.

"Yes. But it's here. I was driving it. Like I told you, she got a ride home with Pam. At least that's what she said she was going to do."

"Yes, ma'am, I understand that. I'm just trying to make sure I have everything straight." He glanced at the clipboard. "I reckon that's all I need for now. I'll take care of that locate, and if your sister hasn't turned up by morning, you check with the station." He smiled.

After the officer had left, Kate stood at the window for a while, wishing every car that passed the house would stop, let Tish out. In her mind Kate saw Tish waving as the car pulled away, then rushing into the house, saying, "Hi, Kate. Sorry I didn't get a chance to call you, but . . ."

Abandoning her vigil at the window, Kate switched on the TV set and sat down on the couch. She thought about the young cop who'd been here, and she wondered whether she had seemed as self-absorbed and uncaring when she'd been a patrol officer. You had to remain aloof, emotionally uninvolved. It was the only way you could do the job—not to mention maintain your sanity. But there was a difference between professional objectivity and callous indifference. Or maybe it was just that she had never seen things from a citizen's point of view before.

Kate had done everything she could for the moment. She felt helpless. Her sister was missing, maybe in trouble, and all she could do was sit here and stare at the TV set. She listened intently every time a car went down the street, but none stopped. They became fewer and fewer. After 1:30 or so, no more cars came. The neighborhood was quiet except for the occasional sound of a barking dog, the distant rumble of a jet passing high overhead, its passengers involved in concerns of their own, unaware that down below Kate Hastings was worried sick about her sister.

She watched the talk shows, the first late movie, and then fell asleep during the second late movie. It was an old pirate film. She dozed off in the middle of a sword fight.

30

THREE

Kate awoke at dawn, stiff and sore, her clothes a rumpled mess. She sat up, swung her legs off the couch, and sat there for a moment, clearing her head. The TV set was still on; Kate got up and turned it off. Then she hurried into Tish's bedroom, thinking that just maybe Tish had come in and slipped quietly into bed, not wanting to wake her sleeping sister. Tish's bed hadn't been slept in. Kate stared at it for a long moment, as if she could make Tish's form appear under the covers through sheer force of will. Finally she turned and headed for the kitchen.

She put coffee and water into the drip coffeemaker, turned it on. While the brown liquid slowly filled the pot, Kate tried to think of every possible explanation for Tish's disappearance. Sure, Tish could have run into some guy that turned her on and shacked up with him for the night. It was possible. Lots of things were possible. She could have flown off to Beirut on a secret mission for the CIA. Unfortunately the only explanation that was probable was that something bad had happened to her.

When the coffee was ready, Kate poured herself a cup and drank it slowly. She heard a car pull to a stop outside and dashed to the window over the sink, yanking back the curtain, and suddenly she was filling with tingly anticipation, because a blue Chevy had stopped right in front of the house. She watched, almost afraid to breathe, waited for Tish to get out of the car. Although Kate could see the driver, a middle-aged man, she was unable to tell whether anyone else was in the car. *Let it be Tish,* something inside her pleaded. *Please, please, please.*

And then, in an instant, the hope that had been churning and swelling inside her vanished, as if it had been sucked out by some machine, leaving only a painful emptiness. A woman had hurried out of the house across the street and climbed into the blue Chevy. Kate watched it pull away, and for a long moment she just stared at the empty street. Finally she returned to her coffee.

When she'd emptied the cup, Kate phoned the hospital again. No one named Patricia Hastings had been admitted. No Jane Does. She called the county sheriff and the Texas Department of Public Safety. Neither office had any information concerning a mishap involving a Patricia Hastings. She considered calling the coroner's office, but decided that the coroner wouldn't be involved unless called in by one of the law enforcement agencies she'd already contacted.

Unbidden, an image of Tish's body lying in a culvert popped into her head. Tish lay there, where some crazed killer had left her, her lifeless eyes staring at the culvert's ribbed sides, flies buzzing around her. Kate shook her head to make the image go away. She was trembling.

It was bad enough to imagine the violent death of someone you loved, but when the victim was your twin, there was an additional wrinkle. You were seeing your own death as well.

Kate called the Leap police, informed the man who answered that she'd reported Tish Hastings missing last night and wanted to know whether they'd learned anything. The man said that to his knowledge there had been no further developments. She had another cup of coffee, then took a shower. As soon as it was no longer too early to go knocking on people's doors, Kate left the house. She was going to let her training take over. She was an experienced detective. She knew how to investigate a disappearance.

Kate arbitrarily picked the house on the right. It was bigger than Tish's place, three bedrooms probably, and its front had a stone facade. A pecan tree stood in the front yard. The door was opened by a woman in her early thirties. She had shoulder-length light brown hair, green eyes, a thin boyish figure.

"Hi, Tish," she said, pushing open the metal outer door, "come on in."

"I'm not Tish. I'm Kate, her twin sister."

The woman put her hand on her forehead. "Oh, my. The two of you do look alike." She proffered her hand. "I'm Marsha Wagner. Glad to meet you."

Kate shook the woman's hand.

"Sit down, sit down. Tish told me you were coming for a visit. First thing in the morning, I didn't even think about it. You even wear your hair like she does."

"It wasn't anything we did intentionally," Kate said as she sat down in an upholstered chair. "I don't think either one of us really knew how the other was fixing her hair."

The living room was nice, the carpeting, furniture, lamps all in compatible shades of green and white, everything apparently chosen with great care. Marsha Wagner seated herself on the couch.

"Tish is real nice," she said. "We all like her. She lends Teddy—that's my son—she lends him books. Just gives them to him over the back fence, lets him keep them as long as he wants. Anyway, what brings you over here so bright and early?"

"I'm looking for Tish."

"She's not over here."

Kate explained what had happened.

"Oh, my," Marsha Wagner said.

"I was hoping you might know something that could help me find her."

"I wish I did. Gosh, that's really not like Tish. She's very reliable and responsible. I hope nothing's happened to her."

"I checked with the police, the hospital, everybody I could think of. No one knows anything."

Marsha said, "I hope Boyd didn't do anything to her."

She leaned forward. "Maybe it's none of my business telling you this, but we were all glad to see Boyd leave." She shook her head. "He's a terrible man. I, uh, I hope I haven't over-stepped."

"No, no," Kate said. "I agree with you. He's a terrible man."

Inwardly Kate groaned at her own stupidity. She hadn't even thought of Tish's former husband. When something like this happens, the first thing you do is take a good look at husbands, wives, lovers, family members. She'd been so worried about Tish, so personally involved, that she forgot to think like a cop.

People who behaved like Boyd already had bad mental problems. Sometimes something would happen that pushed them all the way over the edge, turned them into full-fledged psychos. Maybe Boyd had found out that Tish had divorced him *in absentia*. That might be enough to do it. Again Kate saw the image of Tish's lifeless form abandoned in some dark place. Boyd had already put her in the hospital. How big a step was it from that to killing her?

"I testified when Tish divorced him," Marsha said. "I think I knew more about what was going on than most of the neighbors did. Tish told me some of it. And I saw him hit her more than once. That was the part I testified about."

"If he has come back, do you have any idea where he might be staying? Does he have any friends here? Any rela-tives?"

Marsha considered that. "I know he had a group of drink-ing buddies, but I don't know who they were. I don't think he had any family here. Most of his relatives are from around Lubbock, as far as I know."

"Where did he work?"

Marsha snorted. "He didn't most of the time." She frowned. "I think the last job he had was driving a delivery truck for one of those vending machine outfits. He'd put candy and chips and sunflower seeds and things like that into the machines."

"You remember the name of the company?"

She shook her head.

34

"Why'd he leave the job?"

"I don't know, but I can guess," Marsha said, her eyes on Kate, dead serious. Marsha Wagner was clearly a person of convictions, one of which was an intense dislike for Tish's ex-husband. If you could judge someone by the people she didn't like, then Marsha was thumbs-up.

"What would you guess?" Kate asked.

"Part of the job was putting candy and whatnot into the machines, and the other part was taking the money out." She let it go at that.

"Well," Kate said, rising, "I've got a lot of other people to check with."

"Will you let me know if you learn anything? Tish and I are pretty good friends, and I'm going to worry about her until I know she's home safe and sound."

Kate said she would.

She spent the next hour and a half checking with the other neighbors—nearly all of whom mistook her for Tish—and when she was done she had been to most of the houses on the block. No one knew anything that might help. She got Tish's car and headed for the library.

The Leap public library was a white clapboard-sided house. With its pink roses and big shade trees, it looked a lot like the place in which Grandma might live and very little like a public building. The only thing that gave it away was the small sign suspended between two posts in the lawn: WILLIAM T. GERBER PUBLIC LIBRARY. Kate wondered who William T. Gerber was.

"There you are," a woman said as Kate stepped into the library. She was probably in her seventies, with that extremely pale skin elderly people so often have and white hair that hung limply against the sides of her head. She was sitting at a wooden desk by the front door. A sign on the desk said CHECK OUT BOOKS HERE. She looked at Kate with eyes that were deep clear blue and quite intelligent.

"No, I'm not," Kate said. "I mean I'm not who you think I am."

The woman studied her in silence. Despite the hot summer weather, she was wearing a sweater.

"I'm Kate Hastings. Tish's twin sister."

The woman nodded. "I'm Harriet Fielding. Where's Tish?"

"I don't know. That's why I'm here."

"I think you better explain that."

Kate told her what was going on. "She said she was going to get a ride with someone named Pam."

"Pamela Sue. She works here in the afternoons, after school. Tish is the only full-time employee. I work part-time in the mornings, and Pamela Sue helps out in the afternoons."

"What's Pamela Sue's last name?"

"Jenkins. You'll have to wait until this afternoon to talk to her, unless you want to go by the high school and find out what class she's in, get somebody to fetch her."

"What time does she come in?"

"About two. This is her senior year, and she doesn't have to be in classes the whole day to get the credits she needs to graduate."

Kate took in the library. It was all dark hardwood floors and wainscoting, wooden tables and bookshelves. The place had clearly been a home at one time. This apparently had been the living room. Two smaller rooms, presumably former bedrooms, had hand-painted signs over their doorways indicating that they were now the children's library and the reference room. The place smelled of old books and oiled wood.

"Does Tish have an office?" Kate asked.

"Over there," Harriet Fielding replied, indicating a closed door on the other side of the room.

"Would you mind if I had a look inside? I might find something that could help me figure out what happened to Tish."

The old woman thought about that for a moment, then shook her head. "It doesn't really belong to your sister. It belongs to the town. It would be okay if you were the police, but I don't think civilians should be nosing around in the librarian's office—even if they are the librarian's twin sister."

Kate considered telling her that she *was* the police, but

then dropped the idea. She was the police in New York, not here. "Has Tish ever disappeared like this before that you know of?"

"No, never." And for the first time Kate saw the concern in the old woman's eyes.

"Do you know anything that might help me figure this thing out?"

The woman shook her head. "I hope you find her soon."

Kate asked her for directions to the high school.

Leap's high school wasn't big as such institutions went. It was a one-story structure of brick and glass with a flagpole out front from which the U.S. and Texas flags flew. The walk leading to the main entrance went around the pole like a traffic circle. Inside, Kate found glass cases displaying the trophies won by the Leap Leopards. It occurred to her that that sounded awfully close to leaping lizards. It also occurred to her that the kids attending the school would have to say they went to Leap High.

She located the office and told the woman behind the counter what she wanted. The woman got the assistant principal whose name was McFeeney, and Kate explained it again. He said he'd tell Pamela Sue Jenkins she was here, but it was up to the girl whether she talked to her. He returned about five minutes later accompanied by a heavyset girl with short brown hair. She was the first high school girl Kate had seen in a long time who wore glasses and who didn't wear eye makeup or dangly earrings.

The assistant principal introduced them, then returned to his office, apologizing that there was no place private for them to talk. They sat down on a wooden bench that reminded Kate of a church pew.

"Thank you for talking to me, Pamela Sue."

The girl made a face. "Just call me Pam. Half of everybody in Texas has two names. I've always thought it was stupid."

"Okay, Pam. Uh, I understand you gave Tish a ride home yesterday afternoon. Is that right?"

"Yes."

"Did anything unusual happen?"

"No, I just drove her to her house and let her off. That's it."

"Did she seem upset about anything?"

"No. Mr. McFeeney said Miz Hastings is missing. Do you have any idea what might have happened to her?"

"Not at the moment. Apparently she went out again after you dropped her off, and no one's seen her since."

"I hope she's okay. I've always really liked working with her at the library."

"Did she say anything to you about going anywhere?"

"No, not a thing."

"Was there anybody hanging around when you let her off?"

"I didn't see anybody."

Kate hesitated, trying to decide whether there was anything else she should ask, and the girl said, "Mr. McFeeney told me you were Miz Hastings's twin, but for a moment, I thought someone was pulling a joke on me. You look *exactly* like her. You even sound like her."

Unable to think of anything to say to that, Kate simply nodded.

"You're from New York, aren't you?"

"I'm really from West Texas, but I've lived in New York the last ten years."

"And Miz Hastings told me you're a police detective."

"Yes." It seemed funny to hear Tish referred to as Miz Hastings.

"I think that's neat, for a woman to be a detective on a big police force like that." She sighed. "It would never happen here. Have you met the Leap Police yet?"

"I've met one of them."

"Which one?"

"Officer Schultz."

"Wait'll you meet Chief Colton."

Kate didn't ask for an explanation. She thanked Pam for her help, then drove back to the house. As she pulled into the garage, Kate looked for some sign that Tish had returned. It was a foolish hope, and she knew it. What would Tish say,

38

that she went jogging and lost all track of time, just now got tired?

No, there were no innocent explanations. For Tish to have been gone this long without anyone hearing from her meant that something bad had happened to her. Sure, people did weird things. They flipped out or opted out. Some guy would decide he couldn't handle the pressure of job and family and hop a freight train headed west one day instead of going home to the wife and kids. Kate was no psychologist; she couldn't say for sure Tish hadn't done anything like that. But she'd seen a lot of bizarre human behavior, and her experience along with her instincts told her that Tish wasn't merely acting weirdly. Tish was in trouble.

Kate switched off the engine of her sister's car, then sat there in the hot garage, staring through the windshield at the hoses and garden tools hanging from the wall. A mud dauber flew slowly into her field of vision, and she followed its progress until it lighted on the small earthen nest it had constructed on the ceiling. There were other mud nests there, Kate noticed, and she wondered how the wasps got in. She had always heard they lived on spiders, a thought she found appealing, since she had nothing in particular against daubers, and spiders gave her the creeps.

But the wasps only held her attention for a few moments. Kate tried to picture Tish and was alarmed to find she couldn't. It was as if Tish was slowly fading from her life, even Tish's image. Which was ridiculous. All Kate had to do to see Tish was look in the mirror. But then that wasn't true, was it? Looking in the mirror would be like looking at a photograph. It wouldn't be the real Tish at all.

Kate felt tears welling up, and she shook her head, forced herself to hold them back. If she was going to help Tish, she had to push her emotions back into some dark recess of her consciousness and slam the door on them. She had to maintain a clear, objective mind. She had to think like a cop.

Getting out of the car, Kate went into the house. She had yet to give the place a thorough going-over, the way a cop looking for clues would. She started with the kitchen, looking in all the cabinets, opening all the drawers, picking over

39

the garbage. Moving on to the living room, she sorted through magazines, looked under tables, moved furniture. Tish had two tall bookcases, both of which were full. Kate took out each volume, looked through it for notations, slips of paper. Even before becoming a librarian, Tish had loved books. In nonfiction her taste ran to essays and history. In fiction she had everything from Fielding and Austen to the latest novels by Elmore Leonard and Stephen King.

Kate went through the room in which she was sleeping and the bathroom, opening drawers, moving furniture, looking through wastebaskets. She saved Tish's bedroom for last. There were bookcases here, too, and again Kate went through every volume. She sorted through her sister's clothes, finding dresses and underwear and blouses and slacks, all of which were exactly her size as well as Tish's. Although the clothes were generally less expensive than those she wore, they came very close to being her taste. Things that looked good even if they were inexpensive, things that were never too revealing or too flashy. Classics. Kate had no idea what she was looking for. She was just looking. If she discovered something useful, she'd know it when she saw it.

Kate looked through her sister's jewelry and cosmetics and shoes; she looked underneath the drawers in the dresser to see whether anything had been taped there, finding nothing. And then she did discover something, although she was uncertain what. Embedded in the carpet was a gray clump of something dry and powdery. Getting a small plastic bag from the kitchen, Kate collected the material. It was like mud, but the consistency was wrong somehow. It apparently had fibers of some sort running through it. Whatever it was, it seemed out of place in Tish's bedroom. And things that seemed out of place were worth investigating. Kate sealed the bag with a plastic-covered twist wire and put it in her purse.

She was about to go out back and poke through Tish's garbage cans when the door chimes sounded. It was Marsha Wagner, the woman who lived next door, and she was accompanied by a boy about ten years old. Kate invited them in. The boy studied Kate intently, apparently taking in the resemblance between her and Tish.

"This is my son Teddy," Marsha said.

The boy smiled bashfully. He was on the chubby side, with a round, lightly freckled face and dark hair that had a prominent cowlick. He looked a lot like Beaver Cleaver.

"Any word on Tish?" Marsha asked.

Kate shook her head. "Sit down." When Marsha and the boy had lowered themselves onto the couch, Kate asked, "Can I get you anything to drink?"

Marsha declined. "We came over because Teddy's got something to tell you. Tell her what you saw, Teddy."

"Uh, it was yesterday," the boy began. "I was going home because it was six-fifteen, and that's when we eat dinner, at six-fifteen."

"You were late," his mother reminded him.

The boy flicked his eyes toward her sheepishly, then continued. "Anyway, I was coming down the alley, and there was this pickup parked behind your house. I got right up beside it, and the gate opened, and your sister and this guy came out. I said hi to her, and the guy said something to her, and then she came around to the side of the truck where I was standing and smiled and asked me how I was doing."

Teddy paused, apparently trying to recall exactly how it went. Kate's heart was beginning to beat faster. There were all sorts of things she was dying to ask, but she waited, gave the boy time to tell it in his own way.

"I . . . well, I guess I wanted to say something that sounded like what a grown-up would say, so I asked her if she was going out to dinner. She said that was right. She was going to a place called Clement's on Sixteenth Street." He looked at Kate expectantly, apparently waiting to see whether this meant something to her. It didn't.

"There is no Sixteenth Street," the boy said. "When I ride my bike down Texas Avenue, I read all the street signs, you know, just for something to do. And the numbered ones only go to Eighth." He nodded his head, as if confirming this with himself, then added, "I'm sure. Eighth Street's the last one."

"And there's no Clement's restaurant," Marsha said.

Kate stared at them, trying to assimilate all this. Tish had

41

left from the alley, saying she was going to a nonexistent restaurant on a nonexistent street. What the hell did it mean?

"What did the man look like?" she asked.

"I don't know," Teddy answered. "He kept his head turned. I never saw his face."

Kate said, "You probably know a lot more than you think you do, Teddy. Let's see what we can find out."

The boy grinned at her. He was enjoying this.

"Okay," Kate said. "Was this guy fat or thin?"

Teddy hesitated, then said, "I guess he was sort of thin. Not real skinny or anything like that. Just thin, regular thin."

"Okay, we're doing good. Was he tall or short?"

"Tall. When he was standing next to your sister, he could look over her head."

Since Kate was five-eight, Tish was, too, which meant the guy was at least six feet tall. "What kind of clothes was he wearing?"

"Levi's and a cowboy shirt. His Levi's were clean but real faded. You know what I mean?"

Kate nodded. "Did he have on a western belt?" Sometimes the buckles were very distinctive.

"I think so. It was brown and kind of wide. And it was faded, like his Levi's."

"Did you see the buckle?"

The boy paused, recalling. "No," he said finally. "He pretty much kept his body turned away from me."

"Describe his shirt."

"It was sort of off-white, and wrinkled."

"Anything unusual about it?"

"Like what?"

"Any writing on it, any fancy designs?"

Teddy shook his head. "Uh-uh."

"Was he wearing a hat?"

"No." Then, anticipating her next question, he added, "His hair was brown, but not real dark brown."

"Was it real thick? Did he have a bald spot?"

"There were no bald spots, but it wasn't real thick either."

"Is there anything else you can tell me about him?"

"I don't think so."

"You didn't by any chance get the license number of the pickup, did you?"

He looked disappointed. "I wish I had."

"What can you tell me about the truck?"

"Just that it was white and not real new. I didn't pay any attention to what kind it was."

"Did it have any dents or scratches or anything like that?"

"I guess it did, but I don't remember where they were."

"Would you recognize the truck if you saw it again?"

The boy shook his head.

"How about the guy?"

He had to think about that one a moment, but then he shook his head again.

"Did you know Boyd, my sister's ex-husband?"

"Sure."

"Could it have been him?"

Again the boy took his time. Finally he said, "I don't know. I didn't hear him talk or anything, and I never saw his face." Teddy looked uncomfortable, as if he'd failed somehow. "Mr. Steuben was about the same size, I guess, but I just didn't see enough of the guy to be sure if it was him—or if it wasn't him."

"That's okay, Teddy," Kate said. "You did good. Real good."

He brightened. "Did I help you?"

"You sure did. I know a lot more now than I knew a few minutes ago."

"Really?"

"Really."

Marsha said, "Do you think it was Boyd, Kate?"

"Boyd's tall and wiry, with brown hair, and he likes to wear western clothes." She stopped, let it hang there.

Marsha studied her for a moment, then said, "Kate, Boyd's . . . he's dangerous. He's sick."

"I know."

"What are you going to do?"

"I'm going to go down and have a talk with the local police."

FOUR

The Leap police station occupied one end of the city hall, a one-story cement building with small windows. It was located across the street from a municipal park that was practically ablaze with flowers. The park was beautiful; city hall looked like a bunker.

Leap, Kate had discovered, was laid out like Manhattan, with streets running one direction, avenues the other. At least until you got into some of the newer residential areas, where streets curved around, ended in cul-de-sacs, and did other things incompatible with the street-avenue directional uniformity. Texas Avenue was the main drag. Gerber Avenue, on which the city hall/police station was located, paralleled Texas one block from it. Kate assumed the avenue and library were named for the same Gerber.

She pulled into the lot at the police station end of the building and parked next to a white patrol car. She told the woman at the desk that she wanted to see the chief.

"What do you want to see him about?" She was about fifty, gray-haired, and spoke in a slow Texas drawl.

Kate showed her her gold NYPD detective's shield. "I'd consider it a matter of professional courtesy if he'd see me."

"Hold on," the woman said. She picked up a phone, said

there was an NYPD detective here to see the chief, listened a moment, then hung up. "Down the hall, second door on your left."

There was no outer office. Kate stepped through the open doorway to find herself facing a man of about forty with wavy dark hair and a thick, carefully groomed mustache. When he rose to shake her hand, Kate discovered that he was tall, maybe six-three. He looked like Texas's answer to Tom Selleck. He identified himself as Jack Colton, chief of police.

"How can I help you?" he asked when she'd seated herself. Although he gave her a good-ole-boy Texas smile, his eyes were hard, cold, appraising.

Kate told him about Tish's disappearance, and he said, "We've already taken a report on this."

"Yes. I didn't know it had been called to your attention."

"I read all the reports from the night before when I come in in the morning. I like to keep abreast of what's happening. That way I don't get any unpleasant surprises." He leaned back in his chair. "If you've already reported it, I'm not sure just what help you think I can be."

"There's more," Kate said. She told him about questioning the neighbors, the woman in the library, and Pam Jenkins. She repeated Teddy Wagner's account of Tish's leaving with the man in the white pickup who could have been Boyd.

"Does that mean anything to you," Kate asked, "Clement's on Sixteenth Street?"

The chief fiddled with a rubber band, thinking. "The boy and his mother told you right about there being no such place and no such street. But I don't see any meaning in it. Seems to me it could have been a lie she came up with on the spur of the moment. Because she didn't want to admit where she was really going."

"And where was that?" Kate asked, uncertain where Colton was heading with this.

"Seems pretty likely to me that she ran off with the guy in the white truck."

"Tish wouldn't do that. There's no way."

Colton fiddled with his rubber band for a moment, then said, "You know, when one of my officers finds himself

45

working on something he's personally involved in, I get him off of it real quick. You know why that is?''

His words caught Kate by surprise. "You trying to tell me that I'm too involved to see the thing clearly?''

He nodded. "That's right. Because if you were seeing the thing like a police officer, you'd realize that there was nothing in what the boy saw to indicate that your sister wasn't leaving with this guy voluntarily. And there's nothing to indicate a struggle in the house. But you're not seeing these things because you're not thinking like a police officer. You're thinking like a sister.''

"Tish wouldn't just run off like that, without telling me. She wouldn't just walk out on her job.''

"And how many times have you heard people say things like that?''

"A few.''

"And how many times have you seen people just walk away from it all, disappear?''

"I've seen it.''

"And if that person's over twenty-one, there's nothing the police can do about it. No law says a person can't run off.''

Kate's dislike of Chief Colton was growing rapidly. She tried not to let it show. "Tish didn't run off. The sister says so, and the cop says so, too.''

He sighed. "We'll check into it, but I'm going to have to remind you that you have no authority here. You're going to have to let us handle it. We don't need you doing our job for us.''

"I'm not trying to do that," Kate said.

Chief Colton frowned. "It sure sounds like it. You've been questioning people at the library, questioning the neighbors, going to the high school. That sounds like investigating to me.''

If you'd do the job, Kate thought, no one else would have to do it for you. She said, "I'm not chasing criminals, Chief. I'm just looking for my sister. Any private citizen has a right to look for her sister, doesn't she?''

"As long as it doesn't interfere with a police investigation.''

What investigation? Kate wondered. She fixed her eyes on the chief's. "Look," she said, "if Boyd has Tish, she could be in a lot of danger. I've met him. I know what he's like. He put her in the hospital with some broken ribs the last time he went to work on her. He's one of those people you were talking about who decided to disappear. Tish divorced him *in absentia*. He's got to find out someday, and there's no telling how he's going to take it."

"We've put a locate out on him," Colton said. "Both locally and through NCIC. As soon as we hear something, I'll give you a call at your sister's place."

Kate wondered whether she should translate that as, "Don't call us, we'll call you." In her purse was the plastic bag containing the powdery material she'd scraped off the floor in Tish's bedroom. She decided not to turn it over to Chief Colton.

"I'm very worried," she said, getting up to leave. "I'd appreciate it if you'd let me know if you learn anything— anything at all."

"You can count on it," the chief said, smiling. As Kate turned to go, he said, "Officer Hastings."

"Yes."

"We may not be the New York City Police Department, but we know what we're doing."

Kate told him she was sure that was right.

As she drove away from the police station she tried to figure out what to make of Chief Colton. It was probably safe to assume that he wasn't real fond of big-city cops, and female big-city cops were probably just that much worse. But that didn't matter much. What did matter was that he was going to be of minimal help in finding Tish. He was going to devote the resources of his department to catching burglars and shoplifters and speeders, not to finding some woman who, to his mind, had most likely run off.

I should have tried harder to convince him, Kate thought, suddenly feeling it was her fault the chief didn't see that Tish could be in real danger. And then she realized there was probably nothing she could have said that would have made

47

any difference. Colton saw things the way he wanted to see them. He wasn't apt to have his mind changed easily.

As she drove along the squeaky-clean streets of Leap, Kate considered what she was going to do next. It was a typical summer day in central Texas. Hot, muggy, and cloudless. There would be clouds during the summer, of course, big black ones, towering thunderheads. Hail. Downpours. Tornado watches and warnings. But today was calm, sunny, sticky, humid, with no likelihood that the winds would lift the roofs off houses or play bumper cars with house trailers. The temperature was probably below a hundred, which was as good as summer weather got in these parts.

Kate thought about Clement's on Sixteenth Street. Why had Tish said she was going out to dinner at a nonexistent restaurant on a nonexistent street? Was Tish trying to tell the boy something specific? Or was it just an attempt to let Teddy know something was wrong? Or was it anything at all?

It had to mean something, Kate decided. A person lying solely to hide the truth would have used the name of a real place. Making up a place increased the risk that the lie would be found out. The best lie was simple, unembellished, the one essential fact the only thing that was untrue. Even inexperienced liars seemed to know that instinctively. But if Tish's words meant something, Kate had no idea what.

And Kate sensed that there was some information in Tish's words beyond what Tish might have intended. But whatever it was, it hung in her subconscious, teasing her, staying just out of reach.

She stopped at a Dairy Queen and had a chili dog and an orange soda. When she was a girl in West Texas, she and Tish and their friends had practically lived on orange sodas. This one didn't taste as good as she remembered them, but then that was one of the things that happened when you grew up, she supposed. Things stopped being as good as you remembered them.

Kate drove back to the house to make sure Tish hadn't turned up there. She hadn't. Next Kate called the library and checked with Harriet Fielding. The old woman still hadn't heard from Tish.

Sitting at the table in Tish's kitchen, Kate checked the local phone book for Clement and Clement's, finding no listings for either spelling. Next she checked the city map and street index in the back of the book for any street names that sounded like Sixteenth. Nothing came close. She called directory assistance and was informed that there was no listing for Clement or Clement's. Then she checked directory assistance for the surrounding communities and Austin. There were a few Clements but none on a Sixteenth Street. Kate took their numbers and called them anyway, asked whether any of them knew Tish Hastings. None of them did.

So what to do now? Kate still needed to find a lab to test the material she'd scraped off the floor in Tish's bedroom, but it was unlikely there were any labs in Leap. She checked the yellow pages. There weren't. Getting the lab work done would mean a trip to Austin then. Which could wait for tomorrow, since she still had things to do here.

She checked the yellow pages under vending machines, finding only one company. Hill Country Vending, 743 Alamo Street. It had to be the place Boyd had worked. Kate wrote down the address. Then she looked up the number of the county battered women's shelter and dialed it. She got a recording saying the number was temporarily out of service. She dialed again, getting the same recording. Grabbing her purse, Kate drove out to the house that stood alone on the edge of town, the house Tish had pointed out the day Kate arrived.

The place had no signs to indicate that it was anything other than an ordinary frame house. As Kate pulled into the gravel driveway, she noticed that the house had a lonely look about it, some indefinable quality that said the structure was something apart from this pretty community in the Texas hills. And then she wondered whether she was just imagining it. She'd come here knowing that this was a refuge, a place to which one came in desperation. Grasshoppers leaped from the weedy lawn as she walked to the front door. Kate pushed the button that rang the doorbell.

"Who's there?" a woman's voice said through the speaker behind a metal grille on the wall.

"Kate Hastings. I'm Tish Hastings's twin sister. I need to talk to you about Tish. I think she's in trouble."

Then Kate heard a sound familiar to all New Yorkers, the buzz of a door being electrically unlocked. Inside was a small counter behind which stood a tall woman in her late twenties with red hair and a face that was almost all freckles.

"Boy, you sure do look like Tish," the woman said. "I'd swear you were Tish pulling a prank on me if she hadn't told me that she had a twin living in New York." She reached across the counter to shake hands. "Chrissie Ann Delaney. I guess you could say I'm in charge here. That's because I'm the only one gets paid. Everybody else is a volunteer."

Kate shook the woman's hand. "I tried to call before I came out, but your phone must be out of order."

Chrissie Ann shook her head. "The phone company disconnected us because we couldn't pay the bill. It's all because of the price of oil. The state's economy is a mess, so the state doesn't have any money to give to the county, and the county cuts our budget. We're trying to get enough money to pay what we owe the gas company and the electric company, as well as the phone company. We're kind of behind with everybody. Before you go, remind me to hit you up for a contribution. I know that's forward, to ask like that, but I'd rather be pushy than see this place shut down."

Kate said she'd be more than happy to contribute something.

"Come on," Chrissie Ann said. "Let's go where we can sit down and be comfortable. Then you can tell me what the problem is with Tish."

Reaching under the counter, she pushed a button, and a door to Kate's left buzzed itself unlocked. Kate opened it, stepping into a living room with worn furniture. Three women were sitting in the room. They glanced up when Kate entered, but didn't say anything. They were young, none of them out of their twenties. One, a blonde with short curly hair, had two black eyes and a bruise on her left cheek. Toys cluttered the floor. A small boy was pushing a toy truck and making engine noises. An infant was asleep in a crib. When women fled, they took the children with them.

"You've got a lot of security here," Kate said as Chrissie Ann joined her.

"Got to. We've had some furious husbands try to break down the door."

"That's a time when you really need the phone," Kate said. "So you can call the police."

Chrissie Ann grunted. "For all the good it does. The chief gives us the minimum amount of help he can get away with. I think he believes that slapping your woman around's good for her, keeps her mindful of her place. I'd give anything if this place was a hundred feet over that way." She pointed toward the street. "We'd be across the city line, and the sheriff would be responsible for us."

"I've met Chief Colton," Kate said.

Chrissie Ann said, "Come on. I've got an office around the corner here."

Her office was barely big enough to hold the old wooden desk, which was covered with papers and empty soft-drink cans. Chrissie Ann was not an organizer. Sitting down behind her desk, she moved a Seven-Up can to the side. Kate sat down in a wood chair.

"Not too many women here right now," Chrissie Ann said. "They come at night. Sometimes we've got people lined up on the floor in sleeping bags. They find their way here from all over the county." Her eyes grew distant for a moment, as if she were considering that; then she said, "Tell me what happened to Tish."

Kate told her what she knew. "Did Tish ever say anything to you that might help me figure this thing out?"

"No," Chrissie Ann said, looking thoughtful. "Not that I can recall."

"What about Clement's on Sixteenth? Does that mean anything to you?"

"Not a thing. Are you sure the boy remembered it right?"

"That's what he said he heard. How about a tall guy with brown hair in a white pickup?"

Chrissie Ann shook her head. "I'm sorry."

"It's possible that it was her ex-husband."

"If it was, you better find her. He's one of the ones who

51

tried to force his way in here one night. You can tell what they're like by their eyes. Some of them are just plain crazy and would probably be better off at the funny farm. Others are more confused than anything else. They don't know what they're doing. And then there's the mean ones, the ones that hurt just for the sake of hurting. Boyd was one of those, one of the mean ones."

"What would he do if he had her?"

"Make her suffer."

"But do you think she'd go with him willingly?"

"Maybe she didn't go willingly," Chrissie Ann said. "Maybe it just looked that way."

Kate nodded. She'd thought of that, too.

"Tish wouldn't just run off with some guy," Chrissie Ann said. "She wouldn't do that."

When Kate left a few moments later—after giving Chrissie Ann a twenty-dollar contribution—she noticed the bars over the house's windows. She hadn't paid much attention to them earlier, in part because they were painted white to match the building, but mainly because they were so common in New York that you just took them for granted. Now that she thought about it, this was the only house in Leap she'd seen with burglar bars. She thought of Tish having to hide out behind barred windows and double sets of locked doors. And then the image dissolved. Tish might have worse problems than that now.

Kate started the car and drove away from the lonely building on the edge of town. Even though she had the windows rolled up and the air conditioner on, the odor from the nearby livestock auction seeped into the car.

Under different circumstances Kate might have considered it a country odor, a reminder of her childhood in West Texas. But at the moment it just smelled rotten. She sped up to get away from it.

"Yeah, I remember Boyd Steuben," the man said. He was a chubby bald guy with a ruddy complexion. While he talked to Kate, he worked on a candy machine. Its back was off, and both his hands were out of sight, doing things to its

52

innards. His name was Quintley. He was the manager of Hill Country Vending Company.

"I had to let him go," Quintley said, looking up. "We have to operate on trust here. My life is guided by my trust in the Lord, and He gives me the faith to trust those who work for me. But every now and then someone comes along who just doesn't seem capable of handling trust."

The machine on which Quintley was working was one of several in the room. There were machines that dispensed coffee and soft drinks and cigarettes and even condoms. Most of them had their innards exposed. One had a sign taped to it proclaiming THIS DAMN THING IS BUSTED AGAIN.

"Was he stealing from you?" Kate asked.

"His job was to stock and maintain the machines. He ran a regular route. He'd check each machine, clean it up, restock it if it was low or if the stuff was stale, and collect the money. He was keeping some of the money for himself. It's as simple as that."

"How'd you catch him?"

"We count the stuff that goes out, the stuff that comes back because it's stale, and we count the money. Sure, there's things that can go wrong with the system. Sometimes a machine will start giving the stuff away for free, things like that. But when a pattern develops with one guy, then you know you've got a problem."

"Have you seen him lately, or heard anything about him?"

"No. Don't imagine I would under the circumstances."

"Did he have any friends who are still around?"

He put down an open-end wrench and picked up a screwdriver, his hand disappearing into the machine again. "I think he used to buddy around with Tommy Gomez and another guy named Mundt. Neither one of them works here anymore. Gomez moved out of the state—California, I think. Mundt's dead. He was killed in a motorcycle accident."

"What was he like, Boyd Steuben?"

Quintley was silent for a long moment. Finally he said, "That's hard to answer. Probably the best thing for me to do is give you an example. When I called him in to fire him, he looked at me like he didn't care if I fired him or not, like it just didn't matter. He turned around to leave, and then he looked at me again, and he was entirely different. There was something in his eyes, like he wanted to stomp the hell out of me. I don't mind telling you that I felt a whole lot more comfortable when he was gone.''

She asked him whether Clement's on Sixteenth meant anything to him. He said it didn't.

When Kate got back to the house, she phoned her uncle Charles in West Texas. He recalled Boyd Steuben all right, hadn't liked him much, wished Tish hadn't married him. Hadn't seen Boyd in years and had no idea where he was. No one in Boyd's family was around anymore. The Steubens had lost their farm and moved out of the area. It was real sad what was happening to farmers these days. People better wise up before the big corporations owned all the farms and people were going hungry because of the price of food. Uncle Charles didn't know where the Steubens had gone. Kate promised she'd call when she found anything more out about Tish. Uncle Charles said he would remember both the twins in his prayers.

When she went to bed that night, Kate wondered whether she'd be able to fall asleep, but she was so exhausted she drifted off instantly. But then the dreams came. She was in the room with the eleven-year-old. Tom Napier and the boy were talking. But this time she knew the kid had a gun hidden under the blankets on the end of the couch. She saw him reaching under the blankets, and she tried to scream, to warn Tom, but no sounds came from her mouth. She tried to rush forward, grab the boy, but her muscles wouldn't work. She stood there, helpless, unable to move or make a sound, while the boy pulled out the gun, aimed at Tom, pulled the trigger. Although Kate's own gun was in her purse, it might as well have been in another solar system for all the good it was doing her. Terrified, she watched as the boy swung the gun toward her and aimed carefully.

''Stupid bitch,'' he said, and pulled the trigger.

Kate sat bolt upright in bed, trembling, her breath coming in short gasps. Finally, when she'd calmed down, Kate lay back and forced herself to think about something else. She saw Tish getting into the white pickup with a man. It wasn't Boyd, but a stranger. And then her mind put the eleven-year-old boy in the truck, sitting between Tish and the man. As the truck drove off, both the man and the kid were grinning at Tish.

Stop it! she told herself. Just stop it.

She made herself think about Clement's on Sixteenth Street. If there was a clue in that, what was it? She ran down every possibility she could think of. Was there a slang meaning for Clement? Was it someone's first name? Did the number sixteen refer to the sixteenth district? Sixteenth largest city in Texas? Sixteenth voting precinct? Somewhere sixteen miles from Leap?

After a while, the possibilities flowed together, becoming a blur, a white noise of thoughts, and she drifted off to sleep. There were no more nightmares.

FIVE

In the morning Kate went to the library. She found Harriet Fielding in the reference room, arranging the library's limited supply of magazines.

"Any news?" the old woman asked.

She told her about Tish's leaving with a man in a white pickup. "Does it mean anything, Clement's on Sixteenth Street?"

Harriet Fielding frowned. "I don't think so."

"Could it mean anything connected with the library? Does sixteen mean anything in the Dewey decimal system? Does anyone have library card number sixteen?"

Harriet Fielding smiled indulgently. "I don't think any of those connections are very likely."

"Have you always lived in Leap, all your life?"

"Since I was six."

"Was there ever a Sixteenth Street here?"

"No. Eighth is as high as the numbered streets have ever gone. And I don't recall ever hearing of a place called Clement's."

Kate nodded, tried to think of something else to say. A loud thump startled her. Turning in the direction of the sound, she caught a glimpse of a man picking up a book he'd dropped near the entrance of the reference room. He disappeared from her sight.

"I wish people would be more careful," Harriet Fielding said. "There was a time when people treated books with respect, kept them, treasured them. Now they break the spines, write on the pages, even tear pages out. It's a sin to treat books that way."

Kate stared at the old woman, suddenly angered because Harriet Fielding could worry about library books when Tish was missing and maybe in serious trouble. A book, after all, was only paper and ink and glue. It could be replaced. Then Kate's anger drained away as quickly as it had come. Harriet Fielding was concerned about Tish, and at the same time she was concerned about the books. There was nothing wrong with that. Tish would want someone to look after the books in her absence.

As Kate was leaving the library she noticed a display of books with a sign that read REGIONAL HISTORY, LEAP AND THE TEXAS HILL COUNTRY. She wondered whether some clue to the meaning of Clement's on Sixteenth might be found in one of the volumes, then dismissed the notion. If it pertained to the history of Leap, Harriet Fielding probably would have known about it.

As she drove toward Austin Kate again had the feeling that there was something in Tish's words that she was missing, something that could be deduced if she only thought about it. Whatever it was, it continued to elude her.

The place she was headed was called Capital City Testing Laboratory. It was located near the University of Texas, just off Martin Luther King Boulevard. This morning, before leaving the house, she'd phoned the sheriff's office, told them who she was, and asked for the name of a lab that could identify a sample for her. The officer she'd spoken to said they usually sent their stuff to the state police lab, but when it was too busy they'd sometimes use Capital City.

Following the directions given her by the sheriff's office, she found the place with no difficulty. It was a small one-story brick building on a tree-lined street. Inside was a counter with no one behind it and a bell with a small cardboard sign beside it that said RING FOR SERVICE. Kate rang, and a young dark-haired man wearing a plastic apron appeared.

"Help you?" he asked.

"Sheriff's office said I should ask for a guy named Starzynski."

"That's me."

Kate handed him the plastic bag containing the material she'd collected from the carpet in Tish's bedroom. "I want to know what that is," she said.

"How quick do you need to know?"

"Can I wait?"

"Sure, I guess. I can do a couple of simple things right away. Then if it looks like it's going to be complicated, I'll let you know."

Starzynski turned to go back into the lab, then hesitated. "Mind if I ask you something?"

"What?"

"I, uh, I like to listen to accents and try to figure out where people are from. Usually I'm pretty good, but you've got me completely stumped."

Kate was unsure whether Starzynski was coming on to her. She decided it really didn't matter one way or the other at the moment. She had more important things to worry about. "I was raised near Lubbock," she said. "But I've lived the last ten years in New York."

He grinned. "No wonder I couldn't figure it out."

Starzynski stood there a moment, apparently hoping Kate would continue the small talk. When she didn't, he said, "Uh, I'll check this out for you," and disappeared through the doorway behind the counter.

Although Starzynski was attractive and seemed nice enough, the timing was all wrong. Trifling with men was not something you did when your twin sister was missing and could be in serious trouble.

Kate sat down in a chair made of tubular steel and plastic. On a small table in front of her were a number of magazines devoted to chemistry and such things. She flipped through

58

one, put it back. Less than ten minutes after Starzynski had taken Kate's sample, the lab man was back.

Grinning, he said, "You've been away from Texas too long if you didn't recognize what was in that plastic bag."

"What was in it?" Kate asked, returning to the counter. "Dried armadillo? A chunk of the Alamo?"

He laughed. "It's what Texas probably has the most of—right after sand."

"You going to tell me what it is or make me guess till I get it?"

"Cow manure."

"Oh."

"You probably would have figured it out for yourself if you'd smelled it."

"This ordinary cow manure, or is there anything about it that might help me figure out where it came from?"

"Cow'd been eating mainly hay, as opposed to green grass or grain or whatever else cows eat."

"What does that tell me?"

"Nothing, really. Any time cows are penned, they're usually fed hay. And over winter they have to eat hay a lot of times. This was fairly old manure. The cow probably dropped it months ago."

Kate nodded, trying to figure what—if anything—this meant in terms of figuring out what had happened to Tish.

"You sure you were raised in West Texas?" Starzynski asked.

"My daddy grew sorghum. He didn't raise livestock." But Kate was only answering mechanically now. She was wondering whether the manure had come from the shoe of the man Kate had left with. It seemed likely. He'd been wearing western clothes and driving a pickup, which pretty much fit the image of someone who'd have cow shit on his soles. But what did this tell her that she didn't already know?

"Why'd you go to New York?" Starzynski asked.

"To seek my fortune, get rich and famous in the big city."

"You rich and famous?"

"No. I'm a cop. Joseph Wambaugh's the only one of us ever became rich and famous."

Kate left the lab. On Martin Luther King Boulevard she passed a green bus that was made to look like an old-time trolley. On its side were the words ARMADILLO EXPRESS. Austin was a pretty city that spread out along the terraced bluffs overlooking the Colorado River. Kate had wanted to go to college here, at the University of Texas. Instead she and Tish had gone to West Texas State in Amarillo because it was closer to home.

As Kate headed toward Leap she recalled driving this road a few days ago with Tish. Things had seemed good then, full of hope. The bad things had appeared to be behind them. Kate's vision fogged, and she realized she was about to cry. For a moment she considered pulling over to the side of the road, letting the tears come, but then she blinked them back. Crying would not help her find Tish.

And then Kate remembered how she and Tish had hugged each other and cried as they stood at the bus stop in West Texas. The flat land had stretched off in all directions, acre after acre of cotton and sorghum and wheat.

"You sure?" Tish had asked.

"No," Kate had answered, "but I made it all the way to the bus stop, and I'd be too embarrassed to change my mind now."

"Who'd know who wouldn't forgive you?"

"I would. Because if I don't do it now, I'll never do it."

The whole journey had reminded Kate of Jon Voight's in *Midnight Cowboy*. The long bus trip, the excitement of her first glimpse of the New York skyline, the cheap hotel, the loneliness, desperately trying to find work before the money ran out. Her degree from West Texas State had impressed no one, and she'd worked as a waitress, then a ticket seller at one of those places that sold tickets to all kinds of events. The customers were going to plays, orchestra performances, operas, and rock concerts, events she was usually unable to afford.

Many times she'd been on the verge of bagging the whole thing, going back to Texas. Her pride kept her from it, for going back beaten meant going back in shame. So she stuck it out, applied for every decent-sounding job she heard about. When she was applying for jobs with the city, she spotted a notice announcing openings for police officers. The salary beat the hell out of what a ticket seller made, so she applied.

Kate had all but forgotten about the police department when the notice came stating that she had been scheduled for an entrance examination. She passed the test, had the preliminary interviews, underwent psychological screening, and one day found herself in the police academy. Kate took to it instantly. She liked the academy, liked being a beat cop, liked everything. When she was eligible, she applied for plainclothes and got accepted, propelled into detectives largely by her unquenchable enthusiasm.

Which had remained undiminished until the day she was forced to blow away an eleven-year-old boy who'd just killed her partner, murdered him so the kid could prove his manhood, show he was ready to join a goddamn, stupid street gang.

The kid had thought it out well; she had to give him credit for that. He'd broken into the apartment. The people living there didn't know him, had no connection to him. If he'd pulled it off, there would have been nothing to connect him to the shooting. Only the gang members would have known, and even if one of them had broken the code of silence and given up the killer, there were no witnesses. And no evidence if he was smart enough to get rid of the gun.

But thinking about these things was wasting time. She needed to think about finding Tish. The words "Clement's on Sixteenth Street" came to her again, and it occurred to her that there were streets beyond Eighth, streets that simply didn't have numbers. What if she continued counting, found the street that would be Sixteenth if the numbers continued?

As soon as she reached Leap she tried it. The highway from Austin became Texas Avenue. Kate followed it until the numbered streets began. She counted them out loud.

"Sixteenth," she said finally. It was called Travis, a two-lane residential street that crossed Texas. Kate turned right and followed it into a neighborhood of three- and four-bedroom houses. In one block nearly everyone had pecan

61

trees. In another most of the homes had concrete driveways and basketball hoops mounted above the garage doors. Conformity, the American way.

Travis Street ended where it made a T with Ockner Avenue. Kate turned around, drove back to Texas Avenue, and crossed it. Travis Street on this side of Texas was almost indistinguishable from Travis Street on the other side of it. There was nothing suspicious here, no cross streets named Clement, no signs indicating that this clapboard house or that brick one belonged to the Clement family. There were only the homes of middle- and upper-middle-class people, folks who watched cable TV, went fishing, mowed their lawns. Most likely not a kidnapper in the lot. This time Travis Street ended in a vacant lot.

Kate made her way back to Texas Avenue. As she was heading for the house she thought about the cow manure she'd found. Assuming it had been left there by the man in the white pickup, Kate saw two possibilities. He was either someone Tish knew well enough to invite into her bedroom or he was an intruder. Boyd would fit into both categories, Kate supposed. Although he was no stranger, Tish would never have invited him into her bedroom.

Kate wished she knew where Boyd was. She wished she knew something—anything—that would help her figure out what had happened to Tish. It was possible she had the clue she needed and simply hadn't figured out its significance yet. It was possible. But it sure seemed unlikely.

Kate slept fitfully that night, frequently awakened by her dreams. Although she was unable to remember some of them, others lingered, replayed themselves again and again, tormenting her until she was finally able to doze off and have still more dreams.

She saw Tish hugging her at the bus stop along the West Texas highway. Although her parents had been dead by then, she saw them standing there, too, the concern for their departing daughter obvious on their suntanned faces. Her mother's graying hair was pulled back into a bun. Her dad's craggy face was shaded by a dusty, sweat-stained cap with the John Deere logo on it.

"It'll be okay," Kate told them.

Her parents just stared at her silently. Finally her mother said, "Let's see if the bus is coming."

Kate's mother and father moved into the middle of the two-lane highway, staring in the direction from which the bus would come. Kate heard the distant rumble of a diesel engine. Turning, she saw the truck, a big eighteen-wheeler, black smoke pouring from its twin stacks. It was bearing down on her parents.

Kate started to run into the highway to grab them, but then she heard Tish scream. Spinning around to find out what was happening, she saw Tish being dragged away by a man in cowboy clothes. It was Boyd. He was forcing her into a white pickup. Kate hesitated, uncertain whether to rescue her parents or her sister, and then she knew she'd hesitated too long, and it was too late to rescue any of them. She screamed and found herself lying in bed, trembling, sweating despite the steady stream of coolness from the window air conditioner.

In another dream, Kate saw the eleven-year-old boy pull the gun, but this time she was the one he shot, not Tom. As she felt the bullet slam into her body, Kate experienced both panic and relief. The relief came from knowing she wouldn't be the one whose partner died, from knowing she wouldn't be the one who had to kill an eleven-year-old kid. And strangely, from knowing that she was about to die.

In the morning Kate phoned the Leap police while she was sitting at the breakfast table having coffee. She asked for the chief and was told he was unavailable.

Hanging up the phone, Kate considered what she knew about Tish's disappearance. The most recent information she'd acquired was that the powdery stuff on Tish's bedroom floor was cow manure. What did that tell her? If it was left by the man in the white pickup, then he'd recently stepped into some old cow shit. This was cattle-ranching country. People who worked at the ranches could step in cow dung. So could people who went hiking or camping or hunting. There were also dairy farms around. And people who lived in the country and had a cow or two for fresh milk. Then there were the feed lots, the livestock auction, the stockyards.

And all those places had people who drove pickups and wore western clothes. Kate had a momentary image of Tish being abducted by the Marlboro man, but then that was the New York side of her personality speaking. She'd known a lot of Texas cowboy types, and there hadn't been a Marlboro man in the lot.

Was abducted the right word? She was assuming Tish had been taken away against her will. But she had no proof of that. According to the only eyewitness, Tish had gone with the man in the white truck quite willingly. Kate shook her head. She was unwilling to believe that Tish would have simply left, told no one, abandoned her job, her twin sister.

When she'd finished her coffee, Kate sat at the table for a while, trying to figure out what to do next. She had no idea. She had made all the obvious moves, and there was nothing else to do. If this case had been assigned to her, it would be just one of many. While waiting for something to develop, she would work on her other cases. But under these circumstances she had only two options: to sit and worry or to pace and worry. Getting up, she went into the backyard. At least it would be a change of scenery.

Tish's backyard had a few rosebushes that seemed to be growing wild and some weedy grass that was in need of watering. Tish enjoyed things like reading. For her, yard work was about as pleasurable as unstopping clogged drains. And Boyd had certainly never kept up the yard. Boyd had never done anything—except provide pain, of course.

Kate stretched. It was a pretty morning, the inevitable oppressive heat still a couple of hours away. A mosquito landed on Kate's arm and prepared to dine. She slapped it into oblivion.

"Twenty-three to two," a boyish voice said. "You in position?"

"This is two. Ten-four."

"Okay, let's move in."

Looking over the vine-covered fence into the Wagners'

yard, Kate saw Teddy crouching behind a bush. He was holding a walkie-talkie in his hand.

"Hi," Kate called.

"Oh, hi," the boy said, coming over to the fence. Into his walkie-talkie he said, "Never mind, Steve. I'm talking to the lady next door."

"You're supposed to use the code," Steve said over the radio.

"I forgot."

"What are you doing?" Kate asked.

"Just playing with the walkie-talkies. Do you use walkie-talkies in New York City?"

"Sure do."

"Do you have codes you use? I mean, like on TV they'll tell the police to go to a four-eleven or something like that."

"I think that's mainly in California. Most police departments use ten codes."

"You mean like ten-four?"

"Uh-hum. A lot of the codes are different. In one department a ten-thirteen can mean officer in distress. In another it can mean weather and road conditions."

"That's really interesting," Teddy said, showing a youngster's enthusiasm for such things. "How many crooks have you arrested?"

"I don't really know the exact number, but quite a few."

"You ever shoot anybody?"

Although the question was asked with childish innocence, it hit Kate like a blow in the gut. What the hell was she supposed to say? That the only vicious criminal she'd blown away was a boy maybe a year older than the one she was talking to? That what she'd done was so terrible she'd freaked out afterward? She was about to lie, tell him she'd never shot anyone ever, and then another boy appeared from the far side of the Wagners' house and saved her from having to answer the question. He had curly brown hair and wore glasses. He had a walkie-talkie just like Teddy's.

"Hi," he said as he joined Teddy at the fence.

"Hi," Kate replied. "What's your name?"

"Steve Baker."

"This is my neighbor, Miz Hastings. She's the twin sister of the lady who lives here. And she's a detective with the NYPD."

Steve's eyes widened. "Really?"

"Really," Kate said.

Teddy frowned. In case he was debating whether to tell Steve all about Kate's missing sister, she preempted him. "What's that code you're using over your two-way radios?" she asked.

"Well, I'm number two because my last name's Baker," Steve explained. "Teddy's twenty-three because his last name begins with a *W*. When Kenny Johnson plays with us, he's number ten." The boy watched Kate's expression to see whether she got it.

"I get it," Kate said after a moment. "If you played with someone named Connors, he'd be number three, because *C* is the third letter of the alphabet. Like that."

The boys nodded.

"Well, I guess I'd better get back inside," Kate said, wanting to get away from Teddy before he realized she'd never answered his question concerning whether she'd shot anybody. The boys waved, then dashed off.

Kate paced through the house for a while, finally deciding to go for a drive just as a way to stop pacing. Although she had seen Leap itself and the road coming in from the east, she had never explored the country lying to the north, west, or south of the community. For no particular reason she headed north. She would simply drive, try to clear her mind, and maybe something would come to her, something that would help her find out what had happened to Tish.

The countryside was no different than what she'd already seen. Rolling hills. Scrub oak and mesquite. An occasional entrance to a ranch.

Glancing in the rearview mirror, she saw a green Pontiac behind her. There had been a green car behind her back in town, and she wondered whether this was the same one. She hadn't been paying much attention. She watched it a moment, then dismissed it as unimportant.

What could she do to find out what had happened to Tish?

She was an experienced investigator, a detective in the nation's largest city. If anyone should know how to handle this thing, she should. And yet she was stumped. She could picture Tish chained and gagged, held prisoner in a damp basement somewhere. Or traveling across the country, forced to accompany her brutal ex-husband. Or—and she tried not to think about this—Tish could be lying dead in a shallow grave somewhere. No matter how unpleasant that thought, Kate knew she had to allow for the possibility.

No! a part of her screamed. Not that. *Anything but that.* And something inside her tried to will it not to be so through sheer mental force.

The green car was passing her now. The driver's western hat was pulled down low so she couldn't see his face. Kate realized something was wrong just a moment before the Pontiac swerved in toward her, smashing into her car.

The blow caused her car to fishtail, and while she struggled to regain control of it, the green Pontiac bumped her again. Ahead was a cement underpass for some railroad tracks, and Kate realized she was going to slam into it. She yanked the wheel to the right. The car skidded, and then she regained a modicum of control over it. It flew off the edge of the road, bounced into the air as it came out of the depression at the edge of the shoulder. Although Kate had jammed on the brakes, the car was still bouncing forward, throwing up dust. A barbed-wire fence appeared in front of her, and then she was through it, mowing down scrub brush. When the car came to a stop, it was enveloped by a cloud of dust. Kate just sat there, her heart pounding. The first thought that came to her was that she was glad she'd worn her seat belt. The car had lurched sharply a couple of times, and she'd felt the belt restraining her.

Then she remembered what had happened. The driver of the green car had deliberately tried to run her off the road. He'd followed her, tried to kill her. Kate looked back toward the road. Through the settling dust she could see the green Pontiac, motionless at the side of the road, the driver's silhouetted form staring at her. Automatically her hand reached for her purse, which had fallen to the floor. And then she remembered that she'd left her service revolver in New York, not wanting to have with her the thing she had used to kill an eleven-year-old boy.

Pushing the button that unlocked her seat belt, she found that it was jammed. She saw an image of the man in the green car opening her door, finding her strapped to the seat . . . but then the seat belt released and she quickly climbed out of the car. The green Pontiac started to drive away. Although Kate was still unable to see the driver, she did see the license number.

Suddenly Kate's knees grew weak, and she had to sit down. Resting her back against the side of the car, she sat in the dirt, trying to understand what had just happened. Someone had followed her. Someone had tried to . . . to what? To kill her? To scare her?

What was it all about? Until a few days ago the only person she'd known in this part of Texas was Tish. She had no enemies here; she hadn't been here long enough to make any. The only conclusion was that this had something to do with Tish's disappearance.

And then something else occurred to her. The man with whom Tish had left had been wearing western clothes. So had the person who'd just tried to make her have an accident. But then in Texas people who dressed western weren't exactly rare.

"You okay?" a man's voice asked.

Kate looked up to see a pickup with a camper on it parked at the side of the road, a man walking toward her. He wore the unlikely combination of cowboy boots, a western shirt, and a cap that said "World's Greatest Granddad."

"I'm okay," Kate said. "Do you think you could give me a lift to someplace where I could call the highway patrol?"

"Sure," the man said, helping her up. "There's a phone at the Fina station, about two miles down the road."

SIX

An officer from the Texas Department of Public Safety took a report. The damage was minimal. Scrapes and missing trim on the side of Tish's car and a bent grille, along with a knocked-down section of barbed wire, which the highway patrolman pronounced "bob warr." He ran a check on the license number Kate had given him. It came back a hit on the hot sheet. The green Pontiac belonged to a Leap school-teacher. It had been stolen while she was at work.

The state policeman helped Kate get the car back on the highway. The steering seemed a little loose, and it pulled slightly to the left, but it was drivable. Kate drove directly to the Leap police station, where she marched unannounced into the chief's office.

"Someone just tried to run me off the road," she said. "Someone who followed me from Leap in a stolen car."

"Just how far out of Leap did this occur?" he asked, leaning back in his chair.

"Four or five miles."

"Sounds like the Department of Public Safety's problem to me."

"The point is that it was deliberate. It was an attempt aimed specifically at me."

"I take it you're trying to make a connection between this and the disappearance of your sister."

"Why else would anyone in Leap want to run me off the road? I don't even know anyone here except Tish."

"And what exactly would be the point of trying to harm you?"

"To get me to stop looking into Tish's disappearance," Kate said, exasperated.

"Which I've asked you not to do. Which technically means you're interfering with a police investigation, which means you're violating the law."

"Shit," Kate said, and then stopped herself before she said anything she'd regret.

The chief simply stared at her, a somewhat smug expression on his face. After a moment he said, "If there's any investigating to be done, it's up to us to do it."

"Have you done any investigating?"

"We've looked into it. There's no evidence of foul play, nothing to indicate that your sister didn't leave of her own free will."

"Dammit," Kate said, "I keep telling you that Tish—"

Chief Colton cut her off. "We checked on your sister's ex-husband. The last anyone heard, he'd gone to Louisiana. I can also tell you that a white pickup was stolen on the day your sister disappeared. I'm not saying there's any connection, but we're checking what needs to be checked. We know how to do our jobs."

Colton leaned forward, giving her a stern look. And at the same time there was something vaguely mocking in it. Some men just plain didn't like women, and Kate wondered whether Colton was one of them. He seemed unwilling to take her seriously.

"Who told you Boyd had gone to Louisiana?"

"Woman he used to know."

"What woman?"

"He wasn't real faithful to your sister. He had a girlfriend, a barmaid he used to visit from time to time."

"You sure she doesn't have any idea where he is now?"

"It wasn't that kind of a relationship, the kind where you'd

70

stay in touch. He spent the night with her the day he ran off, told her he was on his way to Louisiana. That's the last she heard from him.''

He gave her that mocking look again, and it seemed to say, *See, you don't know as much as you think you do.* And he seemed to have enjoyed telling her that Boyd had been cheating on Tish. But as far as Kate was concerned, at least when Boyd was cheating on Tish he couldn't be beating on her. Boyd Steuben was the quintessential no-good son of a bitch. She didn't need Chief Colton to tell her that.

"Chief," Kate said suddenly, "you like women?"

He stared at her for a moment, puzzled; then he broke into a big grin. "My daddy would have been awful disappointed in me if I liked boys.''

Kate decided she should have known he'd say something like that.

"I'll call you if I learn anything about your sister," he said dismissively.

"Please do," Kate said. She started to add that she was very worried, then changed her mind and walked from the office.

Chief Colton watched her go, then rubbed his eyes and leaned back in his chair, thinking women were a pain in the ass. He'd known Boyd Steuben. Used to run into him in the bowling alley and every now and then over at the Dew Drop Inn, where Boyd used to stop for his coffee breaks sometimes. Although they weren't real good friends or anything like that, Boyd had seemed like a fairly good ole boy. Talking to him at the bowling alley was how the chief had learned that Boyd was making it with Tammi Lou Brownwood over at the Galaxy Bar. Hell, half the town was making it with Tammi Lou, but for some reason Boyd had been proud of it, seemed anxious to brag about it.

Colton never had approved of what Boyd's wife had done to him. Sure, Boyd had been wrong to run off. A man had responsibilities, and running away wasn't the way to deal with them. Still, he had to wonder whether Boyd's wife hadn't just maybe driven him to it. Women could be tough on a

71

man, always wanting this or that, always pushing him. Surely she'd had no right to divorce him, take his house, everything he'd worked for, when he wasn't even there to defend himself. That was the thing that bothered Chief Jack C. Colton the most about the whole affair.

"J.C., you keep leanin' back in that chair like that, you're gonna end up on your ass," Dan Rawlins said as he stepped into the chief's office.

Sergeant Rawlins was the department's oldest officer. He was in his sixties, and had a potbelly that hung over his gunbelt. With his kind blue eyes and warm smile, he was the sort of cop you liked to point out to children when you were telling them about the friendly police officer who was always ready to help good, honest, God-fearing little kids. Chief Colton valued Rawlins's opinion because the sergeant never sucked up to him. Probably because, three months away from mandatory retirement, Rawlins was the only man on the force who didn't have to.

"How come you're not out protecting the good folks of Leap from robbers and kidnappers and com-nists and the rest of the scum?"

"Being a com-nist ain't against the law," Rawlins said as he sat down.

"Oughta be."

The sergeant shrugged. "The reason I'm here is because I had to put one of Leap's good citizens in the hoosegow for operating a motor vehicle with more whiskey than blood running through his veins."

Rawlins was the only person Colton knew who ever used the word "hoosegow." The chief wondered whether he'd learned it from watching old westerns on TV. He said, "Who'd you bust? Anybody I know?"

"D. L. Galton."

Colton nodded. Galton owned a hardware store. The man's favorite pastime seemed to be driving while he was too plowed to walk. The judge had taken his license away, but old D.L. kept right on driving. Locking him away was probably the only thing would keep him from it, but everybody

72

in town knew D.L. and thought he was a pretty good ole boy, and the judge just couldn't bring himself to do it.

"I've got a woman detective from the NYPD on my case," Colton said. He told Rawlins about Patricia Hastings's disappearance, and about her twin sister.

"I heard that the woman over at the library was missing," Rawlins said. "What you doing about it?"

"What am I supposed to do? There's nothing to indicate that any laws have been broken."

Rawlins considered that. "I don't know, J.C. The whole thing sounds kinda suspicious to me."

"This isn't exactly the FBI I've got here, you know. I don't have the manpower to look into everything seems a little suspicious."

"What have you done on it?"

"Put a locate out on the Hastings woman. And I talked to her ex-husband's shack job, who tells me he split for Louisiana a long time ago and hasn't been seen since. The woman's twin sister has already talked to everybody else there is to talk to. She's one of those aggressive women, likes to get out there and try to show that she can do the job as good as a man."

"You sure she's not doing what we should be doing?"

Colton didn't respond to that. He'd already said he didn't have the manpower to look into things where no apparent crime had been committed, and he didn't feel like saying it again. The woman cop annoyed him. Sure, she had a right to be worried about her sister, but he didn't need her messing around in his territory. If this thing with her sister did turn out to be something and the woman cop was the one who solved it, people would know about it. It would make him look bad.

"I don't need some woman cop coming out here from New York, telling me what to do," Colton said.

Rawlins nodded, but only in acknowledgment. He wasn't expressing any opinions.

"I think one of the biggest mistakes we made in this country—right after the Supreme Court decided that we couldn't

73

use perfectly good evidence just because of some stupid technicalities—was to put women on a police force."

Again Rawlins nodded noncommittally. He said, "Well, as long as you're the chief, there won't be any women on the force in Leap."

"You agree with that policy?"

"Hell, J.C., what do I know about policy matters?"

"You got opinions, don't you?"

"Yup. And if there's one thing I learned over the last sixty-odd years, it's to keep most of them to myself."

"You're whose sister?" Tammi Lou Brownwood asked.

She was maybe twenty-seven. Her red hair was in jumbo-size curlers, which reminded Kate of how she and Tish used to use old frozen orange juice cans for the same purpose when they were about thirteen. Tammi Lou was a little overweight, but most of it had gone to the right places. The T-shirt she wore clung nicely to her ample breasts. There was nothing wrong with the way she filled out her jeans either.

She hadn't been hard to find. Kate had gone back to Boyd's old boss and asked whether Boyd had had any girlfriends. The man had said, Well, yes, he understood there was this woman Boyd had been fooling around with, but he thought it would be best not to mention it to Boyd's sister-in-law. Although he didn't know her name, he understood she worked at a place called the Galaxy. At the bar Kate was informed that she was most likely looking for Tammi Lou Brownwood, who didn't work there anymore. Last the owner of the Galaxy Bar had heard, she was living in an apartment over on Jay Avenue. He didn't have the address. Kate had found it in the phone book.

While Kate explained who she was and what she wanted, she took in the apartment. It was actually a tiny house. Three rooms. A few pieces of plain, inexpensive furniture that had most likely been manufactured around 1952. The walls were bare except for a single Willie Nelson poster. Kate and Tammi Lou were sitting on a green couch with threadbare arms.

"I just talked to Chief Colton about Boyd," Tammi Lou said.

"I know, but I thought that you might have remembered something else since then."

"He said he was taking off for Louisiana. That's the last I saw of him."

"Did he say where in Louisiana he was going?"

"I don't think he knew. He was just going to see what he could find."

"Why'd he pick Louisiana, do you know?"

"He said he was gonna spend some time with the coon asses—that's just how he said it, he was going to spend some time with the coon asses."

"Spend some time with the what?"

"Don't you know what a coon ass is?"

"Something on the rear end of a raccoon?"

"Noooo," Tammi Lou said, shaking her head vigorously. "I can't believe you don't know what it means. A coon ass is a Cajun."

"Oh."

Tammi Lou sighed. "Listen, I'd just as soon you didn't go around mentioning to people about me and Boyd. That's a past life for me now. I . . . well, I know this is going to sound silly to someone like you, but I've seen the light. I've taken Jesus into my heart. I'm a new person now. I don't work at a bar anymore. And I'm getting married to a man who shares my Christian beliefs. I'm very happy in my new life. I'd never go back to the way I was."

Kate said she was glad Tammi Lou was happy. "I'm very worried about my sister," Kate said. "If you should hear from Boyd or if you should think of anything, I'd really appreciate it if you'd let me know."

"I have heard from him," Tammi Lou said.

"When?"

"I, uh, didn't mention it to Chief Colton because . . . well, to tell you the truth, I don't think he's a very nice man."

"Tell me about hearing from Boyd."

"Well, it was a couple of months after he left. I got this postcard. It said he thought he'd be making a lot of money soon, and that when he did he'd send me the airfare and we

75

could have a real good time together in Louisiana. I didn't believe him for a minute, and I threw the card away."

"Where was the card mailed from?"

"I wasn't lying to you when I said I didn't know where he went in Louisiana, because I don't remember where the card was from. It had a picture of a bayou on it, and the postmark was from some little town I never heard of. I wouldn't recognize it if you said it."

"Did he say how he was going to make this money?"

"No, but knowing Boyd, I bet it wasn't anything legal. He was always scheming, trying to come up with some way to get rich—as long as it didn't involve doing very much work. Boyd wasn't very big on work."

Kate wished her success in her new life and left.

Kate spent the rest of the day locating Tish's auto insurance policy, notifying the company, getting an estimate for repairing the damage. Exhausted from emotional stress and lack of sleep, Kate went to bed early and found herself remembering. She recalled how, when she and Tish were little girls, they'd selected a site to make mud pies that was too far away from the house to reach with the hose. So they'd used one of those red metal wagons all children used to have to haul water to the mud-pie-making site. The water, of course, had all splashed out by the time the wagon reached its destination. They never did get any mud pies made, but they had a great time filling the wagon, one of them jumping in while the other pulled, as if it were a portable bathtub. By the end of the day they were soaked and filthy, but they'd had a good time.

Although they'd never used the fact that they were indistinguishable to play games on anyone, people always suspected them of it. Once Kate answered the door to let in a boy who was taking Tish to his church picnic, and the boy had refused to believe she wasn't Tish, no matter how much she insisted otherwise. They were playing a trick on him, he said, and he wasn't going to be fooled. Maybe other people couldn't tell them apart, but he could. When the real Tish presented herself, the boy finally realized he'd made a mistake and became so embarrassed that Kate felt sorry for him.

And Kate recalled how she and Tish had stood at the phone in the hallway at their college dorm, listening to their mother. Kate had answered, then got Tish to come to the phone, too. She hadn't liked the deadness in her mother's voice. The twins held the receiver so they both could hear what was being said. Kate still remembered her mother's words.

'There's been an accident. Your father was using the tractor. It turned over. He's . . .'' There was a pause while their mom forced herself to say the word. "He's dead."

But even more vividly than Kate recalled her mother's words, she remembered the look on Tish's face—the same look that must have been on Kate's own face. Tish had gone pale, her expression a mixture of disbelief, confusion, and horror.

It wasn't as bad a few months later when their mother died. Not that they loved or missed their mom any less. But they'd learned to deal with death, harden themselves to it. Kate had believed that the deaths of her parents had toughened her enough to cope with anything—until a gun-wielding eleven-year-old boy in East Harlem showed her just how wrong she was.

But Kate forced herself not to think about that. It was the source of too many nightmares, and she was dog-tired; she needed sleep.

When she finally did doze off, she had dreams that brought her close to wakefulness, but never quite all the way. Still, she was sleeping lightly enough to hear the gentle *thunk* that came from somewhere in the house.

Suddenly awake, Kate lay in bed, listening. The house was quiet, as was the neighborhood. No cars moved along its darkened streets. No nocturnal animals attacked garbage cans. Then Kate heard a distant *whoomp* as the gas hot-water heater came on in its enclosure by the kitchen. A moment later the window air conditioner came on with a *clunk*. Kate was beginning to doubt that she'd heard anything at all. Or if she had, it had been a car door slamming or something like that. And then she recalled that someone had tried to run her off the road today, someone who'd followed her in a stolen car.

Forcing her eyes to focus on the digital clock beside the bed, Kate saw that it was 3:22 A.M. She slipped out of bed, her hand automatically reaching for the drawer in which she kept her gun. But the drawer wasn't here. It was in New York. And so was her gun.

Moving quietly, Kate made her way to the light switch, then hesitated. Her eyes were adjusted to the darkness. Turning on the lights would be a shock to her eyes, and it would illuminate her clearly, make her an easy target.

Kate listened for a moment, then stepped into the short hallway, slowly moving past the bathroom. Because the house had a slab foundation, there were no floorboards to creak. And like most such homes, it had wall-to-wall carpeting throughout, except for the kitchen and bathroom. The only sounds Kate made were her breathing and the gentle whisper of her nightgown as it brushed against her legs. And it occurred to her that if anyone was here, the intruder would be equally quiet.

Although some illumination seeped in from the street lamp partway down the block, the house was full of deep shadows. As Kate moved through the dimly lit areas, she felt vulnerable and exposed in her yellow nightgown. There's no one here, she told herself. And yet, every time she stared into the shadows, she saw a man in a cowboy hat crouched there, the same man who'd been a silhouette in the green car.

Reaching the kitchen, Kate looked into the dark room, seeing only shadows. Okay, she decided, it's time to put on the lights and get this over with. As Kate reached into the kitchen, feeling for the switch, she heard a movement behind her, and before she could react, someone grabbed her.

Kate was yanked back into the living room. Strong hands grabbed her and spun her around, slammed her into the wall. And then the hands were on her again, holding her against the wall. Kate smelled sweat, the odor of alcohol. And then hands were on her neck, rough, working hands. Squeezing. Her attacker's weight pressed her chest against the wall.

Caught off guard, she had allowed herself to get into the

position NYPD hand-to-hand combat instructors had told her to avoid at all costs. She was being held by a more powerful adversary, a situation in which most of the techniques of self-defense she knew were useless because it pitted her strength directly against his. Kate fought for breath that couldn't come through her constricted throat.

Knowing that she had only moments left if she was to save herself, Kate pushed against the wall with her hands, making just enough room for her to get her feet up, kick as hard as she could against the wall. Her assailant was pushed backward. Kate attacked him with her elbows, and when one hand let go of her throat to block her elbows, Kate reached back with her foot, hooking it behind his, then pulled his leg out from under him. Her attacker dropped, letting go of her. Air, wonderful, precious air flowed into Kate's lungs. She quickly moved out of the man's reach.

If she'd had her gun, she would have jammed it against his ear, told him that if he even so much as twitched he was going to pay for it with a hole in his head and an irreparably damaged brain. But the gun, the great equalizer, was at least fifteen hundred miles away. The man sprang at her.

But now Kate was ready for him. Stepping out of his path, she grabbed his arm and used his own momentum to bring him down. Again she backed away. There would be no more contests of strength that she couldn't win.

"Give up," she said, putting a lot more confidence into her voice than she really felt. "I can hurt you badly if you keep this up."

Again the man came at her, but more slowly this time, more cautiously. In the darkness of the living room, it was like being stalked by a shadow. He reached for her, coming forward and downward at the same time, apparently planning to fall on her, pin her to the floor. Kate dropped, bringing up her feet, using them to propel the man completely over her, again using his momentum against him. Something splintered, the coffee table most likely. Kate scrambled to her feet, backed away.

"You can't win," she said. "Get up and lean against the

wall, spread your feet. I bet you already know how to do it. I bet the police here in Texas have already showed you how.''

The man crouched a few feet away, breathing heavily.

"Next time you lose your balls," Kate said. "Last guy tried this lost his. I've got them on a plaque back home. Real nice conversation piece."

Kate stared at the shadow crouching before her, wishing she could see his face. And then the man stood.

"Do what I told you," Kate said.

The shape retreated until it was against the wall.

"Turn around. Hands against the wall, legs apart."

The figure complied. Kate backed slowly toward the nearest light switch, which was the one she'd been reaching for in the kitchen when the man grabbed her. She was reaching for it again when he moved. He'd been standing about four feet from the side window. Suddenly he went through it, ripping down the curtains as he went, and Kate realized that was how he'd gotten into the place. The window had been open the whole time, and she hadn't known it.

Hurrying to the window, Kate looked out, seeing nothing. A dog barked about two houses down, and a moment later there was the sound of an engine starting, but Kate didn't see any cars. She stood there a moment, staring out into the sticky heat of the night, trembling. Then she rushed into the kitchen to call the police.

SEVEN

"You didn't get a look at his face at all?" the cop asked. He was about twenty-two with a boy's smooth cheeks and inquiring youthful eyes that the job hadn't hardened and made cynical yet. He was most likely fresh from the academy, starting out on graveyard shift. His name tag said "Hagen."

"I never saw him," Kate said. "I was reaching for the light when he grabbed me."

They were standing by the window through which Kate's attacker had made his escape. The curtain rod had been ripped from the wall. The curtain itself lay in a heap on the floor. The window had been pried open.

"All I can tell you is that it was a man who smelled sweaty, had alcohol on his breath, and had rough hands. He probably weighed around one-seventy, and I'd guess he was about six feet tall."

The officer noted that on his clipboard. "I'm surprised you could tell that much."

"I've had enough experience in self-defense to judge the size of my opponent without seeing him."

"I've got to tell you that I'm really impressed that someone your size could fight off a guy six feet tall." He took in

81

Kate's five feet, eight inches and her hundred-twenty-five pounds.

"I've been trained. I'm a cop."

"Really? Where?"

"New York City."

"No kidding?"

"No kidding."

"Are you in uniform?"

"Plainclothes."

"I'll be darned. I never met anybody from the NYPD before. What's it like?"

Kate had no idea how to answer that. Should she tell him that in some neighborhoods homicide was the leading cause of death? That eleven-year-old kids blew away cops? She said, "The number of officers is at least five times the population of Leap."

"Boy," the young cop said, shaking his head. "I have trouble imagining that." When Kate offered nothing further about life in the NYPD, he said, "Was anything taken?"

"Nothing. It wasn't a burglary. He was here to get me."

"You mean to kill you?"

"Maybe. Maybe just scare me off." She told him what had been happening.

"So you think this relates to the disappearance of your sister?"

"That's right."

"What did the chief say when you talked to him?"

"He said Tish apparently left of her own free will."

The young cop shifted nervously from side to side. If the chief was involved, he was going to be careful, it seemed.

"You can put in your report that I think Chief Colton's full of shit," Kate said.

The cop winced. "Uh, I'd really rather not do that."

"What are you going to do?"

"When I file my report, I'll mark it for the attention of the chief. Maybe you should go down and talk to him again, tell him what happened here."

Kate nodded. "Look, I'm sorry if I'm taking out my frustrations on you. The chief's the one I'm angry with. It's just that you're standing here, and he's not."

"That's okay," he said. "Uh, I'm going to take a look outside. Want to come along?"

"I already looked," Kate said. "Grass grows right up to the side of the house right there, so there's no footprints or anything."

"I, uh, I'm still going to have to look."

"I understand."

Through the open window she saw his flashlight bobbing around. After about two minutes, he returned to the living room, said that she should let the department know right away if she had any more troubles. Kate said she'd do that.

After the young cop left, Kate located a hammer and some nails and secured the window her attacker had forced open. Then she cleaned up the mess. Three of the coffee table's four legs had been broken off, and she put the whole mess in the garage. It was dawn when she finished.

Kate made some coffee, then sat at the kitchen table, trying to understand what was happening. Tish had left with a guy in a white pickup, which might have been his and might have been stolen. No one had seen Tish since. When Kate started looking into Tish's disappearance, someone tried to run her off the road; then someone broke into the house. And it was no burglar. Kate was sure of that.

What had Tish gotten herself into? Had she witnessed a crime? A secret liaison? Had the guy in the white truck been employed by someone, hired to abduct Tish? Why would anyone abduct a librarian? You couldn't get that angry over the fines on overdue books.

Other possibilities swirled through Kate's head, but they were all bizarre. Tish had discovered some historical papers in the library, papers that someone wanted kept secret at all cost. Tish had been kidnapped by a group of fanatics who wanted the books they disapproved of removed from the library. And then a possibility occurred to Kate that made her feel as though icy fingers had just squeezed her insides.

What if someone had followed her here from New York? Unlike librarians, cops did make enemies, deadly serious enemies. Could someone have followed her here from New York, mistaken Tish for her? She knew a cop who'd had something like that happen to him. A detective named O'Connor. O'Connor had busted this guy's girlfriend. She'd been a junkie, hooked bad, and going cold turkey in a cell had been more than she could handle. It had killed her. Her boyfriend had blamed O'Connor. Tried three times to ambush him. Would have kept on trying if O'Connor hadn't blown him away during the third attempt.

But she couldn't think of anyone who seemed likely to come after her. For the past six months, she'd been on a special juvy detail, and it just didn't seem very plausible that some gang kid was going to follow her all the way to Texas.

On the other hand, she'd just killed an eleven-year-old boy. There had to be people out there who'd hate a cop who'd whacked a kid. People who were crazy, who'd become obsessed with an idea, like being an avenging angel, punishing the cop who'd blown away a little boy.

The idea just didn't work. How would the avenging angel know where she'd gone? And how many people from New York wore western clothes, drove pickups, and had cow manure on their boots?

Nothing made sense. Tish simply wouldn't intentionally vanish without telling anyone. But why, if she wasn't leaving voluntarily, would she have shown no resistance when she left with the guy in the white truck? Had he tricked her in some way? Had he threatened to harm her if she tried to let anyone know what was going on?

Clement's on Sixteenth Street. Was there a clue in there somewhere? Kate shook her head. She didn't know what to think. She didn't know what to do.

She closed her eyes, massaged her forehead. And then she saw the eleven-year-old kid, swinging the gun toward her. Kate forced the image to go away, but it was replaced by the picture of Tish at the airport in Austin, rushing forward to hug her. Kate felt her control slipping. She'd been trying to handle this thing like a cop, not like a sister. If she didn't maintain her emotional distance, she'd fall apart; she'd be useless to Tish.

But having your twin sister vanish was sort of like losing yourself. Sure you were a separate, unique individual, but there was a bond between you and your twin that made it seem that whatever happened to her happened to you as well. Once, after learning that Boyd had beaten Tish badly, Kate had looked into the mirror and had seen the bruises, felt the pain.

Suddenly all Kate's attempts to put the incident in East Harlem behind her and to retain her emotional distance from Tish's disappearance began to unravel. Her vision clouded as her eyes filled with tears. She made a halfhearted attempt to hold them back, then gave in and let them come.

Kate sat at the kitchen table, her tears dripping on its wooden surface, her whole body shaking as she sobbed. Whatever mechanism she'd been using to give her the strength to keep on going had just crumbled, and at that moment she wondered whether she'd ever be able to put it back together again.

But Kate did pull herself together again. Her sobbing eventually tapered off, and for a long time she simply sat there, feeling drained. Then, abruptly snapping out of it, she picked up the phone and dialed area code 212 followed by the number of the special juvenile detail she'd been assigned to. She asked for Detective Janice Bernstein.

"Kate," Janice said. "How the hell are you? You back in town already? I thought you were off in the west, turning down offers of marriage from rich Texas oilmen or something like that."

"All the oilmen are broke. The only people out here that are rich own hock shops."

"So make it rich hock-shop owners. Who cares as long as they're rich, right?"

"There might be another consideration or two," Kate said. Like not being a worthless son of a bitch who liked to use his fists. Although Janice and Kate didn't associate much off the job, they were good work friends. They'd meet in the lounge, have coffee, talk. Although they'd never been partners, they thought alike, and Kate believed it would work out well if they were paired someday. She told Janice about Tish's disappearance and the other things that had happened.

"Jesus," Janice said. "And you've got no hint at all as to what all this might be about?"

"None."

"Wow. God, Kate, that's all you needed right now, something else to worry about."

Uncertain how to respond to that, Kate said, "The reason I called is that I want to ask a couple of favors. I know you're busy, but—"

"So ask already. Never mind the apology."

"First I want to find out if this might be something out of New York. I don't know, maybe somebody wanting to get even with me because of what happened in East Harlem. Tish is my identical twin. Maybe somebody snatched the wrong person."

"No problem. I'll spread the word for everybody to keep an ear out, maybe put the question to their snitches."

"Yeah, that would be good. Also, I was wondering whether you could check with Louisiana on Boyd Steuben, see if the name means anything to their computers." She told Janice about Boyd.

"No problem, but why aren't the cops out there doing it?"

She told her about Chief Colton.

"Wow. He sounds like that guy from *Cool Hand Luke*. You know, the redneck prison guard who wore the mirror sunglasses. What kind of a place are you in out there?"

She started to tell Janice that most of the people here in this spotlessly clean community were very nice, that you shouldn't judge a place by its assholes. As long as the assholes were in the minority. But instead of telling Janice this, she thanked her for her help, promised to do her numerous favors someday, and hung up. Janice said she'd call if and when she learned anything.

Leaning across the kitchen table, Kate pulled back the curtain. Outside was another hot sunny day. As she stared at the neat houses and weed-free lawns, she wondered whether Tish was out there somewhere, in one of the innocent homes maybe, or a store, a church, a school. Or was she even in Leap at all? Or Texas? Or the United States?

Where are you, Tish? Kate asked mentally. Though strong, the bond between them didn't include telepathy, and the only reply in Kate's head was the dull babble of her own confused thoughts.

Staring through the crack between two of the boards used to cover the window, Tish could see the rocky bank of a ditch, and that was all. She backed away from the window. She had to move carefully because the trailer was leaning against the bank, which made the floor slope sharply.

Leaning against the wall, Tish slid down until she was sitting on the floor. The trailer was old, junk. The linoleum on the floor was faded so badly that the pattern was no longer discernible. In places it had worn through, exposing the subflooring. Any comforts had been removed except for the thin mattress on one of the built-in bunk beds, where she slept. There was some water in the trailer's tank. When she turned on the tap in the tiny sink, foul-tasting brownish liquid came out. She'd been drinking it because it was the only water she had. At first she'd been afraid it would make her sick, but it hadn't.

Tish moved around very little, sometimes sitting in one spot for hours, shifting her position only slightly when she became uncomfortable. All day the sun beat down on the trailer's metal skin, turning its unventilated interior into an oven. It was too hot to move. It was too hot to do anything except sit. And sweat.

The trailer's chemical toilet had no chemicals in it. The stench, especially during the heat of the afternoon, could become unbearable. She'd tried to break out of the trailer. Again and again she'd tried. But the boards over the windows were apparently bolted on from the outside, and she had no lever with which to pry them off. They were too high to kick, and pounding on them with her hands had no effect. She'd tried lying on the floor and kicking the door, but it did no good, for the door had been reinforced from the outside with two-by-fours. It was held closed on the outside by a heavy padlock.

No, Tish thought, don't give up. She had to keep trying, keep kicking the door. Maybe if she kept at it long enough something would give. She started to move toward the door, then stopped herself as sweat trickled down her forehead. It was too hot now. She'd wait until tonight when it was cool.

Tish was filthy. Her dress was torn and covered with dust, which her perspiration turned to mud in places. A dirt dauber flew past her, its wings making a gentle breeze in the hot stillness of the trailer. It went in and out through the space between the boards covering one of the windows. It was constructing its mud nest in a corner. Tish envied the wasp its ability to leave this place.

She had no idea where she was. He'd made her lie on the floor, looking up at all the wires beneath the pickup's dash. She only knew that the trailer was in a ditch that sloped at one end, enabling him to drive down into it. At first Tish had sensed the smell of death here, but it was gone now, overpowered by the stench of her own making. Or maybe it had just been the musty odor of the old trailer. She wasn't sure anymore.

Or maybe she'd sensed her own death. Tish pushed the thought away.

Tish had no idea why she'd been imprisoned here. He brought her nothing to eat, nothing to drink. "I know you, Jenna Lee," he'd said just before locking her in here. "I know who you are." Although the name was familiar, Tish was unable to recall where she'd heard it. It taunted her, hanging just out of reach. Jenna Lee . . . Jenna Lee . . . Jenna Lee. Tish shook her head. Maybe it would come to her.

He'd only been back once since imprisoning her here. He'd yanked open the door and stared at her, something frantic in his eyes. "You're here," he said. "You're here." Then he'd closed and locked the door.

A tear trickled down Tish's face, clung to her chin, dropped. No more tears followed it. She'd cried the first night in the trailer, cried until she was ready to throw up.

But now the tears only came in moments of sadness, and then only briefly. Crying drained her and served no purpose.

Tish ran her hands through her hair, feeling the tangles and grit. As she'd done numerous times before, she recalled what had occurred that day, looking for something that would explain what was happening. Hands had dragged her from the shower, clamped her mouth shut before she could scream, and then a man's voice had whispered to her:

"Don't holler, or I'll hurt you. Do you understand?"

Tish had turned, blinking her eyes that were still stinging from the soap. The intruder came into focus, and she recognized him immediately. "What are you doing here?" she asked, her voice barely above a whisper.

"Get dressed."

Tish realized then that she was standing there naked, but her nakedness seemed unimportant compared to the danger she might be in. She had no idea what he had in mind, although somewhere in the back of her brain she realized that he probably wasn't going to force himself on her if he was telling her to get dressed. He took her arm, steered her toward the bedroom.

"Wear something like you'd wear if you were going out on a date," he said.

He watched her as she dressed. Not lustfully, not even menacingly. It was as if he were watching TV. Tish's hands were trembling so badly she was unable to fasten her bra, and she was afraid he'd come over and do it for her. The thought made her shiver. Finally she succeeded in getting the hooks in place.

"Hurry up," he ordered.

As Tish slipped into a sleeveless white dress, she started trying to think of ways to get away from him. He sat on the bed, watching her dispassionately. In a way that bland stare made him more frightening than a heavy-breathing potential rapist might have been. At least she'd have known where the rapist was coming from.

Tish was dressed now, except for her shoes. Although she was only a few feet from the bedroom window, it was closed and locked, and by the time she opened it, he'd be on her.

Tish kept her eye on him as she began looking for a suitable pair of shoes—and a part of her questioned just what difference it made how suitable her shoes were under circumstances like these, but the mind worked like that; it clung to the familiar, even in times of terror.

As Tish slipped on one shoe his eyes dropped to his hands for a second, then instantly returned to her. He began using the nail of one thumb to pick at the nail of the other. His eyes lowered again, and Tish jammed her foot into the other shoe and dashed for the door. She was through it, into the living room, reaching for the knob on the front door when he caught her. Grabbing her by the throat, he yanked her back, her feet leaving the floor, and then he threw her down.

The carpet absorbed some of the shock, but there was nothing but cement under that, and the fall jarred her. Before she could collect her wits, strong arms lifted her up, pushed her back against the door. Something cold and hard was jammed painfully into her neck.

"This is a gun," he said, slowly pulling it back into her field of vision. "You try any stupid shit like that again, and I'm going to kill you. You understand that?"

Too confused and frightened to reply, Tish just stared at him. He pressed the gun against the side of her head, just behind her ear. "You understand?"

"Yes," she heard herself say in a tremulous voice that sounded like someone else's.

"Go fix your hair. I want you to look nice, like you're going out on a date. Understand?"

"Yes," the strange distant voice replied.

He stood in the doorway to the bathroom, watching as she used the blow-dryer and curling wand on her hair, then applied her makeup.

"Take your purse," he said when she was finished, and then he was steering her out the back door, through the yard, toward the gate that opened onto the alley that ran behind the house. "If you try to run, I'll kill you," he warned.

And then she was through the gate, and he was guiding her toward a white pickup. Suddenly Teddy Wagner, the boy next door, was there, smiling at her, saying hi.

Behind her a voice whispered: "You let the kid know anything's wrong, and I'll shoot him."

Tish walked around to the passenger side of the truck, where the boy was standing, smiled, asked, "How are you today, Teddy?"

"Just fine, Miz Hastings. Uh, are you going out to dinner?"

Tish hesitated, her mind working furiously. This was her one chance to let someone know what was happening. But how? She had to be careful, or she'd endanger Teddy. And then she knew what to say.

"That's right, Teddy. At Clemens' on Sixteenth Street."

And then she was climbing into the truck, and its engine started, and she was being driven away from her house.

"Get down on the floor," he told her.

Tish did as instructed. Unable to see anything but sky and utility poles, Tish had no idea where she was being taken. And no idea what would happen to her when she got there.

The clue she'd given was aimed at Kate. Kate would try to find her, Tish was sure of that. And her twin sister was a detective, a trained investigator. She might get the clue. Teddy Wagner figured into both parts of it. And it was from the boy that Kate would hear it. Maybe Kate would figure it out. Maybe.

As Tish stared into the gloom of the hot, empty trailer, another tear trickled down her face, for she realized how silly it was to hope Kate would figure out the clue. The boy might have forgotten all about Clemens' on Sixteenth. A child would recall that she was going out to eat, not where. And if he did pass Clemens' on Sixteenth Street along to Kate, there was no reason to think she'd make anything of it. And even if she did, the clue was so vague, she'd probably never figure it out.

Another tear ran down Tish's cheek. Then another. No, she thought, I'm not going to cry. But she was unable to stop herself.

EIGHT

Down the street from the house in which he'd pulled Tish naked and terrified from the shower, her abductor sat in a green pickup, watching. The vehicles he'd used when he abducted Tish and later when he attempted to run her sister off the road had been stolen. This truck was his. It was mud-spattered, and he'd packed enough additional mud on the license plate to hide the numbers. Still, he had to be careful. Sitting in a residential area like this was suspicious; someone might call the police.

He was uncertain what he'd do if he spotted the woman. He had to do something, though. Otherwise everything he'd accomplished would be for nothing. He gripped the steering wheel, squeezing it so hard that his knuckles began to ache. He had to find some way of dealing with the woman. She and her sister—both of them—had to pay for what they'd done.

But what to do? Breaking into the house had been a disaster. He must have made too much noise, for she'd awakened, gotten up to check things out. Still, there should have been no problem. She was, after all, a woman. Although he'd known she was a cop, he had been totally unprepared for her skill at defending herself. Clearly physical confrontation was not the answer.

Relaxing his grip on the steering wheel, he sighed. He would find a way to do what had to be done. It wasn't hard to kill someone. It merely required patience. And when you considered how long he'd waited already, what difference did a few more days make?

He made himself relax all over, letting the positive life forces flow freely through him, renew him. Frustration was a negative thing; it took energy away from the life forces. He had to remain calm, clear-headed, in tune with the gentle hum we could all hear if we just listened for it, attuned ourselves to it. The low but vibrant murmur of all life in the universe.

A calmness had settled over him, and his thoughts began to wander. He recalled being a student at Sam Houston High School. He'd gone out for football, but hadn't made the team. A temporary setback in the lives of most boys, he supposed, but this was Texas. And in small towns in Texas, high school football was everything. The entire community went to the games—merchants, farmers, plumbers, store clerks, everybody. Throughout football season a big maroon-on-white GO MUSTANGS banner hung across Main Street. The games were the main topic of conversation at the Cowpoke Cafe and the feed lot and coming out of church on Sunday and anyplace else people congregated. The most recent game was always on the front page of the weekly newspaper, the *Sentinel*. The sports page was full of pictures of the action.

They also had basketball, wrestling, and gymnastics teams at his high school, but except for the players and coaches, no one noticed.

Of course he'd had plenty of company. There were only eleven guys on a football team, and even when you tossed in all the boys who usually sat on the bench, it added up to a pretty small percentage of the male population of the school. Most people who went out didn't make it. But most of them didn't have his father either.

He'd gone home that afternoon, set about his chores, knowing that no matter how much he wanted to avoid it, dinner would come, and his father would ask him about making the team. It was the one thing he never forgot. It seemed more important to him than the price his crop would bring, more important than the tractor breaking down, the milk cow going dry, the payment on his government loan coming due. The boy sensed without really understanding that his father wasn't happy with his life, that he wanted his son to be a football hero so *he* could be one through the boy.

Sitting at the dinner table, the family said a short prayer, thanking God for the meal, and then his father—always first to serve himself—put a helping of homemade chicken pot pie on his plate and passed it on. No one spoke, but then that was usual. It always took a while for a dinnertime conversation to develop.

The four of them sat at the round wood table in the big kitchen. The table and the room's size were the only things most people would have thought were "country" about the kitchen. The cabinets were ready-mades that had some kind of wood veneer on them. The floor was vinyl, the counters Formica, the appliances shiny and up-to-date.

His sister, Connie, passed him the bread, which wasn't homemade and wasn't too fresh either. He put Safeway raspberry jelly on it. His sister was two years younger, a plain girl with straight hair that was the color of beach sand. She was a thin girl, quiet and obedient. Their father never gave her any trouble. In part because she was so well behaved, the boy supposed. But also because the man didn't seem able to deal with girls. And he didn't have the same interest in Connie, as if girls were somehow less important.

To Connie's left sat their mother, thin like Connie, with the same long, slender face. Their mother's hair was darker, a deep brown, but the boy suspected that she dyed it to hide the gray. Like Connie, she was soft-spoken, almost shy.

"Well?" the boy's father said. Blue eyes as icy as Antarctica stared at the boy from a face that seemed permanently tanned from so many years in the sun.

"Sir?" the boy said.

"They announce who made the cut yet?" the boy's father asked. He was a lean man, tall and muscular, with a pointed

94

nose that gave his face a severe appearance. It matched his personality. His icy eyes were a pretty good indication of how much warmth was in him.

"Yes, sir," the boy said weakly.

"Well, don't sit there staring at your supper. Tell me what happened."

"Billy Johnson made it. So did Greg Janklow."

"I don't care one way or the other about Billy Johnson or Greg Janklow. Did *you* make it?"

"No, sir."

The boy's father stared at him like a biologist looking at some new kind of bug. Finally he said, "Why not?"

"I . . . I don't know."

"Why don't you?"

"They don't say. They just put up a list of who made it. There's nothing on it but the names."

"Did you ask?"

The boy shook his head. His mother and sister were staring at their plates, trying to fade into their chairs. Neither of them would say a thing to help him.

"Why didn't you ask?"

"You're supposed to be man enough to accept the coach's decision. You're not supposed to go crying to the coach if you didn't make it."

"Too bad you weren't man enough to make the team."

"The ones who made it were bigger and faster than me. A lot of guys didn't make it. It's no disgrace." As he spoke, the boy realized that his words could be taken as back talk, and he was in enough trouble without adding to it.

"It's certainly no honor to be rejected," the boy's father said, his voice dropping to a low, threatening tone.

"I tried," the boy said meekly.

"I'd say you didn't try hard enough."

The boy nodded.

"You don't try hard enough, you don't make it."

"Even if everybody tries as hard as he can, only a few of them make it," the boy said, knowing reason was wasted on this man but trying anyway.

"The ones who try hardest of all make it."

"Yes, sir."

"If you *truly* put out every last ounce of effort you have to give, then the good Lord will reward you."

"Yes, sir."

"So you didn't try hard enough, did you?"

"No, sir."

"So, what are you going to do about it?"

"I . . . I don't understand."

"What don't you understand?"

"There's nothing I can do about it now. It's too late."

"You mean you're a quitter."

"I . . ." He didn't know how to respond.

"If you weren't a quitter, you'd be down there at the coach's office, telling him that you didn't try as hard as you could, telling him that you want a chance to show him what you can *really* do."

"I . . . I can't do that."

But when he looked into those Antarctic-blue eyes, he knew he would do it. He wouldn't have any pride left afterward, but he'd do it.

The coach told him the cut was final. Period.

As the memory faded away he realized that he'd been sitting there too long. You could sit in a parked car in a residential area for a while, but eventually you made people uneasy, and if they became real uneasy they called the cops. He started the truck.

And then an idea came to him. He'd never tried anything like it, but he didn't see why he couldn't make it work. The more he thought about it, the more he liked it. It was simple, but just complicated enough to have class. He turned it around in his mind a few times, pictured it happening.

Bye-bye, twin sister, he thought. And then he smiled.

Kate spent the day watching TV and pacing. She didn't understand what was going on, and she could think of nothing to do that she hadn't already done. All in all she felt confused and powerless and wretched.

She did not take the police officer's advice and go to see

Chief Colton. She had absolutely no desire to see Chief Colton.

Before going to bed, Kate made sure all the doors and windows were locked. She thought about nailing the windows shut, then decided against it. Whoever was here last night wasn't likely to try the same thing again so soon. She slept lightly, waking whenever she heard anything. But the sounds always turned out to be harmless night noises. A dog barking, the house settling, the air conditioner switching on and off. Just before dawn a mosquito found her, and drove her crazy going *neeeeeee* in her ear for at least half an hour. It either tired of tormenting her or she rolled over and crushed it. She hoped she crushed it.

When the sun rose, so did Kate. She was sitting at the kitchen table, staring groggily at her half-empty coffee cup when she realized there was something else she could do. Parents of missing children often did it, and sometimes it paid off. She checked the yellow pages of the Leap phone book, finding two possibilities. She noted the addresses.

An hour later she was facing a man wearing an ink-smeared blue apron, who stood behind a counter covered with glass. Beneath the glass were all sorts of business cards. One that caught Kate's eye proclaimed: *Abe's Bail Bonds. We'll get you out—even if it takes years.*

"How many would you want?" the man behind the counter asked. He was a small guy, probably not weighing much over one-thirty, and had thin hair combed up from just above his ear in an effort to cover his baldness.

"Fifteen hundred, two thousand."

"How soon you want 'em?"

"How soon can you get them to me?"

"You want a rush order? It'll cost you fifteen dollars extra for a rush order."

"I need them right away."

He frowned. "I could probably get them out by five."

"Today?"

"Yes, ma'am. Today. But I'll have to have the picture right away."

Anticipating the need, Kate had looked all through the

97

house, finding no recent photos of Tish. "What kind of a picture do you need?"

"Snapshot will be fine. Black-and-white works best, and it should be in focus."

"You got a camera?"

He looked puzzled. "Sure, a Polaroid. But I'm not sure I follow you. I mean, if you knew where your sister was so I could take her picture, you wouldn't need the handbills, would you?"

"You can use my picture."

"Yours? Ma'am, I don't think you've thought this thing through real good. I mean—"

"We're identical twins."

"Oh."

They finalized what the handbills would say; then he took Kate's picture, and she paid him in advance. The man promised once more to have the job done by five. Better than his word, he called her at three-fifteen to say they were ready. Kate picked them up and headed for the Lone Star Mall. She'd phoned the mall's manager to get permission to distribute the handbills there. He'd told her it would be okay as long as she was well mannered and didn't get in anyone's way. Kate had promised to be on her best behavior. It had been a little like talking to your mother.

Kate parked her car and walked to the main entrance with an armload of handbills. Printed on standard eight-and-a-half-by-eleven white paper, they asked in large type, *Have you seen this woman?* Below that was Tish's—Kate's—picture, along with a complete description, a brief explanation of what had happened, and the number to call if anyone knew anything that would help.

Kate considered positioning herself just outside the mall's main entrance, but a few minutes of standing in the oppressive moist heat convinced her to move inside, where there was air conditioning.

She stood by the map that identified all the stores by number. The mall was like malls everywhere. It had Penney's and Ward's, along with Kinney Shoes, Walgreen's, a health-food store, Walden Books, a place that specialized in leather goods, a toy store, and a whole bunch of shops Kate was unfamiliar with, presumably local merchants.

Kate had expected that the shoppers would pretty much ignore her, accepting the proffered sheet of paper if she was insistent enough, but quickly scurrying off without meeting her eyes. But her New York City mentality had created that image. This was a small town in Texas.

"You mean she just disappeared?" the first person to receive a handbill said. She was a middle-aged woman with platinum hair. "You poor thing. Does she have any children?"

"No."

"Well, at least that much is a blessing. You sure look like her. It's pretty obvious you're sisters."

"We're identical twins."

"I can believe that. Well, I'll sure call you if I see her anywhere."

"Thank you very much."

And that was how it went. A couple of people thought she was Tish. One, a gray-haired woman who moved slowly and had to use a cane, walked up to her and said, "You quit your job at the library?"

Still others were tuned in to the grapevine that flourished in all small towns. A man in his thirties who wore a University of Minnesota T-shirt said, "I heard that the librarian was missing. I take it you're her twin sister, the New York City police detective." Kate said she was, and the man promised to help if he could.

"Ma'am," a boy said. He was about fourteen, freckle-faced, and had a bashful smile. A Norman Rockwell kind of kid. "I knew Miz Hastings real good. I—" He blushed. "Uh, I guess you're Miz Hastings, too, huh?"

Kate smiled, said that was true.

"Uh, I . . . she always talked to me at the library, told me what books to get and like that. Uh, is there anything I can do to help you?"

"Do you have anything in mind?"

"Well, I thought that I could take some of those infor-

99

mation sheets you've got and go down to the entrance by Ward's. There's a lot of people come in that way."

"I'd appreciate that," Kate said. She gave him some of the handbills. "What's your name?"

"Tyson Doyle."

"I'm Kate."

The boy, one of those tuned in to the grapevine apparently, said he already knew that, and he knew she was a detective in New York. He hurried off to pass out the handbills at the other end of the mall.

And so it went.

He wished he could wait until it was dark, but he couldn't, because he didn't know how long the woman would be gone, and he had to be finished before she returned. He pulled his truck to a stop beside the gate that led from the alley to Tish's backyard. Boldness, he'd decided, was the best way to go about it. Getting out of the truck, he pulled his cap down over his eyes, got a toolbox from the floor of the cab, walked purposefully to the gate, pushed it open, and stepped into the yard.

Dressed in coveralls and a grimy blue cap, he looked like a repairman of some sort. Anyone seeing him should think he was there to fix something, no big deal, nothing to get suspicious about. His main concern had been that he would run into the boy who'd appeared in the alley when he was leaving with Tish. But the boy wasn't around.

He walked directly to the side of the garage. Here lilac bushes grew along the fence, blocking the view of the neighbors on that side. He got a pry bar from the toolbox, forced it between the window and the sill, and applied pressure, hoping he wouldn't break the glass. The wood to which the catch was fastened was rotten, and the screws pulled loose almost immediately. The window jammed after moving only two inches or so, and it took all his strength to raise it enough for him to squeeze through.

Once in the garage, he hurried to its large metal door and began studying the tracks. Then he opened the toolbox. It would be fairly easy to accomplish what he had in mind.

100

* * *

Kate left when the mall closed at nine. Though still worried sick about Tish, she was heartened by the warmth of the people she'd met at the mall. They were friendly, concerned, anxious to help. Leap was a nice place—if only it didn't turn out to be the place where something awful happened to Tish.

Thinking she needed something besides fast food for a change, Kate pulled into the lot of Maria's Mexican Restaurant, finding it closed. She was still attuned to New York lifestyles, she realized. In small Texas towns, people ate early, went to bed early, and restaurants closed at eight, except for truck stops and the burger places. Kate had a bowl of chili at the truck stop. A burly guy with black stubble on his face and a Mack truck cap on his head kept taking surreptitious glances at her. She kept expecting him to come over and say something like, "Y'all goin' my way, honey?" But he never did.

By the time she got back to the house, Kate realized that the chili was giving her heartburn. Her palate, too, had become attuned to New York apparently. She pulled into the driveway, her headlights reflecting off the garage's metal door. Leaving the motor running, Kate got out of the car. The garage door key was loose in her pocket. She dug it out and unlocked the door. Turning the metal handle, Kate heaved the door upward. It traveled about four inches and jammed.

Kate pulled upward with all her strength. Nothing happened. She pushed downward, and the door moved about an inch, then jammed so tightly she was unable to move it in either direction. She sighed, stared at the door a moment, as if she were expecting it to suddenly open all by itself; then she went into the house through the front door. Turning on lights as she went, Kate made her way to the garage. She tried the door again, finding it every bit as immovable as it had been from the outside.

And then Kate saw the problem. The shaft on one of the rollers that followed the door's metal tracks was bent. Another roller had come off entirely. Kate found it on the cement floor by the lawn mower. The door was shot. Kate went back outside.

"No more nice comfy garage for you," she told the car as she locked it. The car needed to go into the shop for repairs to its scrapes and dents and steering. Although Tish's insurance would pay for it, Kate hadn't made an appointment to have the work done. She didn't want to be without the car. Something might come up; she might need it.

Kate watched the ten o'clock news, which carried no stories about missing librarians being found. Nor were there any stories about the discovery of any unidentified women's bodies—no Jane Does who could be Tish. The heartburn from the truck-stop chili was getting worse. Kate took two Alka-Seltzers and went to bed.

Tomorrow she would go back to the mall, hand out more of the handbills. And she would stop by the office of the *Leap Ledger*, try to get the semiweekly newspaper interested in doing a story about Tish's disappearance. These were the things on Kate's mind when she drifted off to sleep.

She awakened in the middle of the night, certain that someone was in the house.

NINE

Kate lay perfectly still, listening. Whatever had awakened her had been a sound that didn't belong, something other than the air conditioner or the hot-water heater or a passing car. But whatever it was, it didn't come again. The house was silent.

Suddenly it occurred to Kate that, if someone was here to kill her, she was a perfect target lying here in bed. An image from numerous spy movies popped into her head. The shadowy figure slipping into the dark room, pumping several shots into the sleeping victim, the bullet holes appearing in the covers, the silenced weapon's discharges sounding more like sneezes than gunshots.

Kate slipped off the bed and lay on the floor, still listening. Sure, she was a trained professional who was supposed to know how to take care of herself. But she was unarmed. And this stuff was out of her league. This was James Bond stuff. The bad guys she knew were junkies and members of street gangs. They were scumbags. Filth. Slime. But they didn't stalk you like this. Their violence was random, not so much like some kind of . . . of what? A plan? A conspiracy? First Tish disappears; then someone runs Kate off the road, breaks into the house. Kate had no idea what she and Tish had gotten themselves into.

She crawled to the doorway and peered into the dark hall. She saw only shadows. Crouching, she moved along the hall, stopping to peer into the bathroom and the other bedroom, again seeing only shadows, none of which seemed out of place, none of which moved. Promising herself that she wouldn't get grabbed from behind this time, Kate entered the living room, then stopped and listened. A loud click came from behind her, and Kate spun around, ready to defend herself, her heart pounding.

But no one attacked. Nothing moved. Finally Kate decided that the click had been the house settling, or maybe adjusting to changes in temperature or humidity. Houses always made noises. You only noticed them when you were listening.

Moving cautiously through the living room, Kate found nothing. She slipped into the kitchen, discovering no lurking killers there either. She moved to the garage.

There was no way to open the door silently, so Kate yanked it open, quickly moving to the side, out of the line of fire. There were no gunshots. Kate waited, listened, then moved rapidly through the doorway. Still no loud bangs. Even at night the garage was stuffy, and its warm mustiness engulfed her.

Kate wanted a weapon. She tried to recall what was in the garage. The only thing she could think of that might serve as a weapon was a shovel that leaned against the wall next to the door to the backyard. Kate moved in that direction, holding her hands out in front of her. Suddenly her foot hit something, and there was a crash. Kate dropped to the floor.

Feeling in front of her, Kate discovered that the thing she'd knocked over with her foot was the shovel. She picked it up. After all the noise she'd made to give away her location, if someone was here, the intruder surely would have attacked. Still, she had to be sure, so Kate finished her inspection of the garage. She found no one.

Leaving the shovel in the garage, Kate returned to the living room. It was time to turn on the lights and make absolutely certain that no one was here. But first she wanted to look through the windows, make sure there was no one in the yard. She moved through the house, looking out windows that faced the backyard, both side yards, and the front yard. The car stood in the driveway, looking forlorn, as if it desperately wanted to get back into its garage. There were no signs of anything living.

Kate went through the house, turning on lights, checking the closets, even looking under beds. She was alone. Switching off the lights, she went back to bed. It was three-fifty. Too tense to sleep, Kate stared at the ceiling, making shapes out of the shadows, the way you'd sometimes make faces or animals or such out of clouds. When the shapes started becoming monsters, she rolled over.

An hour later she was still wide-awake.

Lying on her back on the sloping floor of the trailer, Tish kicked the door as hard as she could with both feet. It was just before dawn, the coolest it would get. Even so, the humidity hung heavily in the trailer, and Tish was sweating, giving up moisture that could only be replenished by drinking the horrible-tasting stuff that came out of the trailer's tank.

She rammed her feet into the door, lifted her legs, did it again. And again. And again.

Tears were mixing with her sweat now. She kicked and kicked, and nothing happened. The two-by-fours bracing the door weren't about to let go. Nor was the thick hasp with its heavy padlock. Tish's whole body was shaking now, and she gave up trying to batter down the door with her feet.

She was getting weaker. She hadn't eaten since he'd imprisoned her here—however long ago that had been. Had she been here two days? Three? A week? The unbearably hot days and terrifying nights all blended together in a kind of blur. Maybe she'd always been here. Maybe her memories of her house, her job at the library, her twin sister, maybe all of it was imaginary, a prisoner's dream.

How long could she go without food before she had no

strength left at all? She didn't know. It seemed to her that those who deliberately starved themselves, hunger strikers and people like that, usually lived a couple of months or so. But then maybe she'd already been here a couple of months. Again Tish tried to sort out the days and found she couldn't. Maybe that was the first sign that death from starvation was near.

She shook her head. She wasn't that thin. Wouldn't bones be showing through her skin? Wouldn't her stomach be distended? That was how starving people in Africa looked. That was how people rescued from Nazi concentration camps had looked.

Tish felt her arm. Though thin, it plainly still had flesh on it. I'm not ready to die yet, Tish thought. And then she wondered whether the heat would kill her or whether she'd run out of water and die of thirst or whether she'd die like the people in Ethiopia, becoming a *thing* with a face that was shrunken and skeletal, skin that looked like dry parchment clinging to thin bones. Fifty or sixty pounds of wretchedness that looked more like something invented by Stephen King than a human being.

Tish kicked at the door again. It was a feeble effort. I have to try, she thought. I can't give up. But when she tried again, the kick was even more feeble than the first one had been. Her legs seemed too heavy to lift.

Tears were streaming down her cheeks now. She felt a scream building in her throat, but when she opened her mouth to let it out, it was a pitiful gurgle. Suddenly exhausted, she lay on her back, whimpering.

Kate glanced at her watch as she left the house. It was ten till eight. She decided to go by the newspaper office first. If it wasn't open yet, she'd pass out a few handbills, then go back. Unlocking the car, she slipped behind the wheel, inserted the key into the ignition switch, and turned it. The starter turned the engine over, but it didn't start. She pumped the gas a couple of times, tried again. It still wouldn't start. She'd never had any trouble with the car before, and she wondered why it was being cantankerous now.

Getting even with me for leaving it out all night, Kate decided.

She pumped the accelerator some more, tried again. The engine gave no indication that it might start. She smelled gas, which meant she'd flooded it. Pressing the pedal to the floor, she waited for the carburetor to clear itself of the excess gasoline. She tried again. It still refused to start. Pulling the knob that unlocked the hood, Kate got out.

Although Kate was no mechanic, she'd grown up on a farm, and anyone who'd grown up on a farm knew at least the rudiments of making obstinate machinery run. Peering into the engine compartment, she saw nothing wrong, no dangling coil wires or crimped fuel lines or broken distributor caps. She poked a few things, pulled on some others. Nothing seemed amiss.

Closing the hood, Kate leaned into the car and turned on the key so she could check the gas gauge. The needle showed that she had about half a tank. The interior of the car still smelled of gasoline. Maybe the engine was still flooded. She was about to slip behind the wheel and try to start the engine again when she noticed the wires. They came down from under the dash, ran under the plastic floor mat, and disappeared beneath the seat. Two small brown wires, almost unnoticeable against the car's dark carpeting.

Kate studied them for a moment, puzzled. Had they been there the whole time, and maybe she simply hadn't noticed? If so, what were they for? Some internal warning mechanism was telling Kate to be very careful, telling her that there was no good reason for these wires to be here. She lowered her head to the floor of the car, peered under the seat. What she saw made her gasp.

She was looking at a metal can. Although she was unable to read the writing on it, it was the sort of thing paint thinner might have come in. The two wires entered the can through its metal cap. When she'd tried to start the car, she'd literally been sitting on a bomb. Kate backed away from the car. She was trembling.

She recalled the sound that had awakened her last night. It had probably come from outside, from the car. Someone

107

had planted a bomb in her car. If it had worked, the car would have exploded, burned. And she would be dead.

Suddenly Kate felt so weak that she had to sit down on the grass. She stared at the car, her heart thudding. She felt lightheaded, and the world seemed to be swirling around her. This was the second time she had been a whole lot closer to death than anyone should ever get. She felt out of control, as if she'd stepped through some time-space barrier and entered Wonderland. Except this was Horrorland. Kate in Horrorland. And here the Mad Hatter was the Mad Bomber, and the rabbit wore cowboy clothes and made people disappear.

Kate cleared the jumble of thoughts from her consciousness. If she was going to deal with this thing, she needed a clear head. Her twin sister had disappeared, and someone was trying to kill her. It was all connected somehow, she knew that. The most likely explanation was that whoever was responsible for Tish's disappearance didn't want her looking into it and was willing to kill her to prevent her from doing so. Kate shook her head. She still had no idea why anyone would kidnap Tish in the first place. Not even a wild guess.

And like it or not, the thing she had to do now was call the Leap police. Getting to her feet, she went back into the house and made the call.

It looked as though they were having a police convention around Tish's car. The officer who responded to the call had never dealt with a bomb before, so he called his supervisor. A sergeant arrived. And then, apparently because this was the most novel thing to happen in Leap in quite a while, two more patrol officers came to see what was going on. The sergeant informed Kate that the Leap force was too small to have a bomb squad, so they were going to have to wait until the bomb disposal unit from the Department of Public Safety got here from Austin.

Two trucks from the Leap Volunteer Fire Department arrived. Firemen connected their hoses to the nearest hydrants and stood by, just in case. The block was awash in flashing emergency lights. Neighbors came out to gawk, and firemen or police officers chased them back inside, telling them they'd be safer there. More cops showed up and closed off the block at both ends to keep the curious away.

The removal of the bomb was almost anticlimactic. Two guys from the Department of Public Safety, looking like some kind of bizarre knights in armor in their protective suits, removed the bomb, took it to their truck, got inside, and closed the door. A few minutes later the guys reemerged, sans protective suits. One of them walked over to where Kate and a number of Leap police officers waited. He held up two wires from which dangled a spark plug.

"Can was full of gasoline," he said. "This was inside."

"Why didn't it work?" Kate asked.

"Not enough juice in the wires to make a spark. Whoever hooked it up didn't know how to do it right."

The local cop who'd answered the call, a young guy with short blond hair, stared at the dangling spark plug, fascinated. "What would have happened if it had gone off?" he asked.

"The can most likely would have exploded; then the gasoline would have ignited sort of like a Molotov cocktail."

No one seemed to notice that Kate had just sucked in a quick breath.

The bomb squad guys and the local cops stood around for a while, comparing notes, talking about explosives and about more mundane stuff like pay and retirement and how long it took to make sergeant or lieutenant. The fire trucks were the first to leave, followed by the DPS bomb disposal truck. The bomb, now a mere can of gasoline, was left in the hands of the Leap police. The sergeant told the officers to get back to protecting the good, honest, God-fearing folks of the community, and the officers dispersed, leaving only the cop who'd answered the call and thus had the responsibility of taking the report.

"Any chance you might have thought of someone who'd want to blow you up?" the officer asked.

Kate had already told him all about Tish's disappearance and the other attempts on her life and how she figured it all had to be connected. She said, "I've told you all I know."

"I meant that you might have thought of somebody who'd want to get you or something like that?"

"No," Kate said. "The only person I know here is my sister."

The cop nodded. "Do you get along okay, you and your sister?"

Kate stared at him. Surely he didn't think Tish was the one who'd just tried to incinerate her. But then he was just doing what he was supposed to do. He was thinking like a cop, and most violence was done by the husband or wife or lover of the victim. And sometimes brother or sister. Kate sighed. "We've always been quite close. We've never even had a serious argument."

"Would anybody gain anything if you were, uh, out of the picture, so to speak?"

"No. Our parents are dead. There aren't any rich relatives or anything like that."

"Would your sister inherit anything from you if, uh—"

"If I was out of the picture? No. I don't own any property. I don't even own a car. No stocks or bonds. My savings account would cover the funeral if I didn't get planted with too much style."

The policeman nodded. "Well, if you think of anything, let us know, okay?"

"You bet."

As the officer left, Kate noticed a man walking toward her. He was wearing slacks and a short-sleeve shirt, no jacket or tie. Kate had noticed him before, staying in the background, talking to the cops every now and then. He was about sixty, with a head of curly hair that was thick enough to have made Elvis envious.

"Hi," he said, smiling. "I'm Walter List, editor and chief reporter at the *Leap Ledger*." He extended his hand.

"Kate Hastings," she said, shaking his hand. "I was just on my way to see you, but my car wouldn't start."

He glanced at the car. "You were lucky."

"Tell me about it."

"Would you like to tell me what you were on your way to see me about?"

110

"I'd be delighted," Kate said. "But would you mind if we went inside so I could sit down?"

When they were seated in Tish's living room, Kate told him everything.

He said, "I'd heard some rumors about the librarian disappearing. Some people were saying she had simply run away with some guy, but most of them were saying that there was some mystery about it."

"Chief Colton, I'm afraid, is one of those who thinks she's simply run off."

"Even with everything else that's happened?"

"I haven't talked to him this morning, but I'm sure that, to him, the guy who ran me off the road was just a reckless driver, and the guy who broke into the house was just a burglar. Maybe this'll change his mind."

"Maybe," the newspaperman said, but Kate could see the doubt in his eyes.

"How well do you know him?" Kate asked.

"Colton? Well, being the editor of the paper, I run into him pretty often. I guess I'd sum him up by saying he's a good-ole-boy redneck. He's not the best cop I've ever run into. He sort of good-ole-boyed himself into being chief. Him and the mayor and a couple of the guys on the town council were drinking buddies."

"I just plain can't communicate with him," Kate said.

"He probably doesn't like you. He doesn't like feminists, women cops, or anybody from the east, especially New York City. He's not real partial to communists, homosexuals, liberals, or newspaper reporters either." He shrugged.

Kate sighed. "I guess I simply haven't been fully appreciating what a swell guy he is."

"He might not be a problem after November. The *Ledger*'s conducted some polls that show Stiver—he's the incumbent mayor—trailing badly. If Jacobi gets in, Colton's gone. Jacobi wants to shake up the department, make it more modern, progressive."

"I'm tempted to become a resident, just so I can vote."

List smiled; then he glanced down at the reporter's notebook in which he'd been writing while Kate told him her story. Looking up, the newspaperman said, "Is there anything else you'd like to tell me about what's happening to you and your sister?"

Kate shook her head. "I don't think I left anything out."

He closed the notebook. "Thank you for talking to me."

"What are you going to do with it?"

"I'm going to check it out. You know, talk to the cops, look at their reports, that sort of thing."

"And then?"

"Then I'm going to print it. It's a heck of a story."

TEN

The story appeared in the *Ledger* the next morning, on the front page, below the fold. Having spotted the paper on the front lawn, Kate had quickly slipped on some clothes and hurried out to get it. She read the story while she sat in the kitchen, drinking her morning coffee. The headline read:

LIBRARIAN'S DISAPPEARANCE A MYSTERY

The byline was Walter List. The story told how Tish had been seen leaving with a man in a white pickup and how no one had seen her since. It had quotes from Harriet Fielding, Marsha Wagner, and Kate. The gist was that everyone thought Tish was a level-headed librarian who would never just run off. The story went on to report how someone had run Kate off the road, how someone had broken into the house and attacked her, and how a gasoline bomb had been planted in her car, a bomb that could have killed her had it gone off. Chief Colton was quoted as saying the incidents were under investigation.

List had done a good job. The story filled the whole bottom half of the front page, and it had a photo of Tish sitting at her desk in the library. It noted that Tish had spent some time at the battered women's shelter—confirmed by an un-named source at the shelter—and that she had divorced her husband *in absentia*. Chief Colton said that, although Boyd wasn't suspected of anything specific, the Leap police did want to talk to him, but they hadn't been able to locate him.

Now maybe you'll try harder, Kate thought. She read the story again, then put down the paper.

She had fixed Tish's car so that it would start again. The wires leading to the bomb had been spliced into a wire under the dash. Kate had merely spliced the cut wire back together again, wrapping the splice with electrical tape she found in a kitchen drawer. The car had started instantly.

Kate had also gone back and reexamined the jammed ga-rage door, this time noticing the tool marks on the damaged rollers. Then she discovered that the garage window had been forced open. The conclusion was simple. Someone had sab-otaged the garage door to make sure the car was outside that night. So the bomb could be planted without having to break into the garage while Kate was there.

Someone had thought it out and gone to a lot of trouble. And yet the bomb hadn't worked. It hadn't been hooked up properly. Kate thought about that. It seemed to offer two reasonable explanations. First, that the bomb wasn't meant to go off. It was meant to scare her. But what would be the point of scaring her? Surely whoever was doing this had to realize that Kate would never abandon her search for Tish. And the attacks on Kate were adding credibility to her con-tention that something bad had happened to Tish. And the bomb attempt had attracted the interest of the media; the story was in the paper now. Kate could think of no way in which publicity would benefit Tish's abductor—and she was instinctively sure that Tish had been abducted, even if there was no hard evidence to back up that conclusion.

Sure, sometimes people did crazy things because they *wanted* publicity, but to quietly make off with a small-town librarian? It just didn't fit. It wasn't dramatic, like a hijacking or blowing up a building or assassinating someone promi-

114

nent. And at least as far as Kate knew, there had been no letters to the cops or media to claim credit or explain.

That left the second possibility: that whoever was doing this was cunning but made mistakes. Which was as far as Kate's thinking went. She had no idea why anyone would want to abduct Tish. Nor did she know why the same person—and she was convinced it was the same person—would want to kill her.

It was possible that their being twins had something to do with it, but Kate had no idea what. She was allowing herself to believe that Tish was still alive—and not just because she *had* to believe it. There was a significant difference between what had happened to Tish and what was happening to her. Tish had been taken away, alive and well. No one had tried to abduct Kate. All the attempts had been aimed at killing her. On the other hand, killing Tish could have been easily done right in the house. Taking her away in the white pickup truck was extra effort, extra risk.

Why kidnap one sister and try to kill the other? Kate had no answer for that. But she believed Tish was alive, that Tish could be found, rescued.

Kate picked up the newspaper again, turning to the classified ads. The category she sought was labeled GUNS AND AMMUNITION.

Danny Larson aimed carefully at the whiskey bottle sitting atop the fence post, then squeezed the trigger. The bottle exploded off its perch. Danny ejected the spent .22-caliber casing and inserted another cartridge. He had received the single-shot .22 three weeks ago, when he turned fourteen, a birthday present from his dad. It had been his father's first gun, too, given to him by his dad.

"That's the last of our targets," Joel Rinehart said.

"Let's look for some more," Danny said.

The boys started down the slope. Handing the gun to Joel, Danny picked up a rock and hurled it at a prickly-pear cactus. He'd hated the plants ever since he'd backed into one, lost his balance, and sat down right in the middle of it.

"If you got a gun, why you throwing rocks at it?" Joel asked. "Shoot the sucker."

"It's a waste of ammo." Which was true. The bullet sometimes knocked off a small piece of the cactus, sometimes just made a hole. It wasn't nearly as much fun as instantly turning bottles into jillions of little pieces of glass or making cans hop in the air. Cartridges weren't to be wasted, not when they cost as much as they did and you had to buy them out of your allowance.

The boys, both students at Gerber Junior High School, were best friends. Danny lived in a new subdivision on the south side of Leap. Joel lived in the Higgins Trailer Park, about a mile away from where they'd been shooting before running out of discarded liquor bottles.

The boys were following a power line now. There was a road of sorts—two ruts with weeds between them—that ran below the line, and sometimes lovers would use it as a place to park, high school kids mostly. And they'd throw out a lot of beer cans and bottles. At the moment there didn't seem to be anything but some of those little foam boxes burgers came in, along with some large paper cups that said Coke on them. What's wrong with high school kids these days, Danny wondered, don't they drink beer anymore?

"We're kinda cutting back toward town," Danny said. "We don't want to get too close to where anybody lives, or we might get in trouble."

Joel nodded. "Wish my dad would buy me a gun."

"Maybe you didn't ask him good enough. You know, like if you didn't have one, you'd never have any fun ever again until you were twenty-one and too old to have fun anymore."

"Wouldn't work," Joel replied sullenly. He kicked a rock, which bounced into the weeds at the side of the road. "My mom hates guns. She won't even let my dad have one."

Danny's mom hadn't been too big on the idea either, but his dad, who owned a small arsenal of guns, all sorts of them, had prevailed. "My dad's going to get me a membership in the National Rifle Association," Danny said. "He says everybody should own a gun and know how to use it."

Joel grunted.

"Don't worry," Danny said cheerfully. "As long as you keep on buying your share of the ammo, you can shoot mine any time you want."

The boys fell silent then. As they walked along Danny thought about what he looked like. It was something that hadn't concerned him much until just recently. He supposed he'd always figured on growing up to look like his dad, or maybe Luke Skywalker. But now he found himself looking in the mirror a lot, and his blue eyes seemed kind of pale and lifeless looking, and his reddish-brown hair seemed kind of limp. If some of the heavy-metal bands he liked had hair like his, they'd have to wear wigs. And even worse than his hair were his teeth. Ever since he got his adult teeth, they'd looked enormous to him, big, horsey-looking teeth that had been designed for someone twelve times his size. He asked his mom about it once, and she'd assured him that the rest of him would grow and the teeth would look just right someday, but Danny was beginning to doubt it. The teeth seemed to be what was growing, instead of his face.

Worrying about his appearance had begun about the same time he started getting hard-ons all the time, although Danny wasn't sure there was any connection. He was even less sure about what was happening with his dick. If he looked at girls sitting near him in class, it got hard. What was really startling was that it even happened when he looked at some of his teachers—especially Miz Anderson, who was really stacked. And it happened when he saw ads for women's underwear in his mom's magazines. Feeling the tightening in his crotch, he glanced down at the bulge.

Jesus, Danny thought. It even happens when you just think about it happening.

Glancing over at Joel, Danny considered whether to discuss these intimate things with his friend and decided against it. Joel, of course, was the only person he would even consider telling such things to, and Danny knew that eventually he would. But not now. The mood wasn't right for talking about personal stuff. He wondered whether Joel was having the same problems with his dick. If he was, it would make it easier to talk about.

Suddenly Joel stopped, aimed the rifle into a clump of brush. After a moment of sighting on whatever it was he saw, the boy lowered the gun. "Thought I spotted a rabbit," he said, and they continued walking.

Rabbits were the only living things they had ever shot at, and for the first time Danny questioned why they did it. What would be the point of shooting a rabbit? What was the point of shooting anything that was alive? Although he found the implications of these questions troubling, he didn't pursue them.

Instead he started wondering whether Joel was happy with the way he looked. Joel had thick dark hair, brown eyes, a round face. He was heavyset and usually slouched when he walked. Danny's father said Joel was going to grow up to look like one of those Japanese sumo wrestlers. But then Danny's dad said lots of stuff. He was real fond of telling Danny that, if he got any skinnier, the family could always paint him green and say he was a blade of grass. His dad thought it was funny, but it just made Danny that much more apprehensive whenever he looked in the mirror.

"There's something," Joel said, pointing to a shiny object in the weeds at the side of the road. He ran over and picked up a Pearl beer bottle. "Where should we put it?"

"Let's take turns trying to hit it when the other guy throws it up."

"Okay. You throw it. It's my turn to shoot."

Danny tossed the bottle, which turned end over end as it rose, making a low *whooh . . . whooh . . . whooh*. Joel fired and missed. He handed the gun to Danny, who also missed. It was Joel who finally hit it, on the sixth try.

"Got it!" he yelled, proud of himself.

"Yeah, but we sure wasted a lot of bullets."

They took stock, discovering that they had maybe twenty bullets left. Enough to have another couple hours of fun if they didn't waste them. They continued following the power line until it veered to the right and headed toward town. Leaving the road that followed the line, the boys walked up a low hill and found themselves confronted by a barbed-wire fence.

The boys were used to going through fences. The Texas

countryside was full of them, and to the boys they were just something you had to be careful getting through if you didn't want to rip your clothes and get into trouble with your mom. It had never occurred to them that a fence might mean anything more than an inconvenience. They took turns holding the strands apart while the other one slipped through.

Continuing on, they found an old tin can, but it was too eaten away by rust to make it worth shooting at. When they came to the top of another hill, Joel exclaimed, "Hey, look at that!"

Below them was a big pit that someone had carved out with a bulldozer or something like that. In the pit, leaning against a bank, was an old house trailer with the windows boarded up.

"Looks sort of like a garbage dump," Danny said.

"Yeah, a . . . . a whatchamacallit."

"A sanitary landfill."

"Yeah, one of those."

"Why you figure that trailer's in it?"

"Must have been thrown away. Sure doesn't look like it could be good for anything."

They looked at each other to see if they were both thinking the same thing. Simultaneously they both began grinning.

"Should we finish it off?" Joel asked.

"I don't see why not," Danny said.

They moved in on the pit. Although they were too old to play games, like the FBI closing in on the bad guys' hideout, Danny knew that's what they were doing. They just weren't admitting it to themselves. When they reached the edge of the pit, Danny said, "I'm going to see if I can knock off that taillight."

"You sure there's nobody inside?"

"Jeez, look at it. It's all boarded up, and it'd fall over if the bank wasn't holding it up. You couldn't walk around in there. And all closed up like that, it would be so hot inside nobody could stand it."

Joel considered that. "Yeah, I guess you're right."

Danny dropped into the prone position, took careful aim,

119

and fired. The taillight was still there. He might have missed the whole damn trailer.

"My turn," Joel said, dropping down beside him.

Danny handed him the gun. Joel slipped a cartridge into the rifle and closed the bolt. He took a long time getting his arms just right, then sighting in, but he finally fired. He missed the taillight, too, but at least he hit the trailer. The bullet hit it with a loud snap.

"Come on," Danny said, abandoning all pretense that this wasn't a game of storm-the-bad-guys'-hideout, and the boys scrambled down the bank into the pit. When they were so close to the trailer that they couldn't possibly miss it, Danny took the gun, aimed at the taillight, and fired. It shattered. Then Joel shot at the already-airless tires.

Tish had been dozing when she thought she heard something hit the trailer. But the sound only brought her partially awake, and she was soon drifting off again. Then something hit the trailer again, and went whizzing past her ear. She was instantly awake, blinking her eyes.

It's him, her mind told her. He's back. He's shooting at the trailer. And then splinters flew from one of the boards covering a window as another shot was fired into the trailer. Tish flattened herself on the floor, and then she wondered what the point was. If he wanted to kill her, all he had to do was open the door and do it. This was just a game, some sick game of chance, like Russian roulette. Fire into the trailer. Maybe you'll hit her and maybe you won't. See what happens.

And if you find out you didn't, what then? Finish her off? Try again tomorrow?

Another bullet ripped into the side of the trailer, then another. The next shot hit something by the sink and ricocheted off, making that whistling sound that only bullets can make. Since the shooting started, Tish had been stuporous, like being in one of those nightmares where your legs won't work and you know you're going to die. Suddenly the dreamlike grogginess lifted. She was trembling, and she was taking in short little breaths that sounded like a dog panting.

"Stop it!" she screamed suddenly. "Stop it, you hear me! Stop it!"

"There's somebody in there!" Joel yelled.

Danny had just taken careful aim at an orange reflector near the front of the trailer. He lowered the gun. "How . . . how could there be anybody in there?" he asked, his voice revealing how shaken he was.

"We didn't know there was anybody in there!" Joel hollered.

"We didn't," Danny yelled. "Honest."

The boys looked at each other, and Danny realized that Joel was thinking the same thing he was: Run! Get out of here! But before they could move, the woman in the trailer was screaming at them.

"Help me!" she pleaded. "You've got to help me!"

Danny moved closer to the trailer. "What . . . what's wrong? Did . . . did we hit you?"

"I've been locked in here. I can't get out."

Both boys moved to the door. Danny examined the two-by-fours that had been fastened to the door and the massive padlock.

"Think we could shoot it off?" Joel asked.

"We might if we had a three-fifty-seven Magnum, but not with a twenty-two."

"There's no way for us to get the lock off," Joel said to the woman inside the trailer. "What do you want us to do?"

"Go for help."

"Okay," Joel said. "We'll leave right now."

Danny grabbed his arm. "Wait a minute," he said. "Let's find out what's going on here first."

Joel nodded.

"What's your name?" Danny asked.

"Patricia Hastings. I'm the librarian."

Although Danny didn't know Patricia Hastings well, he'd been in the library often enough that an image of her immediately popped into his head. He started to say hi and introduce himself, then decided that might seem silly under the circumstances.

"How'd you get in there?" Danny asked.

"I've been kidnapped. I'm being held prisoner."

"We'll call the police. We're going right now."

The boys started to leave; then Danny turned back to the trailer. "I'm sorry we shot at you. We thought it was empty. We really did."

"It's okay," Patricia Hastings said. "Just get help, okay?"

"Okay."

Although the boys had scrambled down one of the pit's steep sides, getting out that way would be difficult, so they headed for the end that sloped up gradually. They'd gone about twenty feet when a green pickup appeared at the entrance to the pit, stopping hard, throwing up dirt. A man in cowboy clothes got out. Danny had the urge to run to him, tell him about the woman in the trailer. But something held him back. He tightened his grip on the .22.

The man was walking toward them. He had one of those shiny belt buckles that was shaped like the state of Texas. "What are you boys doing here?" he asked.

"We're just out shooting at tin cans and stuff," Danny said.

"Is something wrong?" Joel asked. Danny was glad that Joel was being wary, not blurting out everything.

"Is it okay if we shoot down here?" Danny asked. "It looked like a good place because all the bullets would go into the bank."

"I don't see any cans," the man said.

"We were going to go get some," Joel said.

"Did you boys go near that trailer?"

"We looked at it," Joel said. "But it's locked, so we didn't go inside or anything."

"I guess it's just abandoned," Danny said. "That's what it looks like."

The man studied them. Danny's stomach tightened up as if some unspeakable thing with lots of legs and feelers were running around inside of it.

"There's not anyone inside that trailer, is there?" the man asked, watching them closely.

"In . . . inside?" Joel said, and Danny knew that they'd blown it.

"Yeah," the man said. "Inside."

"What makes you think there'd be anyone in there?" Danny asked, knowing it was pointless to keep up the deception.

"Because I'd have to let them out."

Suddenly, on some unspoken signal, the boys turned and ran. Side by side they dashed toward the other end of the pit, fear making their legs pump so hard it seemed they could outrun almost anything. And then Danny heard the loud pop from behind them, and suddenly Joel gasped and fell. Knowing what had happened but unwilling to accept it, Danny spun around, seeing Joel lying on the ground, the man aiming a pistol at them. Danny was reaching down for Joel, to grab him, pull him to safety, and then the pistol in the man's hand fired again, and the bullet hummed by Danny's face, missing it by inches. Knowing there was no way he could help Joel without getting himself killed, Danny scrambled for the nearest cover, which was the trailer.

It wasn't until he was behind it, trembling, hearing the pounding of his heart and his ragged breathing, that he realized that he was still holding the rifle. He was armed. He could defend himself.

Although Danny was unable to see the man, he could see Joel, who lay motionless on the ground, one arm beneath him, the other extended as though he were reaching out for something. Danny wanted desperately to grab that outstretched hand and drag his friend to safety. A tear ran down his cheek.

It occurred to him suddenly how much this was like the games he'd played when he was younger. Good guys versus the bad guys, shoot 'em up, bang-bang. And he realized suddenly that he should have been feeling sorry and afraid when he saw gunfights on TV. Or the spaceship battles in *Star Wars*. Or sword fights. He'd been entertained, thrilled by these things. And now he knew he should have felt sorry for the people who died. And he should have been terrified. There was nothing exhilarating about facing someone who wanted to kill you. There was only unbelievable, consuming fear.

Danny peeked around the corner of the trailer. A bullet slapped into its metal side, and Danny pulled his head back. He hadn't even seen the man.

"What's going on out there?" the woman inside the trailer screamed.

Danny was afraid to speak. For several seconds he simply stood there, knowing that the man could be sneaking up on him but having no idea what to do about it. Then he crawled under the trailer. Because of the angle at which it was leaning and its deflated tires, it was a tight squeeze, but he made it. He was still unable to see the man. He waited.

Finally Danny heard the man's footfalls. Off to his right. Coming closer. Danny clung tightly to his rifle. If the man's face appeared below the trailer, Danny would shoot. He had no doubts about that. The man had shot and maybe killed Joel, and he would kill him, too. If the man appeared, Danny would shoot him.

The footfalls passed the trailer, then moved closer again. Danny saw a pair of cowboy boots about ten feet away, and he took aim. But he didn't squeeze the trigger. The man hadn't seen him yet, and shooting someone in the foot seemed of doubtful value. It wouldn't kill him, but it would certainly reveal Danny's hiding place. The cowboy boots moved out of his field of vision.

Then the footfalls retreated. Danny waited. Finally he heard an engine starting up, the truck pulling away. Danny continued waiting.

"Can anybody hear me?" the woman asked.

Danny didn't answer. He looked at his watch. He'd resolved to stay put for ten minutes before leaving the protection of the trailer. When the time was up, he came out warily, holding the rifle ready, but there was no sign of the man.

Danny hurried over to where Joel lay. The boy was on his back. Danny touched him, giving him a gentle nudge. "Joel, you okay?"

When his friend didn't respond, Danny pushed him a little harder. "Joel."

124

Although he knew he wasn't supposed to move an injured person, Danny didn't care about that. He had to get some reaction from Joel, something to let him know his friend was still alive. He rolled Joel over. His eyes were open, staring dully into the bright sun. Joel didn't close his lids, didn't move his arm to cover his eyes. And then Danny saw the blood that had seeped into his friend's shirt. The bullet had hit him in the side, the side he'd been lying on until Danny turned him over.

Suddenly Danny was running, heading for the steep bank. It would be a hard climb, but he wasn't about to head for the spot where the man's truck had been parked. Tears ran down his cheeks as he scrambled up the bank, kicking rocks loose, using the butt of his rifle as a climbing stick.

He was nearly to the top, when the rock under his foot gave way, and Danny began slipping backward. He clawed at the earth, breaking his nails on the stones embedded in the bank. Finally he stopped his slide, and he was going up again. Breathless and frantic, his heart racing, he reached the top of the bank.

And then he saw the man.

Standing there. Maybe fifteen feet away. Danny threw himself forward, over the crest of the bank, raising the rifle as he did so. The man fired at him, but missed. And Danny had him in the sights of the .22. He pulled the trigger.

Nothing happened.

Danny's mind worked furiously to identify the source of the problem. He'd loaded the gun, he knew he had. And then he knew what had gone wrong. He'd forgotten to cock it.

The man fired again. This time he didn't miss.

Frantic, Tish moved from one window to another, trying to see out through the slits between the boards. She could see nothing. She'd heard shots, then silence, followed by more shooting, then more silence. All she could do was wait, listen, hope the boys she'd spoken to were all right.

Finally she heard footsteps approaching the trailer.

"Who's there?" she said, and then she realized she'd spoken too softly to be heard through the walls of the trailer. "Who's there?" she said more loudly.

"Just me," a male voice said, and Tish slid to the floor of the trailer, all hope gone, desperately fearing for the boys now. It was *his* voice.

"What happened to the boys?" she asked.

"They've been taken care of."

"Taken care of? What . . . what does that mean?"

"It means I'll be burying them real quick here."

"But . . . but . . ."

"If you're going to ask a question, you'd best hurry, because I've got things to do."

"But . . . why?"

"Why'd I kill 'em?"

"Yes, why?" She was crying now, tears running down her cheeks, dripping on her filthy clothes. "Why did you have to harm those boys?"

"Couldn't have them letting everybody know where you were, now could I, Jenna Lee?"

"That's not my name. You know that's not my name."

He didn't reply.

"Why'd you call me that?"

Still no answer.

"Why?" she sobbed. "Why did you have to hurt those boys?"

She heard his footfalls as he walked away from the trailer.

ELEVEN

When Kate returned to the house, she had a .38-caliber revolver in her purse. Although she was uncertain what the rules were concerning the retail purchase of a handgun in Texas, she had avoided any potential hassles by buying the .38 from a private citizen. No waiting period. No forms to fill out.

The guy she'd bought it from said he worked as an electrician but that he'd just been laid off, and for that reason he was being forced to sell some of his guns. He had numerous others—Magnums, small-caliber target pistols, rifles, shotguns, you name it. Kate had known cops who had large numbers of guns like that, and she'd never understood why anyone would want so many of them. They were expensive, you rarely used them, and burglars usually grabbed up firearms even before they took the TV set.

Kate parked the still-unrepaired car in front of the inoperative garage door. As she was getting out, an unmarked white car with two antennas on its trunk pulled in behind her. Kate instantly recognized the car as an unmarked police unit—and so would any crook who wasn't retarded. Chief Colton got out, walked toward her.

"What can I do for you, Chief?" Kate asked, acutely aware of the revolver illegally concealed in her purse.

"I want to talk to you about the troubles you've been having."

The first words to enter Kate's mind were, It's about time you decided to do something. But what she said was, "Come in." And when he was seated on the couch, she said, "Would you like some iced tea—or anything else?"

He shook his head, and Kate sat down in a small upholstered chair.

"It's possible," Colton said slowly, "that someone is trying to kill you."

"Things would seem to indicate that."

"We're looking into that possibility."

"Have you made any progress?"

Ignoring her question, Colton said, "Here's what I see when I look at the facts. Someone ran you off the road. Someone broke into your place. Someone put a bomb in your car. Right so far?"

Kate nodded.

"Okay. We have only one witness to the incident with the car or the break-in, and that's you."

"What are you trying to say? You can see where someone forced the window open."

"Exactly. I can see that *someone* forced it open."

Uncertain where he was going with this, Kate said nothing.

"Now we also have you wanting us to get busy and find your sister," the chief said, fixing his eyes on hers.

Suddenly Kate understood. "Are you suggesting I made all this up in order to . . . to get you off your ass, to make you start looking for Tish?"

He shrugged. "I'm merely looking at what we have here."

"You think I put the bomb in the car, too? You think I tried to blow myself up? That's a hell of a way to make a point."

"Bomb couldn't have possibly gone off. It could have been put there by someone who wanted it to go off but didn't know how to wire it. On the other hand, it could have been put there by someone who did know how to wire it.''

"And didn't want it to go off,'' Kate said.

Colton simply looked at her, just the hint of a smirk on his lips as if to say, Got you, lady, didn't I?

"You dust the bomb?''

"Yup.''

"Find any of my prints on it?''

"Nope.''

And then Kate realized that her point was worthless. She was a cop. She'd have enough sense to wipe the damn thing off. "Look,'' she said calmly, "you're absolutely right that I want you to do more to find Tish. But if you think I'd make a false report to the police, you're absolutely wrong, and furthermore I resent it.''

On his face was still just the suggestion of a smirky grin. "I'm not accusing you of anything,'' he said. "I'm just looking at all the possibilities.''

"I see,'' Kate said icily.

"Also, since I'm here, I thought I'd remind you again about not interfering in a police investigation. But then that's probably not necessary, you being a police officer yourself and all. You already know how mad that can make the officers with jurisdiction over a case. And you know a person could even get arrested for it.''

Kate hadn't realized before just how hairy Colton was. His khaki uniform shirt was the short-sleeve summer model, and his arm hairs were thick and black, almost like fur. Although he'd no doubt shaved when he got up, the dark shadow of thick facial hair was already apparent on his face. And he certainly had no problem with a receding hairline. The hair on his head pushed down his forehead to within an inch and a half or so of his bushy eyebrows.

"You know what a troglodyte is?'' Kate asked.

He looked puzzled. "A what?''

"Never mind. Is there anything else you want to talk to me about?''

"I think I've covered everything.''

The hint of a smirk tried to reappear, but it came out

looking more like his lips wouldn't close quite right. Kate watched through the window as he drove away.

Lowering the scoop, he drove the huge front-end loader forward, scraping off another layer of rocky earth. He figured the soil was the reason that nothing but scrub trees grew naturally here. There was maybe a foot or two of topsoil; then you hit granite. There simply wasn't anywhere for the roots of a big tree to go. On the other hand, people had large trees in their yards, so maybe he was wrong about that.

He backed the loader up, studying the pit he'd carved out. It was a pit within a pit actually. As soon as he buried the two boys, he'd fill in the small area he'd just scooped out, and anyone looking down from above would see nothing but a large pit with an old trailer in the bottom.

Eventually that, too, would disappear.

It seemed unlikely that anyone else would come here. As a rule no one ever did. Two boys looking for a place to shoot. You couldn't figure on something like that.

He'd been lucky, he knew that. If he hadn't come by when he did, they would have gone for help, and he'd be in jail right now. Climbing down from the loader, he pushed the thought away. It had worked out all right; that was all that mattered.

He'd pushed the bodies under the trailer to keep them from being spotted. He pulled the first one out, a pudgy kid with dark hair. He carried the boy to the pit he'd just carved out and dropped him in. Going back to the trailer, he dragged out the other boy, the skinny one, and carried him to the pit as well. Then he realized that the skinny kid's rifle was under the trailer as well, and he went back for it. Returning to the pit, he tossed the gun in.

He stood there, looking at the boys. The chunky one had taken a bullet in the side. Blood from the wound had soaked into his yellow shirt. He lay in the pit facedown, his arms out to his sides, as if he were trying to fly. The other boy was on his back, one arm bent back beneath him, the other stuck down by his pocket, as if he were reaching for his keys. The bullet had hit the boy dead center in the chest. Only a

130

small amount of blood showed. The kid must have died quick. The blood would have quit flowing out when the heart stopped.

Looking at the two kids he'd slain, he tried to assess how he felt about what he'd done and discovered he really didn't feel much of anything. He'd never killed a human being before. He'd helped his daddy slaughter animals for food sometimes back when he lived on the farm. And he'd helped hold down an injured horse one time while someone got a gun to put it out of its misery. Killing the boys was like killing anything else, he supposed. He didn't enjoy taking life, but there were times it had to be done. And in the overall scheme of things, it didn't make a heck of a lot of difference. Besides, life never really ended. It just went back to where it had come from, waited until it was needed again.

Getting back on the loader, he filled in the pit within a pit, covering over the two bodies.

When he was done, he shut off the loader's diesel engine, got down off the machine, and leaned against it while he lit a cigarette. In the sky was a long con trail heading east, probably left by some commercial jet. On its way from Denver to Atlanta maybe.

The sky fascinated him, especially at night. He liked to look at stars. Out here, away from any big cities, the stars were spectacular. Billions of stars, many with planets of their own. There had to be life out there. There was no way it could have happened only here on Earth, when there were so many other planets. On some of them the conditions had been right, and life had begun. He had no doubts about that.

He'd read a lot of stuff about UFOs. They had visited the earth; he was absolutely convinced of that. There were just too many sightings, too many similarities among the various reports. The government was covering it up. Probably because they figured anyone advanced enough to travel through light-years of space had to have super weapons of some sort. And nothing got the government excited like the thought of bigger weapons.

Some asshole in Washington's going to get pissed at his old lady and push the button just because he thinks it'll serve her right, he decided. *Boom*, no more world. He shrugged. It was a prospect he regarded with indifference.

Getting back on the loader, he fired up the big diesel engine and drove out of the pit.

"Crystal must have put the filter into the coffee machine wrong again," Sergeant Dan Rawlins said. Putting his cup down on the chief's desk, he picked some coffee grounds off his tongue.

Chief Colton said, "What you got on the disappearance of the two boys?"

"You see the report?" the old cop asked.

Colton nodded.

"Then you know as much as I do. They went shooting yesterday with the Larson boy's twenty-two, and they ain't been seen since."

"Think they're runaways?"

Rawlins sighed. "Don't know. I know Reid Larson, the boy's dad, but I don't know the boy himself very well. If he was going to run off, why take the rifle along?"

Chief Colton considered that, then said, "To make it look good so nobody would suspect anything. Two boys going shooting, not lighting out for Houston or New York or Los Angeles or wherever kids run away to these days."

Rawlins looked doubtful. "I don't know," he said. "Most kids that age decide to take off, they know, in the back of their minds anyway, that they're going to end up back home in a few weeks or months—or maybe even a few days. They can't take a rifle to Houston or New York, so what are they going to do with it?"

"Leave it somewhere. Or sell it."

Rawlins shook his head. "Rifle'd be a prize possession. Kid would leave it at home because, like I say, he'd know in the back of his mind that this running-away business would end up just being temporary."

"You been watching too much television," the chief said. "Kids don't think like that."

"It's just food for thought," the old cop said. "You know,

132

one of those little doubts that gets into your head and just sort of floats around in there, refusing to go away."

Colton said, "You got any other reason to believe that they're not runaways?"

"We talked to the boys' parents and some of their friends. There doesn't seem to be anything troubling the boys, no big family problems or school problems—at least not that we found out about. And they weren't spending all their time looking at maps or anything obvious like that. But, hell, J.C., who knows what goes on in the mind of a kid that age? They got their own way of looking at things. They can run off because things are bad at home. On the other hand, you treat them real good, and they'll run away because they're bored. They don't know what they're doing. It seems like an adventure. Go get a job in the big city or whatever."

Yeah, Colton thought, and if they don't get picked up and sent home by the police, they probably wind up selling themselves to a bunch of filthy faggots. He thought about young boys being forced to do unspeakable things. "Ought to do something about faggots," he muttered.

"Come again?" Rawlins asked, looking puzzled.

Colton dismissed the question with a wave of his hand. "Here's how I want you to handle this. Officially we're looking into it and doing everything we can. But unofficially we're figuring they're runaways until something comes up to indicate otherwise. In other words they'll probably turn up in Houston or somewhere like that, so don't spend a whole lot of time looking for them."

Rawlins nodded in that way he had of letting you know he'd heard and understood but didn't necessarily agree. Colton wondered whether Rawlins agreed with him very often. The chief watched as the sergeant left the office, taking his coffee cup with him.

Am I making a mistake here? Chief Colton wondered. And then he put his doubts aside. Missing boys were almost always runaways. Girls usually were, too, but you had to be more careful with girls. There were crazy people out there who liked to do bad things to girls, and some of them traveled around the country. The faggots, on the other hand, usually just holed up in the big cities, waited for the boys to come to them.

Somewhere in the back of Colton's mind, one of those little doubts Rawlins had spoken of sprang up. It warned him that this sort of thinking was narrow and bigoted and most likely unreliable. He pushed these thoughts away. His view of the world was based on years of experience. He knew what people were like.

Tish sat on the sloping dusty floor of the trailer, staring at her bare feet. At some point—days ago, weeks ago—she had kicked off her shoes, and they were somewhere in the trailer, but she was uncertain where. It seemed like a long time since she had seen them.

The hairs on her legs needed to be shaved. Soon she would be as hairy as a man, she supposed. And she wondered whether they would grow to a certain length and stop or whether they would keep on growing. Perhaps shaving them over the years had taken away their ability to grow to a definite length. Maybe they'd grow to be so long she'd trip over them.

But then that idea was silly, wasn't it? She'd be dead long before that.

It was the hottest part of the day, the sun beating down unmercifully on the trailer's metal shell. Tish felt like a big bird of some sort, roasting in an oven. The moisture that soaked into her clothes and beaded on her forehead was basting juice. Looking at her hairy legs, she chuckled. She hadn't been plucked. Here she was getting cooked, and she was unplucked and inedible. Suddenly it was the funniest situation in which she'd ever found herself, and she was laughing so hard she was shaking.

A sound from outside the trailer made her stop.

Getting up, she moved to the nearest window and peered through the space between the boards. Her restricted view revealed nothing out of the ordinary. She moved to another window, again seeing only dirt and rocks. And then something flicked across her field of vision. A shadow? Was someone out there?

134

Tish was mustering what strength she had to yell when she heard someone at the door. Scream, she thought. But something stopped her. And then she heard the padlock being removed. The door opened, and he stood there, looking at her, fresh air and bright light pouring into the trailer. He stepped inside, closing the door behind him, the stale gloom returning to the trailer's interior.

Fear wrapped its icy tentacles around Tish's insides. There was always fear in this place, but it was usually in the background, like a dull ache. Now it was immediate, intense. He was here for a reason, to do something.

"I want you to admit who you are," he said.

Tish backed away from him, stopping when her back hit the wall.

He took a step toward her, stopped. "Admit who you really are," he said.

"I . . . I don't know what you're talking about," Tish said, aware of the obvious terror in her voice.

"You know."

She shook her head.

"I thought you might be difficult," he said, and suddenly there was a big knife in his hand. Tish stared at it. "Know what this is?"

Again Tish shook her head.

"It's a hunting knife. Know what it's used for?"

Afraid to speak, afraid that she would say the wrong thing, Tish shook her head.

"It's used for field-dressing animals. You know, for gutting them and all that. It can also be used for skinning." With his thumb, he gently felt the edge of the blade, checking its sharpness. Abruptly he slipped the knife into a sheath, which he slipped into his pocket. "We'll work up to this," he said.

"Please," Tish said in a voice that was barely audible. Though uncertain whether she should plead, she knew she had to try something, because she had no idea what he was talking about and if she couldn't oblige him he would hurt her.

"All you have to do is admit who you are."

"You know what I am."

He nodded. "Oh, yeah, I know all right. But I want you to admit it." He studied her for a moment, then said, "Who are you?"

Oh, God, Tish thought, I don't know the right answer.

"Tell me your name," he snapped.

"Patricia Hastings."

The blow came so fast Tish didn't even have time to flinch. His fist connected with her face so hard that her head was slammed back against the wall. The features of her attacker swirled before her, and then she was sliding down the wall to the floor.

"Who are you?" he demanded again.

Tish touched her lip; it was swelling. When she withdrew her fingers, they were bloody.

"Who are you?" he demanded again.

"I don't know what to say," Tish said.

He grabbed the front of her dress, lifting her up, pushing her against the wall. "Who are you?" he asked, and she could smell the cigarettes on his breath.

"Patricia Steuben," she said, hoping that was the answer he wanted.

He slapped her, the blow turning her head, and before she could make her eyes focus or her brain work, he backhanded her, hitting the other side of her face this time. He kept it up, hitting her again. And again. And again. Her head felt loose on her shoulders, rocking back and forth like a metronome.

When he finally stopped, he said, "Do you want me to hit you some more?"

"No," Tish said, her voice a whisper.

"Then tell me who you are."

"I . . . I don't know what you want me to say."

He drew back his fist.

"No," she said. "Please."

But the fist struck her, and everything went black.

When Tish regained consciousness, she was lying on the bed. She was aware of the pain in her face, and she remembered what had happened. Maybe he's gone, she thought. Maybe he's not going to hurt me anymore. But he wasn't gone. She sensed his presence somewhere in the trailer. She was afraid to turn her head to make sure, for as long as she lay here completely still he wouldn't hurt her anymore.

Clearly she could not have made it to the bed on her own, which meant that he must have put her here, and she wondered why. Why would he do anything for her comfort? Why hadn't he just left her lying on the floor?

And then she recalled his demand that she tell him who she really was. Tish still had no idea what he was talking about. If he asked her again, she wouldn't know how to answer him, and he would hurt her again. She remembered the knife. The deadly-looking knife that was used for cutting through the hides of animals.

The pain in her face was growing more intense. Tish resisted the temptation to reach up with her hand to feel the damage. Was her face black and blue, swollen? Had he broken her nose, loosened her teeth? Would she ever look the same? And lying beneath these concerns was another, even more horrifying thought. Would she live long enough for these things to matter?

"I see you're awake," his voice said.

It took all Tish's will power to keep her muscles from jerking. Maybe if she just lay still, maybe the pain wouldn't come again.

"Stop pretending," he said.

No, Tish thought. No, no, no.

He kicked the bed. "Open your eyes," he said. "Otherwise I'll have to open them for you, and you won't like the way I do it."

Tish opened her eyes. He was standing over her, looking down at her. "That's better," he said. "Are you ready to tell me who you are—who you really are?"

Suddenly Tish recalled that he'd called her a name before, a name that sounded familiar but one that she was unable to place. What was it? She struggled to remember.

"Admit who you are," he said. "Admitting it won't hurt you. You'll be no worse off."

Tish wondered what he meant by that, then went back to trying to recall the name. It swirled around in her thoughts, a blur, unrecognizable. What was it? she demanded of her memory. What was it? And then the knife appeared in front of her eyes.

"You'll admit it," he said confidently. "There's no doubt about that."

He placed the knife's flat edge against her cheek. The point was a blur, no more than an inch from her eyes. He's going to cut my face, her brain screamed. He's going to disfigure me. And then she realized that he could also blind her. Oh God, she thought, what does he want me to say?

"Say it," he said, his voice suddenly less demanding, almost kindly. He was the good-guy interrogator and bad-guy interrogator all rolled into one.

"I . . . I'm who you think I am," she said. "I . . . I admit it."

He smiled. "We're on the right track now. But you still have to say the name."

"I admit everything," she said. "All of it."

He nodded. "That's good. Now tell me who you are and I'll take this knife away from your face."

"I . . . I'm her. I'm the one."

The knife was withdrawn from her face, and Tish thought it might have worked. She might have said enough. But then the blade was moving toward her midsection, and she involuntarily tightened her stomach muscles. A part of her was screaming that he was about to eviscerate her, and she tried desperately not to listen to that part of herself. The knife moved downward.

But instead of plunging into her flesh, it was cutting through the front of her dress, cutting through it so effortlessly that she could barely feel the material pulling against her flesh. The blade had to be sharper than a razor. In a few seconds her white dress lay open just like a blouse that had been unbuttoned, exposing her bra. He slipped the blade under the portion that joined the cups and slit it, exposing her breasts.

He's going to rape me, Tish thought. Surprisingly the prospect didn't seem all that frightening. She was much too worried about dying to be concerned about anything else.

138

"You're being silly," he said. "You've admitted everything. What's so hard about saying the name?" He rested the flat of the blade on her left nipple.

Names flew through Tish's mind. *Linda, Betty, Jane, Alice, Anne, Connie, Michelle, Roxanne . . .*

The knife slipped off her nipple, and then its point was pressing against the flesh of her breast, just enough to make a slight indentation.

Sylvia . . . Zoë . . . Wendy . . . Delores . . . Ellen . . . Francine . . . Grace . . . And then Tish's mind shut down. It seemed unable to pluck any more names from the jumble of thoughts inside her head. The knife pressed harder, the point poking painfully at her flesh now. *Jenny!* she thought. No, not Jenny. Jenna. Jenna something. Jenna what? Jenna . . . Jenna . . . Jenna . . .

"Jenna Lee," she said.

The pressure of the knife grew less. "What about Jenna Lee?" he asked.

"That's who I am. I'm Jenna Lee."

He withdrew the knife. "Very good," he said.

Several moments passed during which he simply stood there, staring at her. Finally Tish said, "I've told you what you wanted to hear. What happens now?"

"The same thing that was going to happen all along," he said.

"What's that?"

When he didn't answer, she said, "When are you going to let me out of this trailer?"

"I'm not," he said. And then he stood up, sheathed the knife, and slipped it into his hip pocket. He walked to the door, opened it, then turned back toward Tish. Pulling out a white handkerchief, he mopped his brow. "Sure is hot in here," he said, and then he was gone.

Tish heard him securing the padlock. Then she listened to his receding footfalls as he walked away from the trailer. She pulled her bra and dress together, but they wouldn't stay, and she stopped trying. I'm alive, she thought. He didn't kill me.

A feeling of relief settled over her that made her feel light, as if she could float off the bed. He was gone, and she was alive. And then the tears came, streaming down her cheeks. She knew she was still a prisoner, and that he had said he would never release her, but these things seemed unimportant at the moment. All that mattered was that she was alive.

TWELVE

Kate sat down on Tish's couch, putting her purse on the cushion beside her. The bag felt normal now, with the weight of the .38 in it. It had seemed entirely too light ever since she left New York, leaving her weapon behind. Ordinarily she wouldn't worry about carrying a concealed weapon in a state where she had no authority. It was not the sort of thing cops hassled each other about. Here, however, in the jurisdiction of Chief Jack Colton, she would have to be careful.

Kate leaned her head back, closing her eyes. She'd gone to the mall to hand out more of the have-you-seen-this-woman notices. And then she'd gone by the *Leap Ledger* to see whether Walter List had learned anything. And to make sure he continued running stories about Tish's disappearance. Although the editor hadn't come up with anything new, he did plan to keep covering the story, although he warned her that did not mean there'd be something about it in every edition of the paper.

Kate felt defeated. She was doing things just for the sake of doing them. She was no closer to finding Tish than she had been the day Tish got into a white pickup truck and drove off with a guy wearing jeans and a western shirt.

Clement's on Sixteenth Street. The words hung there, saying, *Look at me. I'm a clue.* But Kate had turned them upside down and sideways and asked everyone she could think of to ask, and if there was a clue there, she sure as hell couldn't see it.

What am I going to do? she asked herself. She had no answer.

Would she eventually have to lock up the house, go back to New York, hope that Tish would turn up somewhere someday? She could get more leave from the NYPD just by calling the shrink and telling him that she was still falling apart and definitely not ready to return to duty, that she should stay in Texas and get more rest. But she couldn't do it forever. Eventually she'd have to go back.

No, she thought, I could never just leave, abandon Tish. But she knew that was just emotion speaking. Realistically there were limits. Although she didn't know what they were—weeks? months? years?—the time would come when she would have to give up.

Kate felt her eyes filling with tears. One trickled down her cheek. She was starting to prepare herself for the worst, and she hated it. But rejecting the possibility that she might never see Tish again was nothing but an exercise in self-deception, which could only be counterproductive. The worst was possible. She had to be prepared to deal with it.

Abruptly an image from her childhood came to her. It was a hot, sunny afternoon, the smell of grilling burger patties and wieners and marshmallows being roasted on sticks filled the air, along with the aromas of mustard and potato salad and sliced onions. People milled around a big table laden with food. Men wearing cowboy hats or caps bearing the logos of Caterpillar or John Deere or Massey-Ferguson stood around a big pot of Texas chili, drinking beer and talking about the weather and fertilizers and the price their crops might bring this year. It was the Fourth of July picnic.

Kate was playing center field in the annual softball game. Her team was ahead 5–4 in the third inning. The other team was at bat. There were two away with a runner on second, and the batter, a boy with crewcut blond hair and freckles, had two strikes. There was no plate umpire to call balls and

142

strikes. When you were at bat, you got three swings and you either hit it or you didn't; nothing else mattered. If the pitcher didn't get it over, you waited until he did, even if it took all day.

The pitcher, a kid named Henley, wound up and threw one right over the plate. The blond boy swung a little late, but he still got a piece of it, and it flew over the head of the shortstop, dropping before anyone in the outfield could get to it. The left fielder, a girl with waist-length brown hair hanging out from under her baseball cap, scooped it up and threw it to the plate in time to keep the run from scoring. There were runners on first and third now. The next batter was Tish.

"Easy out, easy out," the first baseman chanted. "She can't hit."

Even though he was her own teammate, Kate resented his taunting her sister that way. She knew it was all in good fun, part of the game and all that, and yet a part of her wanted to tell the kid to shut up.

The first pitch was on the outside of the plate—a piece of scrap wood—and Tish swung wildly at it, not even coming close to the ball. "That's one," the first baseman jeered, and Tish glanced around nervously, as if looking for support. Although Kate desperately wanted to cheer her on, she couldn't cheer for a member of the other team.

Tish tapped the plate with the end of the bat, then swung it a couple of times, getting the feel of it, her eyes on the pitcher. Like Kate, Tish had her dark hair tucked up under her cap. Usually it hung to their shoulder blades. Their mom was always telling them to put it up in hot weather, but they never did. Neither of them liked it that way.

Kate could see on Tish's face a mixture of determination and fear. Determination to hit the damn thing, fear that she would fail, embarrass herself in front of of her teammates. She swung and missed the next pitch. Come on, Kate thought. You can do it. Hit a homer.

But she knew Tish was unlikely to do so. Although the twins appeared to be physically similar, they weren't athletic equals. Kate was better at sports. She played volleyball, basketball, and baseball. She was a good swimmer. And when she got to high school, she'd planned to try her hand at gymnastics, maybe even track. Books were Tish's thing. Tish would much rather read than play games. And when she tried to play, she usually embarrassed herself because of her lack of ability. Kate's first time up she hit a double. Tish would probably strike out.

"Why don't you guys get someone that can hit?" the first baseman taunted.

Tish stared at the pitcher, her expression a mixture of anguish and defeat. She knew she would strike out.

"Just put it over," the first baseman shouted. "She can't hit it anyway." Kate wanted to punch him.

The pitcher took the first baseman's advice and tossed a relatively slow one dead center over the plate. Tish smashed it. The ball sailed over the heads of the infielders and into the outfield. Kate realized it was hers. Waving her arms, she called for it, backing up, keeping her eyes on it. And as the ball descended toward her outstretched glove, Kate realized that if she didn't make the catch, two runs would probably score. Tish would be cheered by her teammates, told how good she'd done, patted on the back.

Drop it! a little voice inside urged. *Drop it for Tish.*

And Kate wanted desperately to do just that. But if she did, she'd be cheating, not to mention betraying her teammates. Sure, it was a silly afternoon game at the Fourth of July picnic with an old piece of wood for home plate, but deliberately throwing the game would be dishonest.

For Tish, the voice said. *For Tish.*

And then Kate's glove closed around the ball, and Tish was out.

The two sisters passed each other as Tish's team took the field, and Tish said, "I hit it pretty good, didn't I?"

"Too bad I didn't drop it," Kate replied sullenly.

Tish shook her head. "That doesn't matter. Look at how good I hit it," she said proudly. "I mean, it won't always go where someone can catch it. If I keep hitting it that good, at least some of the times it'll be a good hit, a double or maybe even a triple." Tish was grinning.

144

Kate told her that was right, but inwardly she chuckled. Tish had hit an easy pitch right to the center fielder, causing the third out and stranding two runners, and she was grinning as if she'd just hit a grand slam.

The memory was already fading when the doorbell rang. Opening the door, Kate found a gray-haired man who was a little overweight and who looked quite hot in the brown suit he was wearing.

"Hi," he said. "Either you're Kate or Patricia has come back."

"I'm Kate."

"I'm John Altman. Uh, I'm the county chairman of the political party that's out of power right now here in Leap. Could I talk you into giving me a few minutes of your time?"

"If you know who I am," Kate said, "then you know that I'm not a resident here. I can't vote."

"No, no, that's not why I'm here. I'd like to talk to you about the difficulties you've been having."

Kate invited him in out of the heat, and when they were both seated on the couch, he said, "I, uh, understand you've met Chief Colton."

"One of the high points of my stay here in the scenic Hill Country."

He nodded. "You're a police officer, too, aren't you?"

Kate told him what she did. Altman was blue-eyed and red-faced, and except for the Texas drawl and his German-sounding name, he could easily pass for one of New York's hard-drinking Irishmen. She noticed that his nose was peeling slightly at its tip. Apparently he was one of those people who never tanned, only burned. He accepted Kate's offer of iced tea, which he took with about four spoons of sugar plus lemon.

He held up the glass of tea, studying it admiringly. "With all those little beads of condensation on there, it looks just like an ad for Lipton's."

"Actually it's Brand X from the discount store."

He took a big gulp. "Whatever brand it is, it tastes mighty good."

He put his glass on the coaster Kate had placed on the

couch's arm. It should have been on the coffee table, but the coffee table had been smashed during Kate's struggle with the intruder.

"Getting back to the point," he said, "would you mind telling me about the dealings you've had with the Leap Police Department since your sister disappeared?"

Kate obliged.

"So, summing it all up, it would be safe to say the chief hasn't been much help?"

"It would be safe to say that," Kate agreed.

"Being a police officer yourself, would you be willing to evaluate the chief?"

"I don't think I can do that. It's pretty obvious I'm not real fond of him, but I don't know enough about him to evaluate him professionally."

Altman nodded. "I can appreciate that. Look, I'm not trying to put you out on a limb. We think we've got a good chance to win the next election. I'm pretty sure List over at the newspaper is going to endorse Jacobi—he's our candidate for mayor—along with most of our candidates for the city council. One of the things we want to do is reorganize the police department. We've got a lot of reasons to believe it's in kind of a mess. Don't misunderstand me. There's some darn good officers in the department, but they're afraid to talk to us. If the other side finds out, they'll lose their jobs."

"Don't you have some sort of a personnel ordinance to protect them?"

Altman shook his head. "The chief hires and fires at will, so a lot of the officers are buddies of Colton's. Unfortunately, in the case of some of them, that's about their only qualification. This is one of the things we want to do. We want to put in a personnel ordinance that sets standards for hiring and firing and promotions."

"I approve," Kate said.

"We need to know everything we can find out about the way the department is being run right now. Since we can't learn much from the inside, we need to rely on people on the outside, people like you."

"I'd truly like to help you," Kate said. "But all I can do

is tell you what's happened. I'm simply not in a position to evaluate the Leap Police Department or Chief Colton.''

"You must have some impressions. Anything you can tell me will be confidential. You don't have to worry about that.''

"I've got an impression of Chief Colton, but I don't think it'll help you much.''

"Yes?''

"I think he's an asshole.''

Altman shrugged. "I'm afraid there's a lot of people around here think that. I need something a little more specific.''

"I wish I could give it to you.''

Altman gave her one of his cards, said to call him if she had any more unpleasant dealings with the chief. "Thank you for the tea,'' he said, rising. "Uh, I understand you've been passing out some handbills.''

Kate stood, too. "That's right,'' she said.

"If you'd like to give me some, I can distribute them through our campaign workers.''

"Thank you. I'd appreciate that.'' There were about a hundred of them in her purse. She pulled them out and handed them to Altman. "That's the last of them.''

"If you decide you want to have some more of these printed up, let me know. I can turn it in along with one of our printing orders, and it will cost less than half of what you probably paid for these.''

Kate thanked him, said she'd let him know. She watched through the window as Altman drove away in a brown station wagon. Despite her feelings about Chief Colton, she really didn't want to be involved in Leap politics. Regardless of what she thought about the chief, she had to deal with him as long as Tish was missing. He already disliked her. If she started working with the opposition, it would just make things worse.

She sat down on the couch again, and her thoughts returned to that Fourth of July picnic when two twin sisters played on opposing teams in the softball game.

* * *

He had no idea what time it was when he woke up. It was dark, quiet, the middle of the night. His eyes surveyed the small bedroom. One of the shadows on the ceiling looked like a giant fist, poised directly over his head, ready to drop. He closed his eyes, and when he opened them again, the fist had disappeared.

The dream had awakened him. He'd been dragging the bodies of the two boys out from under the trailer, dragging them to the pit within a pit. Suddenly, looking up toward the rim, he'd seen a woman standing there, watching him. And then she had disappeared. He scrambled to the top of the pit, but when he got there she was gone. She had seen what he had done. She would go for the police.

Hurriedly, he returned to the bottom of the pit and put the bodies of the two boys in his pickup. If he could get away from there, he might be able to dispose of the evidence. But as he climbed into the truck, the police cars appeared at the entrance to the pit. Leaping out of the truck, he ran to the steep bank and began to climb it. But as he neared the top, he looked up, seeing a woman standing above him. It was his mother.

Suddenly he was beginning to slide backward. Looking beneath him, he saw only space, as if the bottom had dropped out of the pit, creating an endless abyss.

"Help me," he said to his mother.

She looked at him, said nothing.

"Please. I'm falling."

"Your father might not like it."

"Stand up to him. Just this once. Please."

"You know I can't do that."

And then he was sliding down the dirt bank, falling faster and faster. He'd awakened then, momentarily panicked, but finally realizing that it was only a nightmare, a product of his sleeping brain. No one had seen what he did with the boys. No one would ever know.

His eyes explored the shadows on the ceiling again, but they were just shadows, without any meaningful shapes. He tried to locate the fist again, finding he was relieved that he was unable to do so. His thoughts began to wander, and he remembered another dream he'd had, when he was about fourteen or fifteen. This one hadn't been a nightmare—at least not until two days later.

It was Saturday morning, and he was bringing in the eggs he'd collected from out in the chicken coop. His sister collected the eggs in a basket when she did it, but that basket had always seemed like something only girls or sissies would use, so he always collected them in a metal bucket. As he set the bucket on the kitchen counter his father appeared in the doorway.

"Come with me," his dad said.

The boy obeyed and found himself in his own bedroom. It was a stark place, his bedroom, without the usual boyish trappings. There were no pictures of rock 'n' roll singers on the walls, no pennants to proclaim which college teams he supported, no posters. Nor were there any baseballs or footballs or clothes lying about. Everything was put away, everything neat. The furniture consisted of a single twin bed, a bed table with an old radio on it, a bureau with drawers that stuck because they were warped, a small wooden chair. Everything was painted with a cream-colored enamel paint.

The bareness and sterility of the room weren't what the boy would have chosen. His father disapproved of things like posters on the walls, and he hated clutter.

Now, as the boy stood in the room, his father staring at him icily, he was afraid. Clearly he was in trouble for something, but he didn't know what. His eyes darted quickly around the room, finding no clothes that had been absent-mindedly left on the chair, no sock that had been kicked under the bed. Then he noticed the bed itself. It looked as if someone had sat on it. He'd made it as soon as he got up, and he wondered who had messed it up. If his sister, Connie, had come into his room . . . He let the thought trail off.

"I looked at your bed this morning," his father said.

"I made it up real neat when I got up. Honest."

"Shut up," his father said, giving him a withering look. "I'll tell you when to speak."

"Yes, sir," the boy replied, and then wondered whether he should have even said that.

"I'm not talking about making your bed. I'm talking about this."

He yanked back the covers, revealing the bottom sheet. And the spots in the center of the bottom sheet. The boy felt his stomach twist sideways, felt his body try to shrink away until it wasn't there anymore.

He'd thought he could keep the spots hidden. Tomorrow he would take the sheets off the bed so his mother could wash them. She wouldn't look closely at them. She'd just toss them in the washer. It had never occurred to him that anyone would actually unmake his bed to see what was there.

"I . . . they . . ." The boy didn't know what to say.

The spots had been there the morning after he'd dreamed about Sally Owens. He dreamed that they'd been naked, touching each other's bodies, and that she'd lay back, spread her legs, and let him get on top of her. The boy definitely did not want to admit to his father that he dreamed about such things.

His father looked disgusted now, as if he could read the boy's mind, as if he knew what the dream had been about. "You've been doing filthy things with yourself, haven't you?"

"Sir?" the boy said, playing dumb, as if he had no idea what his father was talking about.

"Don't sir me, boy. I know what you been doing."

"I . . . I didn't do anything. It was a dream."

His father stared at him, looking as if he'd just discovered the milk was sour. "Don't add lying to your sins."

"I'm not lying. It was a dream."

"You been playing with yourself in bed, haven't you?"

The boy shook his head. He'd done it a few times, but not in bed. As far as he could tell a lot of boys his age did it. Once, he found Jimmy Hockler and Bobby North doing it together in Bobby's barn. All three of them had been real embarrassed. Then Jimmy had suggested that the three of them all do it, but he'd refused. As far as he was concerned, it was the sort of thing you did by yourself, not with other people. Usually he'd do it out behind the chicken coop because no one ever went there. He often felt guilty about it. Doing it had to be wrong, he knew that. And yet he couldn't seem to stop himself, even when he put his mind to it. Eventually he'd sneak back behind the chicken coop, even if he did know it was wrong.

But the spots in the bed had been an accident. He hadn't done anything, at least not intentionally.

"You been abusing yourself," his father said. "Abusing your manhood."

"It was an accident. It was a dream."

"It's filthy and disgusting."

The boy remained silent.

"You've shamed yourself in the eyes of God. Do you understand that?"

"I couldn't help it. It was a dream."

Unwilling to meet his father's hard gaze, he had lowered his eyes, so he was taken by surprise when the blow came. Its force pushed him backward, and he lost his balance, sitting down hard on the wood floor. He looked up, but his father was only a blur through the haze of tears.

"Look at that, will you. Look at the little baby bawling."

The boy forced the tears to stop. He wouldn't cry in front of his father, even if it took every last bit of strength he had.

"Stand up and take your lickin' like a man."

The boy rose and looked his father in the eye. His father's fist smacked into the boy's cheek, then his mouth. The fists flew, again and again, and finally the boy lost all track of where the blows were landing. He concentrated on standing up, on meeting his father's eyes. He was still standing, blood dripping from his nose, when the last blow landed. Without another word, his father left the room, and only then did the boy sink to the floor, tears pouring silently from his eyes, running down his face and mixing with the blood.

Later that day he sneaked behind the chicken coop. Not because of any physical urge, but as an act of defiance.

THIRTEEN

There was a spot on the side of Tish's face where the skin must have been broken because it burned whenever perspiration ran into it. Her lip, too, was cracked. She could feel it with her tongue. Although there was no mirror in the trailer so she could see the damage, Tish was fairly certain no serious harm had been done. Her nose wasn't broken. The bleeding she'd experienced had apparently come from her split lip.

As she usually did during the heat of the day, Tish was sitting on the floor of the trailer with her back against the wall. It was less comfortable than the bed, but the spot was between the two windows, and often a slight breeze would come in through the spaces between the boards. Although it was only a gentle stirring of the air, it felt wonderful, and this was the only place in the trailer she could take advantage of it.

She had been reduced to desperately seeking the tiniest of comforts, she realized. She thought she understood how people felt who were forced to beg for crumbs, grovel and plead for the smallest of kindnesses. She felt a peculiar kinship with the starving in Ethiopia, political prisoners in South Africa and Chile.

And yet her circumstances were vastly different from those of the oppressed of the world. For her this kind of misery and hopelessness was a whole new experience. For them it was a way of life.

Tish heard some unidentified noise from outside the trailer, and suddenly she was scrambling across the sloping floor, climbing onto the bed. She squeezed herself into a corner, holding her sliced-open dress and bra together, pulling her knees up to her chin. He's come back, she thought. He's going to hurt me some more.

She heard the noise more clearly now. It was a diesel engine, and it sounded a lot like the machine he'd brought down into the pit the day he killed the boys. Maybe he's coming to kill me, she thought. Tish immediately tried to make the idea go away, as if it had never occurred to her.

The diesel sound grew still louder, and then it stopped. Tish could hear the engine idling, close but not close enough to be in the pit. Suddenly the engine revved, then returned to an idle. Some rocks tumbled down the bank. Abruptly the trailer lurched as something hit it.

Tish pulled her knees against her even more tightly, her eyes fixed on the door. Don't open, she told it. Please don't open.

The diesel revved again, slowed, revved once more, and then the sound was growing fainter. Whatever it was— *who*ever it was—was going away. She waited until it was completely silent before getting off the bed. She moved to the window on her right. Through the space between the boards she could see nothing that would explain what had hit the trailer. She tried the window on the other side. As soon as she put her eye to the crack, she saw what had slid down the bank, hitting the trailer.

A dead cow lay on its side, its legs held rigidly horizontal by rigor mortis. It looked like a plastic cow that had been knocked over by the wind, as if it should be righted again, maybe to stand outside a steak house. EAT HERE. FRESHEST BEEF IN TOWN.

Tish shook the image away. Why would someone dump a dead cow here? Had *he* done it? Or had someone spotted the pit, decided it would be a good place to deposit a cow carcass? She shook her head. She had no answers for those questions. She didn't even know where she was.

And neither did anyone else. Except him.

Tish returned to her position on the floor. More sweat ran into the sore spot on her face, again causing it to burn. The cow was unimportant, she decided. He hadn't come back to hurt her again. That was all that mattered.

"How's everything out there in cowboy land?" Janice Bernstein said when Kate answered the phone. "You eating lots of barbeque, enjoying the cattle drives and roundups and all that?"

"It was fun till the Indians went on the warpath, but since then we've been holed up in the house with our Winchesters."

"Any word on your sister?" Janice asked.

"No change," Kate answered. "She drove off with some guy in a white pickup and vanished. I'm . . . I guess I started to say I'm worried sick, but I think I'm beyond worried sick. I really don't know what to do, Janice. I'm at a dead end."

"I checked around like you asked me to, and as far as I can find out there's nobody around here who has it in for you bad enough to follow you to Texas. If anyone's pissed off at you, they're keeping it to themselves."

"I guess that's what I figured, but I had to make sure. I was thinking that maybe somebody wanted to get me for killing the kid."

"We couldn't find anybody that seemed likely. It doesn't fit at all for a juvenile gang to be doing something like that. The kid's mother took the whole thing fatalistically. She's still working as a cook in a restaurant and trying to take care of the other kid. He's eight, so you know he's not doing it. Kid's father hasn't been heard from in years."

"Other relatives?"

"Nothing there either. They all seem to regard what happened with resignation. Their biggest concern seems to be that their own kids will get into trouble, too. You know how it goes. They work hard, struggle to make ends meet, and

154

while the parents are at work, the kids are on the street. They see Mom and Dad working their asses off in jobs nobody else wants, and they don't want to be like that. The street, on the other hand, offers excitement, escape, and the chance to make more money in a few minutes than their parents can make in a month." Janice sighed. "But then why am I telling you all this when you already have firsthand experience with everything I'm talking about? The bottom line is that there's no one in the kid's family who's unaccounted for, who might have slipped off to Texas to get even with you."

"What about his father? Anybody know what happened to him?"

"No, nobody knows. He disappeared more than eight years ago, before the second kid was born. He probably doesn't even know the boy's dead."

"Okay, Janice, thanks, I appreciate your help. I'm sure it was a lot of extra work, and I'm really grateful."

"Nothing you wouldn't have done for me. Besides, it all pays the same, right?"

"Did you check with Louisiana on Boyd Steuben?"

"I checked, but I haven't heard anything from them yet. I'll be in touch as soon as I do."

After thanking Janice again, Kate hung up the phone. She sat at the kitchen table, trying to empty her mind. When there were only unpleasant things to consider, it was better not to think at all. But Kate was incapable of thinking about nothing. Her brain would shut down for a moment or two, and then she'd be thinking about Tish—or more precisely, about her inability to do anything to help Tish. All she could do was sit and wait for something to happen, with no guarantee that anything would. It was maddening and at the same time depressing. And underlying all her other feelings was the constant gnawing fear that something awful had happened to her twin sister, that Tish might even be dead.

Kate shook her head. She could not permit herself to think that. Tish was out there somewhere. Tish could be found, rescued. Tish *would* be found, *would* be rescued.

The doorbell interrupted her thoughts. Since the attempts to kill her Kate had been cautious about things like opening the door. But at the moment she was still thinking about her conversation with Janice Bernstein and still trying to convince herself that things weren't as dire as they seemed. So she was unprepared for the blow that knocked her off her feet and left her lying on her back on the living-room floor.

"I ought to stomp the hell out of you for what you did to me," a man's voice said angrily.

Kate's vision had blurred momentarily, but now it cleared. She was looking up at Boyd Steuben, who stared down at her with rage-filled eyes.

"What the hell kind of law allows someone to take everything a man's got when he's not even there to speak up for himself? And what kind of a woman would do it to him in the first place?"

Keeping her eyes on him, Kate got slowly to her feet. She was a little shaken from the blow, but otherwise unhurt. "At least you didn't have the nerve to say you'd lost everything you *worked* for."

His face reddened. Suddenly whirling to his left, he deliberately knocked a lamp off an end table. It tumbled onto the floor. He kicked its shade, which rolled against the couch, bent and broken.

"Let's see how much good this stuff is to you when I get through with it." He looked at her then, his eyes locking on to hers. "You should never have taken everything that was mine while I was away."

It was clear to Kate that he thought she was Tish. Though uncertain how much good it would do to inform him of his error, she decided she had to try. "I'm not Tish," she said.

He looked at her as though she were crazy. "Uh-huh. Next thing I know you'll be telling me this isn't the right house, that I'm really looking for a place two blocks down."

He grabbed a small green vase and smashed it against the wall.

"I'm Kate," she told him. "Tish is missing."

He didn't seem to hear her. Snatching a watercolor landscape off the wall, he threw it into the kitchen. The glass shattered.

156

"Did you hear me?" Kate yelled. "Tish is missing. I'm Kate."

He turned his attention to the television set. He stared at it, maybe wondering whether he should smash it or take it with him. Suddenly Kate recalled the .38 in her purse. The bag was on the couch. She began moving slowly toward it. She was almost close enough to touch it when Boyd whirled around to face her.

"Before I leave, I'm going to break everything you stole from me. But first I'm going to deal with you."

If Kate tried to get the gun now, he'd be on her before she could get it out of her purse. Because he was stronger than she was, he would probably be the one who ended up with the weapon. He watched her, smiling faintly, apparently contemplating all the things he was going to do to her. He looked thinner than Kate remembered him, but strong and wiry. He wore jeans and a western shirt. How could Tish have married a creature like this?

He took a step toward her. "You going to run the way you used to, try to get away?"

Kate backed away, and he grinned. Good, she thought. Let him be overconfident, think he has the situation fully under control. He began to advance, slowly, steadily. Kate continued to back away.

She considered her options. The more room she had to maneuver, the better off she'd be. But in a small house with a lot of furniture there really was no place with very much maneuvering room. The only thing she could do, she concluded, was to let him make his move and hope his overconfidence got him in trouble.

She backed into the hallway. Although there wasn't much lateral room, she could retreat quickly to the bedrooms. And then she realized that was where he was maneuvering her, to the bedroom. She had no choice but to wait for him to do what he was going to do. Let him think she was too frightened to fight back. Let him think he was totally in charge of the situation.

Come on, sucker, Kate thought. And then she wondered whether she was merely trying to give herself confidence. If

157

so, she hoped it wasn't false confidence. She backed into the bedroom, knowing that whatever was going to happen would happen now.

Boyd grinned at her. "Debt collector's here," he said. "And, honey, you got a really big debt."

He unbuckled his belt, and at first Kate thought he was going to take off his pants. But instead he pulled the belt off, letting it slip ominously through the loops of his jeans.

"Lie down on the bed," he ordered.

Kate hadn't expected this. She had to remain standing to be able to defend herself. And yet she didn't want to do anything to make him wary. She shook her head, looking as terrified as she could—and it was only partly an act.

"Please, Boyd," she whispered. "Please don't."

"Gotta," he said. "You know that."

She wrapped her arms around herself, as if trying to protect her upper body, looked at him as if she were resigned to what was to come. He moved in so quickly, Kate didn't have time to resist. The belt cracked across her shoulder.

"Take your clothes off and lie down on the bed," he said.

Kate did nothing.

"It'll be worse for you if you make me force you to do it."

Kate doubted that. This time when he moved in swinging the belt, she was ready. She stepped in, too close for him to hit her with the belt, bringing her knee into his crotch as she did so, putting so much effort into it that she lifted herself off the ground. Boyd's eyes widened and he gasped as her knee smacked solidly into his testicles. She backed away, ready to deal with the next move.

Boyd had no next move. He sank to his knees, looking up at her with eyes filled with both pain and awe. *"Gaaaa,"* he said.

Deciding that Boyd would hold long enough for her to get her gun, Kate hurried into the living room and removed the weapon from her purse. When she returned to the bedroom, Boyd was still on his knees. Beads of perspiration had formed on his forehead. Quickly moving behind him, Kate jammed the gun into the side of his head.

"I'm Kate. Do we understand each other?"

"Yuh . . . yes."

"Good. You are here illegally. You forced your way inside, attacked me, threatened me. I can blow your goddamned head off with impunity. Do we still understand each other?"

He nodded.

"How are your balls?"

"Bi . . . bitch."

She jammed the gun hard into the side of his head. "What was that?"

"Nuh . . . nothing."

"Good. I'm glad to see you're getting the right feel for this conversation. What do you know about Tish's disappearance?"

"I . . . I don't know what you're talking about."

"She disappeared. The last time she was seen, it was with a guy who looks a whole lot like you."

"It wasn't me."

"I got plenty of time. This gun's not getting heavy or anything. So why don't you convince me?"

"I was in prison. In goddamned 'Gola. I just got out a couple of months ago."

"How long you been here?"

"About two days."

"And you didn't know Tish was missing."

"Not till just now."

"It was on the front page of the *Leap Ledger*."

"I haven't seen the *Leap Ledger*."

"Where you staying?"

"Motel on Texas Avenue."

"What motel?"

"The Relax Inn Motel."

"How'd you get here?"

"I drove."

"Drove what?"

"A car. The transmission on my skateboard was out."

If he was starting to wise off, it meant the pain in his

testicles was easing a little, which meant he was becoming more dangerous. As the pain left, his courage would return.

"I think you did something to Tish. I think this little trip here today was just an attempt to fool us, to make us believe you didn't even know she was missing."

"I didn't know. I thought you were her."

"Uh-huh. And I'm the tooth fairy."

"You'll wish you were the tooth fairy."

"What?" She jammed the gun in hard again. "Did I hear a threat?"

He remained silent.

"What'd you do with Tish?" she demanded.

"I got nothing more to say to you."

"I think we're going to have a little talk with the Leap police, you and me."

"I don't know anything about Tish being missing," he said. "You can't prove that I do."

"We'll see. In the meantime there's the matter of breaking and entering, assault and battery, destruction of property. And only two weeks out of Angola. Judge might think you're a career criminal, lock you away and throw away the key."

Boyd gave a bored sigh.

"Get up real slowly," Kate said. "You and me are going into the kitchen and call the police." Kate could sense the tension in the man. She would have to handle him carefully. She moved away from him, holding the gun in both hands. "Come on," she said. "Up."

It was hard to believe this man had been her brother-in-law. The person on his knees in Tish's bedroom was an animal, destined to spend much of his life with all the other animals in places like Angola or Huntsville or Attica. She rejected the notion that this creature could ever have been a member of her family. As he started to rise he groaned, and a shudder passed through his body.

"Come on," Kate said when he was standing. "Let's go. And don't do anything stupid, Boyd, okay? I don't like you very much, and we've already established that I can shoot you with impunity."

She made him walk in front of her to the kitchen. He

160

moved slowly, taking small steps, as if his legs were hobbled. Kate wasn't a cruel person, but she knew Boyd had to be wincing as he took his little awkward steps, and she felt nothing for him.

"Lean against the stove," she said. "Spread your legs. Just like you'd do if I was going to pat you down and cuff you." She wished she did have some handcuffs. They'd make things much easier.

Boyd complied, groaning. "You don't know what you're asking. You might have ruined me, you know that? You might have ruined me by kicking me like that."

And what were you going to do to me? Kate thought. She picked up the phone, dialed 0. Leap had no 911 system.

"Leap police," she told the operator, giving her name, address, and phone number.

Suddenly Boyd groaned loudly and slipped to the floor, pulling a small skillet off the stove.

"Police department," a man said over the phone.

"Get up," Kate told Boyd.

He groaned again, and the cop on the phone said, "This is the Leap Police Department. Is everything all right there?"

Kate told him what was happening.

"I'll get a unit there right way," he said. "Can you stay on the line?"

"No," Kate said. "I've got my hands full here." She hung up, moved toward Boyd, who was on all fours by the stove. "Get back into the position," she ordered.

"Can't!" he said. "Hurts too much."

"Do it!" Kate commanded, moving a step closer.

Suddenly he grabbed the skillet and threw it at her. Deflecting it with her arm, Kate fell backward, knocking over a kitchen chair. Certain Boyd would instantly be on her, she swung the gun up, ready to shoot if she had to. But then she heard the front door being flung open, then a crash. Scrambling to her feet, she ran into the living room. The front door stood open, and the aluminum frame of the screen door was badly bent. Apparently Boyd had run right through it.

Hurrying outside, Kate looked in all directions, seeing no sign of Boyd. Dammit, she thought. I let him get away. What the hell kind of a cop would let him get away that easily? Suddenly Kate felt weak all over. The man who'd just escaped was the only person who might know anything about Tish's disappearance. Dammit, she thought. Dammit. Hot tears of frustration rolled down her cheeks.

A white Leap police cruiser rolled to a stop in front of the house. A young officer got out, hurried toward her. Suddenly the cop inside Kate reasserted itself.

"He got away from me," she said. "Get it on the radio right away. White male, mid thirties, brown hair, blue eyes, six feet tall, slender but wiry, dressed in jeans and brown western shirt. He just got away. I didn't see a vehicle, but I think he had one."

"Ma'am, before we do anything else, you'll have to give me that gun."

Kate handed it to him. "I'm a cop," she said. "From out of town. That man broke in and assaulted me. We need to get his description out."

"Okay," the young officer said. "But you better come to the car with me. I'll never remember everything you just said, and you're not acting like you want me to take the time to write it all down."

FOURTEEN

"He could have done it just to fool us," Kate told Chief Colton. "To make us believe he had nothing to do with Tish's disappearance."

They were sitting in the living room. The chief had shown up shortly after the young officer put the information out over the radio. The police search for Boyd had been unsuccessful. He had vanished.

"That's a lot of trouble for him to go through," Colton said. "Especially considering that he didn't do a very good job of convincing you."

"I said he was trying to fool us. I didn't say he was clever enough to pull it off."

Colton considered that. "Still seems kind of complicated, you ask me. The explanation he gave you seems more plausible. He got out of prison and came here looking for his wife—ex-wife, I guess you'd have to say. He found out she'd divorced him, and he wanted to know what the hell was going on. Makes sense to me."

"Then why did he know Tish had divorced him when he didn't know she was missing? How'd he manage to find out the one part without learning the other?"

"Maybe he was notified in prison."

"Tish divorced him *in absentia*. Nobody knew where he was."

Colton looked thoughtful, said nothing.

As she always did around Colton, Kate was becoming exasperated. She had been working not to let it show, but the effort wasn't worth it. "Chief, why is it you'd believe a slimeball like Boyd before you'd listen to me?"

Colton held up his hands, palms outward. A *who-me?* gesture. "I'm just looking for the truth," he said.

It was Kate's turn to say nothing.

"Where'd you get the gun?" he asked.

"Private party. I saw an ad in the paper."

"Why'd you decide to buy one?"

"There have been attempts on my life, remember? Like the bomb in my car."

He nodded. "I checked with the police department in New York. Talked to a Lieutenant Cappello. He says you blew away an eleven-year-old kid."

"Did he also tell you that the kid had just shot my partner and that my partner later died and that the kid was turning the gun on me?"

"Yeah, he told me that. He also said you were on medical leave, you'd had a breakdown or something like that."

"That's right. How would you feel after having to shoot an eleven-year-old kid?"

Ignoring her question, he said, "So what I've got here is a woman who just had a breakdown running around with a gun."

"No one said anything about running around with a gun. I had one in the house. That's legal. And it's understandable, considering that someone's been trying to kill me."

The front door opened, and the young cop who'd responded to the call came in. "Steuben checked into the Relax Inn Motel two days ago. He hasn't checked out, but there's nothing in his room, not even a suitcase. If he knows we're looking for him, he probably won't go back there."

"What name was he registered under?" Kate asked.

The cop glanced at Colton to see whether he had any objections to his answering her, then said, "His own name."

"Check with the motor vehicle department," Colton said. "See if he's bought a car since returning to Texas." Looking at Kate, he said, "I'll check with Louisiana later, see if he bought a car there, see if what he told you about being in prison is true."

"Why do you think he registered under his own name?" Kate asked.

Colton frowned. "Why wouldn't he? He's served his time. He's free to do what he wants. Why would he want to use an assumed name?"

"It's all pretty convenient, isn't it, him telling me which motel he's at, and then sure enough he was there, registered under his own name?"

"To throw us off the track, right? So we'd think he came here figuring to find his wife, him not knowing anything had happened to her."

"It's possible."

"Anything's possible. Not everything's likely though."

"Why would he go to a motel at all? Why not just come straight here?"

"Maybe he wanted to work up his nerve. Maybe he was trying to figure out a way to sweet-talk her into taking him back." For some reason, the notion made him grin.

"What a way to make up. I open the door, and he hits me in the face. How you figure he acts when he's feeling mean?"

"He thought you were his wife."

"Oh. Well, that explains it."

"These things happen between men and wives. He wouldn't have done it if he'd known you were somebody else."

"I see," Kate said. "Can't go around beating up strangers. They might not understand."

Colton stared at her for a moment. That knowing smile of his appeared on his lips, then slowly faded away. Finally he stood up, said, "If Boyd Steuben's here in town, we'll find him."

"I'm glad to hear that."

"If he knows anything about your sister, we'll find out about that, too."

The words "Keep up the good work" popped into Kate's head, but she didn't speak them. Instead she dutifully asked the chief to keep her posted and then walked him to the door.

When he was gone, Kate sat down and surveyed the room. She seemed to be overseeing the destruction of everything Tish owned. The coffee table had been smashed beyond repair. The garage door had been sabotaged. The car had been in an accident—not to mention nearly being firebombed. Today a lamp, a vase, a picture, and the screen door had been added to the list. Tish would have nothing left by the time she returned.

If she returns, something inside Kate's head whispered.

Kate abruptly shifted her thoughts elsewhere, pretending she hadn't heard the voice that whispered the unthinkable. Boyd was the only person she could think of who had a reason for wanting to harm Tish. And he was here, fresh out of the pen, if he was telling the truth. He'd been wearing jeans and a western shirt, and so had the man with whom Tish had left. He was about six feet tall, and so was the man who'd broken in and attacked her. Boyd probably considered himself clever enough to devise a bomb and put it into her car. And he was probably dumb enough to build one that would fail.

Carrying that one step further, could she say that Boyd would think it a clever idea to come to the house, pretending to think she was Tish, pretending that he didn't know Tish was missing? She nodded to herself. That sounded like Boyd. Always inventing silly schemes, never willing to work for anything. But of course those things weren't what drove him. They were peripheral things. In the core of the man, burning like a well-stoked furnace, was pure meanness.

Okay, she decided, let's say it is Boyd and see how well it fits. It fit real well until she got to the attempts on her life. Why would Boyd want to kill her? So she couldn't come after him? So he could try to get the house back without any interference from Tish's closest relative? Because he disliked her? It was all kind of weak, but then anyone who'd storm into the house, punching her and trying to whip her with a belt didn't have a real good grip on sanity. Maybe it made sense to him.

In any case she knew what she had to do. Find Boyd. Kate was considering exactly how she was going to go about trying to do that when the phone rang. It was Janice Bernstein.

"I heard from Louisiana," Janice said. "They don't know where Steuben is now, but they know where he's been. Serving time in the state pen at Angola. Got out a couple of months ago."

"I know where he is now."

"There?"

"Here." Kate explained what had happened.

"Someday I want you to tell me in great, explicit detail about kicking him in the balls. Concentrate on the way he groaned and the look on his face."

"You mean you're not one of those women who just swoons for the macho, belt-swinging types?"

"I'm not going to dignify that with an answer."

"What was Steuben in for?"

"Burglary and auto theft. Him and two other guys were trying to break into an appliance store in Alexandria. Seems they set off the alarm, and the cops showed up while they were loading a forty-inch TV set into a stolen van. It turns out they'd pulled a number of burglaries, so one of the guys arrested with Steuben turned state's evidence. In exchange for a light sentence he fingered Steuben and the other guy for all the jobs they'd pulled. Now, are you ready for some irony? Steuben was part of a group of guys let out early because there was no more room in the pen. The guy who turned state's evidence is still in."

"No one ever said life was fair."

"There's something else I think you should know about. It seems the cops out there have been checking on you. I don't know much about it, but apparently somebody talked to Lieutenant Cappello. I just thought you should know."

"The chief of police here already told me he knew I was on medical leave following a breakdown. He's a real great guy. I'll tell you all about him one of these days."

When she hung up, Kate went into the bathroom to see what her face looked like after receiving a blow from Boyd's fist. What she saw made her chuckle, not because there was really anything funny about it, but because it was so ridiculous. She had a black eye, which made her look like a ten-year-old boy who'd stood up to the school bully and was proudly going home with his first shiner. An old *Saturday Evening Post* cover or something like that.

The absurd notion vanished, and Kate realized that what she really looked like was a battered woman. And she wondered how many black eyes Tish had received from Boyd Steuben.

Abruptly she turned away from the mirror and left the bathroom. Find Boyd, she thought. Find Boyd.

Tish hadn't bothered to climb onto the bed this time. When she heard the noise, she'd simply curled into the fetal position right where she was sitting on the trailer's floor. But the diesel engine noise stayed above her, up on the rim of the pit. Maybe it would be okay. Maybe he wouldn't hurt her again.

She had stopped kicking the door at night. She had tried to convince herself it was because she was running out of strength. It was true; she was. But she knew the real reason she had stopped working on the door was because she was terrified that he would see any damage she caused and do something horrible to her.

The diesel noises were still coming from above her, and she finally worked up the courage to get up and look out. Peering through the cracks between the boards, she could see the dead cow and that was all. The cow was getting pretty ratty-looking. Something had made a small hole in its side, about the size of a silver dollar. Vultures perhaps, or maybe a predator. Sometimes, when the breeze was just right, the putrid odor from the decomposing beast would overpower her own stench from inside the trailer.

Suddenly something banged into the trailer, causing it to

shudder. Instantly Tish was scrambling toward the bed, intending to pull herself into a protective ball, but she stopped herself. She stood in the center of the trailer, trembling, telling herself it was all right. Something had been pushed down from above, another dead cow maybe. She moved timidly to the other side of the trailer and put her eye to the crack between the boards. It was a bull, a large one, a massive brown and white beast whose horns pointed forward and downward and came to sharp points at the tips. And although the eyes with which it stared at her were dull and lifeless, Tish looked away.

And then, despite the heat, she shivered. She was in a grave of some sort, a grave for cattle. And she knew it would be her grave, too.

After dumping the dead bull into the pit, he drove the loader back to a spot where some old rusty farm equipment stood. There were pieces of a cultivator, a disk harrow, and a small chisel plow that was probably still usable if it had a little bit of work done to it. Maybe this place had been a farm at one time. Or maybe the owner thought the old equipment looked picturesque, like a photo in one of those country-living magazines.

Maneuvering the big loader around the rusty farm equipment, he pulled up to the other thing that had been left here. A dead cow. Dropping the scoop to the ground, he eased the machine forward, working the scoop up and down a little until he had it under the cow. Then he tilted the scoop up and raised it, picking up the dead animal. Backing up, he turned and headed back toward the burial pit.

He had no idea what had killed the cattle he took to the pit. Cows died for all the same reasons people did, he supposed. Their hearts gave out, or the heat killed them. Sometimes the ones that came up from Mexico were just too malnourished and weak to survive. In any case, when they died, something had to be done with them, and that was his job. Part of it anyway. He supposed a written-out description of his duties would say something like ''doing

169

all the things that are too dirty for the boss to do.'' Something like that.

As he drove toward the pit a brown Ford pickup came toward him, and he pulled the loader into the weeds at the edge of the narrow dirt roadway to give the truck room to pass. But the truck didn't pass. It stopped, and the man driving it got out, waving the loader to a stop. It was Mr. Darnell, the owner.

''Where you been?'' Darnell asked, looking up at him, frowning. He was a tall, thin guy, wearing a cowboy hat. When he took the hat off, you could see how much the sun had affected his complexion. The top of his balding head was white, the lower portion dark brown, with a clear line between them. Sort of like a saddle shoe.

''Taking that bull out to the burial pit.''

Darnell was still frowning. ''It seems like I'm always having a hard time finding you.'' He let it hang there.

''Maybe you should do like you said and get me a walkie-talkie or one of those pagers, so you can let me know when you want me.''

''Maybe,'' he said.

''What was it you wanted me to do?''

''There's some steers up in the corral by the office, and we've got to separate them into two of the other corrals. I'll explain it to you when you get over there.''

''You want me to come now or take this cow out to the burial pit first?''

''Finish with the cow first.''

''Okay,'' he said, driving the loader forward again.

He had to be careful. The reason the boss couldn't find him earlier was because he hadn't been there. He'd been off tending to things Mr. Darnell didn't know about. Things that were more important than separating steers and hauling away dead cows. Although the job was less important than dealing with Tish and her twin sister, he didn't want to get fired. Working here gave him access to the burial pit, the trailer, the loader. And it gave him a place into which he could pretty much disappear.

When he'd finished with the sisters, the job wouldn't matter anymore. He'd be done with the job, the town. Maybe he'd be done with everything that mattered in his life. Maybe. He'd have to see.

The loader bounced along the dirt road. Actually it was more of a track or a trail or something like that than a road. It had never been bladed to smooth it out. It had no crown, no culverts, no ditches along its shoulders to carry rainwater. It was a pathway through the grass and weeds, that was all.

When he reached the edge of the pit, he lowered the scoop, tilting it forward, and the cow dropped out, sliding down the bank, loose stones clattering along with it. Like the other dead animals, this one came to rest by the trailer.

It hadn't been so easy with the bull. Despite the loader's massive scoop, he'd been unable to get the huge carcass into it. Every time he'd tried to raise the scoop, the bull had tumbled out, hitting the ground with a *thud*. It might have fit if he got it positioned just right, but he never managed it, so he finally got a rope, tied one end to the bull, the other to the loader, and dragged the carcass to the pit, untied it, and used the machine to push it over the edge.

He wondered whether his prisoner could see enough through the boarded-up windows to know she was being joined in the pit by dead cattle. He hoped so, because it might make her even more afraid, more miserable. And making her afraid and miserable was the whole idea.

It was what she deserved. For what she'd done to him.

He backed the loader away from the edge of the pit, headed back the way he'd come. Sweat trickled from beneath the band of his western hat, ran down his forehead. There were some dark clouds on the horizon, but it didn't look like they were headed this way. It had only rained twice since he'd arrived in town about six weeks ago. The weather had remained hot and sunny and muggy. Of course, if it rained, it would simply be hot and overcast and muggy. Dallas, Houston, and San Antonio were all among the ten largest cities in the nation. Austin was one of the fastest growing. He wondered whether any of this would be so had air conditioning never been invented.

As he drove the loader toward the spot where Darnell was

waiting for him he considered what he was going to do next. And he decided that very shortly he would pay both sisters a visit. The debt had to be paid. It had been left outstanding way too long.

FIFTEEN

Sitting in her usual position on the floor of the trailer, Tish tried to recall how much time had passed since he sliced open her dress and bra. But it was like trying to determine how long she'd been imprisoned here. Time stretched and contracted like an image in a funhouse mirror. Minutes seemed like weeks, and the months seemed like seconds. Months? Had she been here months?

She'd thought about scratching a mark on the wall for the passage of each day, but by the time the idea occurred to her it was already too late. It would only serve to tell her how many days had passed since a point at which she'd already lost all track of time.

She wondered why she was having this difficulty keeping track of time. Sensory deprivation? Lack of food? Something in the foul water she was forced to drink? Or had her brain been baked into a steaming gray mess by the heat?

One thing for certain was that none of these things were doing her any good. She felt lethargic, weak, run-down. She was caked with dirt that had stuck to her sweaty body. Her mouth seemed furry, as if something were growing in it. Probably the only thing that kept her from gagging from her own stench was the overpowering odor from the empty chemical toilet—empty of chemicals, that was. But then that was her stench, too, wasn't it? At least with no food and with water that very nearly made her puke when she drank it, there wasn't much to pass through her body.

She laughed then, a small chuckle that might have been entirely in her mind. She had nearly phrased that last thought as not having to go to the bathroom very much. In her present circumstances the notion of going to the bathroom was an absurdity. It brought up images of medicine cabinets and bubble baths and powder puffs. Here the reality was much different. She was imprisoned in a foul-smelling cell. There was neither heat nor air conditioning nor ventilation. There wasn't even the stained, vile, leaking toilet she pictured in the typical jail cell. There was no toilet paper, not even a Sears catalog to substitute for it. There was the equivalent of a bucket that was never emptied. The only water was disgusting enough to make you choke. And the prisoner was never fed.

If he comes back, she thought, I'm going to demand a TV set. The thought was not only absurd, a product of her broiled brain, but the notion of his returning made her involuntarily draw up her legs.

Stay away, she thought. Stay away.

Dying slowly of heat and starvation and drinking contaminated water had to be better than what he would do to her. Tish didn't even hope that he'd come back and let her out. Her most fervent wish was that the door would remain shut, that he would stay away, that he wouldn't come back with the hunting knife.

Her left arm itched, and when she rubbed it, Tish realized that she had a rash on her forearm. Looking more closely, she saw that there were numerous tiny inflamed bumps within the rash. She wondered whether a fungus was causing the problem. In her present environment, she was probably a better growing medium than the stuff biologists put in their petri dishes. She had an image of herself covered with mold, a big fuzzy undulating heap with tendrils of the stuff reaching to the floor. Tish made the image go away. She shivered, and

174

a drop of hot perspiration rolled down her face. It was a strange combination.

Fungi, she'd read somewhere, were a lower order of plants that weren't green because they contained no chlorophyll. Plants were harmless enough. They could prick you with thorns or stickers or even make you itch, like poison ivy. But they certainly couldn't eat you. And just who was she trying to fool? Maybe a tree couldn't reach down with its armlike branches and gobble you up, but the little ones without the chlorophyll could sure as hell eat you up. She recalled the vaginal yeast infection she'd had once, and thought of what it might be like to feel that kind of burning pain throughout her entire body. She chased the notion away, only to have it replaced by an image of athlete's foot spreading from her feet to her legs, reaching up toward the rest of her, making running cracks in her flesh as it ate through the surface into the juicy red meat beneath.

Stop it! she told herself, and the picture vanished.

But then what difference did it make if her thoughts were generated by that same portion of her mind that created nightmares? When she stopped seeing the imaginary horror of the athlete's foot fungus eating her legs, she was confronted with the reality of starving to death in conditions so inhumane they constituted torture. Where was Amnesty International? I'm a prisoner of conscience, she thought. If you have a conscience, come and get me out.

That made her laugh, but she choked the sound off as soon as it began. Only a crazy person would laugh in a situation like this. Although her brain might have been baked, she wasn't crazy. Not yet.

She needed food. She knew that was true, but she didn't crave it. The desire went away after a while, and you happily starved to death, not interested in food even if it's put in front of you. Tish had read that, although she was unable to recall where. She'd read so much that her head seemed to be filled to overflowing with facts, and she was never able to trace them to their source. Some book or article by someone about something.

But if that were true, if the urge to eat went away after a

175

while, why hadn't she been hungry at first? But she knew the answer to that, too. You had normal drives, hunger, thirst, sex, whatever. But there were other things that could overpower them. Like fear. A terrified person doesn't think about food or sex or a Pepsi. A terrified person only wants to end the terror. At first Tish had been too afraid to be hungry. And now it was too late. The urge had passed.

Steadying herself against the wall, Tish got to her feet. She swayed as if the trailer were a ship in a relatively calm sea, rolling slightly. She was getting weaker, more wobbly as time passed. The time would come, she supposed, when she'd no longer be able to stand, no longer be able to make it to the chemical toilet that had no chemicals.

Looking through the crack between the boards, she had a view of two dead cows on this side of the trailer now. The bull was on the other side. When had the second cow and the bull arrived? Yesterday? A few hours ago? Last week? Tish shook her head. Time was just so odd, so lacking in substance, so hard to grasp.

The hole in the hide of the first cow was larger now. Whatever had been gnawing or pecking at it had been busy. Tish wondered why she never saw the culprit. Perhaps it only came at night. The cows were Herefords, with their white faces, reddish-brown and white bodies. Actually only the most recent arrival was a cow. The other one was a steer. You couldn't grow up in rural Texas without learning some of these things, even if your daddy was a farmer whose only animals were two or three dogs and an occasional cat.

She stared at the cows for a long time—they were all cows to her, regardless of her upbringing. The latest arrival lay perpendicular to the first one, about ten feet farther away from the trailer. She wondered what had killed them. Disease, old age, heat were all possible, she supposed. She didn't know all the things that could kill cows. If she'd been asked, she'd have said most died becoming steaks and roasts and hamburger meat. But for some reason, these had never made it to the slaughterhouse. Maybe he had killed them, just because he enjoyed killing. But it didn't seem likely. Cows were too valuable to kill for no reason.

Unlike librarians.

Realizing that she could put off drinking water no longer, Tish moved to the sink. She wasn't as wobbly now. Maybe it came from sitting on the floor for such long periods of time. Maybe she should move around more. But she didn't want to do that. It was too hot to move. And it made her sweat, which hastened her need for water.

A plastic cup had been in the sink when she was imprisoned here. She didn't know whether he'd left it here for her or whether it had simply been here. Tish picked it up, studied it. The cup might have been white once, but it was so badly stained now that it was hard to tell for sure. Holding it under the faucet, she turned the tap, and a lazy stream of brownish liquid ran into the cup.

Her stomach lurched. The stuff was darker now than it had been at first, which meant she was getting down to the bottom of the tank where God knew what had settled over the years. Turning off the tap, she sniffed the contents of the cup, smelling nothing through the stench of the trailer. Then she sniffed it again, and she thought she detected a metallic odor, like the smell of water that had stood in the pipe for a long period of time. It looked thicker than it used to. A few brown flakes floated on the surface. She waited for them to settle to the bottom. Then she put the cup to her mouth and quickly gulped down the contents.

Her stomach informed her that it intended to expel the foul stuff forthwith, but she fought to keep it down, and her stomach finally relented. You win this time, it warned, but never again. But she would have to win again, because no matter how terrible the water tasted, it was keeping her alive. She wouldn't last long in the unbearable heat without it.

The water's getting thicker. It's running out.

Tish pushed the thought away. There was nothing she could do about the supply of water. She couldn't ration it, since she already drank as little of it as possible just because it tasted so bad. All she could do was go on, see what happened. With her confused grasp of time, the water might last for three lifetimes.

Tish put the cup back in the sink, again wondering whether

177

he'd left it here for her. Did it make sense for him to make sure she had some way to drink the water when he didn't feed her? If he wanted her to have something to drink, why didn't he fill the tank with clean water? Or did he want to force her to drink the foul stuff? Tish had no answers for these questions, and they floated from her consciousness like gas-filled balloons that had gotten away from a kid.

For a long moment, she stared at the trailer's tiny stainless-steel sink. It was spotted and stained and filthy. Tish imagined a blond woman standing in front of it, holding up a can of cleanser, saying, "Scrubola can make even a sink this dirty gleam like new." The "after" shot comes on the screen, and the woman grins real big, then steps aside to reveal the bright shine coming from the now-spotless sink. The image vanished, and Tish was again looking at the sink's caked-on filth. It would take more than Scrubola to clean it. Dynamite might not take that stuff off.

She turned around, leaned against the sink. She had managed to repair both her dress and bra. She wasn't really sure why she'd bothered, but finding a way to fix the garments had given her something to occupy her thoughts, something to do that seemed constructive. Not looking for anything in particular, she'd carefully gone through the trailer. In the tiny cabinet below the sink she'd found a small nail. And then, in a corner, she'd found a scrap of insulated wire about a foot long. She'd broken the wire into two parts by bending it; then using the nail to poke holes in the cloth, she wired her sliced-open garments back together.

If she was rescued, she'd be ready. She wouldn't have to hold the front of her dress together to cover her breasts. *If.* No matter how hard she tried, she was unable to believe that her being rescued was a very realistic possibility. The two boys had tried to rescue her, and they were dead. Since then, no one had come anywhere near the trailer. Except him. And he was insane.

Moving to the other side of the trailer, Tish looked out at the bull, which looked back at her with its dead eyes. The bull both fascinated and repulsed her. She would stare at it for long periods of time, and it would stare back as if it knew she was there. *I can see you*, it seemed to say. And then it would laugh at her, because she was the one in the zoo, and he was the one who got to spectate. *In this cage we have a librarian; isn't it the most amazing thing you've ever seen?*

"But you're dead and I'm alive," she said to the bull.

And in her head she heard it reply, *For how long, Patricia? For how long?*

Suddenly a shadow passed over the bull, and Tish, her heart pounding, was scrambling onto the bed. Pushing herself as tightly as she could into the corner, she pulled up her legs, wrapped her arms around them. It had to be him. Tish wondered why she had heard no sounds of his approach. She heard the padlock being removed from the door.

It opened, flooding the trailer with sunlight, and he stepped into the doorway.

"God," he said, waving his hand in front of his nose. "It stinks in here."

And then Tish saw what was in his hand. A large pair of loppers, the kind that could snip small limbs from trees. He watched her, his expression impassive. She stared at the loppers.

"I want a written confession," he said.

Tish only vaguely heard him. Those loppers could cut off limbs. *Limbs!* And not just the kind on trees.

"I said, I want a written confession."

"What?"

"I want a confession in writing."

"A confession to what?"

His eyes narrowed, and he moved the loppers from his right hand to his left. Tish's eyes followed the movement.

"I shouldn't have to explain that to you, Jenna Lee."

"I'm sorry," she said. "I'll do whatever you want."

"Good," he said. He pulled some folded-up sheets of paper and a ballpoint pen from his hip pocket, tossed them on the bed. "Write it out on this."

Tish's gaze shifted from the loppers to the paper. She had no idea what to write on it. She didn't think saying she confessed to everything and signing it Jenna Lee would be enough. She looked at the loppers again. Limbs. They cut off limbs.

"I see you fixed your dress," he said.

Had that angered him? Would he punish her for it? "Yes," she said. "I . . . I found a piece of wire."

He nodded. "Very resourceful."

Inwardly Tish breathed a small sigh of relief. He wasn't upset about her repairing the dress. But he still held the loppers. And he still wanted a written confession.

"I need some time to do it right," she said, immediately regretting her choice of words. She should have asked politely whether it would be okay for her to think over how she was going to put it all down, maybe take a few days, do it right.

"How much time do you need?"

She studied his face, finding no indication of how he felt about this suggestion. "A couple of days?" she asked hesitantly.

He studied her, shifting the loppers back to his right hand. Then, to her great relief, he said, "Okay, why not? I want you to do a good job."

"Me, too," she said. "I want to do a real good job." She hoped she sounded sincere. Her eyes again found the loppers.

He stood there looking at her for what seemed to be a long time. Then, as he turned and left the trailer, he said, "I'll be back."

Tish remained on the bed while he locked the door. After she was sure he was gone, she picked up the paper. Six blank sheets of cheap paper, the stuff that was sold in discount stores as typewriter paper. And a Bic pen. She had no idea what to write on the paper. The name Jenna Lee was still just a vague tug at her memory, something she had learned at the library, she thought. Maybe something Harriet Fielding had mentioned. She couldn't remember. And in a couple of days, he'd be back, demanding the written confession.

And he'd have the loppers.

Tish was trembling.

* * *

Kate wasted no time beginning her one-woman manhunt for Boyd Steuben. She went back to see Boyd's former boss at Hill Country Vending. He hadn't heard Boyd was back in town and had no idea where he might be staying. He checked Boyd's employment application, which showed that Boyd had held two previous jobs in Leap. He'd been a driver for Centex Sand and Gravel and a used-car salesman for Square Deal Auto Sales.

The car lot had gone out of business. At the address listed for it in the phone book, Kate found a burger place under construction. There was a gas station across the street. The man who owned it told Kate that the car lot had been run by a guy named Duke, who sold crummy cars at inflated prices, financed by loan companies that charged usurious interest. His word, usurious. The guy had been about sixty, unshaven, dressed in greasy gray work clothes, and he'd constantly chewed tobacco, which he spat into a Styrofoam cup. And yet he'd looked Kate right in the eye and used the word "usurious." Proved that it never paid to assume too much about people. He'd also told Kate that Duke had left town—for which the town was better off—and that most of the guys who'd worked for him had probably gone with him.

"Come in here one time, trying to get me to let him have gas for his cars on credit. You know, bill him each month."

"I take it you said no," Kate said.

"Won't tell you what I wanted to tell him. But my mama raised me never to be rude, so I told him this was a cash business. He told me to do something woulda made my mama blush and chase after him with her broom. Which woulda been a lot worse than it sounds. Mama was hell on wheels with that broom."

Duke sounded like Boyd's kind of guy.

Centex Sand and Gravel was still very much in business, and Kate talked to the foreman in a trailer that served as an office, while outside a crusher turned pieces of granite into gravel, which was then loaded into dump trucks and hauled "out to where they're widening the highway."

Kate had no idea what highway he was talking about. "How long did Boyd work here?" she asked.

"Oh, six months maybe." The foreman was a stocky guy who sweated a lot. His blue work shirt was soaked, even though the trailer was air-conditioned. He was also smoking a cigar, which was making Kate nauseous.

"Why'd he leave?"

"Fired him. He called in sick one time too many." The foreman took a puff on his cigar. "Didn't take real good care of the equipment either."

"Did he have any friends here?"

"Um-um. At the time I only had four other drivers. All of them had been with me a real long time, and I guess you'd have to say they're all pretty loyal. You know, they see that as long as the company's doing good, their paychecks will keep on coming. None of them liked Boyd. Didn't like his attitude."

Next Kate went to see Tammi Lou Brownwood, who hadn't looked real pleased to learn that Boyd was back in town. She had no idea where Boyd might hole up. And if there were people in town who'd take him in, she had no idea who they were.

Then Kate went to the bar where Tammi Lou had worked. The owner said he remembered who some of Boyd's friends were, but he didn't think any of them were around anymore. One was dead; a couple of others had left town. And then he thought of a guy named Ben Rust, who lived in a small place out on County Road 6. Rust had married and settled down, the bar owner said, but he used to be pretty wild, and sometimes he'd hang around with Boyd.

Rust turned out to be a young guy, tall and thin with sunken blue eyes. He told Kate that he had associated with Boyd only because he was young and foolish at the time, and that he had no desire ever to see Boyd again. He also said that Boyd owed him fifty bucks, and that anyone who lent money to Boyd had to either be stupid or not especially fond of his money.

It was about nine o'clock when Kate drove away from Rust's small frame house. Located in a small valley, the place had a few corrals, a barn, a windmill that pumped water into a metal stock tank. Kate had seen a horse and a pig, and she'd heard a cow moo once or twice. She wondered whether, after ten years in New York City, she'd like that kind of life. She thought she might.

When Kate got back to the house, she made herself a dinner that consisted of a tuna sandwich and a glass of milk, watched TV for a while, and went to bed. Tomorrow, Kate decided, she would start canvasing the motels. It would help if she had a picture of Boyd, but Tish had thrown them all away. Still, she could describe him.

And she could get into a great deal of trouble with Chief Colton.

To hell with Chief Colton, Kate decided. It was the last thing she thought before drifting off to sleep. She was dreaming that she and Janice Bernstein were dining in an unidentified but very expensive New York restaurant when the phone started ringing.

Groggily making her way into the kitchen, Kate found the phone in the dark, put the receiver to her ear, mumbled something that sounded like hello.

"Kate, it's me, Marsha, next door."

Just then someone started pounding on her door. "Wait a minute, Marsha. There's someone at the door."

"Kate!" Marsha hollered. "Don't hang up. Get out of the house. Get out of there right now!"

"Marsha, what the hell are you talking—"

"The house is on fire. Get out of there."

"What?"

"Get out! Hurry!"

"Yeah, okay." Kate hung up. The pounding on the front door had stopped.

On fire? Kate's sleep-filled brain tried to make sense out of all this. There was no fire. She looked around her, seeing nothing out of the ordinary. Then she opened the door to the garage. Smoke poured into the kitchen. And through the haze Kate could see the orange flicker of flames.

Behind her, in the hallway, the smoke alarm went off. Kate spun around, headed for the front door. She was reaching for the knob when she changed her mind and rushed back into the bedroom. The flames were confined to the garage; there

183

was time to get her purse, which contained her identification, her badge, and the gun—not to mention all her money. The bag sat on a chair near the bed. Kate grabbed it and dashed from the room, her feet slipping on the hall carpet.

Suddenly flames erupted in front of her, blocking her way. She hesitated, uncertain what to do, and in that second during which she paused the flames engulfed the living room.

Smoke was filling up the house. Kate's eyes were watering. She began to cough. Above her, on the hall ceiling, the smoke alarm continued to scream out its piercing warning.

Kate dropped to her hands and knees to get below the thickest part of the smoke. Still coughing, she crawled away from the flames. Heat washed over her. The first room she came to was Tish's bedroom. Through the window she could see fire burning on the outside of the house. How had the fire spread so quickly? Ignoring the bathroom because its window was so small that escape would be difficult, she crawled rapidly into the room in which she'd been sleeping. The smoke was lighter here, and there were no flames.

Getting to her feet, Kate hurried to the window, unlocked it, and pulled upward with all her strength. Although she'd heard of people lifting cars and huge rocks and things like that in times of panic, no superhuman strength came to her. The window wouldn't budge. The smoke in the bedroom was thickening, and her eyes were running so badly that she could barely see.

Grabbing a chair, Kate smashed the glass out of the window. The change in ventilation sucked the flames in from the hallway. They licked the doorway, blackened the door itself. Kate tried to use the chair to knock away any remaining shards of glass, but she was unable to see and barely able to breathe, so she simply threw herself toward the opening that led to safety. The broken glass tore at the flesh on her shoulders and cut into her hands, and then she was through, landing awkwardly on her chest—like a belly flop, except that the ground was much harder than water would have been. She had knocked the wind out of herself, and she fought for breath that wouldn't come.

"There she is!" a familiar male voice called.

"Kate, are you all right?" It was Marsha Wagner.

Kate tried to answer and couldn't. Suddenly hands had grabbed her and were dragging her away from the fire. Flames were leaping out of the open window now. The roof was on fire. Kate coughed a wrenching, lung-tearing cough, and then she was breathing again. Tears flowed from her eyes, caused in part by the smoke, but also by the emotions that came with having barely escaped with her life.

SIXTEEN

"Do you have the keys to the car in there?" It was Bert Wagner, Marsha's husband.

"Keys?" Kate said, confused. She was sitting on the ground, watching the flames spread along the roof of Tish's house.

"In your purse," Bert said. "If it isn't moved, your car's going to burn, too."

Kate became aware of the purse beside her. She was unable to recall grabbing it, but she obviously had, because here it was. She dug the car keys out of the bag and handed them to Bert.

"I'm the one who spotted the fire," Teddy Wagner said eagerly. "I got up to go to the bathroom and looked out the window and the side of your house was burning."

Until this moment Kate hadn't even realized the boy was here. "I'm glad you got up to go to the bathroom," she said.

"Me, too," Teddy said.

Kate was barefoot and clad only in pajamas. The Wagners were wearing bathrobes over their bedclothes. Marsha was examining Kate's arm.

"I think you've cut yourself pretty badly," Marsha said.

"You want to come inside so I can clean this up and put a bandage on it?"

"No," Kate said. "I want to see what happens."

She heard the wail of sirens, growing louder. The whole house was in flames now. Kate could feel the heat on her face.

"I hope our house will be okay," Marsha said.

The sirens grew louder still, and then the first fire truck arrived, its red emergency lights flashing. Members of the Leap Volunteer Fire Department scrambled off the truck and began rolling out their hoses. A second fire truck arrived, and Bert Wagner appeared, handing Kate her keys.

"Your car's okay," he said. "It's in our driveway."

Kate watched as one end of the roof collapsed, sending up an explosion of sparks. Some part of her mind added another item to the list of Tish's things that had been damaged or destroyed since Kate became responsible for them. Her house, her whole house.

Firemen were spraying the house with water now, most of which seemed to be turning to steam in the inferno. Another chunk of the roof collapsed, sending up more sparks. The faint night breeze shifted slightly, and the heat was suddenly intense.

"Let's move back," Bert Wagner said.

He and Marsha helped Kate to her feet, and they moved farther away from the burning house. Kate heard one of the firemen yell and turned just in time to see the whole structure go. One moment there had been a house there, and now there was nothing but steam and smoke and sparks. Tish's house hadn't made any noise when it went. It just sagged into the flames and disappeared.

Kate and the Wagners stared at the scene, awestruck. Finally Kate broke the silence. "Teddy, did you see anyone around the house when you looked out the window?"

"No, ma'am," the boy replied. "I just saw the fire and ran in to wake up Mom and Dad."

Marsha said, "I called the fire department, then you. Bert went over to knock on your door, see if he could rouse you."

One of the firefighters came over. He was wearing his

fireman's hat and a yellow slicker—or whatever firemen called them. He introduced himself as Assistant Fire Chief Carl Beck of the Leap Volunteer Fire Department.

"Was anyone inside the house?" he asked.

"Me," Kate answered.

"Anyone else?"

"No."

"You need medical attention?"

Kate looked at the blood on the left sleeve of her pajamas. "I could probably use some first aid."

"I'll get the kit and be right back," Beck said.

The firemen were definitely in control now. Although the pile of debris that had been Tish's house was still glowing, there were no more flames. The firemen continued to douse the remains. Water was puddled everywhere; bits of charred wood floated in the puddles.

Assistant Chief Beck returned with the first-aid kit. Kate's wounds turned out to be minor, although there was a pretty good gash in the fleshy part of her left forearm. While Beck tended to her injuries, Kate stared at the soggy ashes and chunks of charred wood that had been Tish's house.

"Why would a house burn up that quickly?" she asked.

"No telling. It's been a hot, dry summer, and a house like that that's all wood can just go."

"The flames seemed to be everywhere at once. They were in the garage, and a moment later they were on the other side of the house."

"The flames can cross over through the attic," he said as he applied some antiseptic to a cut on Kate's hand.

"What would cause it to start?"

"Cigarette butt tossed in a wastebasket, burner left on, electrical problem—there's all sorts of ways a fire can get started."

But Kate didn't believe any of these explanations. This was the work of whoever had been trying to kill her. And this time he'd damn near succeeded.

"Will there be any effort to determine the cause of the fire?" she asked.

"County fire marshal will probably be out in the morning

188

to look it over, but when the destruction's this great, it's kinda hard to tell sometimes.''

Again Kate shifted her gaze to the steaming remains of the house. She very nearly died in there, and although she understood that objectively, she hadn't come to terms with it emotionally yet, as if some internal mechanism were holding her emotions back, giving her a chance to prepare for their onslaught. This was different from a bomb that didn't go off or an attempt to run her off the road, because this had nearly worked.

The last time she had been this close to death had been in a tenement in East Harlem. At least this time she hadn't lost a partner or killed an eleven-year-old kid.

On the other hand, the thing that had happened in East Harlem was something she'd exposed herself to by becoming a cop. She'd known the risks of the job and accepted them. But this was different. This madness had come out of nowhere.

When the assistant fire chief finished with Kate's wounds, he closed up the metal case that contained his first-aid supplies and picked up a clipboard. ''I'm going to have to take a report on the fire,'' he said. ''Who owns the property?''

''My sister,'' Kate said. She spent the next few minutes answering his questions.

''We're just about done here,'' Beck said. ''I'll leave one of the fire trucks here for a while just in case we have flare-up, but I don't think there's much need for you to hang around. Is there a number where we'll be able to get ahold of you?''

It occurred to Kate then that she had no idea where she was going to go. She'd have to go to a motel, she supposed. Then she realized she was wearing pajamas. All the clothes she'd brought with her from New York were in ashes.

''You can reach her at 555-2448,'' Marsha said.

Kate didn't recognize the number. And then she realized that it had to be the Wagners' number, that Marsha was expecting her to stay with them.

''Marsha,'' Kate said, ''I can't impose on you like that. I—''

"And just where do you think you're going to go dressed like that?" Marsha asked.

"Thank you," Kate said. "I really appreciate it. I really do."

"We'd be pretty lousy neighbors if we let you wander off barefoot and with nothing to wear." Taking Kate's arm, she steered her toward the house. "Come on. I'll get the spare room ready for you, and then in the morning we'll see if we can find you something to wear."

As Kate allowed herself to be guided across the damp lawn, she found herself sinking into a confused daze. It seemed as if the coolness of the moist grass beneath her feet wasn't real, as if she were dreaming it. She accompanied the Wagners inside. While Marsha got the spare room ready, Bert escorted her to the kitchen and made them both a drink—bourbon and something. She couldn't tell what, and Bert didn't identify it. They sat down at the kitchen table. Teddy got a canned root beer from the refrigerator and joined them. The boy was wide-awake and didn't want to miss a thing.

"Don't you think you should go to bed?" Bert asked the boy.

"I gotta finish this root beer first."

Bert didn't push it.

Kate didn't know Marsha's husband too well. She'd said hi to him a time or two, and that was about it. He was tall, six feet or more, balding, and beginning to develop a middle-age paunch. He owned a TV repair shop.

"You stay here as long as you need to," Bert said. "Tish was a real good neighbor, and the least we could do is offer a little comfort to her sister."

"As soon as I can get some clothes and figure out what's happening, I'll get out of your hair."

"Don't rush. That room's just sitting there empty. Space is just sort of going to waste with nobody in it."

"It's going to be really neat to have a police detective from New York staying right here in my house," Teddy said.

When Kate had finished her drink, Marsha showed her to the spare bedroom. It had the musty smell of disuse about it. The room contained a double bed, a dresser, and one of

190

those things hotels sometimes had that you could put your suitcase on. It was old and scarred and made of dark wood, an item from a rummage sale perhaps. Kate put her purse on it.

"Would you like to take a shower?" Marsha asked.

Kate knew she was dirty and probably smelled of smoke, but she wasn't sure she had the strength to take a shower at that moment. "Would you mind if I waited until morning? Right now I think I just want to lie down."

"Oh sure. I can understand that. Sleep as late as you want in the morning. No one will bother you. I put a robe in the closet for you."

A few minutes later Kate was in bed, trying to decide whether it had all really happened. Had Tish's house burned to the ground? Had she come within a whisker of dying in the blaze? Of course these things had happened. It was just that the reality of it all had yet to hit her. And then it did hit her. Kate began trembling, and then the tears came, hot streams that ran down her face and were absorbed by her pillow.

Again and again, she saw herself crawling along the floor, choking, feeling the heat. And she saw Tish's house sink slowly into a maelstrom of flames and sparks and steam, as if that was the moment when the house had given up, died.

Tish, I'm sorry, she thought. I didn't do a good job at all. I let him burn down your house.

It was nearly dawn when she ran out of tears and fell into an exhausted sleep.

Kate awoke about midmorning. She found the robe Marsha had left for her and made her way to the shower. When she emerged from the bathroom, feeling much cleaner and wishing she had a toothbrush, Marsha was waiting for her with an armload of clothes.

"We'll find something in here to fit you," she said.

And they did. Blue jeans, sneakers, a blouse with tan and white stripes, and even some panties. Except for the sneakers, everything was a little tight, but it was all wearable. The thing Marsha had been unable to provide her with was a bra.

Marsha was flat-chested, and Kate squeezed out around the cups of every bra she was offered.

"I guess I'll just have to jiggle," Kate said.

Next Marsha gave her coffee and a bowl of cereal, which Kate accepted because she was unable to think of a polite way of turning it down. She recalled Tish saying that the stuff tasted like insulation and pushed the memory away. Marsha avoided the subject of the fire, apparently figuring Kate would bring it up when she was ready to talk about it.

When Kate had finished the cereal and two cups of coffee, Marsha said, "You ready to do some shopping?"

"I'm ready."

As they were getting up from the table, Teddy came in with a book, which he handed to Kate. *The Adventures of Tom Sawyer*, by Mark Twain.

"I got that from Miz Hastings," the boy said. "I mean the other Miz Hastings, your sister. She gave it to me to read, and I forgot to give it back. It's not a library book. It's one of hers. So I thought I'd give it to you." Apparently realizing that he might have committed an impropriety, the boy flushed.

"You didn't have to do it now," his mother scolded. "She doesn't even have a suitcase to put it in."

Teddy reached for the book. "I'd be happy to keep it for you."

"That's okay," Kate said. "Your mother and I are going shopping, and one of the first things I'm going to buy is a suitcase." She hesitated, then added, "Thank you for giving this to me. It's the only one of Tish's books that didn't burn up in the fire."

Kate's eyes filled with tears as she hugged the book to her. Everyone fell silent. Finally Marsha said, "I thought we were going shopping."

Kate got her purse from the bedroom. The brown leather bag was scraped and dirty. It needed to be cleaned, maybe replaced. Slipping the strap over her shoulder, Kate felt the reassuring weight of the .38. It occurred to her that with a boy in the house, she would have to be careful about leaving the purse around. She was unaccustomed to living with children, and the necessary precautions didn't come naturally to her.

As they were leaving Kate walked over to see the remains of Tish's house in the daylight. Marsha followed her. It was a pile of charred wood, and that was all. A burnt odor hung over it.

"If it hadn't been for you, I'd have died in there," Kate said.

Marsha gently took hold of Kate's arm, but didn't say anything.

Kate had known cops who referred to the people who died in fires as crispy critters. A lot of cop humor was like that, seemingly callous, but really just a way to distance yourself from some of the job's horrors. She wondered whether cops here used the term. If she'd burned to death in the house, would Chief Colton say the troublesome Kate Hastings had become a crispy critter?

She thought of the improperly wired gasoline bomb in her car. This was the second time she'd escaped crispy-critterdom. A mosquito landed on her cheek and began helping itself to her bodily fluids. She slapped it, then winced because she'd smacked herself so hard it hurt.

"You okay?" Marsha asked.

Kate nodded. Except for the house itself, the only damage seemed to be to the weeping willow tree in the front yard. The whiplike branches on the side closest to the house had been burned off, leaving blackened stubs. Otherwise the tree seemed okay. Part of it was still green. It would probably survive.

Like the tree, her hair was badly singed on one side. She'd noticed it when she looked into the bathroom mirror this morning. Most of the singed hairs had combed out, and with the aid of some of Marsha's shampoo, Kate had managed to make herself reasonably presentable.

Had Boyd done this? It was easy to make a good argument that he had. To his mind Tish had stolen the house from him. If he reasoned that there was nothing he could do to get the house back—or make Tish pay him for it—then he could well have decided he wasn't going to let her have it either.

Or, Kate thought, he could have burned it down just to kill me. *Someone* had been trying to kill her, and Boyd was the best suspect. Boyd was the *only* suspect.

In one respect anyway, nothing had been changed by the fire. She still had to find Boyd. But first she needed something other than tight-fitting borrowed clothes.

"Let's go shopping," Kate said, turning away from the charred ruins of Tish's house.

SEVENTEEN

He had brought the loppers with him.

Sitting on the bed, her body squeezed into the corner, her legs pulled up protectively, Tish shifted her gaze from the loppers to his face. He stood just inside the doorway, staring at her. His expression told her nothing. In a way, it was blank, as if he were sleepwalking. And yet she could make out the hint of something else, something fiercely determined. It was madness, she supposed, and she was glad she could see no more of it than she did.

Her eyes dropped to the loppers again.

Tish knew her fear of the loppers was obvious, but she was unable to make herself stop looking at them. Of course that's why he brought them, to make her afraid, and maybe if she showed enough fear he wouldn't *use* them.

Some analytical part of her mind had taken up the question of which of her appendages the loppers would be able to handle. For this part of her brain, it was a purely intellectual exercise, and it kept trying to offer up its conclusions, despite her efforts to shut off the flow of terrifying information. This analytical part of herself concluded the loppers would easily take care of things like fingers and toes, and most likely her hands and arms as well. Her legs were the questionable part. She didn't know whether the loppers could handle her legs.

Her whole body twitched, and something like a squeak came from her mouth. He continued to stare at her, his expression neutral.

She'd tried to convince herself that he wouldn't come back, that he'd only meant to frighten her, that he really had no interest in having her compose a written confession. How much time had passed since he gave her the pen and paper? It seemed like weeks ago, but it couldn't have been. A day? Two days? Why couldn't she keep track of time?

The reason was unimportant. How much time had passed was unimportant. He was here. He wanted what he'd asked for. And he'd brought the loppers. Kate's eyes dropped to the pages lying on the other end of the bed. The words she had written covered four pages. At the top of the first one, she had written:

JENNA LEE'S CONFESSION

He moved slightly, and her gaze shot back to the loppers.

"Your house burned down," he said.

"What?" She stared at him, confused.

"Your house. It's all gone. Nothing there now but a pile of ashes."

Tish wasn't sure whether she believed him. Maybe he was telling her a lie, just to add to her suffering. But something told her that this wasn't the case, that her house had indeed been destroyed by a fire. And if the house had been destroyed . . .

"What about Kate? Did she . . ."

"Did she get out?"

"Yes."

"According to the story in the *Leap Ledger*, she wasn't hurt except for a few cuts she got climbing out a window." He frowned. "I'm surprised you didn't know that."

"How could I know?"

"Because she's Jenna Lee, too." He looked thoughtful for a moment, then said, "But then I suppose you're not in

196

communication with each other, or she would have rescued you by now."

Tish had no idea what he was talking about. But the sheer bizarreness of it added to her terror. His brain wasn't just broken; it was full of dangling wires that swung back and forth, making outlandish and often horrifying connections.

"It would have taken her a while," he continued, "because you don't know where you are. But if you'd been able to tell her what you know, she'd have figured it out by now."

As he was talking he'd begun opening and closing the loppers, and Tish had been gazing at them the way an insect trapped in a spiderweb must stare at the mandibles of the advancing spider.

"Give me your confession," he said suddenly.

Leaning forward, Tish picked up the four sheets of paper on which she'd written Jenna Lee's confession and held them out to him. When he took them, she yanked her hand back.

He stood, the loppers in one hand, the pages in the other, reading. When he reached the bottom of the first sheet, he had to lean the loppers against the wall so he could turn to the next page. Tish watched him intently. She thought she'd figured out what he wanted, but if she was wrong, he would do something to her, something terrible.

Something with the loppers.

He turned to the third sheet and continued reading. "You have nice handwriting," he said.

The normal reaction was to say thank you. Tish could think of nothing she wanted to thank him for. And yet if thanking him or licking his feet or anything else was what it took to avoid having him use the loppers, she would do it.

He turned to the last page. Tish drew her knees up a little tighter, tried not to think about what might happen. When he finished the last page, he folded up the four sheets and slipped them into his hip pocket. Then he picked up the loppers. Tish waited.

"Confession's good for the soul," he said. "Do you feel good?"

Tish hesitated, uncertain how to respond. Then she blurted out, "I'm glad I confessed."

He nodded. "Do you know who I am?"

Tish had no idea what the right answer was. She said, "Of course I know you."

"But who's speaking—Patricia Hastings or Jenna Lee?"

Having no idea what to say, Tish said nothing.

"Answer me," he said.

"Patricia Hastings was speaking."

"And who am I when Jenna Lee's speaking?"

"I . . . I'm not sure."

"Think about it," he said. "The name will come to you." Abruptly he turned and left, locking the trailer door from outside.

Tish stared at the door. He had left so quickly, she hadn't had time to be relieved. But slowly it came, spreading through her until she felt limp and weak and helpless. Closing her eyes, she floated away on her imagination, visiting places that were safe. The grocery store, the mall, the library. She took a journey through her childhood, playing jacks, drinking orange sodas, skinning her knees and running to Mommy, going to church on Sundays.

And then reality was back. The loppers were gone, but she was still a prisoner in conditions that befitted the jails of a military dictatorship. And she was slowly dying of starvation and filth and water that got fouler as the supply diminished. And the loppers weren't necessarily gone for good. They could come back.

At least she had been right about what to put into Jenna Lee's confession. At first she'd had no idea what to put on the paper, and she had been certain he would come back with the loppers and cut her into pieces. But then she recalled where she'd heard the name Jenna Lee. From Harriet Fielding, who'd told her all about the history of Leap. She'd explained it all when Tish had asked about the William Gerber for whom the library had been named.

So she knew who Jenna Lee was. She had gotten the facts

right in the confession. Why did he think she was someone who'd lived in the 1800s? But Tish was no longer able to concentrate on anything for more than a few moments, and her thoughts began to wander again. She wondered how she had managed to fix her mind on Jenna Lee's confession long enough to get it done.

She forced her thoughts back to Jenna Lee. *Think about it*, he had said. *The name will come to you*. Tish thought she had all the information she needed to be able to figure out what he meant by that, but she was unable to sort it all out. Her thoughts began to wander again.

Getting off the bed, she moved to the window and looked out at the dead bull. Something had pecked its eye out, so it was no longer staring at her. She tried to recall whether she'd already observed that the bull's eye was missing and found she wasn't sure.

Suddenly she thought about the house burning down. For some reason she knew it had. All her books were gone. Tish recalled how Boyd had thrown them all on the floor once, and how she'd picked up each treasured volume and inspected it for damage. Losing her books would be like losing her friends.

She began to cry. For Jane Austen and Mark Twain and her old, old copies of Shakespeare and Poe and Dickens. And even for her paperback copies of books by contemporary writers like Stephen King and Robert B. Parker. They had all been her friends. And they were all gone.

"Nobody registered here by the name of Steuben," he said.

"He might not be using his own name," Kate said. "He's a white male, about thirty-five years old, six feet tall, wiry build, brown hair cut short, blue eyes. Likes to wear western clothes and might be driving a pickup."

The owner of the Sleepytime Motel laughed. "I reckon you just described about twenty, thirty thousand Texans."

"Are any of them staying here at the moment?"

"No, ma'am. I had a couple of young guys traveling together last night, and another guy who's a regular, a salesman. All the rest were families—mom and dad and the kids.''

A thin guy with gray hair and pale blue eyes, he was wearing one of those flowered shirts that seemed to say Florida or Hawaii or someplace like that. A faded tattoo on his left arm said U.S.M.C. He stood behind the counter in the motel's small office, looking at Kate impassively.

''You have any kitchenettes or anything like that?'' she asked.

''No. Why? You looking for a place to stay?''

''I might need a room,'' Kate said, ''if the price is right.''

''Like I said, I don't have any kitchenettes, but I can give you a real good break on a weekly rate. Normally I charge twenty-two-fifty a night for a single. I can let you have one for a hundred a week.''

Kate jotted the information down in a notebook. Since she was visiting all the motels in Leap anyway, she might as well look for one that was clean and reasonable. This one looked like a fairly good bet. The Wagners had put her up for two days now, and she simply couldn't stay there much longer. And not just because she was worried about being a burden to them. Her presence there could be putting them in danger. Someone had tried several times to kill her, even burning down the house in the process. The same thing could happen to the Wagners' house. And she could simply not expose the Wagners to that kind of risk.

''You want the room?'' the owner of the Sleepytime Motel asked.

''I'll let you know,'' she said.

She checked two more motels, neither of which had anyone fitting Boyd's description staying there and neither of which had kitchenettes. She went back to the Wagners' house. She'd been there about ten minutes when John Altman showed up, wearing a white suit and looking more like a Good Humor man than someone involved in Texas politics.

''I was sorry to hear what happened to your sister's house,'' he said when they were both seated in the Wagners' living

200

room. They had the room to themselves. Teddy and his friends were out playing with their walkie-talkies, and Marsha was in the kitchen, fixing dinner.

"I checked with the fire marshal before coming over here," Altman said. "He says he's probably going to have to put it down as cause unknown because the destruction was so complete."

"It was no accident," she said.

He frowned. "Lot of things can cause a fire. Water heater, cigarette butt, bad wiring."

"Someone tried to run me off the road, attacked me in the house, and put a bomb in my car. Then the house burns down. I have a hard time putting that down as a coincidence."

Altman nodded. "Is there anything I can do to help?"

"I don't know what it would be," Kate said. Then she thought of something. "I could use some cooperation from the local police department. A picture of Boyd Steuben would come in real handy, and they could get me one with no trouble."

"That's one place where I don't have any influence. I'm probably less popular with Chief Colton than you are."

"That would be hard to accomplish."

"Have you given any more thought to helping us change things?"

"I still don't want to get involved in Leap politics. I really don't think I can help you all that much, and it would just make my relationship with Colton even worse—if it can get any worse."

"I thought you'd say that, but I'll give you something else to think about. I'm pretty confident that Jacobi will win the election. That means that Colton will be out, which means we'll be needing a new police chief. We don't have anyone in mind for the job. It's not going to be political. Jacobi and the city council are going to solicit applications and pick the best from among those who apply."

"Are you suggesting that I apply?"

"Someone who's been a detective in the biggest city in the country might have a pretty good chance."

"You really think Leap, Texas, is ready for a woman police chief?"

He shrugged. "We'll never know if no women apply for the job."

Kate could think of nothing to say to that.

"I realize it's nothing you want to think about right now, not with everything else you've got on your mind. But a few months on down the road . . ." He let it hang there.

Altman left a few minutes later, again offering to do anything he could to help—anything that didn't involve Chief Colton. Kate thought about what he'd said. The idea of being a police chief had never occurred to her. She tried it on for size and found herself warming up to the notion.

Abruptly she pushed the idea from her mind. She had gone to New York to get away from things like farms and small towns, she reminded herself. Maybe her attitude was changing, but this wasn't the time to think about it. She had to find out what had happened to Tish. Nothing else could matter until she did.

Boyd Steuben pulled his car to the curb in front of the pile of charcoal that used to be his house. He considered getting out for a closer look, then decided that he could see all he needed to from the car. The house was totaled, no question about it. And Boyd wasn't sure how to interpret this development.

He wasn't at all sure that he believed this business about Tish's having disappeared. Tish had to have known he'd just been released from prison. Although he wasn't sure how it was supposed to work, it seemed that the whole disappearance business could be designed to keep him from getting his hands on his share of the things they'd owned jointly—not to mention getting his hands on Tish.

And now, suddenly, the house wasn't there anymore. Everything was gone, everything he was entitled to a share of. And then a word occurred to him that made everything clear. Insurance. The house was insured. If the house and his ex-wife were both gone, there'd be no reason to hang around. And once he was gone, Tish would reappear; the insurance company would rebuild the house, replace its contents.

It occurred to him that this was a tremendously risky and complicated scheme just to prevent him from claiming the property—and the vengeance—he was entitled to, especially when the law was fully on the side of his ex-wife. He realized, too, that it was a scheme in which Tish could easily be found out. But then just because Tish was book smart didn't mean she had any common sense. In fact, this was exactly the kind of thing that someone might have done in one of her stupid books.

Hot anger flashed through him when he thought of Tish and her books. She always had her nose in one, as if she was better than everyone else. As if she was too good to watch TV or go bowling or do the things normal people did. If he could do the whole thing over again, he would carry all her books into the backyard and burn them, and he was suddenly furious at himself for not having done so when he had the chance.

None of this would have happened if he hadn't been so lenient. He should have laid down the law, seen to it there were no violations, not even minor ones. Had he done that, things would have worked out very differently.

He thought back to the beginning, when he'd married her. She had been real cute then; she and her sister had been among the best lookers in the country. And with Tish having gone to college and all, it had seemed like a way to say something, to make a statement. *Look at me. I married this cute little college graduate. Eat your hearts out, guys.*

Shoulda known better, he thought.

All she ever did was to tell him to get a better job, work harder, try to be on time, do this, do that, you got to better yourself. It was like having a mother even when you were a grown-up. And all she ever did was read her damn books, act snooty.

At least she'd been fair to middlin' in bed at first. But then that had changed. She got to where she didn't even want to do it with him anymore. He had to force her. And

203

sometimes she'd looked disgusted, as if someone had rubbed her face in dog shit or something like that. No wonder he'd taken up with Tammi Lou Brownwood. Now there was some fine stuff, a woman who knew how to make a man happy. Tammi Lou really liked it. She'd scream and claw your back when she did it. Tammi Lou was a real woman, not some snooty-snoot with her nose in a damn book.

He wondered what had happened to Tammi Lou. If she wasn't married, maybe he should look her up. Hell, maybe he should look her up even if she was. He could worry about that later. For now he was doing just fine with Debbi, a girl he'd picked up at a place called Billy's Lounge. She was about thirty, divorced. Face wasn't much, but she had a nice little body. She didn't know how to use it the way Tammi Lou did, but she was okay. And she was providing him with a place to stay, a place the cops didn't know about, including Tish's twin sister, the New York cop.

He didn't like knowing that a woman could do to him what Kate had done. He'd always figured that whenever he was with a woman, he was the master. But then Kathleen Hastings wasn't an ordinary woman. She was a cop. She'd had special training. This made him feel a little better, but he still didn't like thinking about what she'd done to him.

He thought about prison then, about Angola, and what a monstrous black guy named Elwood had made him do. That was different. You can't stand up to a guy as big as Elwood. Besides, it was prison, and there were different rules there, different standards. He wondered what the guys back in 'Gola would have said if they'd known how easily the woman cop had handled him.

"Come on, little pussy," they'd have called. "Come on, sweet thing."

This was an image Boyd wanted no part of, and he shoved it into some dark recess of his brain, slammed the door on it.

Shifting his gaze from the ruins of his house to the rest of the neighborhood, he spotted Tish's car—*his* car—

parked in the Wagners' driveway. They'd had two cars, Tish's compact and his pickup. He'd left in the pickup when he decided he couldn't take it anymore. The pickup was gone now, wrecked a few months after he got to Louisiana, but that car in the driveway was still in one piece. It was all that remained of what had been his property. He felt like going over there and claiming it, but he knew better than to do that.

Apparently the Wagners had taken Tish's twin sister in. He wondered whether the Wagners were in on whatever was going on here. If so, was Tish in their house, keeping out of sight? Or were the Wagners being fooled like everyone else? He would have to keep an eye on the house if he wanted to learn the answers to those questions.

Boyd started the engine. He would have to begin his surveillance of the house some other time. He had to get back to Debbi's place so he could take her to the Crestview Cafe, where she worked as a waitress. When he'd asked to borrow her car, saying he needed it for a while to conduct a little personal business, she'd just handed him the keys. No questions. No warnings to be careful with her car. She'd asked him real nice if he could be back in time to take her to work at four, and that was all she'd said. Debbi understood how a woman was supposed to act. Too bad he hadn't had someone like Debbi to teach Tish how to behave. No matter. If he found her, he would teach her a few things himself.

He drove away from the remains of his house, passing the Wagner place. Absently he glanced at the mud-spattered green pickup to his left, wondering where it had been to get so dirty. There was no one in the truck, but it seemed to him that when he'd arrived here there had been somebody sitting in the cab. His eyes shifted to the rearview mirror, and he saw someone abruptly sit up in the truck, as if whoever it was had ducked down when he passed. He continued toward Debbi's place, thinking about what had just happened.

He'd gone about two blocks when he realized that whoever had been in that pickup could have been watching the Wagners' house. In the next instant he was sure that someone *was* watching the house. He turned around, headed back toward the block on which he used to live. But when he got there, the muddy green pickup was gone.

EIGHTEEN

Boyd was back that evening. He parked four houses away from the Wagner place, which put him about twice that far from the spot where the green pickup had been earlier. It wasn't here now. Boyd made himself as comfortable as he could in Debbi's small Japanese car.

He preferred big American cars, like the Cadillac convertible he'd had once, before he got married. Hadn't been a new one, of course, but that big old car sure had cruised down the highway. Big old V-8 engine. Guzzled gas like crazy, but who cared? You could always scrape up a couple of bucks for gas. Besides, it had only cost thirty-five or forty cents a gallon in those days.

Tish had hated big cars. Tanks, she called them. Small cars were economical, she said, easy to park. So he'd never been able to have another Caddy. With the next woman, it would be different. He'd make sure the rules were clearly understood right from the outset.

He'd lied to Tish's sister when he told her he'd driven here. He sure as hell hadn't come out of Angola with enough money to buy a car, even a junker. And in the six weeks that had passed since then, he'd briefly held one job: pumping gas. That hadn't paid him enough to buy a car either. He'd gotten to Leap by hitchhiking. On the day of his run-in with Tish's sister, he'd gotten to the house by walking there from the motel.

But then he met Debbi, and his fortunes began to change. He had a place to stay now, a car he could use, and something to keep him warm at night. It was good he'd found her when he did, because the police would have come for him at the motel—and because he was out of money.

He shifted his weight a little, trying to make some more legroom. He'd been trying to figure out why someone would want to watch the Wagner house. *He* was watching it, but his situation was unique. He was Patricia Hastings's ex-husband. He had what you might call a vested interest in what was going on.

Boyd had tried any number of explanations, without coming up with one he was really happy with. It had even occurred to him that someone could have stumbled on to Tish's scheme and might be trying to cut himself a piece of the action. But the scheme, if there was one, was to cheat him, Boyd Steuben, out of what was rightfully his. There wasn't enough in it to attract the interest of anyone else.

Other explanations he'd tried included: The person in the truck was a cop. The person was a bodyguard hired by Tish or her sister. The person was waiting for someone who lived in one of the other houses. None of them felt right. Sitting there like that just didn't seem like a cop thing to do. And Tish's sister sure as hell didn't need a bodyguard. She could *be* a bodyguard. And the guy—if it was a guy—had been watching the Wagner house, not waiting for anybody.

Boyd shook his head. Something was going on, something he had every intention of learning about.

Tish's car was still in the Wagner's driveway. All he could do was wait, watch. Maybe the car would back out of the driveway, and he'd see who was in it. In his mind he saw both Tish and her sister in it. But then he realized that they wouldn't go together; it would be too risky. They'd take turns. People would assume it was Kate no matter which one was actually in the car.

If one of the twins did go somewhere, he'd follow, see

where she went. If he kept at it, the way a private detective would, eventually things might begin to make sense.

The sun was setting, the sky beginning to take on the grayness of dusk. Boyd shifted his position again. Although he'd only been at it a few minutes, he already knew he wasn't going to like surveillance. He should have brought himself something to drink. Coffee would be best, he supposed. Of course, if he drank coffee, then he'd have to find someplace to take a leak. He shifted his butt about an inch to the left. It didn't help. He hated small cars.

"Well, well," Boyd said softly to himself. "What do we have here?"

The muddy green pickup had just showed up. It pulled to the curb on the other side of the street, about six or seven houses away from him. The driver was hidden by the reflection of the sun on the windshield. But then the driver was looking into the sun, which meant that he'd have a hard time seeing Boyd.

"Welcome to the street the Wagners live on," Boyd said. "Do you know that I used to live on this street, too, right there where that pile of burned-up old wood is?" He smiled. "Before this evening's over, good buddy, I'm going to know who you are and what you're up to. Yes sirree bob."

The pickup stayed there for nearly an hour. When it finally pulled away from the curb and came toward Boyd, it was his turn to duck. As soon as it was by him, Boyd started his car, used a driveway to turn around, and followed the pickup.

It moved at a leisurely pace, turning left when it reached a through street. When that street intersected Texas Avenue, the pickup turned right. Boyd stayed behind it as it passed gas stations, grocery stores, and other places that were open at night. When Boyd went by Strider Ford, he noticed all the small triangular flags suspended over the used-car lot. He wondered whether they had any Caddys on the lot. The pickup kept going, passing Schroeder Lumber Company. It was almost out of town. They were heading west, toward Fredricksburg. Boyd wondered where the guy was going.

The sun had set, and it was that gray time when you were never really sure whether to turn on your headlights, and

209

when you finally did turn them on, you couldn't see them on the pavement.

Ahead was a tall sign with big lighted red letters that said TRUCK STOP. The pickup slowed, turned in. Boyd did the same. The pickup rolled across the gravel parking lot, stopping next to an eighteen-wheeler with chrome wheels and a fire-engine-red cab. Boyd pulled to a stop about fifty feet away, next to a pickup someone had customized. It was shiny black, with chrome exhaust pipes, a roll bar, flames expertly painted on the fenders. For a moment Boyd studied the truck with the admiration of one who has to drive a borrowed car; then he shifted his attention back to the muddy green pickup he'd followed here.

A guy got out of the truck, walked toward the restaurant. He was wearing jeans, straw cowboy hat, and a western shirt. Boyd waited until he was inside the cafe, then followed him.

The place had a counter along one wall, booths along the opposite wall, and tables between. The man was sitting at the counter. Boyd slipped into a booth. He watched as a pale and rather plain-looking blond waitress took the man's order.

Boyd was sure he had never seen the man before. He was about Boyd's age, tall and lean, and he looked comfortable in the clothes he was wearing, as if he'd dressed like that his whole life. His jeans were faded and worn soft, his boots scuffed and dusty, his skin sun-darkened. The blond waitress brought him a glass of iced tea. The man stirred in some sugar.

A sandy-haired waitress who looked to be about sixteen and had a large headless pimple on her chin put a glass of ice water in front of Boyd and asked him what he wanted. He ordered a hot roast beef sandwich and a cup of coffee.

"Say," he said, keeping his voice low, "is that old Jack Martin sitting over there at the counter?"

She glanced at the counter. "That guy wearing the cowboy hat?"

"Yeah, him."

"Dunno. I've seen him in here a few times, but I don't know his name."

Boyd dismissed the matter with a wave of his hand. "I

don't guess he looks that much like Jack anyway, now that I think about it.''

The waitress at the counter brought the man a hamburger, all laid out on a plate the way restaurants always seemed to serve them, as if a burger that came opened up had more class then one that came all wrapped up in one piece. The man popped a fry into his mouth, then assembled his burger and began to eat it.

Boyd's own dinner arrived. Dry overcooked roast beef laid on some bread and smothered with gravy. That was Texas for you. A Texan's idea of a rare steak was a thin line of brown between two layers of charcoal. Boyd wondered how he'd managed to end up liking rare steaks and pink roast beef. Growing up in the High Plains, he'd only had beef cooked Texas style—well burnt. He couldn't recall having even seen a rare steak until he was twenty or so. And then it came to him. Tish had taught him to like rare meat. At least she'd been right about that much.

The man got the waitress to give him a refill of iced tea, then finished off his dinner leisurely. Boyd finished his, too, turned down a coffee refill, and asked for the check. After paying at the counter, Boyd walked into the parking lot. It was fully dark now, and once you got away from the restaurant the only illumination in the lot was the red glow from the big TRUCK STOP sign. Boyd headed for the green pickup.

The license plate was completely covered with mud. Boyd kicked enough of it loose to tell that it was a Colorado plate. The truck was unlocked. When Boyd opened the door, the interior light came on, and he glanced toward the restaurant. No one was coming. The cab needed a good vacuuming. Sand nearly deep enough to plant in covered the floor. A dried hunk of mud mixed with manure clung to the brake pedal. There was nothing of interest in plain sight, so Boyd looked in the glove box. He found the registration. The pickup belonged to Mark Prescott of Rocky Ford, Colorado.

Boyd put the registration back into the glove box and climbed out of the truck. The eighteen-wheeler with the chrome wheels and red cab was gone now, but a moving van had taken its place. Boyd moved into the shadows behind it, waited.

About a minute passed, and then the man emerged from the restaurant, headed for his truck. Boyd waited until the man was reaching for the door handle, then stepped out from behind the van.

"Hey, Mark, that you?" Boyd said.

The man spun around to face him, the confusion on his face obvious even in the dim red glow from the TRUCK STOP sign. "I know you?" he asked.

"We haven't met until just now, but I know your name's Mark Prescott, and I know you've been watching Kate Hastings." Boyd stepped in close, letting him know who was in command of the situation. The two men were about the same height and build, but then Boyd had learned long ago that it wasn't always being the biggest that mattered, but *acting* the biggest.

"Who are you?" Prescott asked.

"I'm the guy who knows something's going on around here and plans on finding out what it is."

Prescott said nothing.

"Why you watching Kate Hastings?"

"I heard she gives the best blow jobs in Texas, and I wanted to find out for myself."

Boyd didn't care one way or the other about the slur against Kate, but he didn't like Prescott's aggressive tone. He had to be careful not to lose control of the situation.

"If you don't want to tell me, I just might be tempted to let my old friend Jack Colton know about you. You know Jack?"

"I've heard of jacking off. You probably know all about that."

"Jack's the police chief here. He doesn't believe in all this civil liberties crap. He believes the best way to get a confession is in private, with a rubber hose."

"You're scaring me half to death."

Boyd felt whatever advantage his surprise appearance had given him slipping away. "If you really want me to give the police your name and license number, it's your choice. They

212

say the Lord looks out for little kids, drunks, and fools, but you might not want to push your luck."

"I'm not the one pushing."

Boyd was unable to think of anything to say to that, so he just stared at the guy.

"Look," Prescott said. "There's no reason for us to make things difficult for each other. You answer my questions, and I'll answer yours. You already know my name, so you tell me yours."

Boyd wasn't sure he wanted to do that, but he probably wasn't going to get any information from the guy without giving up some himself. He thought about lying and decided to go with the truth—for a while anyway.

"My name's Boyd Steuben," he said.

The guy showed no reaction. Apparently he didn't know Boyd was Tish's ex-husband. Either that or he was faking it.

"What's your interest in all this, Boyd?" Prescott asked.

"I'm Tish's ex-husband."

"My, my, that does explain a few things. You looking to get back together with Patricia?"

"I'm looking to get back together with what belongs to me. She took it all away from me while I was . . . while I was out of the state."

"So you've been watching the house."

"I think it's my turn to do the asking," Boyd said. "What's your interest in all this?"

Prescott heaved himself up so that he was sitting on the sidewall of the pickup's bed. It looked uncomfortable. "I've captured your ex-wife, and I'm holding her prisoner in an abandoned trailer."

Boyd didn't know whether to believe him or not. "Why would you want to do a thing like that?"

"Because she's Jenna Lee."

"Jenna Lee who?"

"She's really only half of Jenna Lee. Her twin sister is the other half."

"What the hell is this shit?"

"Life, Boyd. It's called life." He took off his hat, set it on the roof of the pickup.

213

"Either you're feeding me a pile of shit because you don't want to answer my questions or you're nuttier than a goddamned fruitcake, you know that, Mark?"

"At least I'm not stupid, Boyd."

Boyd felt the heat rush into his face, the way it did when Tish had really pissed him off and he was going to have to teach her a lesson. "I'm through fucking with you," he said, and reached for the guy.

Prescott came off the truck, his hand dropping into the bed, reaching for something. Boyd hadn't spent time at Angola without learning something about surviving in a fight. Seeing that he was going to get clobbered with something, he forgot all about grabbing the guy and starting moving out of the way. He heard a swish, felt the breeze as something barely missed his head, and heard the crash as it hit the truck.

Boyd had a pretty good sense of balance, and he quickly got himself into position to move in whatever direction he might have to. Prescott had a piece of pipe in his hand. He lunged at Boyd, who backed away, ducking under the pipe as it flew by his head.

Quickly Boyd moved in close, too close for Prescott to get a good swing with the pipe. He hit him with a left to the gut, doubling him over, then straightened him up with a right to the face. Prescott staggered backward and sat down hard on the gravel. Boyd recalled how in Angola there were guys you had to take shit from and guys you didn't. The big black dude Elwood had been one of the guys he had to take it from. Prescott would have been one of the guys he didn't have to worry about.

"In Angola they'd eat you alive, you know that, Mark?"

Prescott looked up at him, said nothing.

He'd dropped the pipe, which had rolled up against the rear tire of the pickup. Keeping an eye on Prescott, Boyd leaned down and picked it up. It was a nice piece of one-inch galvanized, about two-and-a-half, three feet long.

"You a plumber, Mark, carrying around pipe like this?" He stepped toward Prescott, tapping the pipe lightly in his hand.

214

"Hey," Prescott said, "maybe I was a little hasty, you know? Maybe we should talk this over."

"That's a real good idea, Mark. Let's start with you telling me what this is all about."

"I told you. I kidnapped your ex-wife. She's in an abandoned trailer."

"Why'd you do it, Mark?"

"Because she's Jenna Lee."

"Don't give me that shit." He slapped the pipe into the palm of his left hand.

"That's why I did it. It's the truth. I didn't know there were two of them. I didn't know she had a twin. When I saw the twin in the library, I dropped the book I was looking at. I thought it was Tish. I thought she'd escaped, but then I realized that she should have seen me standing right there in the library. And that the police would probably have had me already. So I scooted back to the trailer, and she was still there. I got back to the library, and asked the old woman who works there—real casually—who the woman was that looked so much like Tish. She told me it was her twin sister Kate, who's a cop in New York. Then I knew I had—"

"Mark, shut up. Now I was hoping that we were through with this pipe, but if you don't start telling me something that makes sense . . ." He let his words trail off.

For several seconds Prescott just sat silently on the ground, staring at the red glow on the gravel. Finally he looked up. "I can tell you, but you won't believe me."

"I think you better try real hard to make me believe, Mark." Boyd raised the pipe, stepped toward him.

Suddenly, with quickness that surprised Boyd, Prescott had him around the legs, and both men were on the ground, Prescott on top, gravel biting into Boyd's back and shoulders. He tried to swing the pipe, but Prescott had his arm. With his free hand he punched Prescott in the face. Prescott was using both hands to get the pipe away from him, so Boyd's left hand was free, and he hit him again, then again. Prescott scrambled off him before Boyd could hit him anymore.

Prescott stumbled, and Boyd was instantly on his feet, swinging the pipe. He grazed Prescott's shoulder with it, and

215

then it hit a rear tire of the parked van he'd hidden behind. It bounced off the rubber so violently that it flew out of his hand. Not worrying about the pipe, he advanced on his opponent, figuring he could do the job with his fists. Prescott scrambled under the van.

It looked as though he was planning to come out the other side, so Boyd rushed around the van to intercept him. A car drove into the lot, its headlights momentarily shining in his eyes, and then it was dark again. Boyd looked beneath the truck, trying to spot Prescott. He wasn't there.

Suddenly Boyd realized that Prescott was probably climbing into the cab of his pickup, getting ready to start the engine and get the hell out of here. He rushed back around the van. Prescott's truck was still here, and there was no sign of Prescott. Boyd opened the door and looked in, just to make sure Prescott wasn't hiding on the floor or something like that. He heard a noise behind him and moved just in time to avoid having his skull bashed in. Pain exploded in his right arm, and he realized the blow with the pipe might have broken it.

Ignoring the pain, ignoring everything except the need to survive, Boyd moved as quickly as he could, his feet pushing against the gravel, trying to propel him out of danger. But suddenly there was more pain as his feet were knocked from under him. For a moment he saw bright swirling lights, and something in some corner of his mind told him he was seeing the aurora borealis for the first time in his life. Then the pain came back, in his legs as well as his arm now, and the lights went away. Mark Prescott was standing over him, holding the pipe.

Boyd tried to make his mouth work, but nothing came out except a grunt. He shook his head, trying to communicate with the man standing over him.

Please don't.

But Prescott either didn't get the message or ignored it because he swung the pipe. Boyd heard the crack as it struck his head, and then he saw the lights again. They were swirling away from him, though, as if they were being sucked into one of those black holes he'd heard about. There was a

216

joke he'd heard about black holes, something about a black woman's pussy, but he couldn't remember it. Nor was he aware of the *splat* that sounded something like a melon being dropped when the pipe hit his head a second time.

NINETEEN

Kate sat on the couch in the Wagners' living room. They were watching a movie on cable TV, something with a lot of cute little science-fiction creatures in it, creations of Steven Spielberg or the Disney Studio or somebody like that. Apparently it was one of those movies the whole family could enjoy, for both Teddy and his parents seemed totally absorbed in the film. Kate wasn't paying much attention to it.

Her thoughts were on Tish, on Boyd, on how helpless she felt. She had yet to tell the Wagners that she was going to move into a motel. Instead of discussing it while Teddy and Bert were here, she planned to talk to Marsha sometime tomorrow, when the two of them could be alone.

She didn't have a clue where Boyd was holed up. She'd checked all the motels. And as far as she could tell, all his old friends were gone—except for Tammi Lou Brownwood, and Kate didn't believe Tammi Lou would have anything further to do with Boyd. So where was he? Had he left town? With Tish missing and the house and everything in it reduced to ashes, why would he stay? Was Boyd responsible for Tish's disappearance and for the fire that destroyed the house? If so, had he accomplished everything he came here to do? Or did he have more things in mind? If he did abduct Tish and

218

then leave town, would he take her with him, keep her as a hostage? Or would he kill her? Kate winced.

The questions bobbed and sank and reappeared in her mind, like a bottle being tossed about in the rapids of a river. She wasn't even sure she was asking herself the right questions. They were based on so many problematic *ifs*. *If* Boyd had kidnapped Tish. *If* Boyd had set the fire. *If* Boyd had done one but not the other. *If* Boyd was the one who'd put the firebomb in her car, tried to run her off the road. *If* Boyd was still in town.

If Tish was still alive.

Not wanting to think about that possibility, Kate shifted her thoughts to Clement's on Sixteenth Street, but that was something she'd considered so much that she'd begun to visualize the nonexistent street. She could picture the sign at the intersection, white on a green background: 16TH STREET. And she could imagine the houses that lined certain blocks. Clement's restaurant was an old two-story house with big shade trees. It was a fairly expensive restaurant, reservations required, a six-page menu, an extensive wine list.

The image vanished. It was nonsense, the product of a distraught mind. On the TV screen a furry space creature of some sort was floating in the air. It must have done something funny, because Teddy was giggling and the adult Wagners had just chuckled.

The scene gave Kate a pang of doubt about the life she'd chosen for herself. Would she ever know the security of a setting like this? Would she ever be able to sit around the TV and chuckle at Hollywood's furry creations with her family? Those hadn't been the things she'd wanted when she'd gone off to New York to seek her fortune. Now she wasn't so sure.

But then she was too tired and discouraged to be objective about anything. It wasn't the time to evaluate her life.

Again she thought about Clement's on Sixteenth, and again she felt there was something in those words she was overlooking. Not just the words themselves, but something about the circumstances under which they'd been spoken. Tish leaving with the guy in the white pickup, Teddy Wagner coming by just then, asking Tish if she was going out to eat.

Kate shook her head. She still had no idea what she was failing to see. Maybe there was nothing there at all.

"There's some watermelon in the refrigerator, and I'm going to slice me off a hunk," Bert Wagner said, getting out of his recliner. "Anybody else want some?"

"A small piece," Marsha said.

"I want a big one," Teddy said.

Kate declined, and Bert headed for the kitchen. He was nearly there when the doorbell sounded. "I'll get it," he said, changing direction. When he opened the door, Chief Colton was standing there.

"I'm here to see Kathleen Hastings," he said, looking past Bert Wagner and right at Kate.

Bert invited him in. His eyes still on Kate, Colton said, "I've got some questions for you. Would you mind stepping outside?"

Kate accompanied him out of the house. He stopped on the front lawn. Sticky hot night air engulfed her. A mosquito bit her on the arm. Another buzzed her ear, then hurried off to tell the others about all the food it had just discovered.

"Where have you been for the past two hours?" he asked.

"Right here. Why?"

"Have you left the house at all in that time, even just for a moment?"

"No." It was obvious he was questioning her as a suspect—or at least a potential suspect. She wondered what had happened.

"Can the people inside verify that?"

"Yes."

"How long have you been at the house, since when?"

"I got back about five or so."

"And you've been here since then?"

"Yes. I told you that."

"What were you doing before five?"

Out doing your job for you, Kate thought, but she didn't dare say so. Colton would be furious if he found out she was canvasing motels after he'd ordered her to leave the investigating to him.

She said: "It's obvious that the time frame you're interested in is the last two hours. I don't have to tell you what I was doing before that. I don't have to tell you anything at all. If I'm a suspect in something, I want to know what before I say anything else."

"Somebody murdered Boyd Steuben."

Kate stared at him, dumbstruck.

"Bashed his head in with a baseball bat or a tire iron or something like that."

"Where did it happen?"

"Truck stop just west of town. About an hour and a half ago."

"I take it there were no witnesses."

"What makes you think that?"

"If someone had seen what happened, you wouldn't be here talking to me. You're here because you think I might have a motive for killing him, but that's all you've got."

A mosquito bit Kate on the back of her neck. She slapped at it, but she thought it got away. It wasn't easy being a mosquito. The penalty for getting caught was summary execution.

"You wait here," Colton said. "I'm going to check your alibi with the people inside."

Kate watched him go into the house. Here's my chance, she thought. I can escape, make my way to the Mexican border, flee the country. But the thought was frivolous, and she pushed it away. Boyd Steuben, her only suspect in all this, was dead. Someone had bashed his head in at a truck stop. Was it related in some way to Tish's disappearance? Or was it a coincidence—a robbery maybe, or a disagreement over a woman or a bad debt? Before she could pose any more questions for which she had no answers, Chief Colton returned.

"The Wagners confirm what you told me," he said glumly.

"You don't have to look disappointed about it."

He frowned at her, said nothing.

"Was Steuben robbed?" she asked.

"No."

"What was he doing at the truck stop?"

"Eating a hot roast beef sandwich."

"Leave with anybody?"

"No. And that's the last question I'm going to answer."

He walked to his car, and for some reason Kate accompanied him. As he opened the door she said, "I take it I'm free to go."

Turning to face her, he sighed. "You know damn good and well you're free to go. There is one thing you could do for me, though."

"Don't leave town?"

"No. Do leave town." He climbed into his car and slammed the door closed.

As Kate walked back to the house she tried again to make sense out of Boyd's murder. She could come up with all sorts of explanations, one as good as another, all of them pretty useless. He ran into a guy from Angola who had a score to settle. He'd been making it with a guy's wife, and the guy waited for him outside the truck stop. The motive had been robbery, but the robber was scared off before getting at Boyd's money.

When she stepped into the house, all three Wagners were staring at her, the furry creatures on the TV screen forgotten. "What's going on?" Marsha asked.

Kate started to tell her and then stopped. Suddenly the thing that had been bothering her about Clement's on Sixteenth Street hopped from the shadows of her mind into the bright light of consciousness. Tish had told the boy she and the man were on their way to a nonexistent restaurant on a nonexistent street. The man had been standing right there, listening to what Tish said. Listening very closely, no doubt. It meant the man had to be from out of town. If he'd known there was no Clement's and no Sixteenth Street, Tish couldn't have said what she did.

And then something else occurred to her. Boyd would have known there was no Clement's on Sixteenth Street. Therefore the man in the white pickup was not Boyd.

He could have been the one who killed Boyd.

But all this was just spur-of-the-moment speculation, with no thought behind it, and certainly no evidence. Why would Tish's abductor kill Boyd? What connection could have ex-

222

sted between them? About the only thing she could safely conclude at this point was that she was even worse off now than she'd been before Boyd's murder. At least, with Boyd alive, she'd had someone on whom she could focus her efforts. Now she was looking for someone whose identity was unknown. Someone who didn't know the community, a newcomer or somebody just passing through.

Kate tossed that around in her mind, somebody thinking, Gee, here I am in Leap, Texas, for a couple of days with nothing to do, so I think I'll kidnap somebody, just to pass the time. It had to be something more than that.

"Maybe Boyd brought someone with him," Kate thought aloud. "Somebody he met in prison."

"Kate, what's going on?" Marsha Wagner repeated. "Chief Colton wouldn't tell us anything. He was only interested in making sure you were here with us this evening."

"Boyd's dead," Kate said. "They found his body at a truck stop. Someone hit him on the head with something."

Marsha put her hand to her mouth, and the three Wagners exchanged glances. Marsha was the first one to figure it out. "You mean . . . he thought you might have done it?"

"You might say I'm a known enemy of his." Kate repeated her conversation with the chief, then explained some of the things she'd been thinking.

"Did the chief say what he was going to do?" Bert asked.

"I don't think he knows."

"What are *you* going to do?" Teddy asked. His words seemed to imply that she, Kate Hastings, the big-time detective from New York, would know what to do even if Chief Colton didn't.

The big-time detective from New York looked away and collected her thoughts, then said, "I wish I knew, Teddy."

Although she wanted to stay up and let the TV set deaden her mind, Kate went to bed at the same time the Wagners did. It was a small house, and the sound of the TV would easily carry to the bedrooms. For a long time Kate's mind tried unsuccessfully to make sense of Boyd's murder, but she eventually managed to drift off to sleep. She was awakened by someone gently shaking her.

"Kate, wake up," Marsha said.

At first Kate thought it must be morning, but when she opened her eyes she discovered it was still dark out. "What time is it?" she asked.

"About four-fifteen. There's a phone call for you."

"A phone call?" Kate tried to figure out who knew she was here. And then she realized that it could be the police, that they might have found Tish—or at least learned something about what had happened to her. She swung her legs over the edge of the bed. "Who is it?"

"He didn't say."

Kate made her way to the kitchen. The light was on, and the phone was off the hook, the receiver lying on the table.

"Hello," she said, putting the receiver to her ear.

"Kate Hastings?" a man asked.

"Yes." Certain that it was news about Tish, she tensed.

"I know who you really are."

"What?" Her still-sleep-deadened mind tried to make sense of his words.

"I know you, Jenna Lee. I know what you are. I know what you did."

Kate's first impulse was to tell this creep to stuff it, but something kept her from doing so. "Yes," she said. "Go on."

"I know because I'm the one you did it to. Think about that, Jenna Lee. Think long and hard on it." He hung up.

Replacing the wall phone's receiver, Kate sat down at the table. Was it a prank? There were demented people everywhere. Had one of them found out where she was staying, decided to add to her misery? Or was the call connected somehow to Tish's disappearance—and maybe to Boyd's murder? Some inner sense told her it was more than just a four A.M. prank phone call.

Marsha appeared in the doorway. "Who was it?"

"I don't know. He called me Jenna Lee, and he said he knew what I did. The name mean anything to you?"

"No, I don't think so." She looked thoughtful. "Jenna

It's not a name you hear very often. It sounds like an old name, one that your grandmother might have."

Not wanting Marsha to worry, Kate said, "Must have been a prank call. You know, somebody who got one of my hand-bills concerning Tish or somebody who saw the story in the paper."

"I hate people who do things like that," Marsha said. "I got an obscene phone call once, and it upset me so much I was almost afraid to leave the house for the next two days." She shuddered at the memory.

Kate nodded. Clearly she had been right to worry that her presence in the house might put the Wagners in danger. To-morrow she would let Marsha know that she was moving to a motel.

"I'm sorry you had to get woken up in the middle of the night," Kate said.

"Well, I'm certainly not blaming you," Marsha said. "Come on. Let's get back to bed. Maybe we can still get a little sleep."

Kate did manage to get a little more sleep, maybe half an hour's worth, between periods of tossing and turning while her mind churned. In the morning Kate told Marsha she was moving to a motel. Marsha said all the appropriate things, like it wasn't necessary, she was no trouble, they didn't mind at all. But the sincerity seemed a bit forced, as if Marsha, too, had figured out that Kate's presence might be putting them all in danger.

Since she had all day to check into a motel, the first thing Kate did after talking to Marsha was to go to the library. She found Harriet Fielding returning books to the shelves in the children's section.

"Any word about Tish?" the older woman asked as she slipped a copy of Dr. Seuss's *Green Eggs and Ham* onto the shelf.

"No." She told the old woman about Boyd's murder.

"Oh, my," Harriet Fielding said. "I knew someone had been killed at the truck stop. At least two people told me about it, but nobody knew the victim's name. Does it have anything to do with Tish?''

''I don't know,'' Kate said.

''I'm glad to see you're all right. I heard about the house burning down. It must have been awfully frightening for you.''

''It was a little scary there for a while, but I managed to get out okay.''

''Do you know what caused it?''

''No.''

Harriet Fielding just shook her head, as if to say there were too many things going wrong, too many bad things happening.

''Does the name Jenna Lee mean anything to you?'' Kate asked.

''What's that?'' Harriet Fielding asked, looking puzzled. ''I'm sorry. I was thinking about everything that's been happening, I guess.''

''Jenna Lee. Does the name mean anything to you?''

''Of course it does. I couldn't have lived here most of my life without learning who Jenna Lee was.''

''Who was she?''

''Have you noticed the name William T. Gerber since you got here?''

''This is the William T. Gerber Library.''

''William T. Gerber was one of the founders of this community. Jenna Lee Smythe was the girl he married. But there's a lot more to the story than that. Come on, I've got a book that has pictures of both Gerber and Jenna Lee.''

TWENTY

Harriet Fielding led Kate to a table in the reference room. "Wait here," she said. "I'll be right back." She returned a moment later and joined Kate at the table. She had a book, which she put down in front of her. It was entitled *Leap, History of a Texas Town.*

"We'll get to this in a moment," she said, tapping the book with her finger. "First let me give you some background—uh, if you're interested, that is."

"I'm definitely interested," Kate said.

"Does this have anything to do with . . . with everything that's been happening?"

"It might," Kate said. She told the old woman about the four A.M. phone call.

"That's rather odd. Jenna Lee's been dead for a very long time."

"Tell me the story," Kate said. "Tell me about Jenna Lee."

"Let me start by telling you about William T. Gerber. He came to Texas from Pennsylvania in the 1850s, started a ranch, worked hard. The Civil War came along, and Texas seceded from the Union to become part of the Confederacy. Gerber was a Northern sympathizer. In those days they called

227

them Radicals. After the war the Radicals rose to power in Texas politics. I guess you could say Gerber was on the winning side. Anyway, by the time Texas was readmitted to the Union in 1870, Gerber owned most of the land around Leap, and he was quite wealthy.

"It was a very colorful period in history. There were huge cattle drives up the Chisholm Trail to the railroad centers in Kansas. They lasted until the 1880s when the railroads crossed the state."

"What about Jenna Lee?" Kate asked.

"Sorry. I love Texas history, and when I talk about it, I start giving history lessons, I'm afraid. Jenna Lee Smythe was a preacher's daughter, and I guess you'd have to say she fits what you hear about preachers' daughters being bad. She was a pretty thing, with dark curls that surrounded her face, and there were a lot of men after her. Of course, the men outnumbered the women by a wide margin, so a pretty girl like Jenna Lee could bide her time and wait for what she wanted.

"She was eighteen when William Gerber decided he should find a wife. He was in his forties, and he'd never married because he'd just been too busy—at least that's what he said. Apparently the thing that made him decide it was time to find a woman was that he didn't have any heirs.

"Anyway, it shouldn't take too much figuring out to see how the richest man in the county and the prettiest, most sought-after girl found each other. There was a lot of talk about how Jenna Lee didn't deserve to be wearing her bridal white, but nobody would have dared say anything around Gerber.

"She was faithful to him for a while, but eventually she began fooling around with a guy named Frank Bates whenever Gerber was away. After a while Jenna Lee and Bates came up with a plan to murder Gerber. She'd inherit everything, and after a suitable amount of time passed, she could marry Bates.

"No one knows exactly how Gerber found out, but he did. And he just plain went berserk. He found Frank Bates in the Leap barbershop and shot him while the barber was cutting

228

his hair. Killed the barber, too. There are different stories about where he caught up with Jenna Lee, but they all agree that he did catch up with her, and that he would have killed her as well if some men hadn't stopped him.

"In those days, if you were rich, you could pretty much do what you wanted. But two things were working against Gerber in this case. First, although he might have got away with killing his wife's lover, he'd also killed the barber. The second thing was that the circuit judge was one of those dyed-in-the-wool Confederates who hoped the South would rise again. And he was known for having an intense dislike of Radicals. Especially Radicals who got rich while his two sons were dying for the Confederacy. Gerber was tried, convicted, and hanged from a gallows in the center of Leap.

"Gerber, figuring he wasn't going to let Jenna Lee inherit anything that belonged to him, made out a will leaving everything to his foreman, who'd served him faithfully for twenty years. As soon as Gerber was swinging in the breeze with a rope around his neck, Jenna Lee got herself a high-powered lawyer and had the will thrown out. She got everything.

"Jenna Lee quit fooling around with men. She never remarried. I guess she found something she liked better than men. Power. And she used it ruthlessly. She handpicked mayors and sheriffs and candidates for the legislature. She played a role in determining who became governor and who went to Congress. People who crossed her, unless they had as much money and power as she did, usually regretted it.

"She died in 1928, the year before the stock market crashed. She never had any children, but she did have relatives, and they carved up everything between them. Put an end to the Gerber dynasty before it could get started. I was just a girl, but I remember seeing her once or twice. My mother always pointed her out to me. 'See that?' she'd say. 'That's Jenna Lee Gerber. She owns just about everything there is to own around here.' " The old woman's eyes grew distant. She was remembering.

"You know what's funny?" she continued. "Jenna Lee was responsible for all the things that got named after William T. Gerber. Maybe it was just for show, to counter the stories about her and Bates and how they'd planned to kill Gerber. Or maybe it was her conscience, not that many people believed she had one.

"You know what Gerber's last words were before they hung him? He said that he was going to take his hatred for Jenna Lee with him, that he'd wait for her on the other side, and when she got there, he'd get even with her." She smiled. "Now you know a little bit of Leap history. What do you think?"

"It's an interesting story, but I don't see how there could possibly be a connection with Tish's disappearance."

Harriet Fielding frowned. "Maybe he wasn't calling you Jenna Lee in the sense that you could be her. It's pretty obvious you can't be her. But you could be *like* her, I suppose."

"A scheming adulteress?"

The old woman blushed. "I don't mean that you *are* like that. But perhaps someone thinks you are."

Kate considered that. The old woman had a good point. You could call someone a Judas or a Jezebel, so why not a Jenna Lee? But the whole thing made no sense. She wasn't a scheming, power-hungry adulteress. She had never been married, and as far as she could judge, she lacked the other qualifications as well. Why would anyone think of her in such a way?

"Here are the photos," Harriet Fielding said, opening the book. She flipped through it until she found the page she wanted, then turned the book so it faced Kate. "That's William T. Gerber."

The man in the photo was middle-aged. He was wearing a dark suit with one of those ribbonlike ties of that era. He didn't look like a person of wealth and power. His small eyes stared warily at the camera, as if he had been afraid of it. He was holding his white hat in his lap, a Stetson, Kate guessed. He was trim, but then the ranch life probably kept you that way, even if you were the owner. His hair was thinning. It was impossible to judge its color in the old black-and-white photo. If there was an overall feeling to the picture, it was one of nervousness, of not wanting to be there doing what he was doing.

"Now show me Jenna Lee," Kate said.

Without turning the book to face her, Harriet Fielding flipped ahead another ten pages or so. "Oh, dear," she said. "It's missing."

A square had been cut from the upper-right portion of the page. Someone had clipped Jenna Lee's photo.

"That the only photo you've got?" Kate asked.

"Yes, I'm afraid so. There aren't many photographs of her. She never liked having her picture taken, especially after her looks started going. The picture in the book was taken when she was in her early twenties. I can't imagine why anyone would have cut it out."

"Do you have records that show who checked this book out?"

"Yes, I can look that up."

"Get me the name of everyone who checked it out over the last three months."

While Harriet Fielding went to check the records, Kate flipped through the book. There were photos of Leap as it had been in the 1800s. The main and apparently only street was dirt, with horses tied at hitching posts. In one photo she could make out Cartwright's Mercantile and beyond it a sign that said BARBERSHOP. She wondered whether it was the barbershop in which William T. Gerber had blown away Frank Bates, along with the barber.

"Here are the names," Harriet Fielding said, handing Kate a slip of paper. Five people had checked out the book in the last three months:

> Jason Tyler
> Sharon Novotne
> Mark Prescott
> William O'Keefe
> Susan Rogers

"Do you know these people?" Kate asked.
"Yes, most of them."

"Any of them involved with livestock?"

"Jason Tyler owns a ranch."

"Where is it?"

"About twenty miles out of town."

It occurred to Kate that someone living that far from town might not realize there was no such thing as a Clement's on Sixteenth Street. She asked Harriet Fielding how to get there, and the part-time librarian gave her a complicated set of instructions.

"I'm going to go see him," Kate said. "While I'm doing that, will you go through your records and get me the addresses of the others?"

Saying she would, Harriet Fielding looked at Kate quizzically, apparently wanting to know what livestock had to do with anything. Kate didn't offer any explanations. She had withheld evidence by not giving the Leap police the stuff she found on the floor of Tish's bedroom, and that wasn't the sort of thing you went around discussing with people.

Kate's first stop after leaving the library was the Sleepytime Motel, where she took a room for a week after arguing the owner down to eighty dollars. Then she headed west out of town until she came to a narrow paved road that headed off to the right, one of the state's many farm roads. She followed that for about ten miles, turned left on a dirt road, and promptly got lost. Two men in a pickup finally told her she was five miles from where she should be. It was the middle of the afternoon when she finally found Jason Tyler's ranch.

Mesquite trees lined the long dirt drive leading to the house. The house itself was fairly modern, one story, made of bricks. Appropriately enough it was what was sometimes referred to as a ranch-style house. Kate noted the tall tower for the TV antenna. A satellite dish squatted on the ground about ten feet from the tower. As Kate pulled to a stop in front of the place two large dogs ran up to the car, barking furiously.

A woman stepped out of the house, shouted, "Duke! Major!" The dogs instantly fell silent and retreated. Kate got out of the car.

"What can I do for you?" the woman asked. She eyed

232

Kate with a peculiar mix of friendliness and suspicion. Country openness combined with a mistrust of strangers, Kate supposed. The woman was in her fifties, tall and thin, dressed in jeans and a blue shirt.

"I'm here to see Jason Tyler," Kate said.

"Rebecca Tyler," the woman said, offering her hand. "Who are you?"

Kate shook her hand. "Kathleen Hastings. I, uh, I'm hoping Mr. Tyler can help me with something I'm working on."

Rebecca Tyler gave her a look that indicated she didn't think that was much of an explanation. "He's inside watching TV," she said. "Come on."

Kate followed her into the house. The air conditioning felt marvelous after the hot, dusty, frustrating ride on country roads. The interior was just sort of universal American. It could have been in New Jersey, California, Florida, anywhere. Wall-to-wall carpeting, good-sized kitchen, quality furniture of no particular style. Rebecca Tyler took Kate to the den, where Jason was watching a console color TV set. He was watching a soap opera. And he was sitting in a wheelchair while he did it.

"Jason, this lady's here to see you."

The chair whirred as it turned so its occupant could face Kate. He was about his wife's age, gray-haired, and he looked at Kate with eyes that seemed moist and sickly. "Jason Tyler," he said, offering his hand.

Kate stepped forward to shake it. "I, uh, I'm Kate Hastings. I'm from the New York Police Department."

"What would the New York police want with me?"

Kate didn't know how to answer that. She didn't want anything with a man confined to a wheelchair. The man who'd left with Tish had been physically sound, as had the man who'd broken into the house and grabbed her from behind. If she'd only explained to Harriet Fielding why she was interested in people who dealt with livestock, Harriet Fielding could have told her Jason Tyler was confined to a wheelchair.

"Did you check a book out of the library entitled *Leap, History of a Texas Town*?"

Tyler glanced at his wife, who was standing quietly in the

233

doorway, listening; then his eyes returned to Kate. "You mean the New York Police Department is investigating over-due books in Leap, Texas, now?"

"I didn't know it was overdue."

"Three days. It's hard for me to get into town, living out here like I do, so I was late getting it back. The library was closed, so I dropped it into the night return slot." He grinned. "I hope you know I'm just funnin' you."

"I suspected you might be."

"I still don't know what the New York police would want with me."

"It really is about the book," Kate said. "Did anyone else read it while it was here?"

"Becky doesn't care for that sort of thing. I'm the local-history buff."

"No one else had the book, no hired help or anything like that?"

Tyler shook his head. "Most of them only speak Spanish, and none of the others are interested in books."

"Did you notice any damage to the book?"

"Someone had cut out the picture of Jenna Lee Gerber. You know who she was?"

"Preacher's daughter who became a wealthy land baron," Kate said. "Or maybe I should say baroness."

"Probably the nicest thing anybody ever called her. Now would you mind if I asked you what a book about the history of Leap has to do with the New York Police Department?"

"Whoever cut out Jenna Lee's picture might be involved in the disappearance of my sister." Kate briefly explained what had happened.

Jason said he'd read about that in the paper. His wife came in then, said how sorry she was that Kate was having so many difficulties, and they both said they hoped Tish turned up in good condition real soon.

Kate said, "May I ask you a personal question?"

"Shoot," Jason said.

"Why are you in a wheelchair?"

"Cigarettes. There's nothing wrong with my legs. I just

234

don't have the breath to make them work. If I take two steps, I'm wheezing and coughing."

"It's emphysema," said Rebecca, who was standing beside her husband now. "The idiot kept right on smoking even after he could barely breathe."

Jason looked up at his wife with a look that seemed to say, *You just don't understand what it's like.* Apparently Rebecca was a nonsmoker. Kate thanked the Tylers for talking to her.

As she made her way along the dirt roads of the Texas Hill Country Kate considered the other names on the list of people who'd checked out the book on the history of Leap. Sharon Novotne, William O'Keefe, Mark Prescott, Susan Rogers. Although she was tempted to eliminate the women, she knew better than to do so. A woman could have checked out the book for someone or lent it to someone.

And of course there was always the possibility that the picture had been cut out years ago, for reasons known only to the one who did it. But Kate didn't want to think about that, because that meant this was another dead end. She was beginning to feel desperate about the situation. The time for finding Tish was running out. Kate sensed that Tish was slipping away from her, that she might just vanish and be gone, as if the twin sister Kate grew up with had been a product of a little girl's imagination, a pretend playmate who just happened to be a double—the image in the mirror brought to life or something like that.

Kate made herself think about something else—anything else. A line of black clouds had been approaching from the west, and Kate noticed lightning in them. The clouds were big and threatening. And coming her way. She hoped she'd be back on pavement if a storm was coming. In a heavy rain these dirt roads could quickly wash out or turn to mud or both.

She made it to the paved farm road just as the first hailstones fell, clattering against the roof of the car, bouncing off the pavement. There was lightning so close she could hear its squeal and then an enormous clap of thunder. The sun vanished as if there had just been a total eclipse.

Kate knew these kinds of storms from her childhood in

West Texas. She assumed they meant the same thing here that they did there. Tornadoes. She switched on the radio. After a few minutes of country music, the announcer came on and reminded listeners about the tornado watch covering six central Texas counties, including the one she was in. The hail, which had been pea-sized, suddenly became the size of pecans. The noise in the car was nearly deafening.

Unable to see more than ten feet in front of her, Kate pulled over to the side of the road. The wind screamed, and the hail abruptly changed to rain, which was coming horizontally. The ditches at the side of the road became bubbling rivers.

A storm like this made anyone a little nervous, but it would most likely stop as quickly as it had started, with no real harm done—unless there was a tornado. As if on cue, the announcer informed her that a funnel cloud had been spotted near Johnson City. The wind shifted, and the rain was coming horizontally from the other direction.

A few minutes later the rain eased. The announcer told her the funnel cloud never touched down. The sky began to brighten. But it was still raining hard, and Kate had to stay put. Two hailstones hit the pavement beside the car, but no others followed them.

Kate turned her thoughts to the names of the people who'd checked out the history book. Then, for no particular reason, she thought of Clement's on Sixteenth. Suddenly she sat up straight, rain and hail and tornadoes forgotten.

"I'll be damned," she said.

And then she grinned, because she was pretty sure she had just figured out what Clement's on Sixteenth Street meant. By the time she got back to Leap, the storm was over.

TWENTY-ONE

Sitting in his pickup, Mark Prescott watched the house in which Kate Hastings was staying. Her car wasn't there. When she got back, he was going to kill her.

His gaze shifted to the charred remains of Tish's house. Maybe he wasn't too good at making gasoline bombs go off in cars, but he was a hell of an arsonist. The house wasn't burnt a little here and scorched a little there; it was *gone*. He couldn't have made the place any more useless if he'd nuked it.

He didn't understand how the woman had gotten out. He'd started the fire with some gallon cans of charcoal lighter, sloshing huge amounts of the stuff on two sides of the house. The clapboard structure had gone up like wadded newspapers. The woman was lucky to have escaped. His eyes dropped to the .45 automatic beside him in the seat. Maybe this time her luck would run out.

For several moments Prescott watched the steam rising from the pavement as the rainwater evaporated from the warm asphalt. Then a series of memories came to him, each one lasting only a moment or two, sort of like the quick succession of scenes in a movie preview. He was on a stretcher, being carried out of the arena, the crowd noise an unintelligible excited babble, the voice of a child rising above it, asking, "Is he dead, Daddy? Is he dead?" And then he was a boy again, lying on his bed and crying, his back and buttocks beaten bloody by his father's belt, the punishment for using the word "shit" to another boy and being overheard. He recalled standing in front of the mirror in the trailer, checking out his baggy pants, his shirt with the huge checks on it, his silly-looking hat that looked as if it belonged to a nineteenth-century English gentleman. He remembered his mother sitting dazed on the floor, because his father had slapped her so hard he'd nearly knocked her unconscious.

He saw a series of rodeo scenes, along with the faces of many of the bronc riders and calf ropers and steer wrestlers he'd known. He remembered the people better than the events, because you met the people again and again in Calgary and Cheyenne and Santa Fe, and after a while all the arenas began to look the same.

He'd become a rodeo clown the way anyone became anything, he supposed. It just sort of happened to you. It had been the summer after he'd finished high school, and the only thing he had to look forward to was working on the family farm—not that it seemed much like a *family* farm. It certainly didn't seem that any of it was his; that was for sure. The place was more like a prison farm, with his father as warden.

One day while his dad was in Abilene, talking to somebody from the Farmers Home Administration, Mark and Noel Jenkins had gone over to the big rodeo in Stamford in Noel's new pickup. Sitting in the stands about halfway through the show, he'd turned to Noel and said, "I wish I could be in the rodeo instead of working on my old man's farm."

"You know how to ride and rope?"

"No."

"I wouldn't pin my hopes on a big career in rodeoing."

Down in the arena, one of the clowns was driving an old car around in circles. Another clown was running away from it, and the car was lurching and backfiring. Finally the car stopped, and the clown who was being chased pinned on an enormous sheriff's star and loudly demanded that everyone

238

get out of the vehicle. The clown driving it got out, then another guy, and another, and another. The crowd was laughing, and guys just kept climbing out of that car, like they were coming from nowhere.

"I don't have to know how to ride or rope to do that," Mark said.

He put the idea aside until after the show, when he saw one of the clowns walking toward a group of trailers parked outside the arena. Telling Noel to come on, he caught up with the clown.

"Hey," he said, "how'd you get all those guys in the car?"

"Packed 'em in there," the clown said. Up close Mark could tell he was an old guy whose unshaved whiskers were showing through his makeup.

"You couldn't pack that many guys in there," Mark insisted.

"That's the secret, how we pack 'em in there."

The clown continued walking toward the trailers, and Mark kept up with him, asking him what it was like to be a clown. The clown said his name was Joe. Joe's trailer turned out to be one of those small jobs that people mainly used for camping. It was connected to a pickup, one of whose tires was flat. So was Joe's spare. Mark volunteered to help him change it. Noel said he had to get on back, and Mark told him to go, he'd get a ride later.

It was the last day of the rodeo, and by the time the final show began that evening, Mark had talked old Joe into taking him with him to Santa Fe. A compulsive gambler who'd bet on anything, Joe was always broke. After years of living alone, he enjoyed the boy's company. He taught Mark to be a rodeo clown. He became the father Mark had always wished for and never had.

And he talked to Mark about things the boy never considered before. Like UFOs. And reincarnation. He'd get books on the subject, bring them back to the trailer, and Mark would read them. The old man's fascination became Mark's fascination.

Mark wrote his parents once, telling them he was working rodeos, but his folks never answered. Either that or the letter never caught up with him, traveling around as much as he did.

Although he hadn't known it at the time, the beginning of the end came in Montana when Joe died. Mark found him lying in bed in the trailer, stiff and cold and white looking. The hospital said natural causes, and that's as much as Mark ever knew about why Joe died.

Mark continued working as a clown for many years after that. It wasn't the same without Joe, but it was all he knew how to do. He and Joe had been a two-man team, working together, so Mark found a new partner, taught him Joe's part of the routine, and went on. Mark floated along, not really liking it anymore, and then came the day he was gored by a bull.

Montana must have been his bad-luck state, because that's where it happened. A bull rider had been dumped on his ass, and it was the clown's job to distract the animal, giving the cowboy time to scramble to safety. He ran into the bull's field of vision, waving his arms, and the beast came after him. At times like this, one of the things he would often do was leap into a large barrel. Frequently the bull attacked the barrel, knocking it over, rolling it along with Mark inside. The crowd loved it. But on this particular occasion he lost his footing when he leaped for the barrel. The bull's horns caught him in the belly, tossing him a good ten feet before he hit the ground. Some cowboys rescued him.

Although his injuries hurt like hell, there was no serious internal damage. He had a cracked rib, a huge bruise, and some abrasions. He had also lost his nerve. The next time he distracted a bull, luring it away from the fallen cowboy, he froze the instant the beast turned to come after him. He just stood there, staring at the animal, knowing it was going to gore him or stomp him into the ground, but not able to do so much as twitch a muscle. Another clown intervened, saving him. Mark never put on his clown costume again.

He pretty much drifted after that, getting jobs at ranches or feed lots or even rodeos, but only as general help, never as part of the action. And wherever he went, he'd usually visit the library, see what books it had on UFOs and reincarnation.

He and Joe had liked sitting outside at night, looking at the stars, talking about what kind of life must exist up there, what it would think about the people on Earth. Beings from other worlds had visited us, and the government had covered it up. They discussed that a lot, he and Joe, talking about what they might learn if they could see the government's secret files.

And they talked about reincarnation, wondering who they might have been before, who—or what—they might become. People would have thought they were crazy, discussing things like that, so they kept their interest in such matters to themselves.

After Joe died, Mark's interest in UFOs began to diminish, while his preoccupation with reincarnation intensified. He found himself looking at babies, wondering whether any of them could be Joe—and if he did find Joe, whether there was any chance the infant could have any memories, however faint, of his former partner, Mark Prescott.

Raised a good Christian, he believed the soul survived after a person died. The soul, of course, was the spark of life, the thing that glowed in you when you were born and went out when you died. Of course it didn't go out the way a light bulb did; it went back to where it had come from. God could use that spark again, send it out to glow within another human life. And he believed that spark wasn't wiped totally clean, that traces of past incarnations remained. Maybe daydreams or stray thoughts were really disguised memories from an earlier life. Maybe you could bear a physical resemblance to the person you had been in a previous incarnation.

In a few cases, Mark knew, the person remembered who he or she had been, remembered everything. As he recalled having been William Gerber, recalled what Jenna Lee had done to him.

Mark Prescott checked his watch. He'd been there for forty-five minutes. He wished Kate Hastings would hurry up so he could do it and get it over with. Although there was nothing fancy about his approach to killing this woman, it was usually effective. Gangsters had been getting rid of people this way for years. When she got back, he was simply going to drive by and empty the gun at her. It would be at close range. He wouldn't miss.

Phoning the woman last night had been an impulsive thing. He'd simply wanted to start her thinking so she'd remember as her sister had. And so she'd understand why she had to die.

He checked his watch again. Come on home, Jenna Lee, he thought. Your William's here waiting for you.

"Leap, one-thirty-four."

Officer Elvin Conley grabbed the microphone from its holder on his cruiser's dash. "One-thirty-four."

"Ten-thirty-one vehicle at 713 Nesbitt Drive. Complainant describes it as a green pickup. She says it's been sitting there for nearly an hour. One subject inside."

"Ten-four," Conley said.

He passed a small shopping center called the Texas Avenue Plaza and turned right at the next intersection. He was about six blocks from Nesbitt Drive. Ten-thirty-one meant a suspicious person or vehicle—suspicious in the mind of the caller anyway. Half the time it turned out to be no big deal, and the other half of the time the suspicious person or vehicle would be gone by the time you got there.

A fifteen-year veteran of the Leap police force, Conley had never made sergeant. He'd never taken the test. He probably could have passed it. Some pretty dumb guys had done that—but then sucking up to Chief Colton probably counted for more than your score did. The reason he didn't want to become a sergeant was that supervisors had to make decisions, and when you started doing that, people could start blaming things on you. It was easier this way. Work your hours, stay out of other people's arguments, collect your paycheck.

His only problem was his weight. He liked to eat, and he hated exercise. His waist had gone from thirty-two, when he joined the force, to its present thirty-eight, which was creeping toward forty. The captain kept telling him to slim down. He didn't like having the captain notice him.

Conley turned onto Nesbitt Drive, drove a few blocks, and pulled in behind the green pickup.

"One-thirty-four's ten-ninety-seven," he said over the radio.

"Ten-four," the dispatcher replied.

"Run a twenty-eight and twenty-nine on Colorado plate 17J—" He studied the license plate, trying to make out the numbers. "Stand by," he said finally. "There's so much mud on the plate I can't read the rest of it."

As Conley got out of his patrol car the man in the pickup stuck his head out the window, asked, "Is anything wrong, Officer?"

"Just stay put," Conley said. "I'll be with you in a minute."

With the sole of his shoe Conley wiped away enough of the mud so he could make out the numbers on the license plate. Returning to the cruiser, he radioed in the license numbers, asking for the computer checks that would show to whom the plate had been issued and whether the plate or vehicle had been stolen or involved in any other mischief. It didn't matter which state a vehicle was registered in. They were all linked together by computer. The dispatcher could check with computers in Georgia or Massachusetts or Oregon or anywhere else.

Taking his clipboard with him, he walked up to the green pickup. "May I see your driver's license and registration, please?"

The guy got out his wallet and found the license, then rooted through his glove compartment until he found his registration. He handed the documents to Conley. The name Mark Prescott was on both of them, and the picture on the license looked like the guy sitting in the truck. Conley took the license and registration back to his cruiser and ran a computer check on Mark Prescott.

A few moments passed, and then the dispatcher gave him the results of his first computer check. The green Ford pickup was registered to Mark Prescott. The address matched the one on the license and registration. No indication that the truck was stolen or that it had been involved in anything. A moment later she reported, "Subject Prescott is negative."

Conley returned to the pickup. "Would you mind telling me what you're doing here?"

The man looked embarrassed. "Well, it's kind of personal."

"You can tell me," Conley said. "I'm very understanding."

The guy practically blushed. "Uh, well, there's this woman I've been messing around with, and, well, she's married."

"What does that have to do with you being parked here?"

"I'm waiting for her husband to leave. You see that white house two down from the one that burned?"

"Yeah."

"That's the one. The red car belongs to her husband. I can't go in till it's gone. He was supposed to have left two hours ago. I don't know what's going on."

"I ought to check that out," Conley said.

The guy looked scared. "Please don't do that. Her husband will kill her—maybe me, too. You'd be causing all sorts of grief if you did that."

Conley nodded, handed the guy his license and registration. "You'll have to move on for now. You can come back and check later, but the people living on this block are getting kind of upset, seeing you just sitting here. It makes them nervous, and they start thinking maybe you're looking for a house to break into or something like that."

The man started his truck and drove off.

Conley got back in his cruiser, picked up the microphone, and said "One-thirty-four's ten-eight." Which meant he was through with the pickup and available for any other calls.

"Ten-four," the dispatcher said.

It was five-fifteen when Kate parked in front of the library and hurried up the walk to the entrance. The wood door had a window in its upper portion, and taped to the inside of the glass was an index card on which had been typed:

244

Kate had no intention of waiting until eight o'clock in the morning. She hurried back to her car and drove until she spotted a pay phone mounted on the wall outside a convenience store. There was no Harriet Fielding in the phone book, but there was an H. L. Kate dialed the number. Harriet Fielding answered.

"I'm glad I found you," Kate said. "I wasn't sure the H. in the H. L. stood for Harriet."

"Doesn't, as a matter of fact. My late husband's initials were H. L., and I've never bothered to change the listing."

Suddenly Kate realized that she was talking about everything except what mattered. "What can you tell me about Mark Prescott?" she said.

"Who?"

"Mark Prescott. His name is on the list of people who had checked out the book about the history of Leap."

"I don't know him. I know everybody else on the list, but not him."

"Did you get the addresses of the people on the list?"

"I pulled their applications for library cards."

"Where are they?"

"At the library."

"Could you meet me over there? It's important. Very important."

"I take it Jason Tyler wasn't the person you were looking for."

"No. It's Mark Prescott. He's the one Tish left with the day she disappeared."

There was a long pause; then the old woman said, "Those cards are city property, and they might be considered confidential. And you're not really the police here. . . . " Her words trailed off.

"Harriet, please. Don't do this to me. Chief Colton thinks Tish left of her own accord and I'm a pain in the ass for

245

bothering him. Do you believe that Tish would just leave with some guy?"

"No."

"Do you want to leave her fate in Chief Colton's hands?"

The line went dead for several seconds, then Harriet Fielding said, "I'll be at the library in ten minutes."

Kate drove back to the library and waited at the entrance, cursing herself for dashing off to Jason Tyler's place without taking the time to find out anything about the other names on Harriet Fielding's list. Had she done it correctly, she would have learned that Jason Tyler was confined to a wheelchair. And she probably would have discovered that all the names Harriet Fielding recognized were people who had been here a long time, people who would have known right away that there was neither a Clement's nor a Sixteenth Street. That would have left Mark Prescott. Kate was betting his library application would show he was a newcomer.

Tish had been very clever when she devised the clue she gave Teddy Wagner, especially considering that she was under tremendous pressure and had only moments to come up with something. The key was that she had given the clue to the boy.

Teddy had misunderstood. Tish had said *Clemens'* on Sixteenth Street, not Clement's. And the Sixteenth Street was nothing more than the code Teddy and his friends used on their walkie-talkies. The sixteenth letter of the alphabet was P. As in Prescott. Clemens, as in Samuel, was the author of the book Teddy had borrowed. Except it was written under the pseudonym Mark Twain. Mark as in Mark Prescott. Like any puzzle it seemed so terribly simple once you had the solution.

A Ford Escort pulled up behind Kate's car, and Harriet Fielding got out. She unlocked the library. The two women went inside. Harriet Fielding hurried into the library's small office and returned a moment later with five applications for library cards. Some were so old the paper had yellowed. One was crisp and new.

Kate said, "These people, the ones you know, how long have they lived here?"

246

"Oh, a long time. One of those applications was filled out fifty years ago."

Kate picked up the crisp, new application form. The name at the top was Mark Prescott, 1208 Rhinemann Road, Leap, Texas. No phone. Employer: Leap Livestock Auction. The form was dated about a month and a half ago.

"Where's Rhinemann Road?" Kate asked.

Harriet Fielding told her, then asked, "What are you going to do?"

"Find Mark Prescott." Kate dug her notebook out of her purse and copied down the address.

"Be careful," Harriet Fielding said.

TWENTY-TWO

Bud Darnell, owner of the Leap Livestock Auction, sat in his windowless office, wondering whether he'd made a mistake in hiring Mark Prescott. Bud liked to trust people, give them the benefit of the doubt. But some guys just didn't appreciate it. Some guys would just naturally take advantage of you, no matter what.

He'd felt sorry for Prescott, the guy being down on his luck the way he was. And he'd been intrigued with Prescott's having been a rodeo clown. Darnell had loved rodeos when he was a boy, and the notion of following the rodeo circuit had been one of those romantic ideas all boys seem to have. So he'd given Prescott a job, even advancing him a few bucks to get his old pickup running.

But he could hardly ever find the man. And he was beginning to wonder if Prescott was a drunk, if he brought a bottle to work with him, consuming its contents in some secret hiding place. Darnell had hired a guy once before who did that. Came to work in a pickup with an old beat-up camper on it, and spent most of his time in the camper, sloshed to the gills. He'd fired the guy, and he had every intention of firing Prescott if he found out the former rodeo clown was doing the same thing.

Getting up from behind his desk, Darnell went into the outer office, where Leanne was sitting behind her desk. She was a big woman with frizzy platinum hair, a shade he was sure God had never put on the human head and never would. But then Francine's Hair Salon—he'd heard her mention the name—wasn't concerned with the limitations of God. Leanne was his secretary and bookkeeper and anything else that had to do with shuffling paper. She was good at it, and the men who came in all seemed to like talking to her, and none of them had ever complained about her hair.

"Prescott go home yet?" Darnell asked.

"If he did, I didn't see him."

"That's the trouble. Nobody ever sees him."

"That's what happens when you let people work unsupervised." Leanne was examining her nails, which were painted such a bright red that Darnell had trouble looking at them. They matched her lipstick.

"If I had time to supervise him, I could do the work myself."

"I've got three letters here need your Bud Darnell on them. You want to sign them now, or should I leave them on your desk?"

"Put them on my desk. I'm going out to look for Prescott."

"It's almost six. You want me to lock up when I leave or just leave everything open?"

"Just leave the place unlocked, and I'll take care of it when I get back. I don't even know why I lock up at night, to tell you the truth. Nothing here worth stealing."

Outside, Darnell walked past a number of corrals with loading chutes. There really wasn't much of anywhere on the property to hide, and he wondered whether Prescott had simply been sneaking off, visiting a woman or something like that. When he reached the last corral, Darnell turned around and walked back toward the big metal building that housed all the indoor parts of his business. His pickup was parked out front, and he decided to use it to conduct the remainder of his search for Prescott.

He drove past the mountain of manure Prescott had scraped

249

out of the corrals with the loader. The mountain would get bigger and smellier as the year passed. Come spring, he would sell it by the truckload to farmers and gardeners. He hadn't spotted Prescott's pickup anywhere. He hadn't spotted the loader either.

Darnell's truck bounced along the narrow dirt road that led to the far end of the property. The only place left he could think of to check was out by the burial pit. There was the old trailer he'd told Prescott to push into the pit and bury along with the dead cattle, but nobody would use that for anything. The stench in that burial pit would be overwhelming.

The metal building and corrals disappeared behind him. The odor of manure was gone, too. The breeze was almost always such that the livestock smells were carried toward the highway, away from this end of the property. And then a new odor greeted him, the stench of death.

The loader stood at the edge of the pit. Darnell parked next to it, got out, and looked into the pit. There were about half a dozen dead cows in one end of it, along with the old trailer. There was no sign of Prescott. Moving to the loader, Darnell put his hand on the big diesel's exposed engine block, finding it cold. He walked down into the pit.

As he approached the trailer he noticed its boarded-over windows. He'd done that himself, along with the two-by-four reinforcing of the door, because the trailer had been used for storage at one time. Some of the corrals were a long way from the main building, and he'd needed a place to keep ropes and shovels and things like that where they'd be handy for people working out there. He'd replaced the trailer several years ago with a heavy-duty commercial storage shed. As he walked around to the side of the trailer on which the door was located he was surprised to find it locked.

And it was locked with a very substantial-looking padlock. Which meant there had to be something inside. He stared at the locked door, trying to figure out what was going on. Prescott had to be the one who put the lock on the trailer, but why? What was inside? As he was posing these questions to himself, he heard a noise inside the trailer. A *thump*.

Darnell backed up a step. There couldn't be anything in

there. It would suffocate in the heat. And then he realized that, if there was something inside, it was a prisoner. He moved up next to the trailer and put his eye to the slit between the boards over the window. Although it was too dark inside for him to see anything, he did smell something, something even stronger than the aroma of putrifying cattle. And then he heard movement again, from within the trailer. Was there an animal inside?

Or a person?

Although Darnell's brain immediately rejected the idea that there could be a human being locked in there, something made him rap on the side of the trailer.

"Anybody in there?" he asked.

"Help me," a woman's voice said weakly. "Please help me."

Darnell was incredulous. A long moment passed before he had any idea what to say. Finally he asked, "Who are you? What are you doing in there?"

"I was locked in here by Mark Prescott. Please help me get out."

"All right, ma'am. Just hang on a moment. I've got some tools in my pickup. I'll be right back."

All sorts of explanations flashed through Darnell's mind as he hurried out of the pit. The woman was Prescott's girl-friend, and he'd put her in there to teach her a lesson for something she'd done. Prescott was holding the woman for ransom. It was a joke, and Prescott would be right back to let her out. But none of the explanations really made any sense. Prescott was crazy if he'd lock anybody up in a trailer like that. And no matter what the explanation, he was going to fire the man as soon as he found him.

When he got back to his pickup, Darnell pulled the tool-box out from under the seat to see what he had. Although bolt cutters would have been the best thing, he already knew there were none in the truck. But he did find a hacksaw. Taking it with him, he started back into the pit, and then it occurred to him that it would be a lot easier to drive down there in his truck.

He reversed direction just in time to see Prescott standing

there, holding a length of pipe about the way you stood at the plate with a baseball bat. Then the pipe smacked into the side of Darnell's head.

Tish was elated. Someone had found her. She was going to get out of the trailer. Breathe fresh air again. Drink cool, clear water again. Shower and wash her hair and put on clean clothes. Brush her teeth. Sleep in a real bed in a place that was air-conditioned. She was going to eat—eat a big steak, a hamburger, a plate of spaghetti.

She was standing by the window, trying to catch a glimpse of her rescuer when he returned. She prayed that he'd have the right tools with him to open the lock, that he wouldn't have to go somewhere to get what he needed. I'm going to see Kate again, she thought. And the library. And I'm going to drive my car.

And Mark Prescott would get his.

She felt like a prison inmate getting out after a long sentence or a sailor who'd spent months at sea. The world was going to be a whole new experience.

Tish felt weak standing at the window. The heat, the days without food, and the foul water had taken the last of her strength. How long? she asked herself. She still had no idea. When she got out, Kate would tell her.

She heard the clatter of stones rolling down the bank of the pit. The sound had come from the other side of the trailer. As she moved to the window on that side she felt dizzy, as if she might faint. After taking a moment to make sure she wasn't going to collapse, Tish put her eye to the crack between the boards. At first she saw only dead cattle, but then she noticed something that made her suck in her breath. A hand and part of an arm.

The body to which they were attached was up the hill and out of her field of vision. It looked as though the hand were reaching toward the dead animals, as if there were safety there. Tish was trembling. The visions of all the things she would do when she got out of here were evaporating, and although she didn't want to admit it to herself, she knew the

252

arm most likely belonged to her rescuer, that she would stay here in this miserable trailer until she died.

Nooooo! she thought. It's not true. Not true, not true.

But she knew it was.

And then, as if to prove it, the sound of a big diesel engine came from above her. A sound she'd heard many times before. Usually just before a dead cow came sliding into the pit. And once after Prescott had killed the two boys. This time she heard a loud smashing noise, and she put her eye to the crack between the boards again. A brown pickup truck lay on its side by the dead cow, its rear end actually on top of one of them.

A moment later something else came down the bank, jarring the trailer when it hit. Tish could see nothing out the window. She moved to the other side of the trailer. She still had no idea what was happening. She heard more diesel noises from above her, then something jarred the trailer again. She could see dust in the air now.

Moving to the other side of the trailer, she saw a few stones roll down the hill. One clacked off the dead pickup and hit a dead cow. The stones were followed by loose dirt, sliding down the bank until the cows stopped it. Then more dirt. Tish backed away from the window. She knew what was happening.

Diesel noises continued to drift into the trailer. Dirt slid down the bank, sometimes near the trailer, sometimes hitting it. When Tish looked out the window again, it had piled up around the pickup and covered the rear end of one of the cows.

The next time she looked, the cows were nearly all covered.

The dirt continued to slide into the pit. More of the pickup disappeared, and more of the cows. The man's hand disappeared. The dirt got higher and higher. Finally it was up to the window through which Tish was looking. It rose higher still, until sand was trickling in through the boards covering the window. Finally it rose beyond the level of the window, and dirt and stones were hitting the roof above Tish's head.

Tish moved to the other side of the trailer. Through the

crack she could see daylight, more dead cows, dirt sliding down the bank to cover them up. Again the earth rose, leaving her six inches of daylight through the crack, then three, then two.

And then there was none.

Tish was in total darkness. She could still hear the diesel noises, the earth coming down, but these began to grow fainter. She told herself she should scream, but no scream came. She should at least cry, she thought, but no tears came either. Finally she felt her way through the dark trailer until she found the bed. She lay down on it.

I'm going to sleep, she thought. I'm going to die in my sleep.

Then the scream came. And so did the tears.

Prescott drove the loader forward, into the pile of earth he'd made while carving out the pit. When the scoop was full he raised it, backing away from the pile, then moving forward again to the edge of the bank and dumping the earth into the pit. The trailer and pickup were covered now. Soon there would be nothing here but a patch of soft, weed-free earth.

As he headed back to the pile of dirt to get another scoopful it occurred to him that none of this would have happened if his truck hadn't broken down while he was passing through Leap on his way to Austin. There hadn't been anything special waiting for him in Austin. He'd always heard it was a nice place, and even though he'd grown up near Abilene, he'd never been to the state's capital city. Besides, he liked to watch "Austin City Limits" on TV. These reasons seemed as good as any for going to Austin.

After following the rodeo circuit for as long as he had, wandering just seemed to be in his blood. Although he'd given up the rodeo, he'd never been able to settle down in one place for any length of time. He'd been living in Arizona before going to Rocky Ford, Colorado. He'd gone to Colorado last September to see whether there was anyone he knew at the Rocky Ford rodeo. There'd been a few, but more new faces than familiar ones. He'd hired on as a stock handler and general doer of dirty jobs, and after the rodeo ended he worked on a sugar-beet farm for a while, then got a job at a feed lot. He finally got tired of Rocky Ford, as he got tired of every place sooner or later, and headed for Austin in his old pickup, with a small suitcase full of clothes and just about enough money to get there. He would have made it if the fuel pump hadn't gone out on his truck.

But then he never would have learned the identity of his previous incarnation.

In Leap, as he did most places he went, Prescott checked out the library first thing. It was a small library, and the supply of books on UFOs and reincarnation was limited. Prescott had read all but one of them, a small volume devoted to UFO sightings in Texas. He read it, finding it of no particular interest, then explored the library's card catalog to see what else was available. He was on the verge of reading a book on firearms of the Old West when he spotted the volume on the history of Leap. He took the history book instead.

It was Joe got him interested in reading. Mainly books on UFOs and reincarnation, but other things, too, like westerns—especially westerns by Louis L'Amour. "There's anything you'd want to know in books," Joe used to say. "Only a fool wouldn't learn some of it." Every time they went to a new town, Joe took him to the library. Prescott learned to love libraries and books and learning things—even though he'd hated all those things when he was in school.

The book on Leap's history had fascinated him. At first he wasn't sure why. Things like the range wars in Lincoln County, New Mexico, and Johnson County, Wyoming, certainly made more exciting reading if you were interested in the history of the Old West. And yet, when he finished *Leap, History of a Texas Town*, he read it again.

What had captured his interest, he realized, was the story of Jenna Lee and William T. Gerber. There were pictures of both of them in the book, and the more he looked at the photos, the more he felt . . . something. Then he started dreaming about Gerber and Jenna Lee, dreaming that he *was* Gerber. He felt Gerber's pain at having been betrayed by the scheming woman. He experienced Gerber's rage as they led

255

him to the gallows. Gerber's voice was his voice as he vowed publicly to have his revenge, even if he had to wait for her in the afterlife.

Not the afterlife. The next *next* life.

For William T. Gerber's soul—his life force, his spark of existence—had been reborn in Mark Prescott. And Mark Prescott *knew*. The memory had been reborn as well. He began to dream about settling the score, finishing the revenge that had been interrupted in that past life. He dreamed about finding Jenna Lee in her new life, seeing the expression on her face when she realized that retribution had followed her from the Void.

Then one day in the library he noticed the resemblance between the picture of Jenna Lee in the book and the librarian. He was amazed that he hadn't noticed it before. He'd spoken to her many times. She knew his name, and he knew that hers was Patricia Hastings, and that everybody called her Tish. He went back to the library several times just to study her. Finally he was sure. Patricia Hastings was the reincarnation of Jenna Lee. And now he would get his chance to pay her back for what she had done. The phone book told him where she lived.

His intention when he kidnapped her was to force her to endure the heat and loneliness of the trailer, to live in fear of what would happen. When she had suffered enough, he would have done what he was doing now. Fill in the hole and bury her alive. The punishment would have been long. And it would have been fitting, considering what she'd done to him.

Everything seemed to be going just as he'd planned it until he saw Patricia Hastings in the library—*after* he'd kidnapped her. Dumbfounded, he'd dropped the book he was examining. Nothing made sense. How had she escaped? Why hadn't she recognized him?

Thoroughly confused, he'd rushed to the trailer, finding that his prisoner was still there. So who was the woman who looked so much like Tish Hastings? Going back to the library, he casually struck up a conversation with the old woman who worked there. And he'd learned all about Patricia Hastings's twin sister.

Now he had a problem. Jenna Lee's life force had divided itself between two identical women. If he killed Tish, it would flee to Kate, and Jenna Lee's spirit would simply go on, perhaps pausing briefly to laugh at him. The solution was to kill Kate; then the spark of life would flow to the one who was already his captive. And the spirit of William Gerber would have its revenge.

If only it had worked that way. But Bud Darnell had discovered the woman in the trailer, and Prescott had killed him. The police would come around, trying to figure out what had happened to Darnell. Prescott had to get rid of the evidence.

Soon Patricia Hastings would die, and the entirety of Jenna Lee's current incarnation would be in the other sister. He wasn't sure he could handle Kate Hastings well enough to kidnap her, which meant he would probably be unable to punish her the way he'd punished Tish. He had had his revenge on half of Jenna Lee's life force, but not the other half. But if that's the way it had to be, then that's the way it had to be. He would have to settle for killing her.

Some people believed that what you did in one life determined what you would be in the next one. Kate Hastings was pretty, a police officer. Instead of being punished for what she had done as Jenna Lee, she was being given another chance to redeem herself. If nothing else, Mark Prescott—William T. Gerber—could take that chance away from her.

After he had moved the last of the earth back into place, he drove back and forth over it with the loader, packing it down.

TWENTY-THREE

Parked across the street, Kate studied the house. Number 1208 Rhinemann Road was a white clapboard house on the edge of town. It was surrounded by big shade trees and set well back from the street. The neighborhood still showed traces of the rural area it must have been at one time. There was a lot of space between the houses. A few hundred feet down the road stood the remains of what must have once been an orchard. A couple of places used former barns as garages.

There were two cars in the driveway at 1208, a mid-sized four-door and a station wagon. Both looked fairly new. Not the sort of thing you'd expect an employee of the Leap Livestock Auction to drive.

Kate slipped her fingers into her purse, felt the reassuring butt of her .38. Then she got out of the car. As she walked toward the white house she reminded herself to be careful, to use the knowledge her police training had given her. She wasn't exactly at the top of her form; she knew that. The way she'd run off to the Tyler ranch proved it. She should have waited until Harriet Fielding could provide her with more information—such as Tyler being a cripple, such as Mark Prescott being the only newcomer on the list.

She'd been through a lot lately. The man she'd been seeing had abruptly broken off the relationship. Then an eleven-year-old boy had killed her partner, and she had blown away the kid. When she came to Leap to recuperate, her twin sister vanished, and then someone began trying to kill her, nearly succeeding the night the house burned down. Kate felt used up, as if events had sucked so much out of her there was nothing left to take.

She was already breaking the first rule you should adhere to when doing something like this. Don't go by yourself. Get backup. But there was no backup. There was only Chief Colton, who might very well arrest her if he knew what she was doing. Resting her fingers on the top of her shoulder bag, just inches from the butt of the .38, Kate rang the doorbell. From inside the house, she heard the sound of someone approaching, and then a middle-aged woman opened the door.

"Mark Prescott here?" Kate asked.

"He lives around back. In the trailer. But I don't think he's there right now. You're welcome to check. If there's no green pickup there, then he's out somewhere. I can take a message for him if you want."

"How long has he been living here?" Kate asked.

"Five, six weeks. Something like that. I was running an ad in the paper, and he's the one got here first with the rent money."

"What's he like?"

"Quiet, never gives me any trouble. Why?"

"Just curious. I'll go see if he's there."

A driveway ran past the house to a clump of trees about fifty yards away. Beneath the trees was the trailer, one that was probably large enough for a family of three if they didn't mind bumping elbows a bit. It sat on blocks, and it looked as if it had been here for a long time. There was no sign of a pickup. As she approached the mobile home Kate withdrew her gun, held it at her side so it couldn't be seen by anyone watching from the house. Standing to the side of the trailer's metal door, Kate knocked. She waited, then knocked again. Apparently no one was at home.

Kate tried the door, finding it unlocked. She moved quickly inside, holding her gun with both hands now, ready to do what she had to if she was threatened. She saw no one in the living room or kitchen. Moving quickly through the trailer, she checked the bathroom, the two tiny bedrooms, then the closets. No one was here. She put her gun away and returned to the living room.

It was easy to see why the trailer hadn't been locked. There was nothing inside it to steal. No TV set, no stereo equipment, no gun collection, no microwave oven. Kate began to search the trailer thoroughly. She found that the cooking utensils consisted of a cast-iron frying pan and an aluminum saucepan. For cleaning equipment, there was a broom, a dustpan, a toilet brush, a can of scouring powder, and a plastic bottle of pink dishwashing liquid. Three shirts hung in the closet. The dresser contained socks, underwear, and two pairs of jeans. Mark Prescott was a man with almost no possessions.

Kate took everything out of the dresser. Under Prescott's jockey shorts, she found a photograph that had been cut from a book. Small boldface type identified the woman in the photo as Jenna Lee Gerber.

At first it just looked like an old photo of a pretty dark-haired woman, but then Kate noticed the nose, the shape of the chin, the way the hair framed her face. It looked a little like her. The more she looked at Jenna Lee, the stronger the resemblance seemed to become. Was that what this was all about? Had everything that had happened somehow revolved around the resemblance she and Tish bore to a woman who died in the 1920s? It made no sense.

Slipping the picture of Jenna Lee into her purse, Kate continued her search. In the living room she looked beneath all the cushions on the couch, then turned her attention to the only reading material in the trailer, the two paperback books that lay on the wobbly coffee table. One was entitled *Perpetual Life Through Reincarnation*. The other one was called *Transmigration of the Soul*. An idea took shape somewhere in Kate's mind, but she couldn't quite drag it into her consciousness. Or maybe she just wasn't letting herself, because the whole explanation was just too bizarre. She flipped through the two books to see whether there were any underlined passages. There weren't.

Taking the books with her, Kate left the trailer. She had just committed a felony, she supposed, but she wasn't going to worry about that now. She could either wait for Prescott to show up or check out the place he worked, the Leap Livestock Auction. She got in the car and started the engine. She had no intention of sitting and waiting.

It was dusk when she pulled up in front of the big metal building that housed the offices of the Leap Livestock Auction. It was a dreary-looking place with pens and chutes and the like. Kate supposed that to the animals that came here it was a temporary prison, a stopover on their way to death. The odors of manure and hay hung heavily in the air.

Her car was the only one here, and the place looked closed. Kate got out of the car and went to the door, thinking maybe she could pound on it and raise the attention of the janitor or a watchman—someone who might be able to tell where Mark Prescott was. She pulled on the door. It was unlocked.

Lights were on inside, indicating the place was open for business. But after looking around for a few minutes, Kate hadn't found anyone. The unlocked building was an open invitation to burglars. There were office machines, including a small computer, and all the other things you'd expect to find in a business. The place even had a small coffee shop with a sign taped to the door that said OPEN ON AUCTION DAYS. There was also a lounge with tables and vending machines that was presumably open all the time. And there was a big room with lots of seats, no doubt the place where the auctions were held.

Back outside, Kate drove along the dirt road that led to a series of corrals. Although a few steers eyed her with no real interest, there were no people about. The road ended when the corrals did, so Kate turned around and followed it in the other direction. She passed more corrals, all empty, and then the road headed off into the property. Kate noticed some old farm equipment and a huge pile of manure—she recalled the

261

powdery substance she'd found on Tish's bedroom floor. Kate felt the seat belt restraining her when the car bounced over one particularly bad bump.

Fresh tire tracks showed in the sandier portions of the road. Some had been made by a car or a light truck, others by some kind of heavy equipment. Kate kept going. A few moments later, she came on a big yellow front-end loader. And then she saw what was on the other side of it. A green pickup.

Stopping near the pickup, Kate studied her surroundings. As far as she could tell, no one was here. Ahead of her was a large area of bare earth, a spot where all the vegetation had been scraped away or plowed under for some reason. It was crisscrossed with big tire tracks, presumably made by the loader.

Kate got out of the car, drawing the gun from her purse. The pickup was old and mud-spattered. She looked inside the cab. The ragged upholstery was covered with a blanket. The glass covering the speedometer was cracked. So was the windshield. She checked the glove compartment, finding Colorado registration in the name of Mark Prescott. The only other things in the glove box were some road maps and a three-year-old ticket stub from the New Mexico State Fair Rodeo in Albuquerque. She looked under the seat, finding nothing except a toolbox. The only thing in the back of the truck was a length of pipe.

Kate moved on to the loader. When she got close to it, she could feel the warmth coming from the engine. The machine had been used recently. She was walking around to the other side of the machine when pain erupted in her shoulder. She staggered backward, her stunned brain trying to force itself to function, and then she realized that she'd heard a shot, that she'd *been* shot. Suddenly Kate was unable to stand up anymore, and she fell, her arm hitting the ground hard, the gun flying out of her hand.

"I really hadn't expected to get this lucky," a man's voice said. "I figured if I kept trying, I'd kill you, but I hadn't even hoped for this much luck."

For a moment Kate was back in East Harlem, except this

time the boy had been faster, and she was the one who'd been shot. And then the silly notion vanished. She was lying in the dirt in Leap, Texas, and the person who'd just spoken was a man, not a boy. Kate tried to make her eyes focus. At first all she could see was gray dusk sky, and then a man stepped into her field of vision. He was aiming a .45 automatic at her.

"You must be Mark Prescott," Kate said. Her voice was tremulous, and speaking sent a shudder of pain through her wounded shoulder.

"Part of me is. But you should think of me as William Gerber."

"William Gerber died a long time ago."

"Not his soul. That continued."

Tish recalled the books on reincarnation she'd found in Prescott's rented trailer. Did he think he was the reincarnation of Gerber? "What have you done to Tish?"

"Your other half is dying."

"Where is she?"

"Very close. Don't you feel her?"

"Goddammit, Prescott—" Her outburst sent pain quivering through her shoulder. And then her stomach lurched, and she threw up. She was shivering and starting to perspire. She hoped she wasn't going into shock.

"When your other half dies, Jenna Lee, I'll have all of you. You know what I'm going to do then?"

Kate just stared at him.

"I'm going to get even."

It was clear to Kate what he thought, but she didn't understand how anyone could be crazy enough to believe the things he clearly believed. That he was the reincarnation of William Gerber. That she and Tish, jointly, were the reincarnation of Jenna Lee. The man was completely, totally loony tunes.

She wanted to look for her gun, but she was afraid to shift her eyes because she didn't want to remind Prescott of the weapon. Maybe it had landed somewhere he couldn't see it. Maybe.

Kate tried to analyze her condition. It was hard to tell how

263

bad her shoulder wound was without being able to see it. There was nothing vital in the shoulder, so the main danger would be blood loss. She tested the fingers of her left hand. They moved.

As a police officer she had met a lot of crazy people. One woman thought she was in contact with beings from outer space. A man thought he was being slowly killed by death beams being tested by the NYPD—if he'd said the CIA it might have been believable. Most nuts were harmless. A few were dangerous. And a handful of those were *extremely* dangerous. The mass murderers and serial killers and the like, the people who put the poison in baby food or climbed to the top of the tower with a sniper rifle and began killing. They were the people with the brains that had been wired wrong. Mark Prescott was one of those, and Kate had no idea how to handle him. She wasn't sure that, in her present condition, she could handle him.

Suddenly something that Prescott had said, something that her brain had somehow failed to lock on to, slammed into her consciousness with the force of a battering ram. *Dying.* He'd said Tish was dying.

"What have you done to Tish?"

"I'll explain it to you after a while," he said. "Get up."

"Tell me about Tish."

In a movement so fast that Kate had no time to prepare for it, Prescott grabbed her by her arm and yanked her to her feet. Pain exploded in her shoulder, and darkness closed in around her, but she didn't faint. She was standing, albeit wobbly, the blackness slowly going away. Her stomach churned but held on to its contents. Her eyes, guided by that part of her that hadn't forgotten she was a cop, searched for the gun she'd dropped. She didn't see it.

Keeping his gun trained on Kate, Prescott backed away from her. When he reached the driver's compartment of the loader, he reached into it and pulled out a piece of rope. Kate's eyes scanned the ground, looking for her gun. It was getting dark. She could barely see her feet, much less the weapon. Returning to where Kate stood, Prescott pulled her arms behind her, causing Kate to cry out when pain shot through her shoulder. Then he began to tie her.

Realizing this was the only chance she would have to get away, Kate marshaled all her strength, then slipped her foot behind Prescott's. He realized what she was doing and quickly moved to the side. It was the wrong move. He could have knocked her to the ground or simply hit her wounded shoulder, letting the pain do the job for him. But he reacted instinctively, and when he did, he loosened his grip on Kate's arms. She spun out of his grasp, forcing herself to ignore the searing agony in her shoulder.

Prescott reached for her, another mistake because it pulled him off balance, and Kate drove her knee into his ribs, wishing she'd had a shot at his crotch from this angle. Prescott grunted and fell. At full strength Kate could have seized the advantage at this point, but she was so weak and in so much pain that simply standing was taking all her strength. Prescott had apparently put the gun in his belt at the small of his back, because he was reaching behind him. Kate took a step toward him, and the world started fading to black again. She stopped, waited a moment for the blackness to lift. It did, and instead of finding Prescott aiming the gun at her, she saw him feeling around himself on the ground. When he fell, Kate suddenly realized, he lost the gun. She spotted something on the ground about four feet from him. If it was the gun, she knew Prescott would grab her before she could pick it up, so she charged the object, kicking it away from him. It disappeared into the shadows. Prescott lunged at her.

Kate moved out of the way; then, knowing she didn't have the strength to fight him anymore, she ran. Actually it was a drunken trot. Kate kept expecting to hear Prescott's footsteps behind her. He'd have no trouble catching her at the rate she was going. But no footfalls came.

He's looking for the gun, Kate thought. But no shots rang out either. Kate kept going, trying to move in a straight line. She had no idea where she was heading other than away. Away from Prescott. She was gasping for breath. The pain had stopped coming in sharp jabs of agony. Now it was constant. And excruciating. She kept moving. To stop was to lose. To lose was to die.

Kate heard the pickup start, and for just an instant she allowed herself to hope that Prescott was leaving. But then she heard the truck's motor screaming, and its headlights were illuminating the ground in front of her. They were getting brighter, the sound of the truck louder. He was going to run her down with the truck. Ahead was a fence. Kate forced her legs to keep working. The ground ahead of her got still brighter. Kate nearly tripped when a large rock, a boulder-size hunk of granite, appeared in front of her, but she kept her balance, desperately commanding her legs not to quit. The truck was within fifteen or twenty feet of her now, coming fast. Kate knew there was no way she could make it.

Suddenly she heard an enormous crash, and the beams from the headlights shifted to a new angle. Kate stopped and turned around. The truck had hit the rock, ridden up onto it and high-centered itself, both front wheels off the ground. The engine revved, and the rear tires spun, but they were only digging holes. The pickup was going nowhere.

Kate kept moving. When she reached the barbed-wire fence, she climbed through it, tearing her clothes on the barbs. She kept going in the same direction she'd been heading. Maybe she was heading out into the middle of nowhere; she didn't know. But she staggered forward, away from Mark Prescott. Away.

And then she heard his footfalls, his heavy breathing. He was coming after her on foot.

Kate was out of the illumination from the headlights now. It was fully dark, and there was no moon. Maybe she could lose herself in the night. Her knees nearly buckled. She kept moving. Behind her Prescott cursed. He must have gotten tangled up in the fence.

Kate was barely moving now. A little old lady with a walker could pass her as though she were standing still. The stupid image popped into Kate's head of her asking the little old lady to get help, the old woman turning and throwing her the finger. Prescott had apparently freed himself from the fence. He was gaining on her rapidly. Suddenly something was stinging Kate's left leg in what seemed like a hundred places at once. She nearly screamed. Not from the pain—this was nothing compared to the agony in her shoulder—but from fright. It took her a moment to figure out that she had walked into a cactus. Prescott was still coming, but off to her left now. He hadn't seen her.

Kate stepped away from the cactus. Its spines tugged at her pants leg, then let go. There might be some of the smaller stickers in her flesh, but at the moment that was the least of her worries.

She made herself start walking again. Sweat trickled down her forehead, burned her eyes. The effort it took to move her feet made the act seem comparable to pushing a car on an upgrade. It took everything you had. And maybe a little you didn't know you had.

Then she saw something that made her find one last supply of strength. Off to her right were some lights. She headed for them.

As she approached the lights with agonizing slowness she saw that they came from a house. And beyond it were the lights of moving cars, a highway. Kate didn't know where Prescott was. She hadn't heard him since she walked into the cactus. The house grew larger, and yet it still seemed so far away. She felt like someone lost on a desert, chasing a mirage.

But the house was real. When she finally reached it, she saw that the stoop was cement, the walls wood. She pushed the button that rang the doorbell. A few moments passed, and the door opened.

"Oh, my God," a woman said. "Tish, what happened to you?"

"I'm not Tish," Kate heard herself say.

"Kate?" the woman asked.

But before Kate could respond, the woman pulled her inside. A buzzer sounded, and then Kate was taken through another door. She was being led somewhere, but she never found out where, because her legs just sort of dissolved out from under her, and she sank to the floor.

"Get me some help here," the woman said. "Get Mandy. She'll know what to do."

Kate noted that the woman had red hair. She looked familiar. "Call the police," Kate said.

"I can't," the woman answered. "We still haven't come up with enough money to pay the phone bill."

Kate knew who the woman was now. Chrissie Ann Delaney. This was the battered women's shelter. In addition to Chrissie Ann, other faces were staring down at her. There was a blond woman with a bruised cheek, a freckle-faced woman whose runny eyes stared at her from behind wire-framed glasses, an extremely pretty woman with long and very shiny black hair. There were others as well, but before Kate could focus on them, a small woman with a sunburned nose that was peeling badly pushed her way through the group, saying, "Let me see."

"This is Mandy," Chrissie Ann said. "She's with the volunteer fire department. She's a trained emergency medical technician."

"Get something to put under her feet," Mandy said.

Kate's feet were raised, something shoved under them to hold them up. Then Mandy began cutting away the cloth around Kate's wound. She felt cool air on the spot, the tug of the fabric being gently peeled from her flesh.

"How many times were you shot?" Mandy asked.

"Just once."

"Bullet hit some bone and came out again then. That's good . . . that it's not in you, I mean. And you're not bleeding too badly. Biggest problem you'll probably face is bone chips. Doesn't look like there's any major muscle damage. I'll put a bandage on that to take care of any bleeding. Then all we'll have to do is make sure you don't go into shock while we're waiting for the ambulance to get here." Mandy looked up. "Anybody called one yet?"

"I'll go," said a pale woman with short brown hair.

"I'll go with you," another woman said.

Then, from across the room, another woman said, "There's a man out front."

"Man" had been uttered with all the affection one would

put into a word like carcinoma. This was not a place where men were regarded fondly. Suddenly there was a loud *thud.*

"He's trying to kick the door in," someone yelled.

There was another *thud,* then another, and another. And a splintering sound. A woman screamed something. More sounds of destruction.

"What's going on?" Kate asked, but no one heard her.

She heard what sounded like scuffling, and then there was a crash. Kate raised her head enough to see that the inner door had just been kicked in. Mark Prescott stepped into the room, his eyes instantly finding Kate.

"Hello, Jenna Lee," he said.

Mandy stepped in front of him. "Leave her alone, you son of a bitch," she said.

But Mandy weighed about ninety-eight pounds, and Prescott shoved her aside effortlessly. He walked over to Kate, kicking the thing that had been holding up her feet out from under them. Kate saw that it was a cushion from the couch. He reached down for her.

"No," Chrissie Ann said, and there was something about her voice that made Prescott turn to look at her. She and two other women were holding baseball bats. "We bought these with the last of our money," Chrissie Ann said. "Just in case somebody's husband tried to break in here and beat on his wife a little more."

The three women took a step toward him, and suddenly all the women in the room had joined them. For a long moment Prescott and the women stared at each other.

"What the hell?" Prescott said finally.

With two quick steps he closed the gap between himself and the two women, grabbed Chrissie Ann's bat out of her hands and tossed it across the room.

"You don't want to get hurt, stay the hell out of my way," he said.

He turned around and started back toward Kate. She saw the surprise when a bat hit him squarely in the center of his back. Then another bat hit his legs, knocking them out from under him. Some kind of mass reaction took place then, because suddenly all the women were kicking him or hitting him with their fists.

"Bastard!" one woman shouted. She was on her knees, a fierce expression on her face, lifting her fists and then bringing them down on Prescott like twin hammers.

Kate realized what was happening. To these women who'd been forced to seek refuge here, Prescott had become the symbol of the men who had brutalized them. They were getting their revenge. They were settling the score for all the bruises and broken noses and maybe most of all for having been forced to live in fear. Prescott wasn't resisting. He had passed out.

"Stop!" Kate shouted, but no one heard her. A baseball bat smacked into Prescott's legs.

"Stop it," Chrissie Ann yelled. "Stop it! You're going to kill him!"

Abruptly the women stopped. There was dead silence in the room. The women looked at each other and at Prescott. They didn't seem to know Kate was there. Suddenly someone began to sob.

"I know him," Mandy said. "He works over there at the livestock auction. I took a long walk the other day, just to get out of the shelter and away from everybody, and I came to this big pit. He was driving a loader. There was a dead cow in the scoop. He dumped it into the pit. There were a bunch of other dead cows down there. And an old trailer. I watched him till he drove off in the loader. I don't think he saw me."

"Mandy," Kate said. "Check him. See if he's okay. He's the only one who knows where Tish is."

Mandy got down on the floor, checked Prescott's pulse, his eyes. "He's unconscious," she said. "I don't know how bad he's hurt."

"He's the only one who knows what happened to Tish," Kate said again.

Dying, he'd said. Tish was dying. How long did she have? Days? Hours? Minutes? And then something else he'd said came to her. *Very close*. Tish was very close.

"Mandy," Kate said, "tell me exactly where you saw this pit."

Mandy told her in more detail.

Kate said, "Call the police. Quickly."

"I'll do it," Chrissie Ann said. She started for the door.

"And call an ambulance," Mandy said.

"For Prescott," Kate said. "I don't need one."

"You've got to be treated by a doctor," Mandy said. "A gunshot wound is nothing to fool with."

"No," Kate said firmly. "Not yet." Then to Chrissie Ann, she said, "As soon as you call the police, call Walter List. If he's not at the newspaper, call him at home. And call John Altman. He's a political guy, county chairman. He's probably in the book. Tell them all what's happened and that I need their help right away."

Chrissie Ann looked at her in confusion.

"Please just do it," Kate said. "There's no time to explain."

The loader along with a bulldozer that had been provided by a construction company were working in the pit. Even though it was getting deeper by the moment, to Kate the process seemed painfully slow.

Kate stood with Chrissie Ann, Mandy, Walter List, and John Altman. She was glad she'd sent for List and Altman. Although she had no proof that Chief Colton wouldn't have believed her, there was no way he could simply ignore what she had to say when the editor of the newspaper and the county chairman of a political party were there. And what she was suggesting was indeed bizarre, that Tish might be buried alive in a trailer.

Kate prayed Tish was there, that she was alive, for she knew that if they found the trailer and Tish wasn't in it, she would most likely never see Tish again.

An ambulance and a rescue unit were standing by. Their crews were standing with Colton and two of his men. The pit was about five feet deep now. Kate had no idea how much air a trailer held or how long it would take to use it up. She

271

could only hope she was right, hope the air would be enough. Hurry, she thought. Hurry.

Although Kate was standing, she was barely managing to do so. Mandy and Chrissie Ann were on each side of her, giving her support. If it weren't for her need to know whether Tish was and alive, she would have collapsed long before this.

Altman said, "I've got one of those folding canvas seats in my car—for when I have to go to fund-raising picnics and listen to all the exciting speeches. I'll get it for you if it'll help."

"I'd better not," Kate replied. "If I sit down, I may just decide to give up and lie down."

"Let me know if you change your mind."

"You should be in a hospital," List said.

"I've been trying to tell her that," Mandy said.

The machines had stopped working in the pit; the drivers were holding a conference. Finally they hurried toward the onlookers, and Kate's group merged with Chief Colton's so everyone could hear what was going on.

"We've got to start doing it by hand," the woman who'd been operating the bulldozer said. "The machines are so heavy that we could crush the trailer if we get over it."

Kate's heart sank. Doing it by hand would take forever.

"There's some shovels in my pickup," the man who'd been operating the loader said. Everyone went to help dig except Chrissie Ann, who stayed with Kate.

Cars and pickups were parked around the deepening pit, their headlights on for illumination. The rescuers had been digging for about ten minutes when one of them yelled, "We just hit metal."

Kate started forward, but Chrissie Ann held her back. "You're in no condition to go down there. You'd never make it."

A couple of minutes later a police officer came scrambling out of the pit. "It's not the trailer," he told Kate and Chrissie Ann. "It's a pickup. I'm going to run a computer check on the plate, see who owns it."

The people in the pit had cleared most of the dirt away

272

from the truck by the time the officer hurried back from his patrol car. It passed through Kate's mind that, if she were in charge of the Leap police force, she would buy some hand-held two-way radios. "Truck's registered to Bud Darnell. He's the guy who owns this place. We've been trying to reach him."

The cop hurried back into the pit to pass along his information. Kate wondered whether Chief Colton approved of his subordinate telling the hated female cop from New York City what he'd learned. She also wondered whether Darnell's body was in the truck.

"We found the trailer!" someone shouted up from the pit.

Again Chrissie Ann had to hold Kate back. A few more minutes passed, which to Kate seemed like centuries, and then came another shout:

"She's here! We found her!"

Another few millennia passed before Mandy hollered, "She's okay! She's weak and dazed, but she's okay!"

With her good arm Kate hugged Chrissie Ann, and then she started to cry. A few moments later the twin sisters were both in the ambulance. When the paramedic attending them moved out of the way, they held hands.

EPILOGUE

Kate sat at her desk, doing the paperwork on two Vietnamese gang members who'd been charged with extorting money from an elderly Vietnamese shop owner. Whatever happened to the Oriental custom of respect for one's elders? Kate worked in a room with about fifteen desks in it, old wooden ones whose drawers usually stuck. Rumor had it that they'd been scrapped by the county assessor's office and picked up cheap by the police department. It was January, the worst month of the year anywhere this side of Australia, and it had been snowing on and off all day.

"Hi, Chief," Janice Bernstein said, stepping up to Kate's desk.

"I'm not the chief yet," Kate said. "I haven't even been offered the job."

"Uh-huh. I bet they're bringing you all the way to Texas just to talk over old times."

"It's called a job interview. Lots of people go to them and then don't get hired."

"If they do ask, you going to accept?"

"Depends on how good the restaurant is when they take me out to dinner."

"What if they don't take you out to dinner?"

274

"Would you accept a job from somebody didn't take you out to dinner?"

"The NYPD take you out to a nice place?"

"My standards were lower then."

Janice just shook her head, making her blond curls bounce. Kate had always wished she had hair that would do that. As she walked toward her own desk Janice glanced over her shoulder and said, "See you later, Chief."

Kate didn't know whether she should take the job, assuming it was offered. She didn't know whether she belonged in New York or Texas. There were parts of her that felt at home in both places, parts that felt vaguely uncomfortable in both places. If she knew which parts to oblige, she'd know better how to feel about the possibility of being Leap's police chief.

And then there was the what-I'd-do-if-I-were-in-charge syndrome. Kate had fun with that one, lying in bed at night, thinking about getting hand-held radios and how to divide a town that size into patrol districts and how to handle the resentment some of the men might have over being forced to work for a woman chief. Again she was of two minds. A part of her wanted to jump at the challenge, while another part feared it.

See if you get the offer first, she told herself. Then you can decide what to do.

Tish was fine. She'd arrived at the hospital dehydrated, malnourished, and exhausted, so the hospital had given her plenty of liquids, plenty of food, and plenty of rest. Kate's bullet wound hadn't been too bad. No bones were broken, and the doctors found only one small chip. It didn't hurt anymore, except for an occasional dull ache on days that were cold and damp.

The people digging in the pit that night also found a lot of dead cows and the body of Bud Darnell. The next day the police looked for the two boys Tish had told them about, but they didn't find anything. Two days later a German shepherd owned by a family living half a mile away got into the pit and dug up the body of Joel Rinehart. The police found Danny Larson's body next to the Rinehart boy's.

They found a pipe in Prescott's pickup from which they

got blood and hair samples that matched Bud Darnell. They also found blood and hair belonging to someone else. Eventually they matched these samples up with Boyd Steuben. Mark Prescott had killed four people. And he'd tried real hard to make it six.

Although Prescott had been half dead when they got him to the hospital, he survived. When the doctor told him just how close he'd come, Prescott had said, "No one ever dies." He'd grinned at the doctor. The last Kate heard, he was still grinning at people and hadn't spoken a word to anyone since telling the doctor no one ever died. He was in the loony bin, playing out his fantasies on the inside now, where no one else could see. Maybe he was killing Jenna Lee inside there, over and over again.

Tish's house had been rebuilt. Her insurance company had picked up the tab for everything, including the house's contents, and paid her motel bill while the construction was going on. There had been remarkably few hassles, and Kate thought that if she ever owned a house, she would want the same insurance company.

As far as Kate could tell, Tish had rebounded mentally as well as physically. Kate had called her frequently while the house was being rebuilt, and Tish had been full of excitement, talking about how the house would be better insulated and have better wiring than it had before. The only note of sadness came when Tish had mentioned her lost books, but she had set about replacing most of them, which gave her a chance to visit the bookstores in Austin and San Antonio, and there was nothing Tish enjoyed more than spending hours poking around in bookstores.

Ed Jacobi was the new mayor of Leap. Two days after he took office, Chief Colton resigned. Jacobi formed a committee to seek out a new chief, and John Altman was one of its members. Kate had yet to tell Tish that Altman had called, asking her to come for an interview. She picked up the phone, dialed the operator, and charged the call to her personal long-distance credit card. Tish answered the phone herself.

"Leap public library," she said.

"Hi, sis, it's me. Can you meet me at the Austin airport

the day after tomorrow at one o'clock, or should I rent a car?''

"Of course I'll pick you up," Tish said. "Tell me everything."

And as she started explaining what had happened Kate realized that if she was offered the job she would take it.

ABOUT THE AUTHOR

B.W. Battin is also the author of ANGEL OF THE NIGHT, THE BOOGEYMAN, PROGRAMMED FOR TERROR, THE ATTRACTION, THE CREEP, and SMITHEREENS, all published by Fawcett. A former TV writer and news director, he now lives in New Mexico.

Fawcett brings you
Edgar Award winning author

KENN DAVIS

M000034109

FOODS
THAT MAKE YOU
LOSE
WEIGHT
FAT-FIGHTING FOODS
FOR A HEALTHIER YOU

Gayle Alleman, M.S.,R.D.
Susan Male Smith, M.A.,R.D.
Densie Webb, Ph.D.,R.D.

PUBLICATIONS INTERNATIONAL, LTD.

Contributing Writers

Gayle Alleman, M.S., R.D., holds degrees in both alternative and conventional nutrition. She manages the nutrition education program for Washington State University Cooperative Extension and teaches nutrition at Bastyr University and other colleges. She is also a freelance writer and speaker in the area of food, nutrition, and health, specializing in holistic nutrition to promote optimum health.

Densie Webb, Ph.D., R.D., is a nutrition writer and registered dietitian. She is editor of *Environmental Nutrition* newsletter and has written several nutritional analysis books. She also contributes to consumer magazines such as *American Health, Woman's Day,* and *Family Circle.* Dr. Webb has also served as health editor of *McCall's* magazine.

Susan Male Smith, M.A., R.D., is a registered dietitian and nutrition consultant who writes for such consumer magazines as *Family Circle, Redbook, McCall's, American Health,* and *Baby Talk.* In 1994, she was nominated for a James Beard Journalism Award. Ms. Smith is assistant editor of *Environmental Nutrition* newsletter.

Cover photo credit: **R. Pleasant/FPG International**

Note: Neither the Editors of Consumer Guide and Publications International, Ltd., nor the authors, consultants, editors, or publisher take responsibility for any possible consequences from any treatment, procedure, exercise, dietary modification, action, or application of medication or preparation by any person reading or following the information in this book. The publication of this book does not constitute the practice of medicine, and this book does not attempt to replace your physician or your pharmacist. Before undertaking any course of treatment, the authors, consultants, editors, and publisher advise the reader to check with a physician or other health care provider.

CONTENTS

Introduction 5
Amaranth 39
Apples 41
Apricots 43
Artichokes 45
Asparagus 47
Bananas 49
Barley 51
Beans & Peas, Dry 53
Beets 57
Blackberries 59
Bran Cereal 61
Bread, Whole-Wheat 64
Broccoli 68
Brussels Sprouts 71
Buckwheat 73
Bulgur 75
Cabbage 77
Carrots 80
Cauliflower 83
Corn 85
Dates 87
Fish 89
Garlic 93
Grapefruit 96
Grapes 98
Greens for Cooking 100
Greens for Salads 103
Herbs & Spices 106
Kale 109

– CONTENTS

Kiwifruit 111
Lemons & Limes 113
Lentils 115
Mangoes 117
Melons 119
Milk, Skim 122
Millet 125
Mushrooms 127
Nuts & Seeds .130
Oats 134
Onions 138
Oranges & Tangerines 141
Parsnips 143
Pasta 145
Pears 148
Peas 150
Peppers 152
Pineapple 155
Plums 157
Popcorn 159
Potatoes 161
Prunes 164
Pumpkin 166
Raspberries 168
Rice 170
Soybeans 173
Spinach 176
Squash 178
Strawberries 180
Sweet Potatoes 182
Tomatoes 184
Wheat Germ 186
Yogurt, Nonfat 188
Index 190

INTRODUCTION

By opening this book, you must be ready to lose weight. Congratulations! That decision will mean a healthier you, and we will help you get there. By dropping those extra pounds and keeping them off, you'll not only feel better and more energetic, you'll also lower your risk of health problems such as heart disease, diabetes, and certain cancers. And the best part is, the foods you'll be eating are delicious and filling.

In the search for the "perfect" diet, there are many choices. The most successful ones are not diets at all, but actually new ways of eating that become a part of your normal lifestyle. You can lose weight easily—almost magically—when you enjoy foods that promote weight loss by their very nature: foods that are low in calories and fat, rich in fiber and nutrients. This book will show you how to use those foods to make tasty and satisfying meals.

Don't be fooled by diet schemes that make unrealistic demands such as drinking a liquid diet, focusing on one food group, fasting or starving yourself, or requiring unbalanced meal plans. To succeed at long-term weight loss, it's important to learn new ways of eating that you enjoy enough to continue doing. If you "diet" for awhile, restricting whatever foods the current fad diet suggests, but then return to your old eating habits, the weight will come crashing back on—just what you don't want.

The best plan for achieving a healthy weight and maintaining it is to gradually change the foods you eat. This book will help you do just that! The food profiles that appear later will show you how to choose foods that can help you get trim. The profiles also provide tips on how to select and prepare these fat-fighting foods. There's no gimmick about them—they're chock full of satisfying complex carbohydrates, brimming with fiber to give you a feeling of fullness, and rich in nutrients to keep you naturally healthy, so your body doesn't crave more food than it needs. Let's discover just how these wonder foods do this.

A Diet that's More than Skin Deep

Compared with the standard American diet, the eating plan you are about to embark on is much healthier. It encourages you to eat a variety of complex carbohydrates such as fruits, vegetables, legumes, and whole grains with a few dairy and protein foods to keep your body in tip-top shape. You'll get full enough on these foods that you won't feel the need to reach for those boxes and packages of processed crackers,

Healthy Side Effects

By basing your diet on the foods in this book you can lose weight AND:

Lessen your chances of heart disease, heart attack, and stroke

Reduce your risk of colon cancer

Lower your blood cholesterol levels

Lessen your chance of developing adult-onset diabetes

Get all the benefits of disease-fighting phytochemicals

cookies, and snack foods. This not only makes it easier to keep calories under control, but your wallet will appreciate it, too. Processed foods are expensive; the natural, whole foods in this book are not. So you end up trimming your waistline while fattening your wallet at the same time.

For years, researchers have noticed that people who eat less meat or who are vegetarian are not only slimmer than their meat-eating counterparts, they also have less incidence of heart disease, heart attacks, and stroke. The eating strategies in this book will let you enjoy these health benefits too, since the plan is primarily vegetarian with the inclusion of fish and low-fat dairy products. Fish provides heart-healthy omega-3 fatty acids, which will be discussed in detail shortly.

The fiber in these foods will not only provide satiety and quell your appetite, they will also fight colon cancer at the same time. Standard American fare, which is usually very low in fiber, is linked to many intestinal disorders, such as diverticulosis and colon cancer. Studies repeatedly show that people who eat more fiber, especially the insoluble type, have a lower incidence of colon cancer. So as you embark on this high-fiber eating plan, you're protecting your colon, too.

The other kind of fiber, soluble fiber, lowers blood cholesterol. As you enjoy the foods in this book, you'll be driving your cholesterol level down and protecting your blood vessels and heart. In fact, this eating plan can help reverse clogged arteries, as you eat more soluble fiber each day.

Both kinds of fiber help to slow the absorption of sugars—natural or added—which means they help stabilize blood glucose levels. A carefully monitored, fiber-rich diet is sometimes enough to enable a person with diabetes who only takes oral

THE FACES OF FIBER

Insoluble Fiber: This is what you traditionally think of as fiber—as in bran cereal and bran muffins. This kind of fiber can be likened to a sponge. When you eat fiber then add water, it swells and gets soft, just like a sponge. The increased bulk pushes on your intestines, creating the rhythmic movement needed to evacuate. And a softer stool is easier on your intestines. Foods rich in insoluble fiber include bran cereals, brown rice, corn and popcorn, fruits (especially apples, berries, and pears), whole grains, and vegetables (especially asparagus, kale, peas, potatoes, and spinach).

Soluble Fiber: This is the gummy stuff that gunks up the works. But that's its job. As its name suggests, soluble fiber dissolves in water. In doing so, it forms a gel-like substance, which captures bile acids and cholesterol in its wake. Foods rich in soluble fiber include barley, dried beans and peas, fruits (especially apples, figs, oranges, plums, and rhubarb), lentils, oats, and vegetables (especially broccoli, cabbage, carrots, okra, and potatoes).

medication to stop doing so. Dropping extra pounds can prevent or even reverse adult-onset diabetes.

Phytochemicals are "plant chemicals," substances that a plant naturally makes that happen to be beneficial to those who eat them. Many phytochemicals are antioxidants, which help protect cells from cancer, protect blood vessels from tiny injuries that start atherosclerosis, and protect eyes from developing cataracts. Other phytochemicals help boost immune function and still others improve the health and integrity of your blood vessels. A plant-based diet is rich in phytochemicals.

STOP THE DIETING

Repeated weight loss and gain carries health risks that you don't need, such as a greater likelihood of heart disease than if you had never lost weight at all. And as you may have heard, it is harder to lose weight each time you do it. Here's why: If your "diet" includes skipping meals, fasting, or eating less than 1,000 calories per day, it lowers your body's metabolic rate. The metabolic rate is the amount of energy, or calories, a resting, awake body needs just to breathe and stay alive. If you don't eat on a regular basis or eat too little, the body thinks it's starving, so it begins to shut down and conserve resources. This is part of the human body's evolutionary design, slowing down to survive periods when food is scarce. Your body doesn't know you're dieting; it thinks the world is on the brink of a famine, so it switches into "starvation mode" to conserve fat stores. The lower your metabolic rate goes, the more difficult it is to lose weight. In fact, just skipping breakfast every day lowers your metabolic rate by four to five percent, resulting in a one-pound weight gain every seven weeks without eating any extra food.

To make matters worse, when this process happens, your body hangs on tightly to its fat stores, because those are concentrated sources of energy it might need if the famine lasts a long time. So instead, it sacrifices protein from your muscles to make the energy it needs. As you lose muscle—the body's main energy burners—your metabolic rate drops even lower, beginning a downward spiral. What you want to do instead is preserve lean muscle tissue, because it has a higher metabolic rate, and get rid of fat tissue, which has a low metabolic rate.

To prevent your body from switching into this "starvation mode" and burning up muscle, you need to eat at least 1,200 calories per day divided up into at least three meals. You'll probably need to eat about 1,200 to 1,800 calories, depending on your size and sex, to get all the vitamins and minerals you need and not feel hungry or deprived.

Many people try to diet by purchasing nonfat convenience foods and snack foods. Never before have there been so many nonfat or reduced-fat products in the supermarket, yet the rate of overweight and obesity in America is at an all-time high. This is due in part to the plethora of non- and low-fat foods that are stripped of their fiber and loaded with sugar and, consequently, calories. These simple carbohydrates, or sugars, give you calories but few nutrients—what you want instead are complex carbohydrates, which are starches. It's much better to eat nature's low-calorie foods, such as grains, vegetables, legumes, and fruits, than to fill up on sugar-laden, fiber-deficient processed foods.

Some popular diet plans advocate eating large amounts of protein and quite a bit of fat while reducing calories overall. It's the calorie reduction that makes these plans work...for a little while. Plus the fact that since your body is starving for carbohydrates, it is forced to break down muscle, which has a considerable amount of water in it. It's usually not long before the dieter gets so tired of the limited foods that they "fall off the wagon" and go back to their old eating habits.

A high-protein diet can carry other risks with it, too. Excessive amounts of protein on a daily basis can cause dehydration, tax the kidneys, and send you into ketosis—a condition in which your body is struggling to make the carbohydrates it needs for energy since you aren't eating enough of them. Ketosis can upset the body's delicate pH balance, and if severe enough, it can lead to coma and even death. Carbohydrates are the clean fuel your body's engine wants to burn; protein is like dirty fuel that can gum up your engine.

Your body needs carbohydrates not only to provide you with energy to walk, think, problem solve, love, play, and do all your daily activities, but also to burn up fat. The body must have some carbohydrates to combine with the fat being released from fat cells in order to turn that fat into energy. It's this simple:

Fat + carbohydrates = energy

Fat with no carbohydrates = dangerous ketones

Most diet plans are strict regimes that don't let you experience making healthy food choices for yourself. Learning and practicing new eating behaviors is the only way you'll be able to maintain weight loss.

SHED POUNDS THIS WAY

So the best way to get rid of fat cells is to pump your body full of unrefined, complex carbohydrates, add a little protein and fat, and mix with physical activity. It's the perfect recipe for weight loss, and the eating plan and foods in this book will help you do just that. You'll get not only plenty of carbohydrates, but you'll learn how to combine them to get good quality protein, plus a little fish for those heart-healthy omega-3 fatty acids, and a few servings of skim milk or nonfat yogurt every day to keep your bones rich in calcium.

The Food Guide Pyramid (shown on the following page) promotes this type of eating. Just by looking at it, you can tell that basing the diet on the bottom of the Pyramid, the grain foods, is the way to go. Eat more of what you see the most of—grains, vegetables, and fruits. Eat less of the foods you see less of—dairy and protein—these are concentrated and your body doesn't need large amounts of them. Make sure your choices are low in fat and added sugar, and you're on your way to successful weight loss.

Notice that the Food Guide Pyramid recommends a number of servings from each food group. This may seem like a lot of food until you realize the size of a serving (see the chart "What Is a Serving" on the following page). For instance, a small apple, about 2½ inches in diameter, makes up one serving of fruit—the large apples you usually buy may actually be almost two servings. A half cup of rice or pasta or half of an English muffin equals one serving of grains. Since your aim

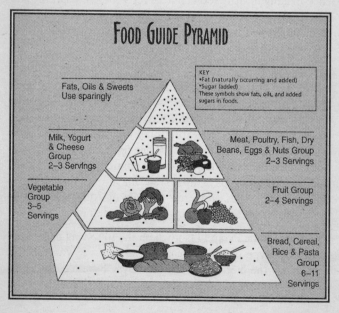

FOOD GUIDE PYRAMID

KEY
•Fat (naturally occurring and added)
•Sugar (added)
These symbols show fats, oils, and added sugars in foods.

Fats, Oils & Sweets
Use sparingly

Milk, Yogurt
& Cheese
Group
2–3 Servings

Meat, Poultry, Fish, Dry
Beans, Eggs & Nuts Group
2–3 Servings

Vegetable
Group
3–5
Servings

Fruit Group
2–4 Servings

Bread, Cereal,
Rice & Pasta
Group
6–11
Servings

WHAT IS A SERVING?

The Food Guide Pyramid indicates how many servings of each food group we should aim for, but what kind of serving are they talking about? Eleven servings of grains sounds like an awful lot. Relax. What the USDA people mean by a serving is not necessarily what you and I sit down to eat. You're probably eating two to three "servings" of pasta at a sitting without even realizing it. On the other hand, many people think they eat more fruits and vegetables than they do. A few spoonfuls of peas or a couple of lettuce leaves do not a serving make. What does?

Bread, Cereal, Rice, and Pasta (Grains)
1 slice bread
1 oz ready-to-eat cereal (see package for cup equivalent)
½ cup cooked cereal, rice, or pasta

Fruit
1 medium piece of raw fruit (an apple, banana, orange, peach, or plum, for example)
½ cup of cut-up raw fruit
½ cup of canned fruit
¾ cup of fruit juice

Vegetables
1 cup raw, leafy vegetables
½ cup cut-up raw vegetables
½ cup cooked vegetables
¾ cup vegetable juice

Meat, Poultry, Fish, Dry Beans, Eggs, Nuts
2–3 oz cooked, lean meat, poultry, or fish

May substitute for 1 oz meat:
½ cup cooked dry beans
1 egg
2 Tbsp. peanut butter

Milk, Yogurt, Cheese
1 cup milk or yogurt
1½ oz natural cheese
2 oz processed cheese

Fats and Sweets
Use sparingly

is to lose weight, check out what makes up a serving, and aim for the low end of the range for each food category.

Here's the number of servings we recommend for weight loss. Make sure the serving sizes are no larger than what the Food Guide Pyramid indicates.

Breads, Cereals, Pasta	6 servings
Vegetables	3–4 servings
Fruits	2 servings
Dairy products (nonfat)	2 servings
Fish or protein foods	2 servings

Here's one way to put these servings together to get a balanced, weight-reduction meal plan every day. It provides you with a lot of flexibility to choose the foods that you like and as much or as little variety as you enjoy.

Breakfast—Eat breakfast within two hours of getting up, every day, to get your metabolism revved up. As you choose foods from each of these groups, make sure your choices are low in fat and added sugar.

1 bread, cereal, or grain (such as toast or cereal)

1 fruit (such as 1 piece or ½ cup of juice)

1 dairy (such as nonfat milk or sugar-free nonfat yogurt)

Snack—Eat one serving of a low-fat, low-sugar bread, cereal, or grain (such as ½ bagel).

Lunch—Eat one or two servings from these food groups, as indicated. Make low- or nonfat choices.

2	bread, cereal, or grain (such as a sandwich or tortillas)
1	protein (such as baked fish or beans)
2	vegetable (lettuce and tomato on sandwich or in tortilla, carrot sticks)
1	fruit (or save until dinner)
1	dairy (or save until afternoon snack)

Snack—Eat one serving of a low-fat, low-sugar bread, cereal, or grain (such as reduced-fat graham crackers) or save until dinner. If you saved your second serving of dairy from lunch, enjoy it now.

Dinner—Eat one or two servings from these food groups, as indicated. Make low- or nonfat choices.

1 or 2	breads, cereals, or grain (2 servings if you saved one from afternoon snack)
1	protein (such as spicy black beans)
2	vegetable (such as steamed vegetable and salad)
1	fruit (if saved from lunch; try a baked apple or pear for dessert)

Snack—Don't do it. Brush your teeth instead. The sweetness of toothpaste often alleviates late-evening cravings.

You can mix these categories around if you like, as long as you don't exceed the total number of recommended servings. Keep in mind your metabolism will run at a higher rate if you eat several small meals and snacks throughout the day, instead of going for long periods of time without food, making your body wonder if starvation is imminent. Learn to lis-

TRICKS OF THE TRADE

Use some of the following tried-and-true tips to enhance your new eating style and make it even more effective for you:

Shop when you're not hungry.

Store tempting foods out of sight; leave preferred foods in sight.

Use smaller plates and bowls.

Set your fork down between bites.

Chew thoroughly and swallow before taking another bite.

Eat mindfully, not in front of the TV or while reading.

Twice a week, write down everything you eat and drink in a 24-hour period. Does it match your plan and goal for number of servings from each group?

Plan nonfood rewards for following your new eating style.

ten to your body's cues; eat when you're hungry without putting it off. If you're not hungry between meals, skip the snacks and add those portions in somewhere else. It's better to eat the majority of your food earlier in the day, rather than close to bedtime, so that it is processed before you go to sleep.

Prepare complex carbohydrates in ways that are tasty to you. Check the food profile pages for new ideas. You'll lose interest in your new eating plan if you don't like the way your food tastes. Treat yourself to a new cookbook or a cooking magazine that focuses on light or low-fat eating.

BENEFITS OF CARBOHYDRATES

Complex carbohydrates, such as those found in whole grains, legumes, fruits, and vegetables, help to jump-start your metabolism. A number of research studies using both animals and people show that a high-carbohydrate diet boosts T_3 levels. In fact, some research indicates that carbohydrates are a very important regulator of T_3 production in humans. T_3 is a thyroid hormone that's responsible for revving up the body's base metabolic rate. There's also some scientific evidence that carbohydrates boost your body's production of norepinephrine. Norepinephrine is another hormone that stimulates metabolic rate. So by eating complex carbohydrates, you can help prevent your metabolism from becoming sluggish. Exercise works much the same way, but you'll learn more about that later.

One of the major benefits of complex carbohydrates is that they're naturally low in calories. Carbohydrates have only four calories per gram. Compare that to the nine calories in every gram of fat and you begin to get the picture. See for yourself in this chart that shows the amount of calories found in a typical serving, versus the amount of calories in a processed form of the food:

Fruit (1 piece)	60 calories	Fruit pie (1 piece)	300 calories
Vegetables (½ cup raw)	25 calories	Potato chips (20)	215 calories
Bread (1 slice)	80 calories	Glazed doughnut	242 calories
Legumes (½ cup)	115 calories	Ground beef patty	250 calories

Of course, what you put on your carbohydrates makes a difference, too. If you add sauces full of butter, cream, or cheese, that's going to drastically increase the calorie count. If you slather butter onto your bread or baked potato or douse your salad with an oily or creamy dressing, that, too, will ruin the low-calorie benefit of those foods. Likewise, turning your fruit into pie will dramatically change its calorie count for the worse. Instead, just follow the serving suggestions listed in the food profile section to help you enjoy the true taste of foods such as juicy pineapple, sweet corn, fresh baked whole-wheat bread, and spicy bean dishes.

Another exciting benefit of eating complex carbohydrates is that you automatically boost your fiber intake. It is recommended that everyone eat 20 to 35 grams of fiber each day. You'll want to aim for the higher end of that range. Fiber is especially helpful when you're trying to lose weight because it helps you feel full, so you don't overeat. Fiber slows the rate at which your stomach empties and takes a while to work its way through your digestive system. It also enables the sugars in your meal to be absorbed slowly. Both of these feats help that feeling of fullness last just a little longer, which, in turn, means your appetite is delayed; you don't feel hungry again so soon. Don't fret too much about overdoing fiber. It takes more than 75 grams per day before adverse effects set in, and it's hard to eat that much fiber.

It's absolutely essential that as you begin to eat more fiber-rich complex carbohydrates, you also begin to drink more water. Without enough fluid, the extra fiber will backfire on you and make you gassy and constipated. Drink at least six 8-ounce glasses of water every day, and drink other beverages, too. Coffee and black tea don't count since they have diuretic properties, making you lose water.

A CALORIE IS A CALORIE—OR IS IT?

One of the secrets behind eating a diet rich in complex carbohydrates is that the body processes carbohydrates differently than it processes fat. It's easy for the body to break down fat, absorb it, and store it. Nature arranged for the body to store fat without much ado, so that it has plenty of stored energy in case of unexpected scarcity or famine.

Carbohydrates and protein, on the other hand, are more difficult for the body to break down, absorb, process, store, and use. It's a much more complicated chemical process to get energy out of carbohydrates and protein than it is to get energy from fat.

As we've mentioned, fat contains nine calories per gram, whereas carbohydrates and protein each contain only four calories per gram. But some scientists wonder whether these numbers should be adjusted. Since it doesn't take much energy for the body to use fat, researchers speculate that it may actually have a caloric value that is closer to eleven calories per gram. And because carbohydrates take a lot of energy to process, their true caloric value might be closer to three calories per gram. Although the official numbers have not been changed yet, the underlying principal still remains: A diet that is high in complex carbohydrates, low in fat, and accompanied by some protein can help you shed unwanted pounds.

Here's an example to illustrate how this works. When you eat 100 calories of carbohydrates, you only get about 74 calories out of that food by the time the body processes it. In other words, it takes 26 calories to process that 100 calories you ate. On the other hand, when you eat 100 calories of fat, you get about 97 calories by the time the body processes it; it takes only 3 calories to process 100 grams of fat. Quite a difference, isn't it? That's why fat makes you fat; it's not only concentrated, carrying more than twice the amount of calories as carbohydrates, it doesn't take much work or energy for the body to process it. It's a simple matter of math: The more carbohydrates and less fat you eat, the fewer calories you'll have to add to your waistline.

IS THE "NEGATIVE CALORIE EFFECT" TRUE?

Generally speaking, nutrition experts say that the body uses about ten percent of all the calories it consumes just to process food. This is called the thermic effect of food. In light of the previous discussion, we see how this rate can get bumped up. By eating more carbohydrates and less fat, the thermic effect of our meal will be more than ten percent. So this is how the negative calorie effect works. Complex carbohydrates take nearly 25 percent of the energy they give just to be processed.

Some people believe that the "negative calorie effect" means that you'll spend more energy eating and processing a food than you'll get from it. This isn't quite true because you'll always spend just a percentage of the total carbohydrates you eat on processing them. The fallacy comes from the fact that some very-low-calorie foods may come close to that. For instance, one cup of chopped romaine lettuce has 9 calories, mostly from carbohydrates, but you'll net only 6.75 calories from it. Close to zero, but not quite, and certainly not a negative number.

Moderation in All Things

Besides filling up on complex carbohydrates, it's important to make low-fat choices. Foods high in fat, such as nuts or avocados, should be eaten only occasionally; eat high-fat snack foods only rarely.

In your zeal to lose weight, keep in mind that you need some fat each day, and not all fats are bad. In fact, the body has to have dietary fat to provide you with the essential fatty acids that cannot be made inside the body. Without essential fatty acids, skin may become dry, cholesterol and triglycerides in the blood may skyrocket, and blood pressure may rise. Essential fatty acids help your body make substances called prostaglandins that keep all these processes in balance.

Fat in the diet is also the only way we get the essential fat soluble vitamins A, E, and K. The body cannot make these vitamins, so they must come from the diet.

The minimum amount of fat recommended in the diet is 10 to 15 percent of calories. Research indicates that lowering fat intake to 10 percent of calories does not increase weight loss or improve cholesterol levels any more than having fat at 15 percent. A diet that contains 15 percent fat is easier to prepare and easier to maintain over the long run—you're more likely to adopt such a diet as a lifestyle change and not consider it a "diet."

Now that people have been eating low-fat diets for a number of years, scientists are able to study the effects of such diets. They're finding that if people eat less than ten percent of calories from fat for very long, they actually experience adverse effects:

- Higher blood cholesterol levels

- Higher blood triglyceride levels

- Higher blood sugar levels

- Higher insulin levels

These four factors set the stage for heart disease. People who thought that if cutting some fat from the diet was good, then cutting even more was better, actually ended up in poorer health. The body likes moderation in all things, and this apparently includes fat. So in your eagerness to drop the pounds, don't drop all of the dietary fat.

Figuring out how much fat is in a food when it has a label is easy—that will be explained shortly—but for foods that you make or that don't have labels on them, think about what the typical ingredients are. For instance, muffins are nothing short of small cakes. They're packed with fat and sugar, even though they don't look like it. Anything that has oil, butter, cheese, cream, or other fats added to it are suspect.

WATCH THE FAT

Not only is it necessary to maintain some fat in the diet, but the type of fat you eat is important, too. Here's the lowdown:

Saturated Fats—These fats are called "saturated" because chemically speaking, all of their bonds are saturated with hydrogen. But what's important to remember is that saturated fat is one of the least healthful of the fats. Saturated fat causes the blood's cholesterol level to rise, which can cause clogs in important arteries. Saturated fat is found in animal foods such as meat and dairy products, as well as in vegetable

FERRETING OUT FAT

Simple ways to cut the fat:

- Make the move to skim milk. If you can't do it "cold turkey," switch first to two percent, then one percent, then skim.

- Build your meals around whole grains, beans, and vegetables. Include a variety of grains and plant foods, like barley, bulgur, couscous, oats, maybe even getting adventurous with millet, quinoa, and teff.

- Experiment with low-fat and fat-free foods on the market. Some work; some don't. In general, low-fat (one or two grams of fat per serving) cookies and crackers fare better than fat-free cookies and crackers. The fat-free cheeses are more of a gamble; some lose their ability to melt. Fat-free dressings and condiments are a good bet because you don't eat them solo, so you're less likely to miss the fat.

- Substitute plain, nonfat yogurt for sour cream.

- Use evaporated skim milk instead of cream in recipes.

- Switch to a "diet" or "light" margarine for everyday uses. But don't substitute them in baked goods because you'll be disappointed with the final product.

- Stick to whole-grain breads for everyday uses. For variety, supplement that with bagels, English muffins, French and Italian bread, pita bread, and corn tortillas.

- Use the "napkin test" on baked goods: Lay the item on a napkin; if you see a grease stain, the item is loaded with fat. Croissants are notoriously high in fat, as are most muffins, biscuits, scones, doughnuts, and pastries.

oils that make you think of warm places, such as coconut and palm kernel oil. Steer clear of saturated fats as much as possible. They should make up no more than a third of the total fats you eat.

Monounsaturated Fats—*Mono* means one, and these fats have one place in their structure where there's a double bond without hydrogen. What this means to you is that it's healthier. In fact, monounsaturated fats are considered to be the most healthful of the fats. They do not cause a rise in cholesterol levels the way saturated fats do; in fact, they help to lower the low-density lipoprotein (LDL), or "bad," cholesterol level in your blood. Monounsaturated fats are predominant in olive oil and canola oil.

Polyunsaturated Fats—*Poly* means many, and polyunsaturated fats have many double bonds where there is no hydrogen. However, they are only a moderately healthy fat. It's true that they do not cause a rise in cholesterol like saturated fat does, but there are other problems. Polyunsaturated fats' double bonds are susceptible to attack by free radicals, which can destroy some of their bonds and allow rancidity to set in. Free radicals damage not only the polyunsaturated fat does, but also cells. High intakes of this type of fat have been associated with an increased rate of cancer. Additionally, these fats tend to lower your high-density lipoprotein (HDL), or "good," cholesterol levels even though they also lower your "bad" LDL cholesterol levels. Polyunsaturated fats are the main type of fat in most vegetable oils, such as safflower, soybean, and corn oils. Use this type of fat sparingly.

Hydrogenated Fats—These fats are polyunsaturated fats that have had hydrogen forced onto the double bonds, making

YOUR DAILY FAT BUDGET

Here's a chart that shows what your daily fat budget would be if you maintained 15 percent of calories from fat.

Average calorie intake	Daily Fat Budget (for 15% fat), in grams
1,000	17
1,200	20
1,400	23
1,600 (Many women, most older adults)	27
1,800	30
2,000	33
2,200 (Active women, teen girls, most men)	37
2,400	40
2,600	43
2,800 (Teen boys, active men)	47

them a saturated fat. And the body isn't fooled; it treats them just like saturated fat, causing cholesterol levels to rise. Research shows that hydrogenated fats—sometimes called *trans* fats, short for *trans* fatty acids—disrupt cell membranes and cause cellular damage. These fats are linked to cancer and decreased immune function. Be diligent about limiting the amount of hydrogenated fats you eat. Unfortunately, this can be rather difficult, since food manufacturers put it in most processed and packaged products.

Essential Fats—These are the essential fatty acids your body cannot make. These fats promote a favorable cholesterol ratio in your blood. (You're aiming for HDL cholesterol levels to be more than 35 mg/dL, LDL cholesterol levels to be less than 130 mg/dL, and total cholesterol levels to be less than 200 mg/dL). In addition, the prostaglandins that essential fats prompt the body to make will also keep blood pressure in line, keep the blood from clotting too easily, and keep a lid on inflammation. The omega-3 essential fatty acids are abundant in fish, especially fatty fish such as salmon, tuna, albacore, herring, sardines, mackerel, bluefish, and Atlantic halibut. The omega-6 fatty acids are found in most vegetable oils, particularly safflower, corn, and sunflower oils.

Despite the "good" and "bad" fats, remember: All fats carry nine calories per gram and count in your total fat intake. Even if all your daily fat intake comes from monounsaturated fat, you still need to limit it to 15 percent of calories. Fat—even the beneficial kind—adds up in terms of calories.

SORTING IT OUT WITH LABELS

When comparing products to decide which will fit into your low-fat, high-carbohydrate eating plan, the Nutrition Facts portion of the label will come in handy.

First, look at the serving size. Is this about how much you eat at one time? If not, you'll need to adjust the numbers on the label accordingly. For instance, if the serving size is one-half cup but you normally eat about one cup at a time, then you'll need to double all the numbers on the label.

Here are some tips on what to look for on food labels:

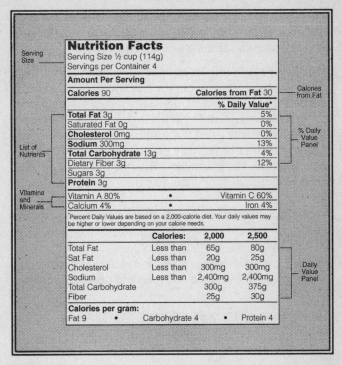

Nutrition Facts	
Serving Size ½ cup (114g)	
Servings per Container 4	

Amount Per Serving	
Calories 90	**Calories from Fat** 30

	% Daily Value*
Total Fat 3g	5%
Saturated Fat 0g	0%
Cholesterol 0mg	0%
Sodium 300mg	13%
Total Carbohydrate 13g	4%
Dietary Fiber 3g	12%
Sugars 3g	
Protein 3g	

Vitamin A 80%	•	Vitamin C 60%
Calcium 4%	•	Iron 4%

*Percent Daily Values are based on a 2,000-calorie diet. Your daily values may be higher or lower depending on your calorie needs.

	Calories:	2,000	2,500
Total Fat	Less than	65g	80g
Sat Fat	Less than	20g	25g
Cholesterol	Less than	300mg	300mg
Sodium	Less than	2,400mg	2,400mg
Total Carbohydrate		300g	375g
Fiber		25g	30g

Calories per gram:			
Fat 9	•	Carbohydrate 4	• Protein 4

Labels around the figure: Serving Size · Calories from Fat · % Daily Value Panel · List of Nutrients · Vitamins and Minerals · Daily Value Panel

Total Fat tells you how many grams of fat are in one serving. The percentage to the right, called the *% Daily Value*, tells you how much of your daily fat budget is used up by one serving of the food, if you typically eat 2,000 calories and aim to get 30 percent of your calories from fat. You, however, are on a slightly different track because you're aiming for about 15 percent of calories from fat and your calorie intake may be considerably lower than 2,000. It's easiest just to use the grams of total fat and keep them tallied throughout the day.

Labels are also required to list the amount of saturated fat in a product. Remember to choose foods that are low in saturated fat, since this is not a healthy type of fat.

Some labels voluntarily list amounts of monounsaturated and polyunsaturated fats. You can use this information to choose products that are higher in monounsaturated fats and lower in polyunsaturated fats. On labels that do list all three types of fat, you may notice that if you add up the number of grams of all three types of fat, they equal less than what is listed under *Total Fat*. The hidden amount of fat you don't see listed is the hydrogenated, or *trans* fats. You can also check the

---

Label Lingo

Finally, manufacturers are being held accountable for those claims they make on food labels. Here is what they have to mean:

Low calorie—40 calories or fewer per serving

Light or Lite—⅓ fewer calories or 50% less fat than the regular version

Fat free—less than 0.5 gram of fat per serving

Low fat—3 grams or less of fat per serving

Low cholesterol—20 milligrams or fewer per serving

Lean—fewer than 10 grams total fat, 4 grams saturated fat, *and* 95 milligrams cholesterol per serving

Extra lean—fewer than 5 grams total fat, 2 grams saturated fat, *and* 95 milligrams cholesterol per serving

---

ingredient list to choose foods that have little or no hydrogenated fat. Ingredients are listed in order of weight, from greatest to least.

If you need to watch your salt or sodium intake, pay attention to that portion of the label, too. Reduced-fat foods often have more salt added to them to make up for the flavor that the fat contributed.

Next, check out the amount of fiber in the food. Dietary fiber is listed beneath *Total Carbohydrates*. Remember all the benefits of fiber, and choose foods that have as much as possible. For example, when choosing a loaf of bread, select one that offers two or more grams of fiber per slice, rather than one that offers only one or none.

Also beneath the *Total Carbohydrates* section you'll find sugars. If the product does not contain fruit or dairy products, then you can be assured that the amount listed comes from added sugars. Whether it's white table sugar—known as sucrose—or corn syrup or honey, they all provide calories and few nutrients. Keep your total added sugar intake below 50 grams per day. Products containing milk and primarily fruit don't count, because the natural sugars in these items are combined with any added sugars that might be present. It's impossible to know from labels on these foods how much sugar is added and how much occurs naturally.

Pick Your Protein

Yes, even complex carbohydrates can provide all the protein you need. It's just a matter of know-how when it comes to combining them. Cultures all around the world have done this well for thousands of years. Meat was not always available and, in more modern times, may not be affordable. Yet people are strong, healthy, and robust, consuming little or no meat.

Complex carbohydrates contain not only starches, but substances called amino acids, which are the building blocks of protein. There are many amino acids, but the body is unable to make eight or nine of them, depending on your stage of life. So these particular amino acids are considered essential and must be obtained from food.

The problem is that most foods contain an abundance of certain essential amino acids while they lack other essential ones. So foods must be combined or eaten together in order to provide the body with all the essential amino acids in good proportions. Don't despair, though; it's much easier than it sounds.

By combining these foods it's usually very easy—and delicious—to get the amino acids your body needs. Even if you don't combine the appropriate foods within one meal, it's OK to combine them within the same day or even over a period of a couple days. Amino acids float throughout your system all the time, and they'll wait a day or two to hitch up with just the right one they need.

Most Americans eat twice as much protein as they need, so don't be concerned about getting enough. As long as you include beans, grains, and dairy foods, you'll be set. Even athletes don't need huge amounts of protein. Muscle strength and endurance is based on repeated exercise and consumption of complex carbohydrates. Protein merely builds the matrix that the body fills with carbohydrates to make muscles grow.

AMINO ACID ARITHMETIC

Combine these foods to make complete proteins your body can use:

Legumes with Grains

> Legumes include all dry beans, peanuts, split peas, and lentils. Examples of this combination are: pinto beans with corn tortillas, black beans with rice, peanut butter on bread, tofu (made from soybeans) with rice, lentil or split pea soup with wheat or rye bread, black-eyed peas with cornbread.

Grains with Dairy

> For instance, cereal and skim milk, toast with nonfat yogurt, sandwich and skim milk.

Legumes with Seeds and Nuts

> Top a bean dish with a sprinkle of toasted almonds or sesame seeds, make humus with garbanzo beans and sesame seeds, or mix up a tofu and cashew stir-fry to serve over rice.

Too much protein can actually be detrimental, as discussed earlier. Protein, especially from animal products, can tax the kidneys, make you dehydrated, and even leach calcium from your bones. Animal proteins are also often accompanied by quite a bit of fat and cholesterol, things you're trying to cut down on. Meeting your protein needs with mostly complex carbohydrates is the healthy and weight-dropping way to go.

As you probably know, nuts are high in fat, but mostly monounsaturated fat, the healthy kind. Still, you don't want to overdo it. Nuts are rich in protein and minerals, so it's a good idea to occasionally include small amounts. For example, toast chopped nuts in a dry skillet until they're fragrant and golden brown, then sprinkle over rice. Limit your intake of nuts to two tablespoons per day.

Fish is another excellent protein source that goes well with many complex carbohydrates. Are you one of those people who say, "I don't like fish"? Perhaps it would help if you tried a very mild variety, such as cod. Find a cookbook on fish at your public library or bookstore and fix fish in ways you have never tried before. Who could resist baked cod encrusted with toasted bread crumbs and served with lemon and dill? It's important to include fish because of the heart-healthy omega-3 fatty acids they contain. In fact, the fattier the fish, the more of these precious fats you'll get. So this is one arena in which it's alright to eat moderate amounts of a high-fat food—as long as the fat is naturally in the fish and not added fat. Eat fish in 3- to 4-ounce serving sizes, which is about the size of a deck of cards, several times per week.

The omega-3 fatty acids in fish can actually benefit your weight-loss plan because they help the body metabolize fat well—so that too much fat doesn't end up in your bloodstream on its way to be deposited into fat cells.

You Can Still Enjoy Eating Out

It's fun to eat out, and any eating plan that doesn't make room for you to do so is not one you're likely to stick with for long. By studying the menu and asking your server a few questions, you can get an enjoyable meal that fits into your eating regime.

First, scan the menu for vegetarian or fish entrees. The vegetarian entree will undoubtedly be rich in complex carbohydrates, but beware of what might be added to it. Identify added ingredients (see chart below) such as a cream sauce, as in fettuccine Alfredo. If available, choose a red sauce, which will be based on tomatoes rather than on cream or butter.

Be aware, too, of words used to describe how the item is prepared. Is it fried or baked? Sauteed or steamed? Choose preparation methods that use little or no fat. Ask your server questions if it's not clear on the menu, or if it doesn't say. Some people are too shy to ask, but keep in mind that the server is there to serve you—you're paying for their time as well as the food so you might as well make use of their knowledge.

Make special requests when eating out. For instance, ask for salad dressing on the side, or if you've ordered anything from pancakes to a baked potato, ask for the butter and other top-

BE A MENU SLEUTH

Be on the lookout for ten telltale words that, when translated, loosely mean "fat":

Alfredo	Creamy
Batter-dipped	Crispy
Béarnaise	Stuffed
Béchamel	Supreme
Breaded	Tempura

pings on the side. Anytime you can, get the sauce or toppings served separately so that you can control how much you eat of them. Dipping your fork first into the salad dressing then forking a bit of lettuce will still give you plenty of flavor with hardly any fat. If you find it difficult to make special requests, practice at home before going out.

Planning ahead is instrumental in eating out, too, whether you're going to a restaurant, a banquet, or a friend's house. Think about what's likely to be served, and plan the things you'll look for to eat. Advance planning is a remarkable way to prevent temptation and overeating. For example, you might plan to eat tossed salad if you expect to splurge on dessert. It's often a good idea to eat a low-calorie snack beforehand to dull your appetite. Also plan what you'll say to politely decline food that doesn't fit into your eating pattern, especially if it's friends or relatives who will be offering.

Fast food can occasionally fit into your complex carbohydrate plan, too. Just be picky about your choices. When given the chance, choose a fast food restaurant that has reasonable options. For instance, at some Mexican fast food places, there are bean and rice burritos or wraps available—just beware of sauces. Fast food fish places typically offer a baked or grilled version in addition to breaded and fried. Quick teriyaki places are ideal, as you can get heaps of rice and steamed vegetables instantly. At a hamburger restaurant, it gets a little tougher— sometimes a salad and bread are the best you can find.

Whichever fast food restaurant you choose, be sure to ask for a nutrition brochure. Most chains have them behind the counter. The brochure will tell you not only which items are full of carbohydrates, but also the fat and calorie content of each menu item so that you can make an informed choice. Collect the brochures from the fast food restaurants you typically go to, look them over, and plan your order options at each of them so you'll be ready when the time comes.

ACTIVITY: THE FINAL INGREDIENT

You've heard it before. You know it's true. But now there are more reasons than ever to get moving!

For starters, did you know that for several hours after physical activity your metabolic rate stays elevated? That's right. If you take a brisk walk or go cycling while your spouse stays home, then come back and you both watch TV, you'll be burning more calories than your spouse for several hours, just because you exercised. Activity raises your metabolic rate while you're doing it, plus it takes one to three hours for it to return to previous levels.

Another bonus: Whenever you're active, you're building lean muscle tissue. Even if you're just walking around the block a few times, you're toning your muscles more than if you were reading a book. The more muscle you have, the higher your metabolic rate will be. If you're getting more muscular and your spouse is flabby, and you're both sitting around playing cards, you're going to be burning more calories than your spouse is, automatically, just because you have more muscle tissue.

Whenever you can raise your metabolic rate, you're promoting weight loss. The rate at which you burn calories while at rest is one of the biggest burners of calories all day long. So if you can pump it up to be burning more even when you're not active, you'll shed pounds more easily.

Assuming your goal is to lose weight, it's important to do aerobic exercise as well as strength-training exercises. Aerobic activity, such as brisk walking, cycling, jogging, swimming, and so forth, helps you lose fat tissue. During the first 20 minutes of aerobic activity, your body burns mostly stored carbohydrates and just a little bit of fat. But at the 20-minute mark, something wondrous happens. Your body shifts gears and begins to burn more fat. Visualize it this way: at the 20-minute mark, an alarm goes off and your control center commands fat cells to open up and release their load. And they do! You start burning mostly fat after 20 minutes of exercise. So the best way to get rid of unwanted fat is to keep moving for more than 20 minutes to take full benefit of your body's fat-burning command mechanism.

How do you know if you're exercising aerobically? Aerobic exercise is when the heart and lungs can still keep up with the oxygen demands of the muscles. If you're breathing rate is increased but you're still able to talk while you're exercising—without too much huffing and puffing—you're in an aerobic state. If you overdo it and go beyond this point, you push your body into anaerobic metabolism, and you don't burn any fat at all. So aim for a more moderate pace, and keep talking. Be sure to check with your doctor before undertaking any new exercise regime.

The other type of activity that will make it easier for you to drop unwanted pounds is to do strength training. You can even do this in front of the TV! Strength training builds and tones muscles. And remember, the more muscle tissue you have, the more calories you'll burn even when resting because of the boost it gives to your metabolism.

How Many Calories Do You Burn?

Weight (in pounds) ...	100	130	150	170	190	210
			Calories Burned Per Hour*			
Basketball	414	486	564	636	714	786
Card playing	78	90	102	114	132	144
Cycling (9.4 mph)	300	354	408	462	516	570
Eating	72	84	96	108	120	132
Fishing, active	186	222	252	288	318	354
Running (11.5 minutes per mile)	408	480	552	630	702	774
Swimming, slow crawl stroke	384	456	522	594	660	732
Tennis	330	384	444	504	564	624
Walking, normal pace	240	282	324	372	414	456

*These are estimates; the actual number of calories you burn during these activities may vary.

Start with one-pound weights and your favorite show. Purchase weights or use plastic one-gallon milk or water jugs partially filled with water or sand. Stand in front of the TV and lift the weights out to the side, over your head, in front of you—any way that's comfortable. (Stop if you have pain.) Start out with three sets of 12 to 15 repetitions. When you can do those easily, increase the weights slightly. Continue until you build up to three- or five-pound weights for each hand. Increased repetitions will tone, whereas increased weight will build muscle. Both are important.

To develop your leg muscles, get ankle weights or use resealable plastic bags each filled with a pound of rice or sand. Strap on the ankle weights or use rubber bands to attach the weighted plastic bags. Do sitting and standing leg lifts, 12 to 15 repetitions, three times. Again, these can be done painlessly as you concentrate on your favorite TV show. Increase the weights as you're able, building up over the course of several weeks or months.

Alternate aerobic and strength-training exercises on an every-other-day basis. Muscles need a day in between workouts to recuperate; so alternating activities is ideal.

GET GOING!

Now that you know the basics, it's time to look over the food profiles and begin to plan your new eating habits. Clean out your cupboards, give away foods you no longer want, and make a list of all the delicious new foods you can stock up on. Eat simply, stay active, and enjoy!

AMARANTH

This ancient grain of the Aztecs has been recently rediscovered by Westerners, although you'll probably need to visit a health-food store or check a mail-order catalog to find it. Technically, it's not a grain; it's the fruit of a plant. And that's the reason it contains a more complete protein, and more of it, than other traditional grains. It has a distinctive sweet but peppery taste—one that many people prefer combined with other grains, for a more mellow flavor.

HEALTH BENEFITS

Even when just a little is included in a recipe, the benefit is worth it. For anyone cutting down on meat, amaranth offers a bonanza of near-complete protein. It's not missing the amino acid lysine, as many grains are. It is also much richer in iron, magnesium, and calcium than most grains, so it can help keep anemia and osteoporosis at bay. It excels as a source of fiber, mostly insoluble, which is of help in reducing the risk of a variety of diseases, including certain cancers and digestive-tract conditions.

SELECTION AND STORAGE

Amaranth is a tiny, yellow grain. It can be bought as a whole grain ("pearled" amaranth), as a flour, or as rolled flakes. It's also found as an ingredient in cereals and crackers. Expect to pay more for it; amaranth is not widely grown and is difficult to harvest, so it is more expensive than other grains. But, remember, you get a lot of nutritional bang for your buck.

Keep amaranth in a tightly closed container to prevent insect infestation. And store in a cool, dry location to prevent the fat in it from turning rancid.

Preparation and Serving Tips

This versatile grain can be cooked in liquids and eaten as a porridge or pilaf. It can even be popped like corn. But because of its strong flavor, you may like it best combined with other grains. For baking, amaranth must be combined with another flour, such as wheat, because it contains no gluten by itself.

To cook: Cook one cup of grains in three cups of water (yield: three cups). Bring to a boil, then simmer for 25 minutes. The final consistency will be thick, like porridge. If you want to cook it with another grain, such as oatmeal or rice, just substitute amaranth for about a quarter of the other grain, then cook as you would for that grain.

To pop: Stir a tablespoon at a time over high heat, in an ungreased skillet, until the grain pops, like corn. This can be used as a breading for fish or chicken or to top salads and soups.

AMARANTH
Serving Size: ¼ cup dry, uncooked

Calories	183	Calcium	75 mg
Protein	7.1 g	Copper	0.4 mg
Carbohydrate	32.4 g	Iron	3.71 mg
Fat	3.2 g	Magnesium	130 mg
Saturated	0.8 g	Phosphorus	223 mg
Cholesterol	0 mg	Potassium	179.5 mg
Dietary Fiber	5.1 g	Zinc	1.6 mg
Sodium	10.5 mg		

APPLES

Chances are, you've only tasted a few of the many varieties of apples because supermarkets offer a small selection that typically includes Cortland, Granny Smith, McIntosh, and the most popular—Red Delicious. Regardless of the type, apples are a perfect addition to your fat-fighting diet since they provide ample amounts of fiber. Enjoying a fiber-packed apple, especially before a meal, is a good way to curb your appetite. It's also a great low-fat snack when you're on the run.

HEALTH BENEFITS

Even though it's not bursting with nutrients like some of the other fruits, an apple a day may do more than keep the doctor away. For starters, apples are a good source of vitamin C, an antioxidant, and research has shown that antioxidants may help prevent the formation of some cancers. They have heart-healthy effects, too—apples are loaded with pectin, which may keep blood cholesterol levels in check. Plus, when it dissolves in water, soluble fiber creates a gummy, gel-like substance that binds bile acids and draws cholesterol out of the bloodstream. Soluble fiber's stickiness also ties up carbohydrates, keeping blood sugar levels on an even keel. And apples may contribute to a healthy smile and fresh breath by stimulating your gums and promoting saliva production.

SELECTION AND STORAGE

A few varieties, like Cortland, Jonathan, and Winesap, are all-purpose apples. But in general, choose apples for their intended purpose. For baking, try Golden Delicious, Rome

Beauty, Cortland, Northern Spy, or Rhode Island Greening; they deliver flavor and keep their shape when cooked. For just plain eating, you can't beat tart Macouns or award-winning Empires.

If possible, buy apples from an orchard. Apples prefer humid air, so the crisper drawer of the refrigerator is the best place to store them. Some varieties will keep until spring, though most get mealy in a month or two. Golden Delicious must be enjoyed right away before their skins shrivel.

Preparation and Serving Tips

Always wash and scrub your apples. Though Alar, the infamous pesticide, is no longer used by apple growers, supermarket apples are often waxed, which seals in pesticide residues that may be on the skins. Peeling apples will remove the film but also a lot of the fiber. All apples will brown when cut, but the rate varies among varieties. To prevent browning, sprinkle a little lemon juice on cut surfaces.

Apple, Fresh
Serving Size: 1 small

Calories	81	Protein	<1 g
Fat	1 g	Dietary Fiber	3 g
Saturated Fat	<1 g	Sodium	1 mg
Cholesterol	0 mg	Vitamin C	8 mg
Carbohydrate	21 g		

APRICOTS

Despite their size, fresh apricots are well-suited for low-fat diets because they are particularly rich in fiber, especially insoluble, which absorbs water and helps contribute to a feeling of fullness. But their fragrant aroma alone makes fresh apricots a dieter's delight.

HEALTH BENEFITS

Apricots are also abundant in good-for-your-heart soluble fiber, which dissolves in water to form gels that bind with bile acids, forcing your body to draw cholesterol from the bloodstream to make more bile acids. But the real heart-healthy news about apricots is that they are brimming with beta-carotene—an important antioxidant that's a member of the vitamin A family. Researchers have linked beta-carotene–rich foods to the prevention of certain cancers (especially lung), cataracts, and heart disease.

Since this fruit's season is short and sweet, canned and dried apricots offer a delicious alternative to fresh. Canned apricots, unfortunately, are not nutritionally equivalent to the fresh variety; sugar is often added during the canning process, and the high heat used in the process cuts the amount of beta-carotene and vitamin C in half.

The drying process concentrates the carbohydrates, so a single serving contains a hefty amount of calories. In fact, a half-cup serving of dried apricots yields three times the calories of a single serving of fresh. So read the labels and pay attention to serving sizes to make sure your portions don't play a role in a calorie overload.

APRICOTS, FRESH
Serving Size: 3 medium

Calories....................51	Dietary Fiber ....3 g
Fat..............................1 g	Sodium......................1 mg
Saturated Fat.........0 g	Vitamin A............2,769 IU
Cholesterol................0 mg	Vitamin C...................11 mg
Carbohydrate ....12 g	Potassium ....313 mg
Protein......................2 g	

SELECTION AND STORAGE

Apricots are delicate and must be handled with care. One of the easiest ways to preserve these fragile gems is for growers to pick them before they are ripe. So you'll need to ripen the fruit for a day or two at room temperature before you can enjoy them. But don't pile them up or the pressure will cause them to bruise as they ripen. Once they are ripe, store them in the refrigerator.

For the best flavor and nutrition, look for plump, golden-orange apricots that are fairly firm or yield slightly to thumb pressure. Avoid those that are tinged with green or have a pale yellow color; they were picked too soon.

PREPARATION AND SERVING TIPS

Be gentle when washing fresh apricots or they'll bruise. To reap the fat-fighting benefits of apricots, it's best to eat them skins and all. But if you would rather peel them, here's an easy way to get the job done fast: Dip the apricot in boiling water for 30 seconds, then immediately peel with a sharp knife under cold running water.

ARTICHOKES

Fibrous artichokes are a dieter's delight—low in fat and loaded with fiber. Yet many would-be artichoke lovers shy away from this delicate, buttery-flavored vegetable since they don't know how to handle it. Actually, artichokes require little prep work; the time-consuming step is the process of eating—that's why this odd vegetable should be included in your low-fat diet. Because it's labor-intensive to consume, you are forced to eat at a leisurely pace, giving your stomach time to tell your brain it's full, which may prevent you from overeating.

HEALTH BENEFITS

Artichokes' high fiber content is also a bonus for your digestive tract. Insoluble fiber is nature's laxative, absorbing water and creating bulk to move things along. Artichokes are also a super source of folic acid, which is especially important for women during their childbearing years, as this vitamin helps prevent neural-tube birth defects. New research has also linked long-term deficiencies of folic acid to an increased risk of developing heart disease.

SELECTION AND STORAGE

Green globe artichokes are grown in the United States. Baby artichokes come from a side thistle of the plant; artichoke hearts are the meaty base. A Jerusalem artichoke is not an artichoke at all; it's an unrelated root vegetable.

Look for heavy artichokes with a soft green color and tightly packed, closed leaves. Bronzed or frosted leaf tips signal delicate flavor. Avoid moldy or wilted leaves.

Artichoke, Fresh, Cooked
Serving Size: 1 medium

Calories	53	Sodium	79 mg
Fat	<1 g	Vitamin C	9 mg
Saturated Fat	0 g	Folic Acid	53 mcg
Cholesterol	0 mg	Iron	2 mg
Carbohydrate	12 g	Magnesium	47 mg
Protein	3 g	Manganese	<1 mg
Dietary Fiber	6 g	Potassium	316 mg

Store artichokes in a plastic bag in the refrigerator; add a few drops of water to prevent them from drying out. (Do not wash artichokes before storing them.) Although best if used within a few days, they'll keep for a week or two if stored properly and handled gently.

PREPARATION AND SERVING TIPS

Wash artichokes under running water. Pull off outer, lower petals and trim the sharp tips off of the outer leaves. Boil, standing upright in the saucepan, for 20 to 40 minutes, or steam for 25 to 40 minutes or until a center petal pulls out easily.

Artichokes are versatile; they can be served hot, at room temperature, or cold. Though they're best served as appetizers, they are well suited for a variety of uses including dips and sauces. Or stick to plain lemon juice. Butter, of course, is a no-no for those who want less flab and more muscle.

ASPARAGUS

This vegetable has garnered a reputation for being elitist, probably because it's rather expensive when bought out of season. But if you're like many people, you may swear it's worth its weight in gold. Gourmet or not, you can't beat the nutrition you get for what asparagus "costs" calorie-wise. At less than four calories a spear, you can't go wrong unless you unwisely top it with Hollandaise sauce. Asparagus not only has few calories, but it also has major flavor, which is often missing in many of the new low-fat and fat-free products in the supermarkets. Most people like to savor their spears, a practice that extends the dining experience and so may prevent you from overindulging in other foods.

HEALTH BENEFITS

Asparagus is ideal for young women; it's a winner when it comes to folic acid—a vitamin that helps prevent neural-tube birth defects. Two major antioxidants—beta-carotene and vitamin C—are also abundant in asparagus. By neutralizing damaging particles in our bodies like smog and cigarette smoke, antioxidants are thought to be major contenders in the fight against heart disease, cancer, and cataracts.

SELECTION AND STORAGE

Spotting the first asparagus in stores is a sign of early spring. Look for a bright green color; stalks that are smooth, firm, straight, and round, not flat; and tips that are compact, closed, pointed, and purplish in color. Thick stalks are fine, but choose stalks of similar size so they'll cook at the same rate.

Asparagus, Fresh, Cooked
Serving Size: 4 spears

Calories....................15	Dietary Fiber ....1 g
Fat..............................<1 g	Sodium.......................3 mg
Saturated Fat.........0 g	Vitamin A................498 IU
Cholesterol.................0 mg	Vitamin C ....16 mg
Carbohydrate ....3 g	Folic Acid ....59 mcg
Protein........................2 g	Potassium ....186 mg

Keep asparagus cold or the stalks will deteriorate, losing flavor and vitamin C. Wrapped loosely in a plastic bag, the stalks will keep for almost a week. To enjoy asparagus year-round, blanch the spears the day you buy them, wrap them tightly in foil, and freeze for up to 12 months.

PREPARATION AND SERVING TIPS

Snap off the whitish stem ends. Add these to soup stock instead of just tossing them out. Boil, steam, or microwave asparagus, but avoid overcooking it. When cooked correctly, the spears should be crisp-tender and bright green. Overcooked spears turn mushy and a drab olive green. Simmer for three to five minutes only. For more even cooking, stand stalks upright in boiling water, with the tips sticking out of the water, for five to ten minutes. This way, the tips steam as the stalks cook. Microwaving takes two to three minutes in a dish with a quarter-cup water. You can serve asparagus hot, warm, or cold. For a change of pace, try adding cut-up asparagus to your next stir-fry or pasta dish.

BANANAS

Bananas come in their own perfect package, so there's no mess, no fuss—they're the perfect take-along snack. No wonder they're one of the most popular fruits in the United States. Admittedly higher in calories than most other fruits, their calories are nearly fat-free calories.

HEALTH BENEFITS

Bananas are loaded with potassium, and researchers now believe that adding potassium may play a stronger role in the control of high blood pressure than restricting salt. Magnesium is also abundant; many researchers think this mineral helps keep blood pressure levels in check, too.

Generally, fruit is a poor source of vitamin B_6, but bananas are the exception; a single serving has more than 30 percent of the RDA. Vitamin B_6 helps to keep your immune system performing at its peak, and recent studies have found that, like a deficiency of folic acid, a long-term deficiency of B_6 may increase your risk of heart disease.

SELECTION AND STORAGE

There are different types of bananas, but Cavendish, the yellow bananas, are the most familiar. To appeal to a variety of cultures, supermarkets are now expanding their selections to include red bananas and plantains, those seemingly underripe bananas that never lose their mossy green color.

Most bananas ripen after picking, and as they do, the starch in them turns to sugar. So the riper they are, the sweeter they

BANANA, YELLOW
Serving Size: 1 (8½-inch) banana

Calories.................105	Sodium......................1 mg
Fat...............................1 g	Vitamin C ....10 mg
Saturated Fat.......<1 g	Vitamin B$_6$ ....1 mg
Cholesterol................0 mg	Magnesium ....33 mg
Carbohydrate ....27 g	Manganese ....<1 mg
Protein.......................1 g	Potassium ....451 mg
Dietary Fiber ....2 g	

are. Look for plump, firm bananas with no bruises or split skins. Brown spots are a sign of ripening. If your banana skins are tinged with green, allow them to ripen at room temperature (don't refrigerate unripe bananas; they'll never ripen); refrigerate them once they are ripe to stop the process. They'll turn an unsightly, but harmless, black color.

PREPARATION AND SERVING TIPS

Yellow bananas are great on their own, but when mashed, they make a great low-fat, nutrient-packed spread for toasted bagels. Sprinkle lemon juice on banana slices to keep them from darkening. To salvage bananas that are too ripe, combine them in a blender with orange juice and skim milk for a healthful "smoothie"—a great take-along treat for dashboard dining. For the kids, try frozen banana pops: Peel and cut a banana in half; insert a craft stick into each half. Dip the bananas into orange juice, roll them in wheat germ, and freeze them until they are firm.

BARLEY

When baked in casseroles, stuffed into vegetables, or served in place of rice, this flavorful, fiber-packed, Middle Eastern grain curbs your appetite for higher-fat fare—the bulking ability of fiber fills you up and reduces the likelihood that you'll overindulge in fat and calories.

HEALTH BENEFITS

You may have heard about oat bran and its cholesterol-lowering ability; new research suggests that barley may have a similar effect on cholesterol, too. Barley contains the same cholesterol-fighting soluble fiber, beta-glucan, found in oat bran and dry beans. Farmers are jumping on the bandwagon and are growing varieties—such as hulless and waxy barley—that are super-high in beta-glucan. The soluble fiber pectin fights cholesterol, too.

Barley is rich in insoluble fiber as well; the whole, hulled form contains more than whole wheat. As insoluble fiber absorbs water, it adds bulk and speeds intestinal contents through your body, which may reduce your risk of developing colorectal cancers since contact between harmful substances and your intestinal wall is limited. And there's another bonus—insoluble fiber may help keep digestive disorders, like constipation and hemorrhoid flare-ups, at bay.

SELECTION AND STORAGE

Whole, hulled barley—brown, unpearled—is the most nutritious. It has twice the fiber and more than twice the vitamins and minerals of pearled. It's available in health-food stores.

Scotch barley, or pot barley, is refined less than the pearled type, so part of the bran's goodness remains.

Pearled barley is the easiest variety to find. While nutritionally inferior to the other two types, it boasts decent fiber and iron, and it is certainly not devoid of nutrients.

Store pearled and Scotch barley in airtight containers in a cool, dark location for up to one year; nine months for all other varieties.

PREPARATION AND SERVING TIPS

To cook: Add one cup of pearled barley to three cups of boiling water (or one cup of whole barley to four cups of boiling water). Simmer, covered, for 45 to 55 minutes (1 hour to 1 hour 40 minutes for whole barley).

As barley cooks, the starch in it swells and absorbs water, making it soft and bulky. This makes it the perfect thickener for soups, stews, and traditional Scotch broth soup. Barley can be successfully substituted for rice in almost any recipe. It has more flavor than white rice though it isn't as strong as brown rice—the perfect compromise.

BARLEY, PEARLED, COOKED
Serving Size: ½ cup

Calories	97	Dietary Fiber	4 g
Fat	<1 g	Sodium	2 mg
Saturated Fat	<1 g	Niacin	2 mg
Cholesterol	0 mg	Iron	1 mg
Carbohydrate	22 g	Manganese	<1 mg
Protein	2 g		

BEANS & PEAS, DRY

If you had to pick one food to be stuck on a desert island with, it would have to be beans. They'd provide you with almost complete nutrition and you wouldn't have to worry about offending anyone. Yes, beans can be gassy, but there are ways around that. So don't let their "explosive" nature scare you away from some of the best fat-fighting nutrition around.

When your diet's based on beans and other complex carbohydrates, you're more likely to follow a low-fat, high-fiber diet. Complementing beans with other low-fat types of protein, like rice, makes them a great substitute for high-fat protein sources like meats. Beans are also filling enough to stave off hunger. The low-fat, high-fiber nature of a bean-centered diet means that chances are good that you'll lose weight eating this way.

HEALTH BENEFITS

Not only are beans low in fat and high in quality protein, but they also have the added bonus of soluble fiber's disease-preventing qualities. The soluble fiber in beans dissolves in water, trapping bile acids in its gummy goo. This lowers blood levels of damaging LDL cholesterol, especially if LDL cholesterol levels were high to begin with, without compromising the level of protective HDL cholesterol.

Because beans are singled out for their soluble fiber, you may not realize they also provide substantial insoluble fiber, which helps combat constipation, colon cancer, and other conditions that afflict your digestive tract. How? Insoluble fiber absorbs water, which swells the size of stool, puts pressure on the

Fiber Content of Selected Dry Beans & Peas
(grams per ½ cup serving, cooked)

Kidney beans	6.9	Great Northern beans.	5.0
Butter beans	6.9	Black-eyed peas	4.7
Navy beans	6.5	Chick-peas	
Black beans	6.1	(garbanzos)	4.3
Pinto beans	5.9	Mung beans	3.3
Broad (fava) beans	5.1	Split peas	3.1

intestines, and moves everything along faster. To help combat the gas problem—caused by indigestible carbohydrates—let your body get used to eating beans. Start slowly, eating only small amounts at first, and try to eat them when you know you'll be active afterward; it helps break up the gas.

As for vitamins and minerals, beans are a bonanza of folic acid, copper, iron, and magnesium—four nutrients that many nutrition experts agree we don't get enough of. Indeed, most dry beans and peas are rich sources of iron—ideal for people who don't eat meat.

The nutritional content of most beans is very similar to the black beans we've chosen as a representative example. (Soybeans are in a class by themselves, so are listed separately.) Exceptions? White beans have almost twice the iron of black beans, while kidney beans are somewhere in between. And fiber does vary. Most differences, however, are minor.

Selection and Storage

Dry beans are available year-round, are inexpensive, and can be found in any well-stocked supermarket (check the ethnic food section). You may need to visit a health-food store for more exotic varieties. Packaged or loose, select beans that look clean, are not shriveled, and are uniformly sized with even color and uncracked hulls. Discard any pebbles, as well as any beans with pinholes, a sign of insect infestation. Some varieties of beans are available canned. They offer convenience but are rather mushy and very salty, although researchers have found that rinsing canned beans under cold running water for one minute eliminates up to 60 percent of the added salt.

If stored properly, dried beans last for a year or more. If packaged, keep them in their unopened bag. Once open, or if you bought them in bulk, store them in a dry, airtight glass jar in a cool, dark spot. Store cooked beans in an airtight container for up to one week in the refrigerator or freeze for up to six months.

Preparation and Serving Tips

When cooking dry beans, it's best to plan ahead; they do not qualify as "fast" food. Before soaking or cooking, sort through the beans, discarding shriveled or discolored beans, pebbles, and debris; then rinse the beans under cold running water. It's best to soak beans overnight for six to eight hours. This softens the beans, reduces the cooking time, and removes the gas-promoting undigestible carbohydrates. But if you haven't planned far enough ahead, you can quick-soak them (although you'll end up with less-firm beans): Put the beans in water and boil for one minute, turn off the heat, and let them stand in the same water for one hour.

After soaking, discard any beans that float to the top, throw out the soaking water (which contains the gas-producing indigestible carbohydrates), and add fresh water to the pot before

BLACK BEANS, COOKED
Serving Size: ½ cup

Calories 113	Thiamin ....<1 mg
Fat.............................<1 g	Folic Acid ....128 mcg
Saturated Fat.......<1 g	Copper ....<1 mg
Cholesterol.................0 mg	Iron...............................2 g
Carbohydrate ....20 g	Magnesium ....60 mg
Protein.......................8 g	Manganese ....<1 mg
Dietary Fiber ....6 g	Phosphorus............120 mg
Sodium......................1 mg	Potassium ....306 mg

cooking. Add enough water to cover the beans by two inches. Bring to a boil, then simmer, covered, until tender—about one to three hours, depending on the bean variety. They're done when you can easily stick them with a fork.

Beans are notoriously bland-tasting, but that makes them versatile. They take on the spices of any ethnic cuisine. Many other cultures have perfected the art of combining beans with grains or seeds to provide a complete protein. For instance, try Mexican corn tortillas with beans and tomatoes, or classic Spanish rice and beans, or traditional Italian pasta e fagioli (a pasta and bean soup). You can't beat black bean soup with complementary corn bread on the side.

BEETS

Beets have only been appreciated as fat-fighting root vegetables in modern times. Before that, the beet greens were favored, most likely for their medicinal qualities, over the actual beet. Maybe back then, people were put off by the red urine and stools that sometimes appear after eating beets; some people inherit an inability to break down the red pigment in beets, so it passes right through their systems and is excreted. It's harmless enough, but you may want to lay off beets a few days before your next doctor's visit. Beets contain a wealth of fiber—half soluble and half insoluble. Both types play roles in fighting fat.

HEALTH BENEFITS

Beets are particularly rich in folic acid, calcium, and iron. Consuming adequate amounts of folic acid during the child-bearing years is a must for women; a deficiency in this critical nutrient has been linked to neural-tube birth defects. But this important vitamin is critical to life-long health for men, women, and children, because long-term deficiencies have been linked to heart disease and cervical cancer, too.

SELECTION AND STORAGE

Your best bet for beets is to choose small, firm ones that are well-rounded and uniformly sized for even cooking. The freshest beets are those with bright, crisp greens on top. The skins should be deep red, smooth, and unblemished. Thin taproots, the roots that extend from the bulb of the beets, are good indicators of tenderness.

BEETS, FRESH, COOKED
Serving Size: 2 beets

Calories.................31	Dietary Fiber.............3 g
Fat...........................<1 g	Sodium.....................49 mg
Saturated Fat........0 g	Folic Acid ....53 mcg
Cholesterol.............0 mg	Magnesium ....37 mg
Carbohydrate ....7 g	Manganese.............<1 mg
Protein.....................1 g	Potassium ....312 mg

Once home, cut off the greens because they suck moisture from the beets. Leave two inches of stem to prevent the beet from "bleeding" when cooked. Keep beets in a cool place; refrigerated, they'll keep for a week or two.

PREPARATION AND SERVING TIPS

Wash fresh beets gently, or broken skin will allow color and nutrients to escape. For this reason, peel beets after they're cooked. Watch out for beets' powerful pigments; they can stain utensils and wooden cutting boards. Microwaving retains the most nutrients. Steaming is acceptable but takes 25 to 45 minutes.

Beets have a succulent sweetness because, unlike most vegetables, they contain more sugar than starch. Beets taste great on their own, but if you'd like to enhance their delicious flavor, add a dash of salt or pepper.

BLACKBERRIES

Anyone who's experienced summer in the country knows the joys of picking berries in the hot sun. What luck that these luscious berries are good for you, too. These juicy, plump berries are low in fat and calories; in fact, a cup has approximately 70 calories. So it's easy to fill up on these flavorful berries without sabotaging your weight-loss goals.

HEALTH BENEFITS

These delightful berries are packed with pectin. By dissolving in water and forming gels that tie up blood sugar and cholesterol, pectin helps keep blood-sugar levels on an even keel.

Two thirds of blackberries' fiber is insoluble, the kind that keeps your digestive tract running smoothly. It absorbs water and swells, speeding stool and toxins through your system. Blackberries also contain a monster amount of manganese, which is important for keeping bones strong.

SELECTION AND STORAGE

Blackberries are often confused with black raspberries and related hybrids. The loganberry is a cross between a blackberry and a raspberry. The boysenberry is a cross between a blackberry, a raspberry, and a loganberry.

Indulge in blackberries in season. Though never truly economical, they are less expensive in summer. Look for berries that are glossy, plump, deep-colored, firm, and well-rounded. The darker the berries, the riper and sweeter they are. Avoid baskets of berries with juice all over the bottom—a sure sign of crushed berries. Refrigerate blackberries, but don't wash them until you're ready to eat them; otherwise they'll get moldy. Use within a day; they do not last long. For a mid-winter pick up, try freezing the berries: Arrange them in a single layer on a baking sheet, cover, and freeze. Once they are frozen, place them in an airtight container and thaw them as needed.

PREPARATION AND SERVING TIPS

Do not overhandle blackberries; their cells will break open and they will lose juice and nutrients. Wash them gently under running water, drain well, and pick through to remove stems and berries that are too soft.

Who can resist a simple bowlful of fresh berries for breakfast or a snack? You may need to sprinkle them with a little sugar if they are too tart, but go easy or you'll lose their natural low-calorie benefit. And forgo the cream—try skim milk. Served over sorbet, blackberries make a divine low-fat dessert. Don't forget the jams. Use them instead of butter or margarine on toast and muffins for the perfect fat-fighting spread.

BLACKBERRIES, FRESH
Serving Size: ¾ cup

Calories	56	Dietary Fiber	4 g
Fat	<1 g	Sodium	0 g
Saturated Fat	0 g	Vitamin C	23 mg
Cholesterol	0 mg	Manganese	1 mg
Carbohydrate	14 g	Potassium	212 mg
Protein	1 g		

BRAN CEREALS

You might not look forward to it, but you still pour that bowl of bran cereal every day to keep yourself regular. Little did you know your bowlful was fighting fat, too.

First, let's define what we mean by bran. Bran is simply the outer layer of any kernel of grain, where most of the fiber and nutrients reside. Here, we're just focusing on wheat bran cereals. (Oat bran is covered in the entry on oats.)

Now, back to fighting fat. Fiber, especially the insoluble kind, fills you up. It has an amazing capacity to absorb water and expand. This bulk fools your belly into thinking you've eaten a lot, so it can shut down your hunger signals.

Moreover, bran fiber requires a bit of chewing. That gives your body time to realize you're full before you shove in more. You complete the fat-fighting breakfast scene if you pour skim milk over that bowl of bran, mix in fresh fruit, and have a glass of orange juice on the side.

HEALTH BENEFITS

No other food packs such a wallop of insoluble fiber at one sitting. There's no underestimating the health boost from a daily bowl of bran cereal. Here's a chronicle.

Constipation: Eat enough insoluble fiber, such as bran, and you're practically guaranteed to avoid constipation—as long as you increase your fluid intake, too. By absorbing water, bran creates bulk, which stimulates the intestines to contract and move things along.

Colon cancer: By increasing stool speed, bran ensures that bowel contents don't stagnate, so that means carcinogens, or cancer-causing agents, can't hang around long enough to cause trouble. And if carcinogens are present, a bulkier stool dilutes them.

Other digestive-tract conditions: A soft, swift-moving stool may prevent and ease the pain associated with many other digestive conditions, such as hemorrhoids.

All this should be enough to convince you to dig into your bowl of bran with vigor. It gets your system going in the morning while providing as much as half the suggested fiber goal of 20 to 35 grams a day (and more than half your insoluble goal of 15 to 26 grams a day).

SELECTION AND STORAGE

You don't need to swallow bran cereal as if it's medicine. Try different brands to find one you like. Bran-bud cereals provide a lot of fiber per spoonful, but flakes may be more palatable. Check labels to compare fiber and calories. Some raisin brans supply almost twice the calories. Be sure to note serving sizes; they may be very different from your usual bowlful. Compare sugar, sodium, and fat, too. But don't get paranoid about these ingredients. You're better off getting the fiber. You can make up for extra sugar, sodium, and fat at other meals.

Store opened cereals in a dry location. Once opened, they will keep for a few months before going stale. If you live in a humid environment, transfer cereals to plastic bags and refrigerate them.

KELLOGG'S® ALL-BRAN®
Serving Size: ⅓ cup (1 oz)

Calories	70	Riboflavin	<1 mg
Fat	1 g	Niacin	5 mg
Saturated Fat	na	Vitamin B₆	<1 mg
Cholesterol	0 mg	Folic Acid	100 mcg
Carbohydrate	22 g	Copper	<1 mg
Protein	4 g	Iron	5 mg
Dietary Fiber	10 g	Magnesium	122 mg
Sodium	26 mg	Phosphorus	278 mg
Vitamin A	750 IU	Potassium	320 mg
Vitamin C	15 mg	Zinc	4 mg
Thiamin	<1 mg		

PREPARATION AND SERVING TIPS

As American breakfasts go, a bowl of bran cereal with skim milk is much, much healthier than an old-fashioned farm breakfast. While having bran for breakfast may be the best way to wake up your digestive tract, it's just as healthy as an afternoon pick-me-up or a bedtime snack. Dare to be different; top yours with nonfat yogurt instead of milk. Or sprinkle bran cereal on yogurt, salads, or cut-up fruit. Use it to coat fish or to top a tuna casserole. These are painless ways to add fat-fighting fiber to your family's menu.

BREAD, WHOLE-WHEAT

You probably know whole wheat is the best type of wheat, but just because your bread is brown doesn't mean it's whole wheat. Even if the label proudly boasts "wheat" bread and lists "wheat flour" as the first ingredient, your bread may still not be whole wheat. Confused?

"Wheat" simply refers to the grain the flour comes from. Anything made with the flour from wheat—even refined white bread—can be called "wheat" and can list "wheat flour" as an ingredient. (The brown color often comes from caramel coloring.) Are manufacturers lying to consumers? No. But are their labeling practices misleading? We think so. Being informed will guard you from being misled. Learning the facts will help you choose the right bread.

Mistakenly, many people still think bread is fattening. On the contrary, bread can be the best fat-fighting friend in your diet. Bread is naturally low in fat and can be high in fiber. Because it is so versatile, you can easily eat many servings a day in place of other more fattening foods. As long as you don't pile on fatty spreads or fillings, bread can help you lose weight. In fact, studies have proved that people who eat 8 to 12 slices of bread a day still lose weight as long as their total diet is low in fat and calories. The trick is keeping yourself from slathering that hearty bread with butter or margarine.

HEALTH BENEFITS

Whole-wheat bread, in particular, is good for you for a number of reasons. It's high in complex carbohydrates, low in fat, a source of protein, and a storehouse of nutrients and fiber—a microcosm of what your diet should be.

To understand what's so special about whole wheat in particular, you need to understand the structure of wheat grain. There are three basic layers to the grain—endosperm, germ, and bran. When whole-wheat flour is milled (refined) to make white bread, the germ and outer bran layer are removed, leaving only the inner endosperm. Unfortunately, more than half the fiber of wheat is in that bran and germ, along with almost three quarters of the vitamins and minerals. Besides nutrients, the milling process also removes nonnutrient components—phytoestrogens, phenolic acids, oryzanol, and tannins—that may have health benefits, like reducing your risk of cancer.

What milling removes, manufacturers try to put back in. Lost B vitamins—thiamin, riboflavin, niacin—and iron are added back to form enriched bread products. Many other nutrients, especially minerals and fiber, don't get added back. So if you eat white bread, you're definitely missing a fiber opportunity.

SELECTION AND STORAGE

The key to buying whole-wheat bread is to be sure it says "100% whole wheat." Unless you read the word "whole," you're not getting all the goodness of the bran and germ of the wheat berry.

What about whole-grain or multigrain breads? They sound and look healthy, but refined wheat flour still may be the primary ingredient. Your only defense against being fooled is to read labels carefully. If you want 100 percent whole wheat, whole wheat should be the only grain listed. If you like the taste of multigrain breads, pick one that lists whole wheat first in the list of ingredients. Then you know it's the predominant grain.

Cracked-wheat breads are not always 100 percent whole cracked wheat. Again, check the label. Pumpernickel bread looks hearty but is really just a form of rye bread with caramel or molasses added. Both rye and pumpernickel breads are usually made from refined rye flour with the bran and germ removed, because breads made with 100 percent rye grain are too dense. If you can find it, look for rye bread made from "unbolted" rye and whole wheat.

Check the expiration date of the bread you buy. Many whole-wheat breads lack preservatives that prolong freshness. To prevent bread from going stale, only leave out at room temperature as much as you'll eat in a day or two, keeping it tightly closed in a plastic bag. Freeze the rest. Take out slices as you need them; they'll defrost quickly at room temperature. Don't refrigerate your bread—it only goes stale faster.

If you see mold on bread, throw out the entire loaf, as well as the bag itself. Mold usually starts as a whitish bloom. You can't salvage bread that's moldy, because mold spores spread quickly throughout soft foods. Do not even smell the inside of the bag; you may inhale mold spores.

PREPARATION AND SERVING TIPS

You don't have to resort to stalking the aisles and investigating ingredient labels for the perfect loaf of bread. You can make it yourself. Nothing could be fresher or taste better. Not knowing how to bake bread or not having the time are no longer excuses if you have a bread-making machine. For per-

Whole-Wheat Bread
Serving Size: 1 slice

Calories	61	Thiamin	<1 mg
Fat	1 g	Niacin	1 mg
Saturated Fat	na	Chromium	14 mcg
Cholesterol	0 mg	Copper	<1 mg
Carbohydrate	11 g	Iron	1 mg
Protein	2 g	Magnesium	23 mg
Dietary Fiber	2 g	Manganese	<1 mg
Sodium	159 mg		

fect rising, look for whole-wheat bread flour, which contains more gluten. Add nonfat dry milk powder for extra protein and calcium. Add wheat germ for extra fiber and a hefty dose of nutrients.

BROCCOLI

Best nutritious vegetable? Broccoli wins hands down. Eat it raw or cooked—as long as you don't cover it with cheese sauce, it can be part of your fat-fighting repertoire. You simply can't get a bigger dose of more nutrients from any other vegetable, especially for so few calories. That's key for those who are trying to lose weight; it's hard to meet nutrient needs when you're eating very-low-calorie foods.

HEALTH BENEFITS

Broccoli's noteworthy nutrients include vitamin C, vitamin A (mostly as beta-carotene), folic acid, calcium, and fiber. While the calcium content of one serving doesn't equal that of a glass of milk, broccoli is an important calcium source for those who don't consume dairy products. Calcium does more than build strong bones. Research shows that this mineral may play a role in the control of high blood pressure, and it may work to prevent colon cancer.

Beta-carotene and vitamin C are important antioxidants that have been linked to a reduced risk of numerous conditions, including cataracts, heart disease, and several cancers.

Broccoli is a fiber find. Not only is it a rich source, but half of its fiber is insoluble and half is soluble, helping to meet your needs for both types of fiber.

But the story doesn't end with broccoli's rich array of nutrients. Broccoli provides a health bonus in the form of protective substances that may shield you from disease. Botanically, broccoli belongs to the cabbage family, collectively known as cruciferous vegetables. Health organizations have singled out cruciferous vegetables as must-have foods, recommending we eat them several times a week. Why? They are linked to lower rates of cancer. Like all cruciferous vegetables, broccoli naturally contains two important phytochemicals—indoles and isothiocyanates. Not long ago, researchers at Johns Hopkins University School of Medicine in Baltimore isolated from broccoli an isothiocyanate, called sulforaphane, that increases the activity of a group of enzymes in our bodies that squelch cancer-causing agents.

SELECTION AND STORAGE

Look for broccoli that's dark green or even purplish-green, but not yellow. Florets should be compact and of even color; leaves should not be wilted; and stalks should not be fat and woody. The greener it is, the more beta-carotene it has.

Keep broccoli cold. At room temperature, the sugar in broccoli is converted into a fiber called lignin, which is woody and fibrous. Store unwashed broccoli in your refrigerator's crisper drawer, in a plastic bag. Don't completely seal the bag, but make sure it is tight. Use within a few days.

PREPARATION AND SERVING TIPS

Wash broccoli just before using. Cut off as much of the stems as you like; they contain fewer nutrients than the florets anyway. Steaming is the best way to cook broccoli because many nutrients are lost when it's boiled. Preventing broccoli's unpleasant odor is easy—don't use an aluminum pan and don't overcook it. Steam only until crisp-tender, while stalks are still bright green; five minutes is plenty. Try this trick:

BROCCOLI, FRESH, COOKED
Serving Size: ½ cup chopped

Calories	23	Vitamin C	49 mg
Fat	<1 g	Riboflavin	1 mg
Saturated Fat	0 g	Vitamin B₆	1 mg
Cholesterol	0 mg	Folic Acid	53 mcg
Carbohydrate	4 g	Calcium	89 mg
Protein	2 g	Iron	1 mg
Dietary Fiber	2 g	Magnesium	47 mg
Sodium	8 mg	Manganese	1 mg
Vitamin A	1,099 IU		

Make one or two cuts through the stems before cooking. This helps the stems cook as fast as the tops.

When serving broccoli, skip the cheese sauce. Keep it simple; add a squeeze of lemon and a dusting of cracked pepper.

Broccoli florets can boost the nutrition, flavor, and color of any stir-fry dish. Raw broccoli tossed into salads boosts the nutrition of a midday meal.

Served raw, broccoli is a great finger food. Children love it this way, perhaps because the flavor isn't as strong, or maybe just because it's fun. Double the fun by giving them a dipping sauce to dunk it in, like fat-free ranch dressing.

BRUSSELS SPROUTS

No one knows the origin of brussels sprouts, though it's logical to assume they originated in Belgium. Like all vegetables, brussels sprouts are naturally low in fat. But unlike most vegetables, brussels sprouts are rather high in protein, accounting for more than a quarter of their calories. Although the protein is incomplete—it doesn't provide the full spectrum of essential amino acids—it can be made complete with whole grains. This means you can skip a fattier source of protein, like meat, and rely on a meal of brussels sprouts and grains now and again—truly a fat fighter.

HEALTH BENEFITS

Brussels sprouts are also very high in fiber, and they belong to the disease-fighting cabbage family. Indeed, they look like miniature cabbages. Like broccoli and cabbage—fellow cruciferous vegetables—brussels sprouts may protect against cancer with their indole, a phytochemical. They are also particularly rich in vitamin C, another anti-cancer agent.

SELECTION AND STORAGE

Fresh brussels sprouts shine in fall and winter. Look for a pronounced green color and tight, compact, firm heads. The fewer the yellowed, wilted, or loose leaves the better.

You're better off choosing smaller heads; they're more tender and flavorful. Pick ones of similar size so they cook evenly. Stored in the refrigerator in the cardboard container they came in or kept in a plastic bag, loosely closed, they'll last a week or two.

BRUSSELS SPROUTS, FRESH, COOKED
Serving Size: ½ cup

Calories	30	Sodium	17 mg
Fat	<1 g	Vitamin A	561 IU
Saturated Fat	0 g	Vitamin C	48 mg
Cholesterol	0 mg	Folic Acid	47 mcg
Carbohydrate	7 g	Iron	1 mg
Protein	2 g	Manganese	<1 mg
Dietary Fiber	4 g	Potassium	257 mg

PREPARATION AND SERVING TIPS

Dunk sprouts in ice water to debug them. Then rinse them under running water. Pull off loose or wilted leaves; trim the stem ends a little. Cut an "X" in the bottoms, so the insides cook at the same rate as the leaves. Steaming is your best bet. The sprouts will stay intact, odor will be minimized, and you'll preserve more nutrients than you would if you boiled them.

As with broccoli and cabbage, the odor becomes most pronounced when overcooked. Brussels sprouts also lose valuable vitamin C when overcooked. So don't be afraid to leave your sprouts a bit on the crisp side. As soon as you can barely prick them with a fork they're done—about 7 to 14 minutes, depending on size.

Brussels sprouts are delicious served with just a squeeze of lemon. For more flavor, try a mustard sauce.

BUCKWHEAT

There's more to buckwheat than flapjacks. Eastern Europeans know roasted buckwheat groats as kasha and eat it like porridge. Despite its name, buckwheat is not a type of wheat—nor is it related to wheat. Buckwheat isn't even a grain; it's the fruit of a plant that's related to rhubarb.

HEALTH BENEFITS

Buckwheat contains more protein than true grains and is not deficient in the amino acid lysine as most grains are, so the protein is more nutritionally complete. That makes it a particularly good choice for vegetarians. It's an excellent source of magnesium, a boon to your blood pressure. Presumably, it's relatively rich in fiber, but exact values aren't available.

SELECTION AND STORAGE

Most of our buckwheat comes from New York and carries a premium price, because so few farmers grow it. Look for it in health-food stores or mail-order catalogs. In larger cities, check stores in Russian or Slavic neighborhoods.

Buckwheat is sold as groats, grits, or flour. Groats are pale kernels without the hard, inedible outer shell. You can buy them whole or cracked into coarse, medium, or fine grinds. Roasted groats—kasha—are dark kernels. Very finely cracked unroasted groats are buckwheat grits. They can be found as a hot cereal—sometimes labeled "cream of buckwheat." Buckwheat flour is also available, in light and dark versions. The darker type contains more of the hull, therefore more fiber and nutrients, and imparts a stronger flavor.

Keep buckwheat in a well-sealed container in a cool, dark location. At room temperature, it is more susceptible to turning rancid than are true grains, especially in warm climates. Keep it in the refrigerator or freezer.

PREPARATION AND SERVING TIPS

Take advantage of buckwheat's intense, nutty flavor. If you don't care for kasha plain, mix it in with pasta, grains, potatoes, or vegetables—especially winter vegetables. It makes a hearty, flavorful meal. For pilafs, stuffing, and soups, use whole kasha. Save the medium and fine grinds for cereals.

To cook: Combine ½ cup whole groats with a cup of water and simmer for 15 minutes. It will triple in volume. Or combine ½ cup of cracked kasha with 2½ cups of liquid and cook for 12 minutes, to yield 2 cups.

Buckwheat flour is superb for pancakes, but don't try making bread with it; it doesn't work because it contains no gluten. But you can add ¼ to ½ cup of buckwheat flour into a recipe for bread, as long as the primary grain is wheat or another high-gluten grain.

BUCKWHEAT GROATS, ROASTED, COOKED (KASHA)
Serving Size: ½ cup

Calories	91	Cholesterol	0
Protein	3.4 g	Dietary Fiber	na
Carbohydrate	19.7 g	Sodium	4 mg
Fat	0.6 g	Iron	0.8 mg
Saturated	0.1 g	Magnesium	51 mg

BULGUR

This Middle Eastern staple sounds more exotic than it is; bulgur is what's left after wheat kernels have been steamed, dried, and crushed. This cereal grain has been a food staple for years because it offers an inexpensive source of low-fat protein, making it a wonderfully nutritious addition to your low-fat meal plan.

HEALTH BENEFITS

Bulgur doesn't lose much from its minimal processing; it remains high in protein and minerals. That means it's an ideal foundation for meals, allowing you to skip higher-fat protein sources, like meat.

Bulgur is also a standout in terms of its fiber content, just like whole wheat, and can help keep your digestive tract healthy as a result. The insoluble fiber it contains absorbs water, promoting faster elimination of waste, which prevents the formation of an environment that promotes the development of carcinogens.

SELECTION AND STORAGE

You may need to visit a health-food store to find bulgur. It's available in three grinds—coarse, medium, and fine. Coarse bulgur is used to make pilaf or stuffing. Medium-grind bulgur is used in cereals. The finest grind of bulgur is suited to the popular cold Middle Eastern salad called tabbouleh. Store bulgur in a screw-top glass jar in the refrigerator; it will keep for months.

PREPARATION AND SERVING TIPS

Because bulgur is already partially cooked, little time is needed for preparation: Combine a half cup of bulgur with one cup of liquid and simmer for 15 minutes. Let stand for another ten minutes. Fluff with a fork. It triples in volume.

For cold salads, soak bulgur before using: Pour boiling water over bulgur, in a three-to-one ratio. Soak for 30 to 40 minutes. Drain away excess water. If you like your bulgur chewier, let it sit longer to absorb more water.

Bulgur is used like rice in Mediterranean countries. In fact, you can use bulgur in place of rice in most recipes. Bulgur lends its nutty flavor to whatever it is combined with, allowing you to use it as a main ingredient, thus cutting back on fattier foods.

BULGUR, COOKED
Serving Size: ½ cup

Calories....................76	Dietary Fiber..............4 g
Fat...........................<1 g	Sodium.......................5 mg
Saturated Fat.........0 g	Iron...............................1 mg
Cholesterol...............0 mg	Magnesium ....29 mg
Carbohydrate ....17 g	Manganese ....1 mg
Protein.......................3 g	

CABBAGE

Cabbage is at the head of the cruciferous vegetable family. But it's a vegetable that few people appreciate. Though strong-flavored, it's this feature that makes you less likely to miss the flavor of fat in your diet. In fact, cabbage is a dieter's friend, with among the fewest calories and least fat of any vegetable.

HEALTH BENEFITS

From green cabbage you'll enjoy a fiber boost and a respectable amount of vitamin C. Two types of cabbage, savoy and bok choy, provide beta-carotene—an antioxidant that battles cancer and heart disease. For vegetarians, bok choy is an important source of calcium, which may help prevent osteoporosis and aid in controlling blood pressure.

The phytochemicals in cabbage, called indoles, are also being studied for their ability to convert estradiol, an estrogenlike hormone that may play a role in the development of breast cancer, into a safer form of estrogen—powerful incentives to add cabbage to your diet.

SELECTION AND STORAGE

There are literally hundreds of varieties of cabbage. Green cabbage is the most familiar kind, with Danish, domestic, and pointed being the top three picks of the cabbage family. All sport the familiar pale green, compact head; are similar nutritionally; and shine in fiber. Red cabbage, a cousin of the green, has a bit more vitamin C, but the most nutritious is savoy cabbage, which has a pretty, dark-green, round head that's loose, ruffly, and prominently "veined." It is much higher in beta-carotene—about ten times more—than green or red cabbage. Napa cabbage, also known as celery cabbage or pe-tsai, is often incorrectly called Chinese cabbage. Nutritionally, it's equivalent to green cabbage.

Bok choy, or pak-choi, is true Chinese cabbage. As its dark green color suggests, it's rich in beta-carotene. It's also a good source of potassium and a particularly well-absorbed nondairy source of calcium, providing about ten percent of a day's requirement. It only falls short in the fiber category.

When choosing green and red cabbage, pick a tight, compact head that feels heavy for its size. It should look crisp and fresh, with few loose leaves. Leafy varieties should be green, with stems that are firm, not limp.

Store whole heads of cabbage in the crisper drawer of your refrigerator. If uncut, compact heads keep for a couple of weeks. Leafy varieties should be used within a few days.

PREPARATION AND SERVING TIPS

Discard outer leaves if loose or limp, cut into quarters, then wash. When cooking quarters, leave the core in as this prevents the leaves from tearing apart. If shredding cabbage for coleslaw, core the cabbage first. But don't shred ahead of time; once you do, enzymes begin destroying vitamin C.

Forget old-fashioned corned beef and cabbage recipes. More nutrients will be preserved and the cabbage will taste better if it is cooked only until slightly tender, but still crisp—about 10 to 12 minutes for wedges, five minutes if shredded. Red cabbage takes a few minutes more; leafy varieties cook faster.

GREEN CABBAGE, FRESH, COOKED
Serving Size: ½ cup chopped

Calories	16	Protein	1 g
Fat	<1 g	Dietary Fiber	3 g
Saturated Fat	0 g	Sodium	5 mg
Cholesterol	0 mg	Vitamin C	18 mg
Carbohydrate	4 g		

BOK CHOY, FRESH, COOKED
Serving Size: ½ cup chopped

Calories	10	Sodium	29 mg
Fat	<1 g	Vitamin A	2,183 IU
Saturated Fat	0 g	Vitamin C	22 mg
Cholesterol	0 mg	Calcium	79 mg
Carbohydrate	2 g	Iron	1 mg
Protein	1 g	Potassium	315 mg
Dietary Fiber	1 g		

To solve cabbage's notorious stink problem, steam it in a small amount of water for a short time and do not cook it in an aluminum pan. Uncover briefly, shortly after cooking begins, to release the sulfur smell.

Combine red and green cabbage for a more interesting cole slaw. Keep the fat down with a dressing of nonfat yogurt laced with poppy seeds. Bok choy and napa cabbage work well in stir-fry dishes. Savoy is perfect for stuffing. In place of the meat in traditional stuffed-cabbage recipes, use a grain like bulgur, quinoa, or buckwheat.

CARROTS

If you don't have a bag of carrots sitting in your refrigerator, you should—they're anything but ordinary when it comes to nutrition. Carrots contain an uncommon amount of beta-carotene. And they can masquerade as a fat substitute by serving as a thickener in soups, sauces, casseroles, and quick breads. Because of its terrific replacement qualities, you don't have to add any cream, or fat for that matter, to cream of carrot soup. In fact, their numerous health benefits call for amending that well-known saying to: A carrot a day keeps the doctor away.

HEALTH BENEFITS

One of carrots' fat-fighting features is their respectable fiber content, half of which is the soluble fiber calcium pectate. Soluble fiber may help lower blood-cholesterol levels by binding with and eliminating bile acids, triggering cholesterol to be drawn out of the bloodstream to make more bile acids.

Carrots have few rivals when it comes to beta-carotene. A mere half-cup serving of cooked carrots packs a walloping four times the RDA of vitamin A in the form of protective beta-carotene. One raw carrot supposedly contains as much, though it's not clear if all of it's useable by your body. The strongest evidence for beta-carotene's protective antioxidant effect is against lung tumors (though avoiding tobacco is still your best defense), but beta-carotene may also ward off cancers of the stomach, cervix, uterus, and oral cavity.

The National Cancer Institute is studying the whole family of umbelliferous foods, of which carrots are a member, for protective effects. Recent research results from Harvard University suggest that people who eat more than five carrots a week are much less likely to suffer a stroke than those who eat only one carrot a month.

Finally, like Mom said, carrots do help your eyes. The retina of the eye needs vitamin A to function; a deficiency of vitamin A causes night blindness. Though extra vitamin A won't help you see better, its antioxidant properties may help prevent cataracts.

SELECTION AND STORAGE

Look for firm carrots with bright orange color and smooth skin. Avoid carrots if they are limp or black near the tops; they're not fresh. Choose medium-sized ones that taper at the ends. Thicker ones taste tough. In general, early carrots are more tender but less sweet than larger, mature carrots.

Clip greens as soon as you are home to avoid moisture loss. Store greens and carrots separately in perforated plastic bags in your refrigerator's crisper drawer. Carrots keep for a few weeks; greens last only a few days.

PREPARATION AND SERVING TIPS

Thoroughly wash and scrub carrots to remove soil contaminants. Being root vegetables, carrots tend to end up with more pesticide residues than nonroot vegetables. You can get rid of much of it by peeling the outer layer and by cutting off and discarding one-quarter inch off the fat end.

CARROTS, FRESH, COOKED
Serving Size: ½ cup chopped

Calories	35	Dietary Fiber	2 g
Fat	<1 g	Sodium	52 mg
Saturated Fat	0 g	Vitamin A	19,152 IU
Cholesterol	0 mg	Vitamin B6	<1 mg
Carbohydrate	8 g	Manganese	<1 mg
Protein	1 g	Potassium	177 mg

Carrots are a great raw snack, of course. But their true sweet flavor shines through when cooked. Very little nutritional value is lost in cooking, unless you overcook them until mushy. In fact, the nutrients in lightly cooked carrots are more usable by your body than those in raw carrots, because cooking breaks down their tough cell walls, which releases beta-carotene.

Steaming is your best bet for cooking carrots. Take advantage of the fact that most children love carrots, raw or cooked. But avoid serving coin-shaped slices to young children; they can choke on them. Cut them into quarters or julienne strips.

For that fat-free carrot soup mentioned above, use carrots and leeks for thickening. Add onions, chicken stock, white pepper, and you're in business. In fact, the soluble fiber in carrots can add thickness to lots of foods, taking the place of fattening butter and cream. The stronger the flavor of the soup or sauce, the more it will hide the carrot flavor. You can even use carrots when baking, as long as you puree them.

CAULIFLOWER

Cauliflower, one of several cruciferous vegetables, is an ideal fat-fighting companion for meatless meals. Its strong flavor allows it to stand alone without meat or other fatty foods. And if you're really hungry, raw cauliflower makes a wonderful snack. Because it's extra crunchy, cauliflower takes longer to chew, giving your body time to realize you're full before you eat yourself out of house and home.

HEALTH BENEFITS

After citrus fruits, cauliflower is your next best natural source of vitamin C, an antioxidant that appears to help combat cancer. It's also an important warrior in the continuous battle our bodies wage against infection. Cauliflower is also notable for its fiber, folic acid, and potassium contents, proving it's more nutritious than its white appearance would have you believe. Cauliflower may also be a natural cancer fighter. It contains phytochemicals, called indoles, that may stimulate enzymes that block cancer growth.

SELECTION AND STORAGE

Though cauliflower is available year-round, it's more reasonably priced in season—fall and winter. Look for creamy white heads with compact florets. Brown patches and opened florets are signs of aging.

Store unwashed, uncut cauliflower loosely wrapped in a plastic bag in your refrigerator's crisper drawer. Keep upright to prevent moisture from collecting on the surface. It will keep two to five days.

CAULIFLOWER, FRESH, COOKED
Serving Size: ½ cup

Calories....................15	Dietary Fiber..............1 g
Fat..............................<1 g	Sodium......................4 mg
Saturated Fat.........0 g	Vitamin C.................34 mg
Cholesterol................0 mg	Folic Acid.................32 mcg
Carbohydrate.............3 g	Potassium..............200 mg
Protein........................1 g	

PREPARATION AND SERVING TIPS

Remove outer leaves, break off florets, trim brown spots, and wash them under running water. Cauliflower serves up well both raw and cooked. Raw, its flavor is less intense and more acceptable to children. Let them dip it into fat-free dressing.

Steam cauliflower, but don't overcook it. Overcooking destroys its vitamin C and folic acid. Moreover, overcooking gives cauliflower a bitter, pungent flavor. To prevent this, steam it in a nonaluminum pan over a small amount of water, until a fork barely pierces a floret—about five minutes. Remove the cover soon after cooking begins to release odoriferous sulfur compounds.

Although cheese sauces are popular over cauliflower, they add a hefty dose of fat and calories. Why ruin a good thing? Better to serve cauliflower plain or with a little dill weed. For a low-fat, meatless meal, add cauliflower, broccoli, and carrots to homemade tomato sauce; simmer for 15 minutes, then enjoy over hot pasta.

CORN

Corn is a low-fat complex carbohydrate that deserves a regular place on any healthy table. Unfortunately, as with many other naturally low-fat foods, the American tendency is to smother corn-on-the-cob with butter. But these high-fiber, fat-fighting kernels of goodness are better left alone. Because corn is hearty and satisfying, it can curb your appetite for high-fat foods.

HEALTH BENEFITS

This popular food is high in fiber. In fact, it's notoriously hard to digest. But its insoluble fiber is tops at tackling common digestive ailments (like constipation and hemorrhoids) by absorbing water, which swells the stool and speeds its movement.

Corn is a surprising source of several vitamins, including folic acid, niacin, and vitamin C. The folic acid in corn is now known to be an important factor in preventing neural-tube birth defects. It's just as important in preventing heart disease, according to new studies that show folic acid can prevent a buildup of homocysteine, an amino acid, in the body. Long-term elevation of homocysteine has been linked to higher rates of heart disease; folic acid helps break it down.

SELECTION AND STORAGE

End-of-summer corn is by far the best ear in town. Although you can find good-tasting corn year-round, many out-of-season ears aren't worth eating. When buying fresh corn, be sure

CORN, YELLOW OR WHITE
Serving Size: 1 ear

Calories	83	Dietary Fiber	3 g
Fat	1 g	Sodium	13 mg
Saturated Fat	<1 g	Vitamin C	5 mg
Cholesterol	0 mg	Folic Acid	36 mcg
Carbohydrate	19 g	Niacin	1 mg
Protein	3 g	Potassium	192 mg

it was delivered in cold storage—as temperatures rise, the natural sugar in corn turns to starch, and the corn loses some sweetness. Corn is best eaten within a day or two of picking.

Corn husks should be green and have visible kernels that are plump and tightly packed on the cob. To test freshness, pop a kernel with your fingernail. The liquid that spurts out should be milky colored. If not, the corn is either immature or overripe. Once home, refrigerate corn immediately.

PREPARATION AND SERVING TIPS

Boiling is the traditional method for preparing corn-on-the-cob, though grilling, steaming, and even microwaving will get the job done. A couple of notes about boiling: Adding salt to the water toughens corn; adding sugar isn't necessary; over-cooking toughens kernels. Cook for the shortest amount of time possible—about five minutes.

Though you may be tempted to slather on butter or margarine, keep in mind that each pat you add contributes about five unnecessary grams of fat to your diet. Instead, sprinkle with a favorite herb or fresh-squeezed lemon juice.

DATES

Dates are among the most ancient of fruits, growing along the Nile as early as the fifth century B.C. Perhaps the Egyptians knew dates' sweetness hid a bounty of nutrients. Dates are nuggets of nutrition that satisfy a sweet tooth, making them ideal snacks to stave off hunger. True, dates provide more calories than most fruits, but they are practically fat-free.

HEALTH BENEFITS

Loaded with fiber—both soluble and insoluble—dates are able to fill you up and keep your bowel habits regular. They are an excellent source of potassium and provide numerous other important vitamins and minerals—quite a powerhouse packed in a tiny, portable package.

SELECTION AND STORAGE

Most supermarkets stock fresh dates; you may have to visit a health-food store to find dried dates. For both types look for plump fruit with unbroken, smoothly wrinkled skins. Avoid dates that smell bad or have hardened sugar crystals on their skins.

Packaged dates are available pitted, unpitted, or chopped. Dried dates keep for up to a year in the refrigerator. Fresh dates should be refrigerated in tightly sealed containers; they'll keep up to eight months. If stored in the kitchen cabinet, they'll stay fresh for about a month.

If dates dry out, they can be "plumped" with a little warm water, fruit juice, or for fancier dishes, your favorite liqueur.

Don't store dates near strongly flavored items such as garlic; they tend to absorb outside odors.

PREPARATION AND SERVING TIPS

Dates are great on their own, but for an extra-special treat, try stuffing them with whole almonds or chopped pieces of walnuts or pecans. For a spicy twist, tuck in a piece of crystallized gingerroot.

Adding dates to home-baked breads, cakes, muffins, and cookies adds richness and nutrition to otherwise ordinary recipes. And the natural moisture of dates adds to the quality of the final product. Dates work well in fruit compotes, salads, and desserts. Chopped or slivered, dates can even be sprinkled on side dishes like rice, couscous, or vegetables.

To slice or chop dates, chill them first; the colder they are, the easier they are to slice.

DATES, DRIED
Serving Size: 10 dates

Calories	228	Pantothenic Acid	1 mg
Fat	<1 g	Vitamin B_6	<1 mg
Saturated Fat	na	Calcium	27 mg
Cholesterol	0 mg	Copper	<1 mg
Carbohydrate	61 g	Iron	1 mg
Protein	2 g	Magnesium	29 mg
Dietary Fiber	6 g	Manganese	<1 mg
Sodium	2 mg	Potassium	541 mg
Niacin	2 mg		

FISH

Fish is a delicacy not to be missed. It's a fabulous addition to any healthful diet because its low fat content (generally 20 percent or less of total calories) makes it the perfect protein substitute for fatty cuts of beef and pork. Even shellfish is low in fat and isn't as high in cholesterol as many believe.

HEALTH BENEFITS

Although fish is lean, it does contain some oil. Known as omega-3 fatty acids, these fish oils are thought to offer some amazing health benefits, such as helping to prevent heart disease and cancer, treating psoriasis and arthritis, and relieving the agony of migraine headaches. Fatty fish tend to have more omega-3s than leaner fish, but even "fatty" fish contain less fat than lean beef or chicken.

Even canned fish like tuna, sardines, and salmon have omega-3s, and sardines and salmon, when eaten bones and all, pack your meal with an ample amount of good-for-your-bones calcium, too.

SELECTION AND STORAGE

When buying fresh fish, always smell it. If you detect a "fishy" odor, don't buy it. Whether you buy whole fish, fish fillets, or steaks, the fish should be firm to the touch. The scales should be shiny and clean, not slimy. Check the eyes; they should be clear, not cloudy and bulging, not sunken. Fish fillets and steaks should be moist. If they look dried or curled around the edges they probably aren't fresh.

It's best to cook fresh fish the same day you buy it. (Fish generally spoils faster than beef or chicken, and whole fish generally keeps better than steaks or fillets.) But it will keep in the refrigerator overnight if you store it in an airtight container over a bowl of ice.

If you need to keep it longer than a day, freeze it. The quality of thawed, frozen fish is better when it freezes quickly, so freeze whole fish only if it weighs two pounds or less; larger fish should be cut into pieces, steaks, or fillets to ensure a quick freeze. Lean fish will keep in the freezer for up to six months—three months for fatty fish.

When buying most shellfish—clams, oysters, lobsters, crabs and crayfish—it's imperative they still be alive. Live lobsters and crabs are easy to spot. Clams and oysters are trickier though; you must be sure the shell is closed tightly or closes when you tap the shell.

Fish and shellfish have been dogged by safety questions, including those arising from man-made contaminants. Oysters and clams carry a particular risk of passing on diseases such as hepatitis or Norwalk-like viruses if eaten raw. New

Coho Salmon
Serving Size: 3 oz, cooked

Calories 157	Protein......................23 g
Fat.............................6 g	Dietary Fiber ....0 g
Saturated Fat.........1 g	Sodium.....................50 mg
Cholesterol..............42 mg	Potassium ....454 mg
Carbohydrate ....0 g	

SNAPPER
Serving Size: 3 oz, cooked

Calories	109	Protein	22 g
Fat	2 g	Dietary Fiber	0 g
Saturated Fat	<1 g	Sodium	48 mg
Cholesterol	40 mg	Magnesium	31 mg
Carbohydrate	0 g	Potassium	444 mg

research suggests even typical cooking may not be enough to kill all bacterial threats. Pesticides, mercury, and chemicals like PCB sometimes find their way into fish. Though fatty fish is richer in omega-3s, they're also more likely to harbor environmental contaminants.

Here are precautions you can take to reduce the odds of eating contaminated fish:

• Eat fish from a variety of sources.

• Opt for open ocean fish and farmed fish over freshwater fish; they are less likely to harbor toxins.

• Eat smaller, young fish. Older fish are more likely to have accumulated chemicals in their fatty tissues.

• Before you fish, check your own state's advisories about which waters are unsafe for fishing. Try the Department of Public Health or the Department of Environmental Conservation.

• Don't make a habit of eating the fish you catch for sport if you fish in the same area over and over again.

• Avoid swordfish; it may be contaminated with mercury.

PREPARATION AND SERVING TIPS

For the uninitiated, fish is most perplexing to prepare. But the number one rule is: Preserve moistness. That means avoiding direct heat, especially when preparing low-fat varieties of fish; you'll get the best results if you use moist-heat methods such as poaching, steaming, or baking with vegetables or in a sauce. Dry-heat methods such as baking, broiling, and grilling work well for fattier fish.

Fish cooks fast, so it's easy to overcook it. You can tell fish is done when it looks opaque and the flesh just begins to flake with the touch of a fork. If it falls apart when you touch it, it's too late; the fish is overdone. The general rule of thumb for cooking fish is to cook eight to ten minutes per inch of thickness, measured at the fish's thickest point.

For fish soups, stews, and chowders, use lean fish. An oily fish will overpower the flavor of the broth. Citrus juices enhance the natural flavor of fish. Lemon, lime, or orange juice complements almost any kind of fish. Some favorite fish seasonings are dill, tarragon, basil, paprika, parsley, and thyme.

GARLIC

Through the centuries, garlic has been both reviled and revered for its qualities. Today, the gossip about garlic and its apparent disease-preventing potential has reached a fevered pitch. For garlic lovers, that's good news; adding garlic to dishes can make up for bland low-fat preparations. Once you learn to appreciate its pungency, most anything tastes better with garlic. And once you learn its possible health benefits, you may learn to love it.

HEALTH BENEFITS

The list of health benefits just seems to grow and grow. From preventing heart disease and cancer to fighting off infections, researchers are finding encouraging results with garlic. Behind all the grandiose claims are the compounds that give garlic its biting flavor. The chief health-promoting "ingredients" are allicin and diallyl sulfide, sulfur-containing compounds. The biggest question surrounding them is whether their disease-preventing abilities remain intact once cooked. No one really knows for sure. But it's believed that at least some health benefits survive cooking.

Garlic has been found to lower levels of LDL cholesterol, the "bad" cholesterol, and raise HDL cholesterol, the "good" cholesterol. It may also help to dissolve clots that can lead to heart attacks and strokes.

Garlic has also been found to inhibit the growth of, or even kill, several kinds of bacteria, including *Staphylococcus* and *Salmonella*, as well as many fungi and yeast.

Animal studies have found that garlic helps prevent colon, lung, and esophageal cancers. How much is enough? No one knows. In many studies, garlic extracts were used, making it impossible to translate into a practical prescription for better health.

Selection and Storage

Most varieties of garlic have the same characteristic pungent odor and bite. Pink-skinned garlic tastes a little sweeter and keeps longer than white garlic. Elephant garlic, a large-clove variety, is milder in flavor than regular garlic. But most varieties can be used interchangeably in recipes.

Opt for loose garlic if you can find it. It's easier to check the quality of what you're getting than with those hiding behind cellophane. Its appearance can clue you in to its freshness; paper-white skins are your best bet. Then pick up the garlic; choose a head that is firm to the touch with no visible damp or brown spots.

Don't expect the flavor of garlic powder to mimic fresh garlic. Much of the flavor is processed out. Garlic powder, however, does retain large amounts of active components. Garlic salt, of course, contains large amounts of sodium—as much as 900 milligrams per teaspoon.

Store garlic in a cool, dark, dry spot. If you don't use it regularly, check it occasionally to be sure it's useable. Garlic may last only a few weeks or a few months. If one or two cloves have gone bad, remove them, but don't nick remaining cloves; any skin punctures will hasten the demise of what's left. If garlic begins to sprout, it's still okay to use, but it may have a milder flavor.

GARLIC
Serving Size: 3 cloves

Calories	13	Carbohydrate	3 g
Fat	1 g	Protein	1 g
Saturated Fat	0 g	Dietary Fiber	<1 g
Cholesterol	0 mg	Sodium	2 mg

PREPARATION AND SERVING TIPS

Garlic squeezed through a garlic press is ten times stronger in flavor than garlic minced with a knife, so use pressed garlic when you want full-force flavor to come through; use minced when you want to curtail it; and for a buttery flavor, bake whole cloves until tender. The longer the garlic is cooked, the more mild the flavor.

For just a delicate touch of garlic in salads, rub the bottom of the salad bowl with a cut clove before adding the salad greens. For more flavor, add freshly crushed garlic to the salad.

You can make your own version of fat-free garlic bread by warming a loaf of bread, spreading the inside with a fresh cut clove of garlic, then toasting the loaf under the broiler. You'll get a teaser of garlic without all the fat.

Chew on fresh parsley, fresh mint, or citrus peel to neutralize the pungent aroma garlic leaves on your breath—a common complaint among garlic lovers. This doesn't work for everyone, but it just might help you.

GRAPEFRUIT

No, grapefruit is not a calorie-free fruit, as some diets would have you believe. Despite its reputation as a "fat-burner," grapefruit has no special ability to burn away excess fat. But it is low in calories with essentially no fat, and its soluble fiber content is decent enough to fill you up, discouraging you from overeating. So yes, grapefruit can help you lose weight, just not as easily as some would say. And it's nutritious, to boot. Grapefruit is a tart-tasting fruit not everyone enjoys. But for those who do, grapefruit offers a lot of nutrition for few calories.

HEALTH BENEFITS

Grapefruit is an excellent source of vitamin C. Pink and red grapefruit are good sources of disease-fighting beta-carotene. If you peel and eat a grapefruit like you would an orange, you get a good dose of cholesterol-lowering pectin from the membranes—the same soluble fiber that fills you up by dissolving in water and creating gels. As a member of the citrus family, grapefruit is also a storehouse of powerful phytochemicals such as flavonoids, terpenes, and limonoids. These naturally occurring substances may have cancer-preventing properties.

SELECTION AND STORAGE

Grapefruit isn't picked unless it's fully ripe, making selection a no-brainer. However, choose ones that are heavy for their size; they're juiciest. And avoid those that are soft or mushy, or oblong rather than round. They are generally of poorer quality—possibly pithy and less sweet.

GRAPEFRUIT, PINK OR RED
Serving Size: ½ fruit

Calories	37	Dietary Fiber	2 g
Fat	<1 g	Sodium	0 mg
Saturated Fat	0 g	Vitamin A	318 IU
Cholesterol	0 mg	Niacin	<1 mg
Carbohydrate	10 g	Vitamin C	47 mg
Protein	1 g	Potassium	158 mg

The difference in taste among white, red, and pink varieties of grapefruit is minimal; they are equally sweet (and equally tart). Store grapefruit in your refrigerator's crisper drawer; they'll keep for up to two months.

PREPARATION AND SERVING TIPS

Wash grapefruit before cutting to prevent bacteria that might be on the skin from being introduced to the inside. You might want to bring grapefruit to room temperature before you juice or slice it for better appreciation of flavor.

You don't have to relegate grapefruit to breakfast. Instead of halving and segmenting it, try peeling and eating it out of hand for a juicy, mouth-watering snack. For dessert, sprinkle with a little brown sugar and place it under the broiler until it bubbles.

GRAPES

Grapes, one of the oldest cultivated fruits, are unique because they grow on vines. This bite-size fruit is popular with everyone, especially kids (but be sure to peel or slice them lengthwise for young children to avoid choking). One of grapes' best attributes is that everyone likes them. Moreover, they're portable and neat, making them easy low-fat substitutes for high-fat, calorie-filled snacks and desserts. Bursting with juice, they are a refreshing way to fight the fat. You just have to be sure to have them handy.

HEALTH BENEFITS

Grapes may not be packed with traditional nutrients, but they do contain a collection of phytochemicals that researchers are just beginning to appreciate. Among them is ellagic acid, a natural substance also found in strawberries that is thought to possess cancer-preventing properties. Grapes also contain boron, a mineral believed to play a role in preventing the bone-destroying disease osteoporosis.

SELECTION AND STORAGE

Some varieties of grapes are available year-round. When buying grapes, look for clusters with plump, well-colored fruit attached to pliable, green stems. Soft or wrinkled grapes or those with bleached areas around the stem are past their prime.

There are basically three categories of grapes: the greens, the reds, and the blue/blacks. Good color is the key to good fla-

GRAPES, AMERICAN
Serving Size: 20 grapes

Calories 30	Dietary Fiber ....<1 g
Fat..........................<1 g	Sodium......................0 mg
Saturated Fat.........0 g	Vitamin B$_6$ ....2 mg
Cholesterol.................0 mg	Manganese..............<1 mg
Carbohydrate ....8 g	Potassium ....92 mg
Protein ....<1 g	

vor. The sweetest green grapes are yellow-green in color; red varieties that are predominantly crimson/red will have the best flavor; and blue/black varieties taste best if their color is deep and rich, almost black. If you object to seeds, look for seedless varieties. Store grapes unwashed in the refrigerator. They'll keep up to a week.

PREPARATION AND SERVING TIPS

Just before eating, rinse grape clusters and drain or pat dry. Slight chilling enhances the flavor and texture of table grapes. Cold, sliced grapes taste great blended in with low-fat yogurt. Frozen grapes make a popular summer treat. For a change of pace, skewer grapes, banana slices (dipped in lemon), apple chunks, and pineapple cubes, or any favorite fruit. Brush with a combination of honey, lemon, and ground nutmeg. Broil until warm.

GREENS FOR COOKING

Most often thought of as a Southern dish, collard greens and their cousins—beet greens, dandelion greens, mustard greens, and turnip greens—are gaining new respect as nutrition powerhouses—they're loaded with disease-fighting beta-carotene and offer respectable amounts of vitamin C, calcium, and fiber. All these attributes make cooking greens a wise choice for your diet. As fat-fighters, they play the part of most vegetables, providing little natural fat but filling stomachs with some fiber and furnishing nutrients galore. Just lose the traditional way of cooking them in bacon grease to turn them into true fat-fighting foods.

HEALTH BENEFITS

If you're keeping calories to a minimum, you depend on certain foods to provide more than their share of certain nutrients. And cooking greens fill that role for two nutrients in particular.

First, greens contribute an important nondairy source of calcium that's absorbed almost as well as the calcium found in dairy products. That's good news for those facing the threat of osteoporosis, as calcium is one of many factors crucial to bone health.

Second, most greens are superb sources of vitamin A, mostly in the form of beta-carotene, which has been shown to help protect against cancer, heart disease, and cataracts through its antioxidant properties. Other carotenoids found in greens may be just as potent cancer conquerors as well, but research is still lacking. The outer leaves of greens usually contain more beta-carotene than do the inner leaves. Dandelion greens are bursting with twice the vitamin A of other greens.

Some greens—collard, mustard, and turnip—belong to the cruciferous family, which also includes broccoli, cabbage, and cauliflower. Research has shown that people who eat a lot of cruciferous vegetables are less likely to suffer cancer than those whose diets contain fewer servings.

Some greens stand out individually. Beet greens shine in several minerals, including iron, as well as potassium, but they are also naturally high in sodium. Turnip greens provide folic acid—important for the prevention of birth defects and heart disease—plus manganese and copper. They are much richer in fiber and calcium than other greens.

SELECTION AND STORAGE

Choose greens that have smooth, green, firm leaves. Small, young leaves are likely to be the least bitter and most tender. Be sure the produce department kept the greens well-chilled, or they'll be bitter. Wilting is a sign of bitter-tasting greens.

Collard Greens, Cooked
Serving Size: ½ cup

Calories 56	Dietary Fiber ....<1 g
Fat.............................<1 g	Sodium.....................18 mg
Saturated Fat.........0 g	Vitamin A.............2,109 IU
Cholesterol.................0 mg	Vitamin C ....9 mg
Carbohydrate ....3 g	Calcium ....74 mg
Protein........................1 g	

Unwashed greens store well for three to five days when wrapped in a damp paper towel and stored in an airtight plastic bag. The longer they are stored, however, the more bitter they will be. Be sure to wash greens well and remove the tough stems; cook only the leaves. One pound of raw leaves yields about a half cup of cooked greens.

PREPARATION AND SERVING TIPS

Cook greens in a small amount of water, or steam them, to preserve their vitamin C content. Cook with the lid off to prevent the greens from turning a drab olive color. When you can, strain the nutritious cooking liquid and use it as a base for soups or stews.

Greens will overpower a salad. To eat them as a side dish, simmer in seasoned water or broth until wilted (collards may need to cook longer). Or you can combine greens with other vegetables and a whole grain for a healthful stir-fry dish. Finally, add them to soups and stews, where their strong flavor is an advantage.

BEET GREENS, COOKED
Serving Size: ½ cup

Calories	20	Vitamin A	3,672 IU
Fat	<1 g	Vitamin C	18 mg
Saturated Fat	0 g	Riboflavin	<1 mg
Cholesterol	0 mg	Calcium	82 mg
Carbohydrate	4 g	Copper	<1 mg
Protein	2 g	Iron	1 mg
Dietary Fiber	1 g	Magnesium	49 mg
Sodium	173 mg	Potassium	654 mg

GREENS FOR SALADS

Everyone knows salads are diet food. Yet a heavy hand with dressing will do the healthiest salad in. Still, eaten before a meal, a salad can take the edge off hunger, while filling your stomach with its bulk. This should curb your appetite enough to modulate overindulgence for the rest of the meal. Though Romaine provides decent nutrition, most lettuce does not, so to make the ultimate fat-fighting salad, don't overlook greens. Wonderfully flavored greens like raddichio, arugula, endive, chicory, and escarole make a salad stand out in taste and nutrition. Some greens back up their fat-fighting bulk with a decent amount of fiber.

HEALTH BENEFITS

The darker the color of the salad green, the more nutritious it is. Beta-carotene is the chief disease-fighting nutrient found in the darker-colored greens. As an antioxidant, it battles certain cancers, heart disease, and cataracts. A dark-green color also indicates the presence of folic acid, which helps prevent neural-tube birth defects in the beginning stages of pregnancy. Researchers are uncovering other important contributions folic acid has to offer to your well-being like its role in the prevention of heart disease.

Chicory is a good source of vitamin C, another antioxidant nutrient linked to prevention of heart disease, cancer, and cataracts. Some salad greens, including arugula and watercress, are members of the cruciferous family, adding more ammunition to the fight against cancer.

SELECTION AND STORAGE

Avoid salad greens that are wilted or have brown-edged or slimy leaves. Once they reach this point, there's no bringing them back to life. They should have vivid color, and leaves should be firm. Store greens in your refrigerator's crisper drawer, roots intact, in perforated plastic bags.

Romaine is a produce-department staple, though it may never completely take the place of the boring, yet popular, iceberg. Less-recognizable greens come in a wider variety of sizes, shapes, and colors, and some manufacturers prepack a variety of these delicious treasures in handy salad packs.

Arugula: Also known as rocket or roquette, these small, flat leaves have a hot, peppery flavor. The older and larger the leaves, the more mustardlike the flavor. You're more likely to find arugula in ethnic or farmers' markets than in supermarkets. It's so delicate, it keeps for only a day or two.

Chicory: This curly-leaved green is sometimes mistakenly called curly endive. The dark-green leaves have a bitter taste but work well in salads with well-seasoned dressings.

Endive: Belgian endive and white chicory are names for this pale salad green. The small, cigar-shaped head has tightly packed leaves and a slightly bitter flavor. Endive stays fresh for three to four days.

Escarole: A close cousin to chicory, escarole is actually a type of endive. It has broad, slightly curved green leaves, with a milder flavor than Belgian endive.

Radicchio: Though it looks like a miniature head of red cabbage, this salad green is actually a member of the chicory family, with a less bitter flavor. Radicchio keeps up to a week.

ROMAINE LETTUCE
Serving Size: ½ cup, shredded

Calories	4	Sodium	2 mg
Fat	<1 g	Calcium	10 mg
Saturated Fat	0 g	Potassium	81 mg
Cholesterol	0 mg	Vitamin A	728 IU
Carbohydrate	1 g	Folic Acid	38 mcg
Protein	1 g	Vitamin C	7 mg
Dietary Fiber	<1 g		

Romaine: Also known as cos, Romaine lettuce has long leaves that are crisp, with an oh-so-slight bitter taste. Romaine is hearty, storing well for up to ten days.

Watercress: This delicate green is sold in "bouquets," or trimmed and sealed in vacuum packs. Choose dark-green, glossy leaves and store in plastic bags; use in a day or two. Unopened vacuum packs last up to three days.

PREPARATION AND SERVING TIPS

Dirt and grit often settle between the leaves of salad greens. Separate the leaves, then wash well before using. For small bunches, swish leaves in a bowl of water.

In general, the stronger and more bitter the salad green, the stronger-flavored the dressing should be. Try warm mustard or garlic-based dressings with strong-flavored salad greens. But keep fat down: Rely more on vinegar than oil, or use low-fat yogurt or buttermilk as a base.

HERBS & SPICES

There are dozens upon dozens of herbs and spices, from commonplace black pepper to more exotic turmeric and cardamom. But all share two unique features—they add flavor and aroma to food, especially low-fat dishes where flavor can sometimes be lacking. Herbs and spices, then, are necessities in the fight against fat. Too often, they are relegated to attractively labeled bottles on revolving spice racks. This is unfortunate, because using the right blend of these taste enhancers can literally make or break a dish.

HEALTH BENEFITS

Most dried herbs and spices are low in calories, providing no more than 15 calories per teaspoon. So feel free to use them even if you are following a low-calorie regimen. Some are surprisingly good sources of nutrients. Paprika is an excellent source of vitamin A, parsley is rich in vitamin C, cumin is an unexpected source of iron, and caraway seeds even contribute a little calcium to your diet.

New research findings suggest that several herbs are also rich sources of antioxidants that may possibly prevent the growth of cancer cells and protect delicate arteries from buildup of cholesterol-filled plaque. Among them: allspice, basil, clove, coriander, dill, fennel leaves, mint, nutmeg, parsley, rosemary, and sage.

Aside from their nutrient and antioxidant contents, there are many health claims made for individual herbs. Here are but a few: Mint relieves gas and nausea; cinnamon enhances insulin's activity; oregano has antiseptic properties; sage contains compounds that act as antibiotics; thyme is said to relieve cramps. Most, however, have not been scientifically proved.

Selection and Storage

In our opinion, fresh is best. But it's not always easy to find fresh herbs. Farmers' markets are your best bet. Supermarkets may carry them sporadically, but often only in summer (although many supermarkets will special order them if you ask). You may find them through mail order catalogues, or you can grow your own windowsill herb garden. In any case, buy fresh herbs only as you need them. Wrap them in damp paper towels, place in a plastic bag, and refrigerate. They should last a few days.

When fresh aren't available, dried will do. Store dried herbs and spices in airtight containers, away from heat and light (over the stove is the worst spot). Dried herbs will keep for a year. Whole spices, like cloves or cinnamon, keep much longer. The flavor of dried herbs tends to fade faster than that of dried spices.

Preparation and Serving Tips

Becoming acquainted with herbs and spices is a must if you're committed to low-fat or low-salt cooking. When you remove fat or salt, a lot of flavor goes with it. That loss of flavor can be masked with herbs and spices.

If you're a novice at using herbs and spices, start by using only one or two per dish. If you're using fresh herbs, don't be shy. Their flavors are often subtle, and it usually takes more than you think to overpower a dish. With dried herbs, however, a little often goes a long way, so use judiciously. Start with about ¼ to ⅓ teaspoon until you get a better "feel" for the amount you like in dishes.

If you're cooking with fresh herbs, wait until the end of the cooking time to add them, so they'll retain their delicate flavor. Dried herbs and spices, on the other hand, hold their flavor well—even under intense heat.

Here are some seasoning suggestions to get you started:

Pasta: basil, fennel, garlic, paprika, parsley, sage

Potatoes: chives, garlic, paprika, parsley, rosemary

Rice: cumin, marjoram, parsley, saffron, tarragon, thyme, turmeric

Salads: basil, chervil, chives, dillweed, marjoram, mint, parsley, tarragon

Seafood: chervil, dill, fennel, tarragon, parsley

Vegetables: basil, caraway, chives, dillweed, marjoram, mint, nutmeg, oregano, paprika, rosemary, savory, tarragon, thyme

KALE

Kale is king. Along with broccoli, it is one of the nutrition stand-outs among vegetables. It fights fat through its ability to mingle in a variety of roles—in side dishes, combined in main dishes, or in salads. For a green, kale is unusually high in fiber. This helps create the bulk you need to fill you up. It also pumps you up with nutrients, like calcium.

HEALTH BENEFITS

Though greens in general are nutritious foods, kale stands a head above the rest. Not only is it one of your best sources of beta-carotene, one of the antioxidants believed by many nutrition experts to be a major player in the battle against cancer, heart disease, and cataracts, it also provides other important nutrients.

According to recent research results, kale is an incredible source of well-absorbed calcium, which is one of the many factors that may help prevent osteoporosis. It also provides decent amounts of vitamin C, folic acid, magnesium, and potassium.

Don't forget, kale's a member of the cruciferous family, along with broccoli, brussels sprouts, cabbage, cauliflower, and collard greens. Many researchers believe that loading up on cruciferous vegetables can help ward off certain cancers.

SELECTION AND STORAGE

Kale looks like a darker green version of collards, but with frills. It also has a stronger flavor and a somewhat coarser tex-

KALE, COOKED
Serving Size: ½ cup

Calories 21	Sodium.....................15 mg
Fat.............................<1 g	Vitamin A.............4,810 IU
Saturated Fat.........0 g	Folic Acid ....9 mcg
Cholesterol.................0 mg	Vitamin C ....27 mg
Carbohydrate ....:...4 g	Calcium ....47 mg
Protein.........................1 g	Magnesium ....15 mg
Dietary Fiber ....3 g	Potassium ....148 mg

ture. The smaller leaves are more tender and the flavor is more mild, but it grows stronger the longer it is stored. So unless you actually prefer a strong taste, use kale within a day or two of buying it. Wrap fresh kale in damp paper towels, and store it in a plastic bag in the crisper drawer of your refrigerator.

PREPARATION AND SERVING TIPS

Wash kale thoroughly before cooking, as it often has dirt and sand in its leaves. Hearty kale stands up well to cooking, so just about any method will do. But keep cooking time to a minimum to preserve nutrients and to keep kale's strong odor from permeating the kitchen.

Simmer the greens in a well-seasoned stock for 10 to 30 minutes, until tender. Don't forget that most greens cook down a great deal. One pound of raw yields only about a half cup of cooked. Kale also works well in stir-fries, soups, and stews.

KIWIFRUIT

The funny-looking green fruit in the fuzzy brown package hit this country by storm a few years back. Now it's almost as commonplace as apples and bananas. Though native to China—as the "Chinese gooseberry"—a marketing campaign renamed this unusual fruit to one more suited to its new imported home—New Zealand. Today, it is grown in California. Kiwis carry a lot of nutrition in a small package. They aren't high in calories, yet they pack a powerful punch with their strong tart taste, which allows them to jazz up the flavor of low-fat diets.

HEALTH BENEFITS

Kiwifruit is literally filled with fiber. All those little black seeds combine for a good dose of insoluble fiber, which aids digestion by decreasing the transit time of stools through your system. But kiwifruit also offers soluble fiber, providing bulk that promotes the feeling of fullness—a natural diet aid. By creating gel-like substances that trap bile acids, it has the potential to reduce blood cholesterol levels.

Kiwis are brimming with vitamin C, which is essential for healthy gums and important for wound healing, and boasts ample amounts of good-for-your-bones magnesium and potassium.

SELECTION AND STORAGE

Because New Zealand and California have opposite seasons, and, therefore, opposite harvests, kiwis are available year-round. Choose those that are fairly firm, but give under slight pressure. Firm kiwis need about a week to ripen at room temperature. You can hasten the process by placing them in a closed paper bag. Store the bag at room temperature and begin checking for ripeness after two days. Ripe kiwis keep for one to two weeks in the refrigerator.

PREPARATION AND SERVING TIPS

With its brilliant green color and its inner circle of tiny black seeds, sliced kiwis are the perfect garnish. They don't even discolor when exposed to air since they contain so much vitamin C, which contains antioxidant properties that prevent oxygen from oxidizing the fruit and turning it brown.

Most people prefer eating peeled kiwifruit, though the skin is edible—just rub off the brown fuzz. You can slice kiwi, or peel it and eat it whole. Since kiwifruit contains a "tenderizing" enzyme that prevents gelatin from setting, it's a good idea to leave kiwifruit out of molded salads.

KIWIFRUIT
Serving Size: 1 medium

Calories	46	Dietary Fiber	3 g
Fat	<1 g	Sodium	4 mg
Saturated Fat	0 g	Vitamin C	75 mg
Cholesterol	0 mg	Calcium	20 mg
Carbohydrate	11 g	Magnesium	23 mg
Protein	1 g	Potassium	252 mg

LEMONS & LIMES

Probably the most tart of fruits, lemons and limes are rarely eaten alone. But their tart juice adds life to everything from salads to pies. This gives them *carte blanche* to fight fat by perking up the bland flavor of low-fat foods.

HEALTH BENEFITS

Anyone cutting back on fat or salt should keep a lemon or lime handy. Squeeze on lemon or lime juice, add a few herbs, and you can perk up most any dish. Neither juice adds any appreciable calories, just pizzazz, plus a bit of nutrition, too.

Both lemons and limes exude vitamin C, the antioxidant that helps fight heart disease and cancer. Moreover, lemons and limes contain phytochemicals, such as terpenes and limonenes, that may play a role in preventing some cancers.

SELECTION AND STORAGE

Look for firm, unblemished fruit that's heavy for its size—an indicator of juiciness. Thin-skinned fruit yields the most juice. Refrigerated, they keep for a month or two. Lemons will even keep for a week or two at room temperature, but limes must be refrigerated.

Lemon varieties vary mostly in their skin thickness, juiciness, and number of seeds. The key lime—of pie fame—is more flavorful than other lime varieties because of its greater acidity. Key limes are small and round; other varieties look more like green lemons. Limes typically turn yellowish as they ripen. The greenest limes have the best flavor.

Lime
Serving Size: 1 medium

Calories	20	Dietary Fiber	2 g
Fat	<1 g	Sodium	1 mg
Saturated Fat	0 g	Folic Acid	6 mcg
Cholesterol	0 mg	Vitamin C	20 mg
Carbohydrate	7 g	Calcium	22 mg
Protein	<1 g	Potassium	68 mg

Lemon
Serving Size: 1 medium

Calories	17	Dietary Fiber	3 g
Fat	<1 g	Sodium	1 mg
Saturated Fat	0 g	Folic Acid	6 mcg
Cholesterol	0 mg	Vitamin C	31 mg
Carbohydrate	5 g	Calcium	15 mg
Protein	<1 g	Potassium	80 mg

PREPARATION AND SERVING TIPS

To get more juice from a lemon or lime, bring it to room temperature, then roll it back and forth under the palm of your hand before you cut and squeeze it.

The most flavorful part of the fruit is its "zest," or skin. Scrape it off with a grater or knife and use it to enhance desserts and fruit salads.

A twist of lemon also adds zing to fish.

LENTILS

Because they boast a bevy of low-fat nutrients, lentils are finally gaining the recognition they deserve as a great source of low-fat protein, making them the perfect substitute for meat.

HEALTH BENEFITS

Lentils' high fiber content is a boon to health; it's mostly the soluble kind, so it lowers blood cholesterol by creating gels that bind with bile acids, forcing the body to use cholesterol to replace them. These gels also tie up carbohydrates, so they are absorbed more slowly, keeping you full longer—of benefit to anyone on a diet.

Lentils are exceptionally high in folic acid, which can help prevent certain birth defects and may prevent heart disease as well. Lentils are an important source of iron for vegetarians, serving as protection against anemia.

SELECTION AND STORAGE

Brown, green, and red lentils are the most common varieties in the United States. Most supermarkets carry them packaged, but you can buy them in bulk at health-food stores and gourmet markets.

If you buy them packaged, look for well-sealed containers, with uniformly sized, brightly colored, disk-shaped lentils. If you buy them in bulk, check the lentils for tiny pinholes. Don't buy them if you spot holes; they're a sign of insect infestation.

When stored in a well-sealed container at a cool temperature, lentils keep for up to a year.

PREPARATION AND SERVING TIPS

Red lentils cook quickly and become mushy, so they work best in dishes where a firm texture isn't a concern, like in soups, purees, or dips. Brown or green lentils, on the other hand, retain their shape if not overcooked and can be used in salads or any dish in which you don't want your lentils reduced to mush.

Most lentils cook in 30 to 45 minutes or less and they don't require any precooking soak like dried beans do.

Best of all, lentils are willing recipients of flavorful herbs and spices, taking on the flavors of the foods they are mixed with. No wonder they are common in Indian, Middle Eastern, and African recipes.

LENTILS

Serving Size: ½ cup, cooked

Calories	115	Thiamin	<1 mg
Fat	<1 g	Vitamin B6	<1 mg
Saturated Fat	<1 g	Calcium	19 mg
Cholesterol	0 mg	Copper	<1 mg
Carbohydrate	20 g	Iron	3 mg
Protein	9 g	Magnesium	35 mg
Dietary Fiber	5 g	Manganese	<1 mg
Sodium	2 mg	Phosphorus	178 mg
Folic Acid	179 mcg	Potassium	366 mg
Niacin	1 mg	Zinc	1 mg

MANGOES

This "fruit of India," as it is sometimes called, is unique in its wealth of nutrients and richness of flavor. Though the pungent flavor may be an acquired taste for some, the one-two nutrition punch it delivers is worth it.

HEALTH BENEFITS

If you're limiting your intake of fat and calories, eating concentrated sources of nutrients makes sense. And mangoes deliver. Mangoes are a superior source of beta-carotene. In fact, they are one of the top beta-carotene providers you can eat. Consuming large amounts of this antioxidant has been linked to a reduced risk of some forms of cancers, including lung cancer.

Just one mango provides almost an entire day's worth of vitamin C. Unlike many other fruits, mangoes contribute several B vitamins and the minerals calcium and magnesium.

SELECTION AND STORAGE

There are hundreds of varieties of mangoes in every shape, size, and color. The color of mangoes ranges from yellow to red and will deepen as the fruit ripens, though some green may remain even in perfectly ripened fruits. When ripe, a mango has a sweet, perfumey smell. If it has a fermented aroma, then it's past its prime.

Choose mangoes that feel firm, but yield to slight pressure. The skin should be unbroken, and the color should have begun to change from green to yellow, orange, or red. Though

MANGOES
Serving Size: 1 mango

Calories	135	Niacin	1 mg
Fat	1 g	Riboflavin	<1 mg
Saturated Fat	<1 g	Thiamin	<1 mg
Cholesterol	0 mg	Vitamin B₆	<1 mg
Carbohydrate	35 g	Vitamin C	57 mg
Protein	1 g	Calcium	21 mg
Dietary Fiber	6 g	Magnesium	18 mg
Sodium	4 mg	Potassium	322 mg
Vitamin A	8,060 IU		

it's normal for mangoes to have some black spots, avoid those mottled with too many. It's a sign the fruit is overripe. Ditto for loose or shriveled skin.

If you bring home a mango that isn't ripe, you can speed the process by placing it in a paper bag with a ripe mango. Check daily to avoid overripening.

PREPARATION AND SERVING TIPS

Because mangoes are so juicy, they can be a real mess to cut and serve. You can peel the fruit and eat it as you would a peach, just be sure to have plenty of napkins or paper towels on hand to sop up the juice that runs down your chin.

Try eating chilled mangoes as dessert or as breakfast fruit. For extra zip, sprinkle them with a little lime juice. Mangoes are an indispensable ingredient in sauces and chutneys.

MELONS

Melons may come in different shapes, sizes, and colors, but they all have two things in common: a soft, sweet, juicy pulp and superb, natural low-fat taste—that's why it's hard to say no to melons. Besides being low in fat, melons offer a decent dose of fiber, which helps fill you up. As a snack for dieters, melons can't be beat. Their juicy sweetness is just the substitute for fat-filled snacks and desserts.

HEALTH BENEFITS

Most melons are rich in potassium, a nutrient that may help control blood pressure and possibly prevent strokes. They're also abundant in vitamin C, one arm of the now-famous disease-fighting antioxidant trio. Another arm that's well represented is beta-carotene. Researchers believe that beta-carotene and vitamin C are capable of preventing heart disease, cancer, and other chronic conditions. No matter which way you cut them, when it comes to nutrition, melons are number one.

SELECTION AND STORAGE

The three most popular melons in the United States are cantaloupe, watermelon, and honeydew. In general, look for melons that are evenly shaped with no bruises, cracks, or soft spots. Select melons that are heavy for their size; they tend to be juicier.

Cantaloupes should have a prominent light brown netting that stands out from the underlying smooth skin. If the stem is still attached, the melon was picked too early. Ripe cantaloupes have a mildly sweet fragrance. If the cantaloupe smells sickeningly sweet, or if there is mold where the stem used to be, it is probably overripe and quite possibly rotten. Cantaloupes continue to ripen off the vine, so if you buy it ripe, eat it as soon as possible.

Choosing a watermelon is a little chancier. Watermelons don't ripen much after they are picked, so what you see is what you get. The single most reliable sign of ripeness is a firm underside with a yellowish color; if it is white or green, the melon is not yet mature. A whole watermelon keeps in the refrigerator up to a week, but cut watermelon should be eaten as soon as possible. The flesh deteriorates rapidly, taking on an unappetizing slimy texture.

Ripe honeydew, signaled by a yellowish-white color, are the sweetest of the melons. Avoid those that are paper-white or greenish white; they'll never ripen. If the skin of a honeydew is smooth, it was picked prematurely. It should have a slightly

CANTALOUPE
Serving Size: ½ melon

Calories	94	Vitamin A	8,608 IU
Fat	1 g	Folic Acid	46 mcg
Saturated Fat	na	Niacin	2 mg
Cholesterol	0 mg	Vitamin B$_6$	<1 mg
Carbohydrate	22 g	Vitamin C	113 mg
Protein	2 g	Calcium	28 mg
Dietary Fiber	3 g	Magnesium	28 mg
Sodium	23 mg	Potassium	825 mg

WATERMELON
Serving Size: 1/16 fruit

Calories	152	Niacin	1 mg
Fat	2 g	Pantothenic Acid	1 mg
Saturated Fat	na	Thiamin	<1 mg
Cholesterol	0 mg	Vitamin B₆	1 mg
Carbohydrate	35 g	Vitamin C	47 mg
Protein	3 g	Calcium	38 mg
Dietary Fiber	3 g	Magnesium	52 mg
Sodium	10 mg	Potassium	560 mg
Vitamin A	1,762 IU	Copper	2 mg

wrinkled feel. Honeydews keep longer than cantaloupes, but should still be refrigerated. Try to cut it open within four to five days. When you do, leave the seeds in place until you're ready to eat it; they help keep the fruit moist.

PREPARATION AND SERVING TIPS

Some people like melons only slightly chilled or even room temperature, but watermelons taste best when they're served icy cold. A multicolored melon-ball salad topped with fresh, chopped mint makes a pretty dessert. Chilled melon soup is a refreshing change of pace in hot weather. And the natural cavity left in a cantaloupe after removing the seeds is a perfect place for fillers like nonfat yogurt or fruit salad.

MILK, SKIM

Milk is nicknamed "nature's most perfect food." While it's not truly perfect, skim milk certainly comes close with its high protein and exceptional calcium counts and a bevy of B vitamins. All this for only 86 calories in an eight-ounce glass. In fact, merely switching from whole milk to skim milk can be one of the more significant choices you can make to reduce fat and calories in your diet.

Though milk is often thought of as highly allergenic, only a tiny fraction of people are truly allergic to milk. Gastrointestinal distress after drinking milk is more likely the result of lactose intolerance, a much more common problem. A large percentage of the world's population—though far fewer in the United States—suffer from lactose intolerance, the inability to digest lactose, the natural sugar in milk. New research, however, claims gastrointestinal symptoms are often incorrectly attributed to this condition. Even those in the study who proved to be lactose intolerant were able to enjoy at least a cup of milk a day without experiencing digestive distress.

HEALTH BENEFITS

The advantage of skim milk over whole milk cannot be stressed enough. The fat in whole milk is mostly saturated animal fat—the kind that raises blood cholesterol. And when you compare the percentage of calories from fat per serving, whole milk checks in at 50 percent; skim milk at 4 percent. So you can really see the fat savings you'll reap if you make the switch. And if you do it gradually, switching first to 2 percent, then 1 percent, then skim, the transition is painless.

MILK, SKIM
Serving Size: 8 oz

Calories	86	Vitamin B$_{12}$	1 mcg
Fat	<1 g	Niacin	<1 mg
Saturated Fat	<1 g	Pantothenic Acid	1 mg
Cholesterol	4 mg	Riboflavin	<1 mg
Carbohydrate	12 g	Vitamin D	3 mcg
Protein	8 g	Calcium	302 mg
Dietary Fiber	0 g	Phosphorus	247 mg
Sodium	126 mg	Potassium	406 mg
Vitamin A	500 IU		

Switching to skim milk won't compromise the amount of nutrients in your glass. If anything, you'll get slightly more. Fat takes up a lot of space, leaving less room for nutrients, so when the fat content is decreased, there's more room for nutrients. Skim milk is an excellent source of calcium, which plays a critical role in preventing osteoporosis. And the calcium in milk may be better absorbed than the calcium found in supplements, because lactose, which is also found in milk, but not in supplements, appears to aid its absorption.

Milk in this country is fortified with vitamins A and D and is the major dietary source of both. It's also one of the major contributors of riboflavin, a B vitamin involved in the breakdown of food.

SELECTION AND STORAGE

All milk should have a sell-by date stamped on the carton. Don't depend on milk to stay fresh much longer than the date on the carton.

Milk in translucent plastic jugs is susceptible to considerable losses of riboflavin and vitamin A, much more so than milk in paper cartons. That's because light, even the fluorescent light in supermarkets, destroys these two light-sensitive nutrients. This same light also affects the taste of milk.

Whatever you do, don't buy raw milk or products made from raw milk, such as some cheeses. Raw milk has not been pasteurized and often carries bacteria that can make you sick. It's especially dangerous to give it to children, the elderly, or people with an impaired immune system.

PREPARATION AND SERVING TIPS

Milk tastes best when it's served icy cold. There are, of course, some recipes that just won't work well with skim milk, but most do fine. A tip: When you heat milk, don't allow it to come to a boil. This forms a film on the surface that won't dissolve.

MILLET

In the United States, millet is used mainly for fodder and birdseed, but this nutritious grain is a staple in the diets of a large portion of the world's population, including Africa and Asia. It has been cultivated for about 6,000 years. There are several varieties of millet available throughout the world. In Ethiopia, it is used to make porridge; in India, to make roti (a traditional bread); and in the Caribbean, it is cooked with peas and beans.

HEALTH BENEFITS

Millet is a remarkable source of protein, making it perfect for vegetarian diets. It's also a good source of niacin, copper, and manganese. You may want to give millet a try if you are allergic to wheat. Chances are, you won't suffer a reaction.

SELECTION AND STORAGE

Look for this slightly bland-flavored grain in health food stores, Asian markets, and gourmet shops. Millet is a tiny, pale-yellow bead. Store it in an airtight container in a cool, dry place, and it should keep for up to a month. In the freezer it will keep up to a year.

You may occasionally see cracked millet sold as couscous. But couscous is most often made from semolina.

PREPARATION AND SERVING TIPS

Millet has no characteristic flavor of its own, and it tends to take on the flavor of the foods it is prepared with. To cook millet, add one cup of whole millet and a teaspoon of margarine or oil to two cups of boiling water. Simmer, covered, for 25 to 30 minutes. It should double in volume, once all the water is absorbed. Keep it covered and undisturbed while it cooks, and you'll produce a millet that is fluffy; stir it often and it will have a creamy consistency, like a cooked cereal.

For a change from the same old thing, try millet on its own as a hot breakfast cereal. You can cook it with apple juice, instead of water, and top it off with raisins, brown sugar, or nuts.

Cooked millet can also be combined with cooked beans or peas to make vegetarian "burgers." Simply combine the two (they should be moist enough to hold together), and shape into patties.

Millet also works well in soups and stews. Simply rinse the millet in a strainer or colander and add to the mix. It should take about 20 to 30 minutes for the millet to absorb the liquid and become tender.

Millet
Serving Size: ½ cup

Calories	143	Dietary Fiber	4.3 g
Protein	4.2 g	Sodium	2 mg
Carbohydrate	28.4 g	Niacin	1.6 mg
Fat	1.2 g	Copper	0.2 mg
Saturated	0.2 g	Magnesium	52 mg
Cholesterol	0 mg	Manganese	0.3 mg

MUSHROOMS

Mushrooms may be standard fare in Asian cultures, but Americans are only beginning to appreciate them for their ability to perk up low-fat dishes. Though low in fat, they contain a super-powerful flavor enhancer, glutamic acid, which is the same amino acid (a building block of protein) found in MSG (monosodium glutamate), except the mushroom variety isn't loaded with salt. Besides lending wonderful flavor to foods, mushrooms contribute more nutrition than you might think.

HEALTH BENEFITS

Mushrooms provide an unusual array of nutrients, not unlike those in meat, making them a particularly appropriate food for vegetarians. Cooked mushrooms are an unexpected protein source, which, even though incomplete, is easily complemented by grains. They also shine in iron, riboflavin, and niacin; offer decent amounts of potassium and zinc; and are full of fiber.

When possible, stick to cooked mushrooms. They're higher in nutrients than raw mushrooms; for the same volume, you get two, three, or even four times the nutrients. That's because cooking removes water from mushrooms, concentrating nutrients and flavor. Moreover, hydrazines—toxic natural compounds in raw mushrooms—are eliminated when mushrooms are cooked or dried.

Some researchers have found that cooked enoki, oyster, shiitake, pine, and straw mushrooms have antitumor activity.

BUTTON MUSHROOMS, FRESH, COOKED
Serving Size: ½ cup pieces

Calories 21	Sodium ....2 mg
Fat ....<1 g	Riboflavin ....<1 mg
Saturated Fat ....0 g	Niacin ....4 mg
Cholesterol ....0 mg	Iron ....1 mg
Carbohydrate ....4 g	Potassium ....277 mg
Protein ....2 g	Zinc ....1 mg
Dietary Fiber ....2 g	

Wood-ear mushrooms exhibit blood-thinning properties that may help prevent the dangerous clotting that contributes to heart disease.

SELECTION AND STORAGE

All supermarkets stock the white button mushroom, and many have expanded their selection to include the popular shiitake; trumpet-shaped chanterelle; sprout-like enoki; small, brown, intensely-flavored, spongy-capped morel; huge oyster; hearty-flavored portobello; and crunchy, often dried, Chinese wood-ear.

When selecting button mushrooms, look for those with caps that extend completely down to the stems, with no brown "gills" showing. If mushrooms have "opened"—meaning the gills are showing—they are older and won't last as long. They are perfectly acceptable to use, but they'll have a stronger flavor. The color should be creamy white or soft tan. Avoid those that have dark-brown soft spots or long, woody stems. Growers used to add sulfites to the packages to maintain their white color for longer periods of time, but this practice was discontinued—good news for those who are allergic to these additives.

Mushrooms like cool, humid, circulating air. So store them in a paper bag or ventilated container in your refrigerator, but not in the crisper drawer. Do not store them in a plastic bag; otherwise they'll get slimy. Mushrooms only last a couple of days, but you can still use them for flavoring even after they've turned brown.

A caution: Picking wild mushrooms can be hazardous to your health. There are too many poisonous varieties that fool even the most experienced foragers. So play it safe and stick to cultivated varieties of wild mushrooms.

PREPARATION AND SERVING TIPS

Don't wash mushrooms; they absorb water like a sponge. Use a mushroom brush or wipe with a barely damp cloth. Don't cut mushrooms until you're ready to use them; they'll darken. Use the trimmed stems to flavor soups.

Mushrooms cook quickly. Overcooking makes them rubbery and tough. If you saute, go easy on the butter or margarine; they'll absorb it like water and you'll suffer the consequences. Try cooking them in a bit of wine instead. Due to their high water content, mushrooms add liquid to a dish once they cook down.

NUTS & SEEDS

This category is just a little nutty. Besides seeds, it encompasses some foods that aren't true nuts but have similar nutrition. This includes peanuts (really legumes) and Brazil nuts and cashews, which are technically seeds. Because almost all nuts and seeds are super high in fat, it may surprise you that we are calling them fat-fighting foods. But the fat is unsaturated and may have disease-fighting properties. As long as you can restrain yourself, nuts and seeds can indeed be fat-fighters. By taking the place of more traditional protein sources, nuts and seeds can actually reduce the fat in your overall diet.

HEALTH BENEFITS

Nuts and seeds are good news/bad news foods. They are high in protein and nutrients, though their fat content—75 to 95 percent of total calories—precludes eating too many at a time. Macadamia, the gourmet of nuts, is the worst culprit. Chestnuts are the only truly low-fat nuts—only eight percent of their calories comes from fat.

Of all the nuts, peanuts provide the most complete protein. Other nuts are missing the amino acid lysine. But all are easily complemented by grains. As an alternative protein source, then, their fat content can be forgiven.

Recent research has heartened nut lovers. Studies at Loma Linda University in California found that eating nuts five times a week—about two ounces a day—lowered participants' blood cholesterol levels by 12 percent. Walnuts were used, but similar results have been reported with almonds and peanuts. The researchers theorize that replacing saturated fat in the diet with the monounsaturated fat in nuts may be the key. It makes sense, then, to eat nuts instead of other fatty foods, not just to gobble them down on top of your regular fare.

Some nuts, notably walnuts, are rich in omega-3 fatty acids, which may contribute further to the fight against heart disease and possibly even arthritis. Also, seeds and some nuts contain significant amounts of vitamin E. As an antioxidant, vitamin E can help prevent the oxidation of LDL cholesterol, which can damage arteries. More heartening news: Seeds are a good source of folic acid. Researchers have found that folic acid helps prevent the buildup of homocysteine. High levels of this amino acid have been linked to heart disease.

Seeds, peanuts, and peanut butter are super sources of niacin. Nuts are chock-full of hard-to-get minerals, such as copper, iron, and zinc. Seeds are among the better plant sources of iron and zinc. And nuts do their part to keep bones strong by providing magnesium, manganese, and boron.

Peanut Butter, Smooth Style
Serving Size: 2 Tbsp

Calories	188	Niacin	4 mg
Fat	16 g	Vitamin E	3 mg
Saturated Fat	3 g	Copper	<1 mg
Cholesterol	0 mg	Magnesium	50 mg
Carbohydrate	7 g	Manganese	1 mg
Protein	8 g	Phosphorus	103 mg
Dietary Fiber	2 g	Potassium	231 mg
Sodium	153 mg	Zinc	1 mg

One caution: Brazil nuts are astonishingly high in selenium—perhaps too high. True, selenium is a beneficial antioxidant, but too much selenium is toxic. Stick to only one or two for a snack.

Selection and Storage

Fresh nuts are available in fall and winter. Seeds and shelled nuts are available year-round, but check for a freshness date. If you buy bulk, they should smell fresh, not rancid. Aflatoxin, a known carcinogen produced by a mold that grows naturally on peanuts, can be a problem, so discard those that are discolored, shriveled, moldy, or taste bad. And stick to commercial brands of peanut butter. A survey found that best-selling brands contained only trace amounts of aflatoxin, supermarket brands had five times as much, while fresh-ground peanut butters averaged more than ten times as much.

Because of their high fat content, you must protect nuts from rancidity. Unshelled nuts can keep for a few months in a cool,

---

Cashews, Dry-roasted
Serving Size: 1 oz

Calories	163	Sodium	4 mg
Fat	13 g	Copper	1 mg
Saturated Fat	3 g	Iron	2 mg
Cholesterol	0 mg	Magnesium	74 mg
Carbohydrate	9 g	Phosphorus	139 mg
Protein	4 g	Zinc	2 mg
Dietary Fiber	2 g		

Sunflower Seed Kernels
Serving Size: 1 oz, oil-roasted

Calories	176	Niacin	1 mg
Fat	16 g	Vitamin E	14 mg
Saturated Fat	2 g	Copper	1 mg
Cholesterol	0 mg	Iron	2 mg
Carbohydrate	4 g	Magnesium	36 mg
Protein	6 g	Manganese	1 mg
Dietary Fiber	2 g	Phosphorus	323 mg
Sodium	1 mg	Zinc	2 mg
Folic Acid	67 mcg		

dry location. But once they're shelled or the container is opened, refrigerate or freeze them. Seeds with the hulls intact keep for several months if cool and dry; seed kernels don't keep as long.

PREPARATION AND SERVING TIPS

By using nuts in cooking and baking, you can benefit from their nutrition without overdoing fat and calories, since a little flavor goes a long way. Nuts on cereal can boost your morning fiber intake. Peanut butter on apple wedges or a slice of hearty whole-wheat toast is a superb breakfast or lunch.

A sprinkling of seed kernels over pasta, salads, and stir-fries adds crunch and flavor.

Tips: Brazil nuts open easier if chilled first; almonds should be boiled and then dunked in cold water to make peeling them a snap.

OATS

Whether horse feed or muffins come to mind when you think of oats, you're probably underestimating this truly healthful grain. Although its fat-fighting fiber has been sometimes maligned, rest assured it packs plenty of punch.

HEALTH BENEFITS

In the past few years, oat bran has risen and fallen from wonder-food status. While the media attention has vanished, oats remain as nutritious as ever, with the same fat-fighting potential for reducing the risk of disease as before.

A recent analysis of ten studies highlighted the effect of oats' soluble fiber—the same beta-glucans found in barley—on blood-cholesterol levels. On average, eating three grams of soluble (not total) fiber a day—the amount in two bowls of oatmeal or one cup of cooked oat bran—reduced cholesterol by six points in three months. Participants with the highest cholesterol levels saw the best response; those whose blood-cholesterol levels were over 230 mg/dL saw their levels drop by 16 points. Those who ate the most oat bran benefited the most. Another study showed that in certain individuals, oat bran can be as effective as—and certainly much less expensive than—medication in curbing elevated blood-cholesterol levels.

Similarly exciting results have been seen in people with diabetes and those with high-normal blood-sugar levels. The soluble fiber in oats means slower digestion, spreading the rise in blood sugar over a longer time period. Some people with diabetes who followed a diet high in soluble fiber from sources like oats and beans have been able to reduce their medication. Weight watchers benefit, too. The soluble fiber in oats fills you up by creating gels. The gels delay stomach emptying, so you feel full longer.

Oats have more to offer everyone. They are tops in protein and manganese—providing 50 percent of the recommended intake for this mineral. In addition, they offer an unusual amount of iron, thiamin, and magnesium.

SELECTION AND STORAGE

The bran of the oat grain is the outer layer of the oat kernel, where much of the fiber and many of the nutrients reside. Whole oats—rolled or steel-cut—contain the bran along with the rest of the oat kernel. Oat bran contains the same nutrients and fiber found in whole oats but they are more concentrated. So eating whole oats will give you the same benefits of oat bran, you'll just need to eat more of it to get the same effect.

Cooking time and texture are the only differences among the varieties. Steel-cut oats, sometimes called Scotch oats or Irish oats, are whole oats sliced into long pieces. They have a chewy texture and take about 20 minutes to cook.

Rolled oats are steamed and flattened between steel rollers, so they take about five minutes to cook and are easier to chew than steel-cut oats.

Quick oats are cut into smaller pieces before being rolled, so they cook very quickly—in about a minute. But the time saved from cooking quick oats rather than rolled oats may not be worth it, considering what you sacrifice in flavor and texture.

Instant oats are precooked and pressed so thin it takes only boiling water to "reconstitute" them. Generally, they have a lot of added sodium; the flavored versions also have added sugar.

Store oats in a dark, dry location in a well-sealed container. Oats will keep up to a year. Whole oats are more likely to go rancid, so be sure to refrigerate them.

Preparation and Serving Tips

To make oatmeal, all you do is simmer rolled oats in water on the stove for five minutes (one minute for quick oats). Do not overcook your oatmeal or you'll have a thick, gummy mess. If you like, sprinkle with cinnamon and top with skim milk. You couldn't find a more satisfying, low-fat, high-fiber way to start the day. Oat bran can be served as a hot cereal, too—it takes about six minutes to cook—though the taste might take some getting used to.

Rolled Oats, Cooked (Oatmeal)
Serving Size: ¾ cup (⅓ cup uncooked)

Calories	108	Sodium	1 mg
Fat	2 g	Thiamin	<1 mg
Saturated Fat	<1 g	Iron	1 mg
Cholesterol	0 mg	Magnesium	42 mg
Carbohydrate	19 g	Manganese	1 mg
Protein	5 g	Phosphorus	133 mg
Dietary Fiber	3 g	Zinc	1 mg

Granola is traditionally made with oats. By making it yourself, you can avoid the fat trap that many commercial varieties fall into. First, toast the oats in a shallow pan in an oven preheated to 300°F, stirring occasionally until brown. Then combine the oats with wheat germ, raisins, your favorite nuts or seeds (toasted), dried fruit if you like, and a little honey. Let the mixture cool, then store it in an air-tight container in the refrigerator.

Whole oats can be cooked (simmer for six minutes) and combined with rice for a pilaf, or mixed with vegetables and seeds for a main dish.

Both oat bran and oats (rolled or quick) can be used in baking. Oats alone don't contain enough gluten to make bread, but you can modify your recipes to include half the grain as oats.

ONIONS

The onion is a member of the allium family, which, as your nose will tell you, also includes garlic, shallots, leeks, and chives. Egyptians worshiped the onion's many layers as a symbol of eternity. Today, the onion can be one of the most useful and flavorful ingredients in creating low-fat, healthful dishes.

HEALTH BENEFITS

While dry onions are a surprising source of fiber, they are not particularly rich in any other nutrients. Green onions, on the other hand, have those green tops, which provide a wealth of vitamin A. Without their flavor, some low-fat foods would be far too bland for most of us.

Moreover, like garlic, onions are just now being appreciated for their contributions to health. Research has lagged behind that of garlic, but there are promising signs that onions have similar anticancer and cholesterol-lowering properties. Onions may also play a role in preventing blood clots and alleviating the symptoms of allergies and asthma.

SELECTION AND STORAGE

Dry onions are any common onion—yellow, white, or red—that does not require refrigeration. This distinguishes them from green onions, which will perish quickly when stored at room temperature.

Dry onions come in various shapes and colors, none of which is a reliable indicator of taste or strength. The white, or yellow globe, onion keeps its pungent flavor when cooked. All-purpose white or yellow onions are milder. Sweet onions—Bermuda, Spanish, and Italian—are the mildest.

Choose firm dry onions with shiny, tissue-thin skins. "Necks" should be tight and dry. If they look too dry or discolored or have soft, wet spots, don't buy them—they aren't fresh.

Dry onions keep three to four weeks if stored in a dry, dark, cool location. Don't store them next to potatoes, which give off a gas that'll cause onions to decay. Light turns onions bitter. A cut onion should be wrapped in plastic, refrigerated, and used within a day or two.

Green onions, also called "spring" onions because that's the time of the year when they are harvested, have small white bulbs and are topped by thin green stalks. Though they are often sold as scallions, true scallions are just straight green stalks with no bulb. Look for green onions with crisp, not wilted, tops. For pungent aroma, choose fatter bulbs; for a sweeter taste, smaller bulbs are your best bet.

Green onions must be refrigerated. They keep best in a plastic bag in your refrigerator's crisper drawer.

ONION, DRY
Serving Size: ½ cup chopped

Calories	29	Protein	1 g
Fat	<1 g	Dietary Fiber	2 g
Cholesterol	0 mg	Sodium	8 mg
Saturated Fat	0 g	Vitamin C	6 mg
Carbohydrate	7 g	Vitamin B₆	<1 mg

PREPARATION AND SERVING TIPS

To keep tears from flowing, try slicing onions under running water. Or chill onions for an hour before cutting. To get the onion smell off your hands, rub your fingers with lemon juice or vinegar.

Onions are the perfect seasoning for almost any cooked dish. Their flavor mellows when they are cooked because smelly sulfur compounds are converted to sugar when heated. Onions saute wonderfully, even without butter. Use a nonstick skillet and perhaps a teaspoon of olive oil. Keep heat low or they'll scorch and turn bitter.

Sweet onions are ideal raw, as rings in salads or as slices atop sandwiches. They add bite to a three-bean salad or a plate of homegrown tomatoes.

Wash green onions, trimming roots and dry leaves. Chop up bulb, stalk, and all. They work well in stir-fry dishes, adding an understated bite. Green onions can also be served raw with low-fat dip as part of a crudité platter.

GREEN ONION, FRESH
Serving Size: ½ cup chopped (stalks and bulbs)

Calories	13	Dietary Fiber	1 g
Fat	<1 g	Sodium	2 mg
Saturated Fat	0 g	Vitamin A	2,500 IU
Cholesterol	0 mg	Vitamin C	23 mg
Carbohydrate	3 g	Iron	1 mg
Protein	1 g		

Oranges & Tangerines

Oranges and tangerines are staples of American diets, and fortunately, they fit nicely into a fat-fighting diet; they are sweet enough to satisfy as snacks and desserts, making them wonderful substitutes for fat-filled sweets.

Health Benefits

Oranges are most famous, of course, for their vitamin C. One orange provides 134 percent of the RDA. That's particularly important for smokers, who may require twice as much vitamin C as nonsmokers to help ward off the development of lung cancer. For women in their childbearing years, oranges are a great source of folic acid, now known to help prevent neural-tube birth defects.

Tangerines only have a third as much vitamin C and folic acid as oranges, but they provide three times as much cancer-fighting vitamin A.

Selection and Storage

Oranges are one of the few fruits abundant in winter. There are over 100 varieties in all, but your supermarket probably carries only a few.

The California navels, with their telltale "belly-buttons," easy-to-peel thick skins, and easy-to-segment flesh with no annoying seeds, are the favorite eating oranges. The Valencias, pride of Florida, are the premier juice oranges. Mandarin oranges are small and sweet with thin skins and easily sectioned segments. Tangerines are a popular type of mandarin.

Navel Orange, Fresh
Serving Size: 1 small

Calories	65	Dietary Fiber	2 g
Fat	<1 g	Sodium	1 mg
Saturated Fat	0 g	Vitamin C	80 mg
Cholesterol	0 mg	Folic Acid	47 mcg
Carbohydrate	16 g	Calcium	56 mg
Protein	1 g	Potassium	250 mg

Tangerine, Fresh
Serving Size: 1 medium

Calories	37	Protein	1 g
Fat	<1 g	Dietary Fiber	2 g
Saturated Fat	0 g	Sodium	1 mg
Cholesterol	0 mg	Vitamin A	773 IU
Carbohydrate	9 g	Vitamin C	26 mg

For all varieties, select firm fruit heavy for its size, indicating juiciness. Green color and blemishes are fine. Refrigerated, most varieties, except mandarins, will keep for two weeks.

Preparation and Serving Tips

For fruit salads, choose seedless oranges or tangerines, such as navels or canned mandarins. Use orange juice to make marinades or nonfat sauces. Or blend with a banana and skim milk for a delicious, low-fat shake.

PARSNIPS

Parsnips look like anemic carrots, certainly not as appealing as you'd think, given their medieval reputation as an aphrodisiac. But they're nutritious just the same.

HEALTH BENEFITS

Parsnips shine as a fiber source. They're high in soluble fiber, the type that helps lower cholesterol and keep blood sugar on an even keel. They're a surprising source of folic acid, that B vitamin women planning a family need to help reduce the risk of certain disabling birth defects. And potassium, the aid to blood pressure, is present in ample quantities. Unlike their carrot cousins, however, parsnips lack beta-carotene.

SELECTION AND STORAGE

Parsnips are root vegetables that are creamy yellow on the outside and white on the inside. They're available year-round in some markets but are easier to find in winter and early spring. The later parsnips are harvested, the sweeter they will taste, as the extra time and a frost help turn the starch into sugar.

Choose small- to medium-size parsnips; they'll be less fibrous and more tender. They shouldn't be "hairy" with rootlets or have obvious blemishes. The skin should be fairly smooth and firm, not flabby. If the greens are still attached, they should look fresh.

Before refrigerating, clip off any attached greens, so they won't drain moisture from the root. Parsnips stored in your crisper drawer in a loosely closed plastic bag will keep for a couple of weeks.

Preparation and Serving Tips

Scrub parsnips well before cooking. (They're not for eating raw.) Trim both ends. As with carrots, cut ¼- to ½-inch off the top—the greens end—to avoid pesticide residues. Scrape or peel a thin layer of skin before or after cooking. If you do it after, they'll be sweeter and full of more nutrients.

Because parsnips tend to be top-heavy, they don't cook evenly. Get around this by slicing halfway down the fat end, or cut them in half crosswise and cook the fat tops first, adding the slender bottoms halfway through cooking. Steaming takes about 20 to 30 minutes. To speed cooking, cut them into chunks and steam them for 10 to 15 minutes.

For a change of pace, parsnips make a fine substitute for potatoes. They are a hearty accompaniment to beef and pork. Serve them whole, cut-up, or pureed like winter squash. For the latter, resist the urge to top with melted butter. Instead, try a dollop of nonfat yogurt. To bring out their sweetness, add ginger, dill weed, chervil, or nutmeg.

Parsnips are best in soups and stews. They help make a flavorful stock, or you can puree them for a flavorful thickener.

Parsnips, Fresh, Cooked
Serving Size: ½ cup sliced

Calories	63	Dietary Fiber	3.3 g
Protein	1 g	Sodium	8 mg
Carbohydrate	15.2 g	Vitamin C	10 mg
Fat	<1 g	Folic Acid	45 mcg
Saturated	0 g	Manganese	<1 mg
Cholesterol	0 mg	Potassium	287 mg

PASTA

Pasta has finally shed its fattening image, which was so undeserved. As a complex carbohydrate, it is digested slowly. And as for calories, at four per gram, pasta won't pack on pounds unless you eat platefuls or pile on creamy sauces. Eating healthy pasta dishes with a simple tomato sauce and lots of vegetables fights the fat in your diet by taking the place of fattier meat-based meals.

HEALTH BENEFITS

By glancing at the nutrients listed here, you can tell pasta is a health food. To help process its carbohydrates into energy, pasta even brings along its own B vitamins. Whole-wheat pasta is particularly rich in minerals and fiber, making it even more satisfying as a meal.

SELECTION AND STORAGE

Durum wheat, from which golden semolina pasta is made, is naturally higher in nutrients, including protein, than other types of wheat. But like white flour, durum flour is refined, so it's missing the nutritious bran and germ—the storehouses of valuable nutrients. More often than not, refined flours used to make pasta are enriched with three B vitamins—thiamin, riboflavin, and niacin—and iron, so most aren't nutritionally void. But if you're looking for the most nutritious type of pasta, whole wheat is superior. Its bran and germ are intact so it has many vitamins and minerals, including hard-to-get copper, magnesium, and zinc, which are missing in refined pasta. If you don't like the taste or chewiness of whole-wheat pasta, try mixing it with regular pasta, for at least half the benefit.

Dried pasta will keep in your cupboards for months, especially if transferred to airtight containers. Storing pasta in glass jars makes a pretty countertop display, but the exposure to light will destroy some of the B vitamins. So store it in a cool, dry place and away from light and air. When it comes to taste and texture, fresh pasta is better than dried pasta, but it's not practical for some people.

PREPARATION AND SERVING TIPS

Cooking pasta may seem simple, but note these finer points:

•Use a large pot of water—four to six quarts per pound of pasta. Pasta needs room to move or it gets sticky.

•Add a pinch of salt. It makes the water boil at a higher temperature, so the pasta cooks faster and the strands are less likely to stick together.

WHOLE-WHEAT SPAGHETTI, COOKED
Serving Size: 1 cup (2 oz uncooked)

Calories	174	Riboflavin	<1 mg
Fat	1 g	Niacin	1 mg
Saturated Fat	<1 g	Copper	<1 mg
Cholesterol	0 mg	Iron	2 mg
Carbohydrate	37 g	Magnesium	42 mg
Protein	8 g	Manganese	2 mg
Dietary Fiber	5 g	Phosphorus	124 mg
Sodium	4 mg	Zinc	1 mg
Thiamin	<1 mg		

ELBOW MACARONI, ENRICHED, COOKED
Serving Size: 1 cup (2 oz uncooked)

Calories	197	Thiamin	<1 mg
Fat	1 g	Riboflavin	<1 mg
Saturated Fat	<1 g	Niacin	2 mg
Cholesterol	0 mg	Copper	<1 mg
Carbohydrate	40 g	Iron	2 mg
Protein	7 g	Magnesium	25 mg
Dietary Fiber	1 g	Manganese	<1 mg
Sodium	1 mg	Zinc	1 mg

•After the water reaches a boil, add pasta gradually. This prevents the water from cooling down, which slows cooking.

•Don't overcook pasta, or the starch granules will absorb too much water, causing starch granules to rupture, making it very sticky. Pasta is best cooked al dente—tender but chewy. Five to ten minutes does it.

•Drain pasta immediately. Do not rinse; you'll lose valuable nutrients. To prevent sticking, immediately toss the pasta with a little sauce.

Pasta can fit into your fat-busting diet as long as you forget fat-laden Alfredo sauce or pesto swimming in oil. Try piping hot spaghetti topped with uncooked, chopped, homegrown tomatoes, fresh basil or arugula, and perhaps a light sprinkling of freshly grated Parmesan cheese. Or add your favorite vegetables to a low-fat marinara sauce for pasta primavera.

PEARS

Lucky for us, pears are in season all winter long, making it possible to enjoy their luscious sweetness for months.

HEALTH BENEFITS

The amount of fiber in other fruit pales of comparison to that in a pear. Much of it is insoluble, making the pear a natural laxative. Its gritty fiber may help prevent cancerous growths in the colon, too. Enough of the fiber is soluble so it provides the same stomach-filling, blood-sugar-blunting effect as other fruits. It also fights cholesterol by absorbing bile acids, forcing the body to make more from its blood cholesterol.

Pears provide a decent amount of copper, potassium, and vitamin C. They're also rich in boron, which is needed for proper functioning of calcium and magnesium. So pears may indirectly contribute to your bone health.

SELECTION AND STORAGE

The juicy Bartletts are the most common variety, fresh or canned. The d'Anjos are firmer and not quite as sweet as Bartletts. They are all-purpose pears, like Boscs, which have elongated necks and unusual dull-russet coloring. Bosc pears are crunchier than others, and they hold their shape when cooked. The runts, Seckels, are also a russet color, but they are sweeter than the others. Comices are the premier dessert pears—sweet and juicy. They are cultivated to have less fiber than other varieties. Asian pears look and crunch like apples but taste like pears.

Pears are picked before they're ripe. Left on the tree, they get mealy. Off the tree, the starch converts to sugar. You can't tell a ripe pear from its color; fragrance and touch are better indicators. Because a pear ripens from the inside out, once the outside seems perfect, the inside is on its way to rotting. So don't buy pears ripe; buy them firm but not rock hard. Ripen them at home in a ventilated paper bag, taking care not to pile them up or they'll bruise. Eat them when they just barely yield to pressure.

PREPARATION AND SERVING TIPS

To get a pear's full nutritional value, be sure to eat the skin. Of course, wash it well first. If still firm, pear slices work well in salads.

Of all the fruits, pears are arguably the best for cooking, becoming even more sweet and creamy when heated. For best results, cook only firm pears. The traditional method is poaching; try using wine or juice as the cooking liquid.

PEAR, FRESH
Serving Size: 1 medium

Calories	98	Dietary Fiber	6 g
Fat	1 g	Sodium	1 mg
Saturated Fat	0 g	Vitamin C	7 mg
Cholesterol	0 mg	Copper	<1 mg
Carbohydrate	25 g	Potassium	208 mg
Protein	1 g		

PEAS

Green peas, like dried peas, are legumes, except they're eaten before they mature. As with all legumes, they're chock-full of nutrients and fat-fighting power, and they flaunt twice the protein of most vegetables, so they're the ideal substitute for fattier protein fare.

HEALTH BENEFITS

Their fiber, mostly insoluble, aids intestinal motility and may help lower cholesterol. Of the myriad nutrients peas provide, iron is particularly important since it's hard to find nonanimal foods with much of this blood-building nutrient.

Snow peas and other edible-podded peas don't contain the same amount of protein or nutrients green peas do. But they are rich in iron and vitamin C, which help maintain your immune system.

SELECTION AND STORAGE

Fresh green peas are only available in April and May. Choose firm, plump, bright-green pods.

Fresh snow peas—Chinese pea pods—are increasingly available year-round. Look for small, shiny, flat pods—they're the sweetest and most tender. Avoid cracked, overly large, or limp pods.

Sugar snap peas are edible pods like snow peas, but sweet like green peas. Select plump, bright-green pods.

GREEN PEAS, FRESH, COOKED
Serving Size: ½ cup

Calories	67	Thiamin	<1 mg
Fat	<1 g	Riboflavin	<1 mg
Saturated Fat	0 g	Niacin	2 mg
Cholesterol	0 mg	Vitamin B₆	<1 mg
Carbohydrate	13 g	Folic Acid	51 mcg
Protein	4 g	Copper	<1 mg
Dietary Fiber	2 g	Iron	1 mg
Sodium	2 mg	Magnesium	31 mg
Vitamin A	478 IU	Manganese	<1 mg
Vitamin C	11 mg	Potassium	217 mg

Fresh peas don't keep long. Because their sugar quickly turns to starch, the sooner you eat them the better.

When you can't get fresh peas, try frozen.

PREPARATION AND SERVING TIPS

Wash peas just before shelling and cooking. To shell, pinch off the ends, pull down the string on the inside, and pop out the peas. Steam for a very short time—six to eight minutes. They'll retain their flavor and more vitamin C if they retain their bright green color.

Snow peas just need washing and trimming before cooking. Sugar snap peas need the string removed from both sides. Snow peas are perfect in stir-fries; cook briefly—a minute or two. Try adding peas to pasta sauce or tuna casserole.

PEPPERS

Though a completely different plant, peppers serve a purpose similar to that of peppercorns: Peppers, especially the hot varieties, add flavor to otherwise bland low-fat dishes.

HEALTH BENEFITS

All peppers are rich in vitamins A and C, but red peppers are simply bursting with them. Besides being low in fat, peppers provide a decent amount of fiber as well.

Hot peppers' fire comes from capsaicin, which acts on pain receptors, not taste buds, in our mouths. Capsaicin predominates in the white membranes of peppers, imparting its "heat" to seeds as well. Whether hot peppers are good or bad for you is not clear. At least one study has found that capsaicin benefits people suffering from migraines. And it's been shown to act as an anticoagulant, perhaps preventing heart attacks and strokes. But capsaicin has confounded researchers by exhibiting both anticancer and procancer effects. And though you may think hot foods like peppers cause ulcers, they don't. There's no proof they even irritate existing ulcers.

Easy does it may be the best advice. If hot peppers bother you, cut back. It takes time to develop an affinity for and immunity to capsaicin's fire. Some people never do.

SELECTION AND STORAGE

Sweet peppers have no capsaicin, hence no heat. They do have a pleasant bite, though. Bell peppers are most common. Green peppers are simply red or yellow peppers that haven't ripened. As they mature, they turn various shades until they become completely red. Once ripe, they are more perishable, so they carry a premium price. But many people favor the milder taste that these varieties provide. Cubanelles, Italian frying peppers, are a bit more intense in flavor and are preferred for roasting or sauteing.

Hot chili peppers, or *chilies*—the Mexican word for peppers—are popular worldwide. Ripe red ones are usually hotter than green ones. Still, shape is a better indicator of heat than color. Rule of thumb: the smaller, the hotter.

For example, the poblano, or ancho, chile is fatter than most peppers and only mildly hot. Anaheim, or canned "green chilies," are also fairly mild. Jalapeño is a popular moderately hot pepper. Among the hottest are cayenne, serrano, and tiny, fiery habañero.

With all peppers, look for a glossy sheen and no shriveling, cracks, or soft spots. Bell peppers should feel heavy for their size, indicating fully developed walls.

Store sweet peppers in a plastic bag in your refrigerator's crisper drawer. Green ones stay firm for a week; other colors go soft in three or four days. Hot peppers do better refrigerated in a perforated paper bag.

PREPARATION AND SERVING TIPS

To cool the fire of hot peppers, cut away the inside white membrane and discard the seeds. Wash hands, utensils, and cutting boards with soap and water after handling them and use gloves to prevent the oils from irritating your hands. Avoid touching your eyes while handling peppers.

Bell peppers are delicious raw. They develop a stronger flavor when cooked; overcooked, they are bitter.

What to do if you swallow more than you can handle? Don't drink water; it spreads the fire around your mouth, making the heat more intolerable. Research from the Taste and Smell Clinic in Washington, D.C., has revealed that a dairy protein, casein, literally washes away capsaicin, quenching the inferno; so milk is your best bet. If you don't have any milk on hand, eat a slice of bread.

Sweet Bell Pepper, Fresh
Serving Size: 1 pepper

Calories 18	Vitamin A
Fat................................<1 g	green pepper .....392 IU
Saturated Fat.......<1 g	red pepper ......4,218 IU
Cholesterol.................0 mg	Vitamin C
Carbohydrate ....4 g	green pepper ....95 mg
Protein.........................1 g	red pepper ....141 mg
Dietary Fiber ....1 g	Iron.............................1 mg
Sodium.....................2 mg	

Hot Chili Pepper, Fresh
Serving Size: 1 pepper

Calories 18	Dietary Fiber ....na
Fat................................<1 g	Sodium.......................3 mg
Saturated Fat.........0 g	Vitamin A
Cholesterol.................0 mg	green pepper .....346 IU
Carbohydrate ....4 g	red pepper ......4,838 IU
Protein.........................1 g	Vitamin C................110 mg

PINEAPPLE

Although pineapples from Puerto Rico, Mexico, and elsewhere are cheaper, they aren't as juicy and flavorful as those from Hawaii. But all pineapples share the same fat-fighting characteristics—exceptionally sweet taste and high fiber content.

HEALTH BENEFITS

Serve pineapple for dessert and no one will complain about missing sweets. That's just one benefit of this delicacy. Moreover, its fiber will fill you up and might help keep you regular. Pineapple is also a sweet way to get your manganese, just one of many bone-strengthening minerals. One cup exceeds a day's recommended amount by 30 percent. You also get a decent amount of copper and thiamin, plus more than a third of your recommended vitamin C needs.

SELECTION AND STORAGE

When choosing pineapple, forget all the other tricks; let your nose be your guide. A ripe pineapple emits a sweet aroma from its base, except when cold. Color is not reliable; ripe pineapples vary in color by variety. Don't rely on plucking a leaf from the middle either. You can do this with all but the most unripe pineapples. And it can just as easily mean that it's rotten.

Choose a large pineapple that feels heavy for its size, indicating juiciness and a lot of pulp. The "eyes" should stand out. A ripe pineapple yields slightly when pressed.

— Pineapple

Once a pineapple is picked, it's as sweet as it will ever get. It does no good to let it "ripen" at home. It will only rot.

Preparation and Serving Tips

Tips on tackling a pineapple: Core it and peel the outside first, then cut into slices. Or cut into quarters, then scoop out the inside without peeling it at all. Refrigerate cut-up pieces.

Try fruit kabobs for a unique dessert: Alternate pineapple, strawberries, and other fruit on skewers. Or grill pineapple skewered with vegetables. Try pineapple on brown rice to give it zing—a great alternative to a meat-based dish.

Pineapple contains an enzyme—bromelain—that breaks down protein and is the reason why gelatin won't set when fresh pineapple is added. Use canned pineapple instead.

Pineapple, Fresh
Serving Size: 1 cup diced

Calories	77	Dietary Fiber	2 g
Fat	1 g	Sodium	<1 mg
Saturated Fat	0 g	Vitamin C	24 mg
Cholesterol	0 mg	Thiamin	<1 mg
Carbohydrate	19 g	Copper	<1 mg
Protein	1 g	Manganese	3 mg

PLUMS

If you can't find a plum you like, you haven't tried hard enough. There are over 200 varieties in the United States alone, some quite different than others. It pays to be adventurous and explore unfamiliar plums.

HEALTH BENEFITS

If you eat a couple of plums at a time, you'll get more than a fair dose of vitamins A and C, the B vitamin riboflavin, potassium, and fiber. None is in amounts to bowl you over, but they're important all the same.

SELECTION AND STORAGE

Plums are a summer pitted fruit, called a drupe, with a long season—May through October. Some plums cling to their pits and some have "free" stones.

Plums are generally either Japanese or European in origin. The Japanese types are usually superior for eating. Many European types are used for stewing, canning, or preserves or for turning into prunes.

Plum skins come in a rainbow of colors: red, purple, black, green, blue, and even yellow. Plum flesh is surprisingly colorful, too. It can be yellow, orange, green, or red.

There's no room here to chronicle the characteristics of every type of plum, but here are a few eating plums you're likely to encounter: Santa Rosa, Friar, Red Beauty, El Dorado, Greengage, and Kelsey.

When choosing plums, look for plump fruit with a bright or deep color covered with a powdery "bloom"—its natural protection. If it yields to gentle palm pressure, it's ripe. If not, as long as it isn't rock hard, it will ripen at home. But it won't get sweeter, just softer. To ripen plums, place them in a loosely closed paper bag at room temperature. Check them frequently so they won't get shriveled or moldy. When slightly soft, refrigerate or eat them.

Preparation and Serving Tips

Don't wash plums until you're ready to eat them, or you'll wash away the protective bloom. Like most fruits, they taste best at room temperature or just slightly cooler.

Although Japanese plums are best eaten out of hand, most European varieties are excellent for cooking. They're easy to pit—being freestone—and their firmer flesh holds together better. Try famous Damson or Beach plums for preserves.

A compote of plums and other fruits, such as apricots, is a traditional way to warm up your winter. Poach plum halves, skin on. Plum sauce is a treat on ice milk or mixed into yogurt.

Plum, Fresh
Serving Size: 2 medium

Protein....................1 g	Sodium....................0 mg
Carbohydrate ....17 g	Vitamin A................426 IU
Fat............................<1 g	Vitamin C ....13 mg
Saturated..........<1 g	Riboflavin ....<1 mg
Cholesterol................0 mg	Potassium ....226 mg
Dietary Fiber ....2 g	

POPCORN

You may think popcorn seems undeserving of its own entry, but it's an important snack food and it can also be a healthful one, too. Popcorn is here as much for what it doesn't have as it is for what it does have. It fills you up—but not out.

HEALTH BENEFITS

What snack food do you know that provides fewer than 100 calories, no fat or sodium, and almost four grams of fiber in three cups? Only one—popcorn. The catch is that it must be air-popped popcorn with no added oil, butter, margarine, or salt. But don't knock it. It's chewy, tasty, and filling—everything a snack food should be.

Besides all that, popcorn provides protein. And you can't beat its fiber content, practically all of which is insoluble. Eat plenty of popcorn and with all the fiber you'll be less likely to suffer constipation. Plus your intestinal tract will also be less likely to harbor carcinogens and other toxins.

SELECTION AND STORAGE

Nutritionally, air-popping is the best method and the only way to avoid added oil. Not everyone is pleased with the taste, however. If you prefer popcorn with added oil, keep it minimal since the oil used is often a combination of saturated and *trans* fatty acids. Fortunately, some microwave popcorns have only half the fat and calories of regular popcorn. Some are as low as one gram of fat per serving, so check labels when you shop and try different brands to find one you like.

POPCORN, PLAIN, AIR-POPPED
Serving Size: 3 cups

Calories 93	Protein........................3 g
Fat...............................1 g	Dietary Fiber ....4 g
Saturated Fat.......<1 g	Sodium.......................1 mg
Cholesterol.................0 mg	Magnesium ....32 mg
Carbohydrate ....19 g	Manganese..............<1 mg

What about ready-popped packaged popcorn? Most of them are loaded with fat, especially the popular cheese-flavored varieties—some get as much as three quarters of their calories from fat. So make sure you read the labels.

The good news in all of this is that no matter the variety, you still get the fiber bonus. Figure at least one gram per cup.

PREPARATION AND SERVING TIPS

You can do it the old-fashioned way and pop kernels in oil on the stove, but you'll add extra fat to your diet. If you refuse to air-pop, you're better off sticking with a light microwave popcorn.

If you want added flavor, try dusting popcorn with grated Parmesan cheese, which is tasty but adds some fat. Or flavor it with sprinkle-on butter substitute, garlic powder, or cinnamon.

POTATOES

Whoever coined the phrase "the lowly potato" certainly wasn't aware of its nutrient values. And anyone who still shuns the potato thinking it is fattening is missing out on a food tailor-made for the weight-conscious person; potatoes are extremely low in fat and very high in fiber.

HEALTH BENEFITS

Potatoes may seem high in calories, but they are nutrient-dense, meaning you receive many nutrients for those calories. The fiber is half soluble, half insoluble, so it helps to keep you regular and helps to lower cholesterol. And slowing down digestion helps to keep you full longer.

With the exception of vitamin A, a potato has just about every nutrient. Did you know potatoes are one of the richest sources of vitamin C? They are also very high in potassium, beating other potassium-rich foods. They are a good source of iron and copper, too. In fact, a potato a day is good for your heart, promoting normal blood-pressure levels.

SELECTION AND STORAGE

Boiling potatoes are red or white. They're small and round with thin skins that look waxy, signaling more moisture and less starch. Baking potatoes, also known as russets or Idahos, are large and long with brown, dry skin. Their lack of moisture makes them bake up fluffy. Long, white all-purpose potatoes are also known as Maine, Eastern, or California potatoes. New potatoes are not a variety of potato; they are simply small potatoes of any variety that have yet to mature. They look waxy with thin, undeveloped skins that are often partially rubbed away.

For all potatoes, choose those that are firm with no soft or dark spots. Pass over green-tinged potatoes; they contain toxic alkaloids, such as solanine. Also avoid potatoes that have started to sprout; they're old. If you buy potatoes in bags, open the bags right away and discard any that are rotting, because one bad potato can spoil a bagful.

Store potatoes in a location that is dry, cool, dark, and ventilated. Light triggers the production of toxic solanine. Too much moisture causes rotting. Don't refrigerate them, or the starch will convert to sugar. Don't store them with onions; both will go bad faster because of a gas the potatoes give off. Mature potatoes keep for weeks; new potatoes only a week.

PREPARATION AND SERVING TIPS

Don't wash potatoes until you're ready to cook them. Scrub well with a vegetable brush under running water. Cut out sprout buds and bad spots. If the potato is green or too soft, throw it out.

Baking a potato takes an hour in a conventional oven, but only five minutes in a microwave (12 minutes for four potatoes). Prick the skin for a fluffier potato. If you are baking them in a conventional oven, it's inadvisable to wrap them in foil unless you like steamed, mushy potatoes. When boiling potatoes, keep them whole to reduce nutrient loss.

Remember, the potato itself is not fattening, but what you put on it may help expand your waist. Don't slather your potatoes in butter, margarine, sour cream, or cheese. Instead,

WHITE POTATO, FRESH, BAKED (WITH SKIN)
Serving Size: 1 large baking potato

Calories 220	Thiamin ....<1 mg
Fat.............................<1 g	Niacin..........................3 mg
Saturated Fat.......<1 g	Vitamin B$_6$ ....1 mg
Cholesterol.................0 mg	Copper ....1 mg
Carbohydrate ....51 g	Iron...............................3 mg
Protein.........................5 g	Magnesium ....55 mg
Dietary Fiber :............4 g	Manganese ....1 mg
Sodium.....................16 mg	Phosphorus.............115 mg
Vitamin C ....26 mg	Potassium ....844 mg

eat them plain or top them with nonfat yogurt or nonfat sour cream, and sprinkle them with chopped dill, parsley, or scallions. Pile broccoli or other veggies on top for added nutrition, fiber, and satisfying bulk.

New potatoes are delicious boiled and drizzled lightly with olive oil, then dusted liberally with dill weed.

PRUNES

Though relatively high in calories for their size, prunes have a reputation as a dieter's friend. They add a powerful dose of fiber and some nutrients to your diet that are needed when you follow a lower-calorie meal plan.

HEALTH BENEFITS

Prunes are a sweet way to add fat-free laxative fiber to your diet. A single prune contains more than half a gram of fiber and more than one gram of sorbitol (a carbohydrate that our bodies do not absorb well). Large amounts of sorbitol can cause diarrhea. Prunes also contain the laxative, diphenylisatin. No wonder they prevent constipation. So snack away, just don't go overboard.

In contrast, prunes' reputation for being rich in iron doesn't hold true. In reality, they're a decent, but not spectacular, source. Prunes, however, get overlooked as a source of vitamin A, even though they provide more than ten percent of recommended levels. Potassium is another unexpected benefit you get from eating prunes, which is beneficial for blood pressure.

SELECTION AND STORAGE

When selecting prunes, look for well-sealed packages, such as those that are vacuum-sealed. After opening, seal the package or transfer the prunes to an airtight container or plastic bag. Stored in a cool, dry location or in the refrigerator, they'll keep for several months.

PRUNES, DRIED

Serving Size: 4 medium

Calories 80	Dietary Fiber ....2 g
Fat..............................<1 g	Sodium........................1 mg
Saturated Fat.........0 g	Vitamin A................668 IU
Cholesterol.................0 mg	Iron.............................1 mg
Carbohydrate ....21 g	Potassium ....250 mg
Protein........................1 g	

PREPARATION AND SERVING TIPS

You can eat them out of the box, of course. They make a great portable fat-free snack. Combine them with dried apricots for a delightful mix of sweet and tangy flavors. Or mix them with nuts and seeds for a healthy trail mix. But watch out—the calories add up fast.

If you're not crazy about eating whole prunes, try prune bits in your baking. They'll add sweetness, flavor, and fiber to quick breads, snack bars, even pancakes. Better yet, for real fat-fighting success, puree eight ounces of pitted prunes and six tablespoons of hot water in a food processor for a great fat substitute to use in baked goods. Replace butter, margarine, shortening, or oil in your baked good recipes with half the amount of the prune puree. For example, if the recipe calls for one cup of butter, substitute a half cup of prune puree. Tightly covered, the prune puree will keep about one week in the refrigerator.

PUMPKIN

The pumpkin is an American original. Unfortunately, it seems most people associate pumpkins with Halloween or with Thanksgiving when it's enjoyed as pumpkin pie. Pumpkins, belonging to the squash family, have an understated taste that lends itself well to a variety of dishes. Besides, pumpkins make a great fat substitute in baking.

HEALTH BENEFITS

The distinctive bright orange color of pumpkin clearly indicates that it's an excellent source of that all-important antioxidant beta-carotene. Research shows that people who eat a meal plan rich in beta-carotene are less likely to develop certain cancers than those who fail to include beta-carotene–rich foods in their diet.

SELECTION AND STORAGE

Look for deep-orange pumpkins, free of cracks or soft spots. Though large pumpkins make the best jack-o'-lanterns, they tend to be tough and stringy, so they aren't the best for cooking—try smaller ones.

A whole pumpkin keeps well for up to a month, if stored in a cool, dry spot. Once cut, wrap the pumpkin and place it in the refrigerator; it should keep for about a week.

To prepare, wash off dirt, cut away the tough skin with a knife or a vegetable peeler, remove the seeds, then slice, dice, or cut the pulp into chunks. You might want to save the seeds;

```
                         PUMPKIN
            Serving Size: ½ cup, mashed, cooked

Calories ................. 102      Sodium ..................... 2 mg
Fat ............................ <1 g      Vitamin A ............ 1,320 IU
    Saturated Fat ......... 0 g      Niacin ..................... 1 mg
Cholesterol ............... 0 mg      Vitamin C ................. 6 mg
Carbohydrate ............ 6 g      Calcium ................. 18 mg
Protein ...................... 1 g      Potassium ............. 181 mg
Dietary Fiber ............. 1 g
```

when toasted, they make a great snack. If you prefer something quicker and more simple, you can always opt for canned
pumpkin. It's just as nutritious as fresh. For pies and purees,
many say it tastes as good, if not better.

PREPARATION AND SERVING TIPS

Pumpkin pie is, without a doubt, Americans' favorite food
use for pumpkin. But traditional preparation, with heavy
cream and whole eggs, transforms a virtually fat-free food into
one that's loaded with fat. Instead, substitute evaporated skim
milk for the cream and use only one egg yolk for every two
eggs the recipe calls for. You'll cut the fat to about 30 percent of calories, and we predict no one will know the difference.

Pumpkin can be used to make nutritious, delicious, and moist
cookies. Likewise, you can substitute it for some of the fat in
quick breads. How about pumpkin pancakes?

RASPBERRIES

This fragile, exquisite, and expensive berry is actually a member of the rose family. But there is nothing delicate about the fat-fighting fiber you get from this tiny fruit.

HEALTH BENEFITS

It's hard to believe a food could taste so good and be so good for you. But raspberries fit that description well. They are low in fat and calories and they are also a good source of fiber. Some of the fiber is insoluble, so it helps keep you regular. But much of it is found as pectin, a soluble fiber known to help lower blood cholesterol.

Besides being a good source of vitamin C—an antioxidant beneficial in the fight against cancer—raspberries contain a phytochemical, ellagic acid, believed to have anticancer properties.

SELECTION AND STORAGE

Because they are so fragile, choose and use raspberries with care and eat them right away. Look for berries that are brightly colored with no hulls attached. If the green hulls are still on the berries, they will be tart. Avoid any that look shriveled or have visible mold. They should be plump, firm, well shaped, and evenly colored, with no green. They should be packed in a single-layer container and have a clean, slightly sweet fragrance. When you get them home, don't expect to keep them around for long. It's best to eat them within a day.

Raspberries

Serving Size: ½ cup

Calories 30	Dietary Fiber ....2 g
Fat............................<1 g	Sodium.....................0 mg
Saturated Fat........ 0 g	Niacin.........................1 mg
Cholesterol.................0 mg	Vitamin C ....39 mg
Carbohydrate ....7 g	Manganese ....1 mg
Protein........................1 g	

PREPARATION AND SERVING TIPS

Just before serving, take chilled raspberries and rinse under cool water. For a low-fat dessert extraordinaire, top frozen sorbet or a slice of angel food cake with whole, chilled raspberries. Make a raspberry puree to pour generously (it's terrifically low in calories) over fruit salad, a slice of low-fat cake, pancakes, or waffles. If you're celebrating a special occasion, add chilled, ripe raspberries to your champagne. Raspberries also make a colorful, edible garnish.

Frozen raspberries in light syrup can be used to make a delicious frozen dessert. Puree the berries in a food processor first. Then, add skim milk and fresh lemon juice. Process all of the ingredients on low speed. Pour into an airtight container and freeze the mixture. Then process the frozen mixture in the food processor, and refreeze it. Enjoy.

RICE

Rice is the dietary backbone for over half the world's population. In Asian countries, each person consumes, on average, 200 to 400 pounds a year. Americans eat about 21 pounds per person, per year.

Rice is one reason why Asian diets are so low in fat. While Americans tend to view rice as a side dish to a meat-centered diet, Asians view rice as the focus of the meal. Increasing the amount of rice and decreasing the amount of meat served helps reduce fat intake.

HEALTH BENEFITS

Rice is an excellent source of complex carbohydrates and, if enriched, a good source of several B vitamins. It complements other protein alternatives well, particularly legumes. This makes it a good basis for a diet—a low-fat one at that. Using rice-based meals to replace meat will have a direct impact on your fat intake.

Brown rice provides three times the fiber of white rice. Research shows that rice bran, a small amount of which remains in brown rice, lowers cholesterol. It's also more slowly digested than the carbohydrate of processed white rice.

SELECTION AND STORAGE

Long-grain rice is the most popular variety in the United States. Cooked, the grains are fluffy and dry and separate easily. Medium-grain is popular in Latin-American cultures. Though fairly fluffy right after cooking, it clumps together once it cools. Short-grain, or glutinous rice, has nearly round grains with a high starch content. When cooked, it becomes moist and sticky so the grains clump together—perfect for eating with the chopsticks of Asian cultures.

Brown rice is the whole grain with only the outer husk removed. It is tan in color and has a chewy texture and a nutlike flavor. It is more perishable than white rice but keeps about six months—longer if refrigerated. White rice keeps almost indefinitely if stored in an airtight container in a cool, dark, dry place.

Expensive wild rice is not rice at all but a member of the grass family. It has a rich flavor and is higher in protein than other types of rice.

PREPARATION AND SERVING TIPS

If rice is bought from bins, as in Asia, it must be washed to remove dust and dirt. Packaged rice bought in the United States doesn't need to be washed. If it's fortified, rinsing washes away some of the B vitamins. However, it is a good

---

RICE, WHITE, LONG-GRAIN
Serving Size: ½ cup, cooked

Calories	131	Sodium	2 mg
Fat	<1 g	Iron	1 mg
Saturated Fat	<1 g	Manganese	1 mg
Cholesterol	0 mg	Niacin	2 mg
Carbohydrate	29 g	Pantothenic Acid	<1 mg
Protein	3 g	Thiamin	<1 mg
Dietary Fiber	1 g		

RICE, BROWN, LONG-GRAIN
Serving Size: ½ cup, cooked

Calories	109	Dietary Fiber	2 g
Fat	1 g	Sodium	5 mg
Saturated Fat	<1 g	Magnesium	42 mg
Cholesterol	0 mg	Manganese	1 mg
Carbohydrate	23 g	Niacin	2 mg
Protein	3 g		

idea to rinse imported rices. They may be dirty and are not enriched, so nutrients won't be washed away.

Cooking times for rice vary by variety and size of grain. Long-grain white rice takes about 20 minutes to cook. Long-grain brown rice takes longer—about 30 minutes. Short-grain brown rice takes about 40 minutes. Wild rice takes the longest—up to 50 minutes.

Water isn't the only cooking medium you can use to prepare rice. Try seasoned broth, fruit juice, or tomato juice for a change of pace. Dilute it to half strength with water. Be aware that when you add acid to the cooking water—as with juices—the rice takes longer to cook.

Though rice is often served alongside a main dish, it is better stir-fried and mixed with plenty of vegetables. Or try it as a cold salad with peas, red peppers, and a warm, low-fat vinaigrette dressing.

SOYBEANS

Though the United States is the world's largest grower of soybeans, more than half of the crop is exported. What a waste. Soybeans are one of the best plant sources of protein, nearly mimicking the perfect protein profile of milk. When used as a substitute for meat—which it does well because of its protein profile—a serving of soybeans can save you fat, especially saturated fat. You also get a fantastic fiber boost, both soluble and insoluble.

HEALTH BENEFITS

For fighting fat, you just can't beat soybeans for their versatility. Though surprisingly high in fat for a bean, it's mostly unsaturated. By lowering your blood level of LDL cholesterol (the "bad" cholesterol), soybeans' unsaturated fat is thought to reduce the risk of heart disease. Soybeans also happen to be one of the few plant sources of omega-3 fatty acids, which may aid in the battle against heart disease and cancer as well as arthritis.

Soybeans are loaded with a phytochemical called isoflavone, which may help combat breast tumors by dampening the ill effects of estrogen-like compounds. This fact may partly explain why Asian women, whose diets are typically rich in soybeans, are less likely to develop breast cancer than American women (soybeans are often poorly represented in American diets).

Most soy products contribute some calcium; tofu with calcium sulfate or calcium chloride is an even better source of the bone-building mineral.

SELECTION AND STORAGE

When buying soybeans, make sure packaged bags are well-sealed. Check for insects if buying in bulk; pinholes indicate insect infestation. Store soybeans in an airtight container in a cool, dry place, up to a year.

Many people benefit from soy without ever seeing a bean; they simply rely on its many other incarnations. Textured vegetable protein (or TVP—a meat extender) is used in many soy-based products. Tofu is soy milk that's coagulated and pressed into blocks. Tempeh is fermented soybeans that are formed into a "cake." Miso is a combination of soybeans and barley or rice that is made into a strongly flavored, salty paste. Roasted soybeans, called soy nuts, are sold as snack food.

Tofu can be purchased in bulk, water-packed, or aseptically packaged. If you buy in bulk, follow safety precautions. Because it can harbor bacteria, tofu, except that which is aseptically packaged, must be refrigerated. So unless it's aseptically packaged, don't buy it if it's displayed unrefrigerated. At home, refrigerate unwrapped tofu immediately. For packaged tofu, check the "sell-by" date. Aseptically packaged tofu keeps without refrigeration for up to ten months, but refrigerate it once opened.

Because of their high fat content, all soy products are subject to rancidity. If you smell a rancid odor or see mold, throw the product out.

PREPARATION AND SERVING TIPS

To prepare soybeans: Soak a half cup of soybeans overnight, add two cups boiling water, and simmer for two to two and

TOFU, "LITE" (1 PERCENT FAT)
Serving Size: 3 oz

Calories	35	Carbohydrate	1 g
Fat	1 g	Protein	5 g
Saturated Fat	<1 g	Dietary Fiber	na
Cholesterol	0 mg	Sodium	70 mg

SOYBEANS
Serving Size: ½ cup, cooked

Calories	149	Dietary Fiber	5 g
Fat	8 g	Sodium	1 mg
Saturated Fat	1 g	Folic Acid	46 mcg
Cholesterol	0 g	Iron	4 mg
Carbohydrate	9 g	Calcium	88 mg
Protein	14 g	Potassium	443 mg

a half hours. To lessen soybean's gassy nature, throw out the soaking water, which contains indigestible carbohydrates, and cook them in fresh water.

The flavor of soybeans is bland, but that's their secret. The versatility of this culinary chameleon lies in its ability to take on the flavors of foods it's prepared with—enough so you forget you're not eating meat. Tempeh has the "meatiest" quality and works well as a meat substitute in stir-fry dishes. Miso works best as a taste enhancer, but if you're watching your salt intake, take it easy.

SPINACH

It seems Popeye had the right idea. Spinach is indeed a nutrition superstar, even a fairly good source of iron. It's loaded with vitamins and minerals, some of which are hard to find in other foods, and it's reasonably high in fiber—offering twice as much as most other cooking or salad greens. This helps you fight fat by filling you up with bulk.

HEALTH BENEFITS

Like other dark greens, spinach is an excellent source of beta-carotene, a powerful disease-fighting antioxidant that's been shown, among other things, to reduce the risk of developing cataracts. It fights heart disease and cancer as well.

Served raw, spinach is a good source of vitamin C, another powerful antioxidant. Overcook it, however, and you lose most of this important vitamin. Though spinach is rich in calcium, most of it is unavailable, because oxalic acid in spinach binds with calcium, preventing its absorption. When you cook spinach, it cooks down tremendously. Because cooking concentrates nutrients and fiber, a serving of cooked spinach gives you even more bang for your buck than a serving of raw.

SELECTION AND STORAGE

Two basic varieties of spinach are available—curly-leafed and smooth. Smooth is more popular, because curly-leafed is more difficult to rid of dirt that's buried in its folds.

Choose spinach with leaves that are crisp and dark green; avoid limp or yellowing leaves—an indication that the

SPINACH
Serving Size: 1 cup, raw

Calories	12	Sodium	44 mg
Fat	<1 g	Vitamin A	3,760 IU
Saturated Fat	0 g	Folic Acid	108 mcg
Cholesterol	0 mg	Vitamin C	16 mg
Carbohydrate	2 g	Iron	2 mg
Protein	2 g	Manganese	1 mg
Dietary Fiber	1 g	Potassium	312 mg

spinach is past its prime. Refrigerate unwashed spinach in a plastic bag; it'll keep for three to four days. If you wash it before you store it, the leaves have a tendency to deteriorate rapidly.

PREPARATION AND SERVING TIPS

Wash spinach leaves carefully and thoroughly, repeating the rinsing process two or three times. Even a speck of grit left behind can ruin an otherwise perfect dish.

Spinach is treasured for its versatility—it's tasty whether you serve it fresh or cooked. Either way, it can be added to dishes without adding extra fat. Warm spinach salads are a classic, but they are typically high in fat. For a tasty low-fat version, omit the bacon and egg yolks, and use mushrooms and garbanzo beans instead.

To cook spinach, simmer the leaves in a small amount of water until the leaves just begin to wilt, about five minutes. Top with lemon juice, seasoned vinegar, sauteed garlic, or a dash of nutmeg, and serve.

SQUASH

Because squash is actually the fruit of various members of the gourd family, it comes in a wide array of colors and sizes. Eating squash is particularly satisfying, because the bulk fills you up, allowing you to forgo fattier fare.

HEALTH BENEFITS

Though all varieties of squash are good nutrition choices, winter varieties tend to be more nutrient-dense. They generally contain much more beta-carotene and more of several B vitamins than tasty, summer squash. Butternut squash's beta-carotene content even rivals that of mangoes and cantaloupe. And that's a boon in the fight against cancer, heart disease, and cataracts.

SELECTION AND STORAGE

Despite seasonal growth patterns, most types of squash are available year-round, though winter squash is best from early fall to late winter. Summer varieties—with thin, edible skins and soft seeds—include chayote, yellow crookneck, and zucchini. Winter varieties—with dark skins too hard and thick to eat—include buttercup, butternut, calabaza, hubbard, spaghetti, and turban. Look for smaller squash that are brightly colored and free of spots, bruises, and mold.

The hard skin of winter squash serves as a barrier, allowing it to be stored a month or more in a dark, cool place. An added bonus: Beta-carotene content actually increases during storage. Summer squash only keeps for a few days; store it in your refrigerator's crisper drawer.

SQUASH, BUTTERNUT
Serving Size: ½ cup, cooked

Calories	41	Sodium	4 mg
Fat	<1 g	Vitamin A	7,141 IU
Saturated Fat	0 g	Niacin	1 mg
Cholesterol	0 mg	Pantothenic Acid	<1 mg
Carbohydrate	11 g	Vitamin C	15 mg
Protein	1 g	Calcium	42 mg
Dietary Fiber	3 g	Potassium	290 mg

SQUASH, CROOKNECK
Serving Size: ½ cup, cooked

Calories	18	Dietary Fiber	1 g
Fat	<1 g	Sodium	1 mg
Saturated Fat	<1 g	Niacin	1 mg
Cholesterol	0 mg	Calcium	24 mg
Carbohydrate	4 g	Potassium	173 mg
Protein	1 g	Manganese	<1 mg

PREPARATION AND SERVING TIPS

After peeling (or not, if you like) and removing the seeds, winter squash can be baked, steamed, sauteed, or simmered. Summer squash, on the other hand, is cooked and eaten skin, seeds, and all.

Some savory seasoning suggestions for squash: allspice, cinnamon, curry, fennel, marjoram, nutmeg, sage, and tarragon.

STRAWBERRIES

Luscious strawberries are the most popular berries and are unique because they are the only fruit with seeds on the outside rather than on the inside. In season, strawberries need no extra sweeteners or toppings. They fight fat by eliminating the need for any other fatty sweet.

These delicate heart-shaped berries range in size from tiny wild varieties to larger cultivated ones. Generally, smaller varieties are more flavorful. Unfortunately, today's cultivated berries are bred with durability, not flavor, in mind. Still, in late spring and early summer, you can find superbly sweet strawberries at farmers' markets and green grocers.

HEALTH BENEFITS

As with all berries, they are a fabulous fiber find, with those little seeds providing insoluble fiber that keeps you regular and helps fend off digestive system woes, including hemorrhoids and varicose veins.

Most of all, strawberries are a super source of vitamin C, even better than oranges or grapefruit. Strawberries are also a good source of potassium. Because it keeps blood pressure in check, potassium may keep you from becoming a stroke statistic. Also, strawberries are one of the few fruits that contain ellagic acid, a phytochemical with cancer-fighting power.

SELECTION AND STORAGE

Look for strawberries that are ruby red, evenly colored, and plump, with fresh, green, leafy tops. Big does not translate into

STRAWBERRIES
Serving Size: 1 cup

Calories	45	Sodium	2 mg
Fat	1 g	Vitamin C	85 mg
Saturated Fat	0 g	Calcium	21 mg
Cholesterol	0 mg	Manganese	<1 mg
Carbohydrate	11 g	Pantothenic Acid	1 mg
Protein	1 g	Potassium	247 mg
Dietary Fiber	2 g		

juicy; in fact, smaller berries tend to be the sweetest. Avoid strawberries in containers with juice stains or berries packed tightly with plastic wrap. And walk on by if you notice soft, mushy, or moldy berries.

Strawberries spoil quickly. So it's best to buy them within a day of serving. Refrigerate unwashed strawberries loosely covered.

PREPARATION AND SERVING TIPS

Though they are superb served au naturel, strawberries can perk up any cereal, add pizzazz to any salad, or beef up pudding or gelatin. If strawberries become overripe, puree and add them to fruit drinks (strain the seeds, if you wish) or drizzle the puree over fruit salad for a low-fat dessert.

Sweet Potatoes

In some homes in the United States, sweet potatoes are only served at Thanksgiving, even though they are available year-round. Too bad. Sweet potatoes are one of the unsung heroes of a fat-fighting diet. For reasonable calories, you get a load of nutrients.

Health Benefits

This starchy vegetable has bulk to keep your tummy full for hours. Yet its nutritional profile makes the calories worth it, especially since they are fat free. Its fiber alone is enough to make a sweet potato worth eating.

If a beta-carotene contest were held, sweet potatoes would tie carrots for first place. That may make them top-notch for fighting chronic diseases like cancer and heart disease. Sweet potatoes are also rich in potassium and vitamin C; a small potato provides almost half the daily allowance.

Selection and Storage

Though often called a yam, a sweet potato is a different vegetable. True yams can only be found at ethnic markets. The sweet potatoes in supermarkets are either the moist, orange-fleshed type or the dry, yellow-fleshed variety that resemble baking potatoes in texture. The orange variety has a thicker skin, with bright orange flesh. It is much sweeter and moister than other varieties.

Look for potatoes that are small to medium in size, with smooth, unbruised skin. Avoid any with a white stringy

SWEET POTATOES
Serving Size: 1 potato (4 oz), baked

Calories	118	Pantothenic Acid	1 mg
Fat	<1 g	Vitamin B₆	<1 mg
Saturated Fat	0 g	Vitamin C	28 mg
Cholesterol	0 mg	Vitamin E	.5 mg
Carbohydrate	28 g	Calcium	32 mg
Protein	2 g	Magnesium	23 mg
Dietary Fiber	2 g	Potassium	397 mg
Sodium	10 mg	Copper	<1 mg
Vitamin A	24,877 IU	Manganese	1 mg
Folic Acid	26 mcg		

"beard"—a sure sign the potato is overmature and probably tough.

Though sweet potatoes look hardy, they're actually quite fragile and spoil easily. Any cut or bruise on the surface quickly spreads, ruining the whole potato. Do not refrigerate them; it speeds up the deterioration.

PREPARATION AND SERVING TIPS

To cook sweet potatoes, boil unpeeled. Leaving the peel intact prevents excessive loss of precious nutrients and "locks" in its natural sweetness.

The dry, yellow variety can be used in just about any recipe that calls for white potatoes. The darker, sweeter varieties are typically served at Thanksgiving. Try them mashed, in a soufflé, or in traditional Southern sweet-potato pie. Resist candying them; it adds lots of unnecessary calories.

TOMATOES

Tomatoes are one of the most frequently consumed "vegetables" in the United States, whether raw, steamed, fried, stewed, crushed, pureed, or reduced to a sauce. Though thought of as a vegetable, tomatoes are botanically classified as fruits. They are also one of our best sources of vitamin C.

HEALTH BENEFITS

Tomatoes, it seems, are at the center of low-fat living. They naturally lend themselves to health-conscious cooking, being sweet yet low in calories and fat.

While not bursting at the seams with vitamins and minerals, tomatoes are indeed rich in vitamin C. This antioxidant plays a key role in maintaining a healthy immune system. They also contain beta-carotene and several other carotenoids that may have their own disease-preventing properties, particularly against heart disease and lung cancer. Tomatoes also offer a good dose of that possible stroke preventer, potassium.

SELECTION AND STORAGE

Red or yellow, tomatoes fall into three groups: cherry, plum, and round slicing tomatoes. Cherry tomatoes are bite-sized and perfectly round. Italian plum tomatoes are egg-shaped. Slicing tomatoes are large and round, perfect for sandwich slices. Beefsteaks are a popular variety.

Though available year-round, you may not want to eat what passes for fresh tomatoes in the wintertime. The best-tasting tomatoes are "vine-ripened," that is, they've been allowed to

TOMATOES

Serving Size: 1 tomato

Calories	24	Dietary Fiber	1 g
Fat	<1 g	Sodium	10 mg
Saturated Fat	0 g	Vitamin A	1,133 IU
Cholesterol	0 mg	Vitamin C	22 mg
Carbohydrate	5 g	Potassium	254 mg
Protein	1 g		

ripen on the vine, so they aren't made to ripen artificially. You may have to shop farmers' markets to find them. Moreover, there is no standard definition for the term "vine-ripened." Know your vendor before you trust the claim.

Look for tomatoes that are firm and well-shaped and have a noticeable fragrance. They should be heavy for their size and yield to slight pressure when gently squeezed.

A common mistake is to store tomatoes in the refrigerator. Cold temperatures ruin the taste and texture of a good tomato. Also, wait until you're just ready to serve them before you slice them; once cut, flavor fades.

PREPARATION AND SERVING TIPS

Salads seem more complete with a ripe, red tomato. Sliced tomatoes, served on a bed of radicchio or arugula, drizzled with a flavored vinaigrette or balsamic vinegar, and topped with fresh basil can't be beat. Chopped fresh tomatoes add flavor, color, and nutrition to soups, stews, and casseroles. They're superb on hot pasta.

WHEAT GERM

Wheat germ, a health-food basic, is the embryo of the wheat kernel. It is the portion of the wheat kernel that is removed when it is processed into refined flour. Wheat germ certainly deserves its reputation for being a powerhouse of nutrients, as its profile strikingly illustrates.

HEALTH BENEFITS

When you cut back on fat, you almost certainly cut back on the amount of meat you eat. When this happens, you may also be cutting back on important nutrients, too. Filling the void, though, is fat-fighting wheat germ. It provides a bevy of minerals, including all-important "meaty" iron and zinc.

Face it, wheat germ is a nutrition standout. It's one of the best sources of folic acid. That's good news, since the government is now recommending that all women of child-bearing age get sufficient amounts of this nutrient to prevent neural-tube birth defects. Newer research suggests that folic acid may help prevent heart disease. The fiber boost you get from wheat germ is phenomenal.

SELECTION AND STORAGE

Because of its fat content, wheat germ goes rancid easily, especially if it's raw. Fresh wheat germ should smell something like toasted nuts, not musty. Unopened, a sealed jar of wheat germ will keep about one year on the shelf. Always store opened wheat germ in the refrigerator in a tightly sealed container, where it'll keep up to nine months.

WHEAT GERM
Serving Size: 1 oz, toasted

Calories	108	Thiamin	1 mg
Fat	3 g	Vitamin B$_6$	<1 mg
Saturated Fat	1 g	Vitamin E	4 mg
Cholesterol	0 mg	Calcium	13 mg
Carbohydrate	14 g	Copper	<1 mg
Protein	8 g	Iron	3 mg
Dietary Fiber	4 g	Magnesium	91 mg
Sodium	1 mg	Manganese	6 mg
Folic Acid	100 mcg	Phosphorus	325 mg
Pantothenic Acid	<1 mg	Potassium	269 mg
Riboflavin	<1 mg	Zinc	5 mg

PREPARATION AND SERVING TIPS

Wheat germ makes a nutritious and often undetectable addition to a myriad of dishes, including breads, pancakes, waffles, cookies, cereals, and milk shakes. It's a lower-fat alternative to granola that can be added to yogurt and cereals.

When adding wheat germ to baked goods or quick breads, you can replace one half to one cup of the flour with it. Because wheat germ tends to absorb moisture, you may want to add one to two tablespoons of water for every one-quarter cup of wheat germ you add to a recipe.

Yogurt, Nonfat

There was a time when yogurt eaters were considered "health nuts." Attitudes have changed. Today, yogurt is consumed by all sorts of people. Walk into any supermarket and you'll see a dizzying array of brands and flavors—and not all are so nutritious. Your best bet is to stick with nonfat yogurt.

Health Benefits

Yogurt may not be the miracle food some have claimed, but it certainly has a lot to offer. As a protein source, it is complete, so it can be used as the basis for meals, substituting for high-fat meats. It provides bone-building calcium in a dose as great as that from a glass of milk but can be digested more easily when live, active bacterial cultures are present. It also features riboflavin, vitamin B_{12}, and many minerals.

It's believed that the bacterial cultures used to make yogurt, *Lactobacillus bulgaricus* and *Streptococcus thermophilus*, carry their own health benefits. Research suggests that eating yogurt regularly helps boost immune function, warding off colds and possibly cancer. It's also thought that the friendly bacteria in yogurt help prevent and cure diarrhea. Another study has demonstrated that women plagued with chronic vaginal yeast infections found protection by eating a daily dose of bacteria-toting yogurt.

Selection and Storage

To ensure your carton is a welcome addition to a fat-busting diet, look for three traits when choosing a yogurt carton from the supermarket cold case. First, select one that's nonfat. Second, look for yogurt that contains live, active cultures. And third, it's best to choose plain, vanilla, lemon, or any yogurt without a jamlike fruit mixture added, which adds little nutrition but lots of calories. Also, check for a "sell-by" date on the carton. Refrigerated, yogurt will keep for up to ten days past that date.

PREPARATION AND SERVING TIPS

Yogurt makes a great portable lunch, if kept cold. If you don't have access to a refrigerator, try freezing the carton; it will thaw in time for lunch. Yogurt also makes a delicious low-fat dessert. For either, try adding sliced berries, nuts, wheat germ, bananas, or low-fat granola. You can even top cereal with yogurt instead of milk.

Yogurt substitutes beautifully in recipes that call for high-fat ingredients like cream or sour cream. And yogurt is especially well-suited as a base for dips and salad dressings.

YOGURT, NONFAT, VANILLA
Serving Size: 8 oz

Calories	100	Pantothenic Acid	1 mg
Fat	0 g	Riboflavin	1 mg
Saturated Fat	0 g	Vitamin B_{12}	1 mcg
Cholesterol	5 mg	Calcium	389 mg
Carbohydrate	16 g	Magnesium	37 mg
Protein	12 g	Phosphorus	306 mg
Dietary Fiber	0 mg	Potassium	550 mg
Sodium	149 mg	Zinc	2 mg

Aerobic exercise, 36
Aflatoxin, 132
Amino acids, 30, 39
Antioxidants, 8, 41, 106, 119. *See also* Beta-carotene; Vitamin C.
Arthritis, 89

Beta-carotene, sources of
    apricots, 43
    asparagus, 47
    broccoli, 68
    cabbage, 77–78
    carrots, 80
    grapefruit, 96
    greens, cooking, 100–101
    greens, salad, 103
    kale, 109
    mangoes, 117
    melons, 119
    pumpkin, 166
    spinach, 176
    squash, 178
    sweet potatoes, 182
    tomatoes, 184
Boron, 98, 131, 148
Bran cereals, 61–63
Breast cancer, 77, 173

Calcium, 68, 123, 176
Calcium, sources of
    amaranth, 39
    beets, 57
    broccoli, 68
    cabbage, 77
    fish, 89
    greens, cooking, 100
    herbs and spices, 106
    kale, 109
    mangoes, 117
    skim milk, 122, 123
    soybeans, 173
    spinach, 176
    yogurt, 188
Calories, 9–10, 17–18, 19–20, 37
Capsaicin, 152
Carbohydrates. *See also* Fiber.
    calories in, 17, 19
    complex, 10, 17–18, 19

Carotenoids, 100–101, 184
Cholesterol, 21, 22. *See also* HDL cholesterol; LDL cholesterol.
Colon cancer, 7, 53, 62, 94
Constipation, 18, 51, 53, 61, 159, 164
Copper, sources of
    dry beans, 54
    greens, cooking, 101
    nuts and seeds, 131
    pasta, 145
    pears, 148
    pineapple, 155
    potatoes, 161

Diabetes, 5, 7–8, 134–135
Diverticulosis, 7

Essential fatty acids, 21, 26
Exercise, 35–38

Fiber
    health benefits of, 7–8
    recommended amounts, 18
Folic acid, sources of
    artichokes, 45
    asparagus, 47
    beets, 57
    broccoli, 68
    cauliflower, 83
    corn, 85
    dry beans, 54
    greens, cooking, 101
    greens, salad, 103
    kale, 109
    lentils, 115
    nuts and seeds, 131
    oranges and tangerines, 141
    wheat germ, 186
Food Guide Pyramid, 11–14

HDL cholesterol, 24, 26, 53, 93
Heart disease prevention
    antioxidants and, 47, 68
    body fat and, 5
    fiber and, 7
    folic acid and, 45
    garlic and, 93
    low–fat diet and, 21–22

Heart disease prevention (continued)
  mushrooms and, 128
  phytochemicals and, 8
  saturated fats and, 22–24
  vegetarian diet and, 7
  weight loss and, 5, 7
Hemorrhoids, 51, 62, 180
Hepatitis, 90
Homocysteine, 85, 131

Immune function, 25, 49, 188
Iron, sources of
  beets, 57
  dry beans, 54
  greens, cooking, 101
  herbs and spices, 106
  lentils, 115
  mushrooms, 127
  nuts and seeds, 131
  oats, 135
  pasta, 145
  peas, green, 150
  potatoes, 161
  prunes, 164
  spinach, 176
  wheat germ, 186
  whole-wheat bread, 65

Labels, food, 26–29
Lactobacillus bulgaricus, 188
Lactose intolerance, 122
LDL cholesterol, 24, 53, 93, 131, 173

Magnesium, sources of
  bananas, 49
  dry beans, 54
  kale, 109
  kiwifruit, 111
  mangoes, 117
  nuts and seeds, 131
  oats, 135
  pasta, 145
Manganese, 59, 101, 131, 135
Metabolic rate, 9, 17, 35
Migraine headaches, 89, 152
Monosodium glutamate, 127
Monounsaturated fats, 24, 26, 28

Negative calorie effect, 20
Niacin, 65, 85, 127, 131, 145
Night blindness, 81
Norepinephrine, 17
Nutrition Facts. See Labels, food.

Obesity, 10
Omega-3 fatty acids, 7, 11, 26, 32, 89, 91, 131, 173
Omega-6 fatty acids, 26
Osteoporosis prevention
  boron and, 98
  calcium and, 100, 123

Pesticides, 42, 81, 91
Phytochemicals, sources of
  broccoli, 69
  brussels sprouts, 71
  cabbage, 77
  cauliflower, 83
  grapefruit, 96
  grapes, 98
  lemons and limes, 113
  raspberries, 168
  soybeans, 173
  strawberries, 180
Poisoning
  alkaloids and, 162
  contaminants in fish, 90–91
  wild mushrooms and, 129
Polyunsaturated fats, 24, 28
Potassium, sources of
  bananas, 49
  cabbage, 78
  cauliflower, 83
  dates, 87
  greens, cooking, 101
  kale, 109
  kiwifruit, 111
  melons, 119
  mushrooms, 127
  pears, 148
  potatoes, 161
  prunes, 164
  strawberries, 180
  sweet potatoes, 182
  tomatoes, 184

Prostaglandins, 21, 26
Protein, sources of
  brussels sprouts, 71
  bulgur, 75
  mushrooms, 127
  oats, 135
  popcorn, 159
  skim milk, 122
  soybeans, 173
  whole-wheat bread, 64–65
  yogurt, 188

Riboflavin, 65, 124, 127, 145, 157, 188

Salmonella, 93
Saturated fats, 22–24, 28
Selenium, 132
Serving sizes, 12, 13
Shellfish, 89–92
Smoking, 141
Sodium, 29, 94, 101
Staphylococcus, 93
Strength training, 36–38
Streptococcus thermophilus, 188
Sulforaphane, 69

T₃ hormone, 17
Thiamin, 65, 135, 145, 155
Trans fatty acids, 24–25, 28–29, 159
Triglycerides, 21, 22

Unsaturated fats, 24, 173

Vitamin A, sources of
  broccoli, 68
  carrots, 80, 81
  greens, cooking, 100–101
  herbs and spices, 106
  onions, 138
  oranges and tangerines, 141
  plums, 157
  prunes, 164
  red peppers, 152
  skim milk, 123, 124

Vitamin B₆, 49
Vitamin B₁₂, 188
Vitamin C, sources of
  apples, 41
  apricots, 43
  asparagus, 47, 48
  broccoli, 68
  brussels sprouts, 71
  cabbage, 77
  cauliflower, 83
  corn, 85
  grapefruit, 96
  greens, cooking, 100
  greens, salad, 103
  herbs and spices, 106
  kale, 109
  kiwifruit, 111, 112
  lemons and limes, 113
  mangoes, 117
  melons, 119
  oranges and tangerines, 141
  pears, 148
  peas, green, 150
  pineapple, 155
  plums, 157
  potatoes, 161
  raspberries, 168
  red peppers, 152
  spinach, 176
  strawberries, 180
  sweet potatoes, 182
  tomatoes, 184
Vitamin D, 123
Vitamin E, 131

Zinc, sources of
  mushrooms, 127
  nuts and seeds, 131
  pasta, 145
  wheat germ, 186